Whittled Away

To Capt. Les Pettigrew 15th Texas

Philip McBride

Philip McBride

ISBN-13: 978-0615822167

ISBN-10: 0615822169

Acknowledgments

I must thank my two prime readers: My brother who is an historian and has been my life-long literary guide, Dr. John McBride; and my beloved wife, professional librarian and lover of books, Juanita McBride.

The cover photograph is courtesy of the Liberty Rifles www.libertyrifles.org

This Novel Is Dedicated to
US Army Private Jesse McDonald,
Co. C, 1st Battalion, 175th Infantry, 29th Division
Landed on Omaha Beach on D-Day + 1
Killed in Combat June 18, 1944, Normandy, France

My wife and I travelled to France when <u>Whittled Away</u> was about one-third written. We spent a day touring the World War II D-Day sights at Normandy, including the American military cemetery seen in the film, *Saving Private Ryan*. The cemetery looks down over Omaha Beach and is the final home of 9,000 American soldiers, sailors, and airmen. It's a beautiful, peaceful place, a "thin" place where God seems close.

I was walking alone up and down the long rows of Christian crosses and Jewish stars, reading the names, idly looking for soldiers from Texas. It took a while to find the first Texan, but the name on the cross leapt out at me. I was standing next to the grave of a real Private Jesse McDonald.

I have since learned that Private McDonald was a teenager from Hidalgo County in South Texas. He had been inducted into the army at Fort Sam Houston, in San Antonio, Texas, the same city where the Civil War Alamo Rifles were formed. Coincidence? Perhaps.

Philip McBride

Table of Contents

Part 4   **Tennessee, 1864**

Part 5   **North Carolina, 1865**

Part 1

Chapter 1

Early September 1862, Southwest Arkansas
58 Men Present for Duty

Bain Gill sat staring at his haversack in the dim light before sunrise. He watched a black beetle and a pair of red ants explore the grease spots that had soaked through the cotton bag. It held all the food he was going to get for the next day or two, so gently brushing the insects off, Corporal Gill picked up the lumpy sack and slung it over his shoulder. He stood and stretched, twisting at the waist to work his sore back muscles. Six months away from home and he still ached every morning after sleeping on the ground rolled up in his ratty Mexican blanket. The bed at home hadn't been much more than a sack stuffed with straw laid on a web of ropes, but for all its faults, it was still a bed.

"Bain, *mi amigo*, we movin' now?"

Gill glanced over at the man lying a few feet away, noticing as always the blend of English and Spanish spoken by Private Jesús McDonald. He was only a few months younger than Gill, but was several inches shorter, slighter of build, had a dark complexion and dark hair that looked reddish in the bright sunlight. They had been boys together in Bexar County, growing up on neighboring spreads on Salado Creek just north of San Antonio. Gill smiled to himself as he considered his friend Jesús. His Mexican mother had insisted on naming him Jesús after our Lord and Savior. His red-headed Scottish father had found the idea sacrilegious and called the boy Jesse when the two were away from Mrs. McDonald, and had written "Jesse" in the family Bible. But that made no difference to Consuela Maria Salazar McDonald since she had never been taught to read. She raised her first son as Jesús, even if her Scottish husband and their Anglo neighbors couldn't bring themselves to call one of their own such a holy name.

"I said, Bain, are we movin' out now?" Jesús repeated when Gill didn't answer immediately.

"Reckon soon enough. If you want to eat, you best get the fire stoked and some 'pones cooking. You ain't got time to just lay there."

Gill turned and moved a few feet away from his messmates, unbuttoning his trousers fly to relieve himself next to a pine tree. The day before had been a twelve hour march, so the whole company had just spread their blankets and slept for the few hours until it was each man's turn on the picket line. Since Sergeant Degas always told him to lead a sink digging work party if they were halting for more than one night, Gill figured that meant more marching this morning.

Gill shrugged his canvas knapsack onto his back. Then he collected his battered tin canteen from where it hung on a broken branch, shook it to make sure it was full, and draped it over his shoulder.

"Corporal Gill, a moment, please." Gill looked up and saw the silhouette of the second sergeant walking toward him.

"Sure, Sergeant," Second Sergeant Henry Degas was stocky, middle-aged, brusque, and seemed to Gill to never have gotten over not being elected first sergeant back in Texas.

Gill and Degas moved away from the other men who were now going about their own morning rituals.

Degas spoke first, "You going easy on McDonald 'cause he's your neighbor back home?"

Gill started to reply, then hesitated before answering. Degas's question.

"No, Sergeant, I ain't."

"I hear any more of it, he's going to Smith's platoon and you get that Hawkins boy instead."

Ambrose Hawkins was barely sixteen, small, awkward, and wasn't catching on to soldiering very fast. He hardly seemed strong enough to aim his musket and couldn't remember drill. Yet, he displayed an insufferable good humor, even during the last hours of a long day's march. He wasn't much liked, perhaps because he seemed happy to be where he was.

Gill sighed without showing it, and assured the sergeant that Private McDonald would carry his full load.

"See to it." With that Sergeant Degas walked away and slung on his own knapsack. Gill paused only long enough to realize he didn't have time now to sort this out, but the day's march ahead would give him ample chance to think it over.

"What'd the Sergeant want, Bain?" Jesús held out a tin plate of dark brown fried cornpones still hot and wet with grease. Gill took one, nibbled, and grimaced.

"Damn, Jesse, didn't you ever watch your mama cook? Sergeant Degas just wanted to remind me that our platoon has the scout this morning. So be on your toes, and don't shoot at some blame courier you think is a wild hog." That had only happened once so far, when a nervous and nearsighted private in Company C was startled.

Captain McAllister sat silently, at ease in his saddle. It was a well-worn saddle on which he had spent nearly two decades of endless hours in pursuit of Comanche raiders and Mexican bandits. He knew most of the men in the company, as he had been the driving force in the formation of the Alamo Guards militia company three years earlier. Just about every man in the militia company had enlisted in the new Confederate army at the same time, in the early flush of eagerness that had sucked in men from every town in the south, even San Antonio on the edge of the far western frontier. Most of the men from San Antonio figured riding mustangs and fighting Yankees would be far less dangerous and far more exciting, than trailing Comanche's across endless desolate plains. But, the army had not seen fit to mount this particular group of new soldiers, as infantrymen were needed, not more cavalry. So the Alamo Guards militia company was now the Alamo Rifles, Company K of the Sixth Texas Infantry. It was September and they were marching to Arkansas to take their place protecting the big cannons that guarded the best highways in the South – the rivers.

The captain waited on the side of the road while all fifty-five riflemen in his company marched by. McAllister was not a placid man by nature, and he made mental notes to himself about a number of the men as they passed. McAllister had been a sergeant in the war with Mexico just over a decade ago, and still sometimes displayed a sergeant's intense interest in the details that made or broke soldiers on the march. He would be inquiring of First Sergeant O'Donoghue about weapons that showed spots of rust, nearly empty canteens betrayed by their bouncing too lightly on hips, and straps that were hanging too loosely.

For his part, Sergeant O'Donoghue respected Captain McAllister, since he had ridden with him chasing Indians and rustlers. McAllister's attention to details had saved them more than once, and getting home with one's hair built loyalty. O'Donoghue also approved of Captain McAllister's speech to the company when they had started the march north from Victoria.

"You men know I have spent my whole life as a fighting man. First in Mexico with General Scott, fighting Mescans, and back here in Texas chasin' the Comanche. The damned Comanche are the toughest bastards God ever thunk up. But even God Almighty soon saw the Comanch was ornery and evil and not prone to follow His orders, He was sorry ever to have created them, so He rid himself of their devilment by tossing their boney arses out of The Promised Land, and by damn, but they landed in Texas, here to torment the God fearing white man.

"I hate them red sonsabitches. They are murdering thieving demons from Hell. But they are the best damned horsemen and fighters anywheres. And they taught me a few things, things that kept me alive through ten damned years of chasing 'em, and things that may just keep you alive when we face those black hearted Lincolnites who are marching south to force their ways onto us.

"The first thing I learned from the red heathens was to never draw attention to yourself. Blend in. Don't be the man who draws the eye of the enemy. If you are still wearing that piece of brass on your hat, take it off. God blesses the Texas Star, but He will bless it just fine while it's pinned to your shirt, under your blouse. On your hat that brass star ain't nothin' but a shiny target for some sharp-eyed northern boy with a keen aim.

"I seen and kilt a passel of brave Comanche bucks who so got their blood up that they left their cover, left their fellow braves, and charged out to count coup or kill me with their tomahawks. Hell, boys, lead from Samuel Colt's revolvers knocked down ever damned one of them of them savages that drew such attention to hisself, and a minie bullet from a Springfield rifle will just as surely knock down a wild-eyed Texan hell-bent on glory, ever damned time.

"So mind your sergeants and corporals. If you git so scared you break ranks and run backwards, I'll shoot you dead myself. If you git the killin' fever so bad, you break ranks and try to run over the Yankee, he too will shoot you dead. Your safety is in the men whose shoulders you are squeezed between, so stay there until I tell you different."

It had been a fine stirring speech, the wisdom of his experience at killing and surviving shining brightly on the captain. Yet, Sergeant O'Donoghue still would have preferred that his commander leave more matters to him. Captain McAllister knew that the sergeants ran the company, while the officers fretted over higher matters. But, Sergeant O'Donoghue also knew men don't change all that much, regardless what their rank was.

The forty-two wagons in the brigade supply train trundled along behind the last regiment in the column. The faded red painted wagon belonging to the Alamo Rifles was pulled by four mules and was at the very end of the line.

"Wonder what Cousin Jesús is thinkin' 'bout all these tall trees. I bet he's never seen a tree so tall. Hell, I ain't ever seen the like of these trees, and I been as far as the coast three times. These trees reach to the sky, but they don't even have real leaves, just them long stringy green things," commented Matthew Quinn to his older brother Benjamin who was handling the reins that day.

"Don't cuss. An' them long stringy things is pine needles. The trees are pine trees and their leaves are called needles. And they don't have nuts like oak trees. They got cones. Pine cones, and they ain't no good to eat,'" Benjamin replied.

"When did you git to be the know-it-all of tall trees?" Matthew asked.

"I ain't through, yet. The best part is that the sap out of these here pine trees burns like kerosene. If it's rainin' hard, just find a pine knob on the ground and bust it open. The sap inside will catch a spark easy. An' if you got lucifers, it ain't no problem a'tall."

"Like I said, Ben, where'd you git all this tree learnin'?"

Benjamin answered without taking his eyes off the mules, "I gets around. I gets around."

The Quinn brothers were Jesús McDonald's first cousins. While Jesús's mother had caught the eye of a Scotsman nineteen years ago, two years earlier her sister had left home with a ranger who sometimes rode with Captain McAllister. The ranger had taken an arrow in the shoulder and been left at the family's adobe hut so the rest of the troop could stay on the trail. Juanita was fourteen and her mother would not allow her near the ranger's pallet. But the girl brought food to him after he was able to sit on the bench in front of the hut, and they talked more and more as the days passed. It didn't really surprise Juanita's parents that on the day the ranger saddled his horse to leave, she came out of the hut with some dried goat meat and corn tortillas wrapped in a scarf, and held out her hand to be pulled onto the horse. She was not deterred by the fact Ranger Nathan Quinn was a free black man twice her age. Juanita's father approved of the ranger and saw one less mouth to feed. Her mother couldn't hold back a tear or two, but she also liked the ranger, and she liked that he was not trying to scratch out an existence by raising corn and goats in the brush, but was taking her daughter to San Antonio where he had a job at a livery stable.

By the time Captain McAllister was outfitting his growing company for service in the new Confederate army, Nathan Quinn was no longer an occasional ranger, as his old arrow wound still made riding a painful experience. Instead, Quinn rented a small barn that he operated as a livery stable just off Alamo Plaza in San Antonio. He also owned two old freight wagons. His two oldest sons were now young men and tall like their father. They were also dark skinned like their father, but spoke fluent Spanish like their mother. For over a year they had been muleskinners driving the two freight wagons from San Antonio to Brownsville, where Texas and Mexico joined at the Gulf of Mexico. They hauled cotton bales to the coast for shipment to England, and brought back whatever crates needed transport, offloaded from the same ships that carried the cotton overseas.

When Nathan Quinn acquiesced to Captain McAllister's appeal to lease one of his wagons to the Confederacy, Quinn's two sons pleaded to go as the wagon's teamsters. His father liked the idea of his sons being able to look after his mules and wagon, and took comfort that Captain McAllister would be nearby to watch over his boys. Besides, Captain McAllister had promised the wagon would not be leaving Texas, and would most likely be home by the new year when the war ended. That had been six months earlier in April.

Only the ranking officers of the brigade knew that the last river crossing had put them into Arkansas. The march had been tough on every man in the regiment. When it was dry, the road dust clogged their lungs. When it rained the red mud sucked at their shoes. Knapsack straps dug deeper into shoulders as the hours passed. Shoe soles came apart. The weight of weapons and "essentials" caused every man to rethink how important each item really was to his well-being. An ever increasing array of "essentials" became road litter as the road went on and on through this small piece of the great American forest.

Corporal Gill looked to his right, trying to spot Jesús through the brush. Pine forests were sometimes remarkably clear of undergrowth, but were also sometimes thick with brambles patches that made it hard to control the moving skirmish line. Gill saw Private McDonald walking several yards ahead of the rest of his group of four riflemen.

"Dang it, Jesse, wait on Johnson and the others," Gill muttered, but did not call out. Instead, he moved out of his place in the skirmish line and hurried to catch up with Jesús. Halfway through the bramble patch, Gill's left foot caught on a thick blackberry vine and he tripped and fell. His right thumb had been resting on the musket's hammer in the half-cock position, and when he started falling, Gill reflexively tightened his hand, inadvertently pulling the hammer back to full-cock. An instant later, when he reached the ground, the musket stock bounced off the ground and the hammer fell, resulting in a 58 caliber lead bullet being discharged into Private Hiram Johnson's left calf.

Johnson had been moving some ten yards to Gill's right and had turned towards him at the sound of his falling. The bullet created a nasty inch-long gouge out of his flesh, and landed in the trunk of a scrub oak. However, the sound of the musket shot, followed by the sound of Private Johnson's revelation of being shot, followed by the profanity coming from Corporal Gill, brought the whole skirmish line to an immediate halt.

The rest of the men in the platoon immediately went to ground, scanning the forest to their front for the tell-tale smoke of a fired musket. Seeing nothing, Private McDonald turned his head towards Gill intending to profess his inability to see smoke to their front, when he saw the small white cloud dissipating from around Gill's head as he rose from the bramble patch.

"Corporal G..., huh," McDonald paused as he tried to understand what had just happened, "Are you all right, Bain?"

"Yes, dammit. Now shut up Jesse, will you," Gill uttered sharply as Private McDonald turned and moved towards him.

Gill knew he needed to immediately give Sergeant O'Donoghue a quick and reasonable, if not necessarily truthful, explanation. Since Private Johnson had a bloody wound in his leg, Gill also understood his options were few. Random single shots from the forward platoon were certainly not rare, but nor were they an everyday occurrence. Nonetheless, privates in the forward platoon sporting bullet wounds were rare, and demanded an answer. After all, they were soldiers moving into a region where the Federal army was said to be advancing also, and corporals wounding privates in the forward skirmish line would hardly enhance the regiment's reputation. Realizing all this, Gill knew the truth would not sit well with the sergeant or Captain McAllister. He also quickly recognized that the brush was thick enough to have hidden his musket's accidental discharge on the ground from the soldiers who had been spread out in front of him.

Since the sergeant was still a few yards away, hidden by the brush, Gill quickly moved to Private Johnson who was on the ground hugging his leg to his chest.

"Hiram, move your hands and let me see your leg." Gill pulled up Johnson's trouser leg and plucked a few threads out of the wound. It was bleeding impressively, so Gill poured water from his canteen over the wound, put his right hand on top of it to slow the blood flow, and quickly pulled a large square cotton handkerchief from his pocket and wrapped it around Johnson's leg, covering the wound as tightly as he could.

"Hiram, did you see the smoke of the damned skunk who fired on you?"

"Nah, Corporal, I was just trying to catch up with Jesse and all of a sudden it was like someone hit my leg with a hammer. What happened? Are we about to get into a scrap? I can fight. I can sit here and shoot."

"I see that, and you will get your chance to fight, but not today."

By now Jesús was standing next to him, wide eyed and clearly biting his tongue, eager to ask more questions. Gill gave him a hard look, and loudly ordered, "Private McDonald, take this man to the surgeon's wagon, while I report to the sergeant."

By now both sergeants and the lieutenant were approaching. Gill quickly turned to the men still in the skirmish line and shouted, "Look sharp there, men. There's a bushwhacker out there somewhere."

Without comment, Sergeant Degas moved past Gill to the skirmish line, where he soon vanished into the undergrowth along with the line of skirmishers, who now were moving forward, nervously checking behind every tree trunk for the enemy.

First Sergeant O'Donoghue stood next to Corporal Gill and waited for the lieutenant to question Gill. Before the young man could phrase his first question, Gill announced that a bushwhacker must be to their front, and had given Johnson a flesh wound. Both men nodded, and the trio quickly separated to resume their positions and duties, now like their men, much more alert. Only McDonald had an idea of what really happened, and he figured he would keep his thoughts to himself until he could ask his friend Bain about it later.

Company K's time on advance guard passed without further incident until Company A moved forward to relieve them, by now late in the afternoon. The march route had not left the pine forest all day and when the brigade stopped just before dusk, the men found an abundant supply of dead wood for their cook fires. Those who had not already cooked their beef ration, pulled out the cuts of meat that were fresh last night when they were issued, but after a long hot day in the haversacks, were now sticky and dark. Some men starting boiling the chunks of blue beef, as others tried to fry them with a little pork fat they had saved. Either way, the smell of near rancid beef floated above the campfires. Gill munched on the last of the cold burned cornpones that Jesús had made that morning.

Gill was distracted, realizing that he had skirted a harsh time by his outright lie about the phantom bushwhacker. He also realized that his position as a corporal allowed him to look after friends like Jesús, but as a private his voice would be nothing but sour air.

The first platoon had guard duty tonight, so Gill looked forward to a few hours of uninterrupted sleep. Corporals of the Guard spent most of the night walking between the sentry posts to check on those men who couldn't be trusted to stay awake after the tiring hours and miles on the march. Gill was immensely grateful that tonight was not his night, but he knew he must find Private Johnson somewhere around the surgeon's tent to confirm and reinforce the story that he had indeed been shot by a bushwhacker, and not his own corporal. Also, Gill knew he needed to sit for a few minutes with Jesús. Gill was unsure if he should be truthful with Jesús, or keep to the story of the bushwhacker. On the one hand, self-protection was a powerful incentive, but on the other hand, Jesús was his best friend, as close as his own brothers. The indecisiveness followed Gill as he went about his duties checking on the men and offering them an ear after the long day. He finally decided he would not make the call with Jesús until he had to.

The troubled corporal was walking away from the campfire of the "Hen House Mess," a name given by Sergeant O'Donoghue to four young men who had enlisted together, each with two yard birds tied together and slung over their shoulders. Without warning, he was touched on the arm by a hand reaching out of the shadow of a tree. Turning quickly, fearing another confrontation with Sergeant Degas, Gill saw the deeply lined face of Captain McAllister. Gill had only spoken to the captain a few times, and he stuttered, " Caaaapt..." as he tried to quickly salute. McAllister replied by gripping his arm and pulling him deeper into the shadows.

"Weren't no bushwhacker back there today, was there?"

Gill looked straight at the captain, and made a quick decision that since the dog was out of the kennel and on the trail, he might as well own up to what he'd done. Still he hesitated before he reluctantly said, "Nah, sir, there wasn't. I stumbled on a berry vine and fell and my musket went off."

"So you lied about it to the others. You that scared of losing those stripes?"

"Well, maybe. Not so much for me, though, Captain. I can take care of myself. But for the boys. Some of them don't hardly know which way is up. I, I just don't know how they'll get by and how they'll... handle what's in front of us. And Jesse, well, I been watching over him his whole life. If I get sent

17

off now, I don't know how they, what they..." Gill stopped, having run out of words and resigned to whatever punishment the captain would dole out to him.

After a long pause, Captain McAllister said, "Corporal Gill, you can return to your duties now."

As Gill turned to go, not clear where he stood, the captain spoke quietly once more. "You know you can't protect them past the first shot in the first fight we get into. Then, as if to himself, "I found out quick enough in Mexico." Then more loudly, "I reckon you'll find out yourself soon enough, when we meet those who've come down here to learn us what for."

Chapter 2

Late December 1862, Arkansas Post, Central Arkansas
46 Men Present for Duty

Gill was mightily impressed with the wide Arkansas River that made a sharp bend just below where Arkansas Post lay. The name made the young Texan think of fur traders and river boats. Of course, he had never met a fur trader or seen a river wider than the Brazos, and that up close view of the Brazos came only the one time they had forded it a few weeks ago.

Arkansas Post was most assuredly more than a "post." It was also a fort named Fort Hindman, designed to deter armored Union gunboats and the unarmored troop transports that were said to be bringing a hundred thousand Yankees into Arkansas. It had taken five hundred slaves hired from farms all around the region and five thousand Confederate soldiers three months of dawn to dusk work to construct the star fort for the big cannons. Then they went on to dig the trenches and rifle pits that reached nearly a mile inland from the fort, designed to protect the cannons from an infantry assault.

After a wet, cold fall season, Fort Hindman was also a foul place, a place of deep muddy trenches reinforced with pine logs. Measles and dysentery had struck down many of the soldiers. The daily sick calls continued to take more and more men away from their rifles and left artillery crews at half strength. Yet, Arkansas Post exuded an aura of safety and military might. It

19

was easy to believe that Fort Hindman was an impregnable fortress from which the Confederates would easily repel any Yankee incursion.

One of things Private Jesús McDonald disliked most about army life, and there were many things to dislike, was standing guard post at the headquarters tents of the regiment's commander, Colonel Garland. It was a duty that was rotated among the nine companies, so the chore fell on Company K less than once a week, but McDonald found it to be onerous anyway.

One positive aspect of guard duty at headquarters was the chance to overhear what officers talked about. It didn't take Jesús long to realize they mostly talked about the same things that privates talked about: The war, their families, letters from home, the farm or business they had left behind, who was sick or hurt, the weather, and not infrequently, how bad the food was and how they missed their wives' or mothers' cooking.

One thing that became evident to every guard at headquarters was that staff officers ate better than they did. Not so much because the raw food was more varied and fresher, although it usually was, but because it was prepared every day by body servants – slaves – who knew how to cook. Jesús had noticed that almost all of the senior staff officers enjoyed the services of body servants, as did some of the company captains, mainly those who had large farms back in Texas and had brought a male slave with them when they enlisted.

On a cold morning in early January, Private McDonald was standing guard post near Colonel Garland's tent. Jesús did not own an overcoat, but he wore his good Texas jacket and had his knitted scarf tightly wrapped around his neck and covering his ears. Still, he was close enough to overhear most conversations.

"Colonel," said a captain who had just walked up from the wagon yard, "the goods you ordered from the mercantile store in Pine Bluff are here. Just one crate. Shall I send a detail to bring it up?" The captain was the battalion adjutant and Colonel Garland's twenty-one year old son.

Colonel Garland was sitting in a folding chair, rereading a lengthy missive from Fort Hindman's commander about the growing number of sick soldiers and the need to complete the fortifications before the Federals might steam up the river. He looked up and replied, "No, Captain, the men are all working on the trenches." Garland looked around, saw his body servant, a slender middle-aged man named William, standing at a large pot that was sitting on the coals of a campfire behind the tents.

"William, you go down to the wagon yard and fetch the crate that's there for me."

"Yas, suh," William answered and put down the long wooden stirring stick he had been using to swirl the colonel's dirty shirts around in the iron tub of hot water.

"Captain, write William a pass so he won't be pulled into a work gang at the fort. Can't have that, I need William here. Any man can use a spade, but not many can cook a good biscuit. Right, William?"

"Yas, suh, I does that, sure 'nuf. I knows just how to knead da dough and when to brush da coals off da oven lid. Yas, I does."

"You do indeed, my good William." Colonel Garland looked towards Jesús and pointed at him. "You there, Private. You go with William and make sure he finds his way back with my crate. And if some sergeant tries to put William in a work party, you speak up for me. The pass should satisfy anyone. Can you do that, Private?"

"Yes sir, Colonel." Private McDonald waited until the captain had scribbled out a pass, signed it, and handed it to William. Then Jesús raised his musket to his shoulder, saluted the colonel, and walked away from the tents with Colonel Garland's body servant.

Jesús and William found their way through the muddy paths to the fort's large wagon yard. Dozens of wagons stood in ragged lines and here and there men, both soldiers and civilians, were busy unloading newly arrived wagons. Teamsters were leading unhitched mules and oxen to and from the creek for water and other teamsters were repairing leather harnesses. William and Jesús both stopped and looked at the lines of wagons, not knowing which one held the colonel's crate of purchased goods. Neither man had thought to ask the captain how to recognize the wagon, and since Pine Bluff was the fort's daily source for resupply, there was a steady trickle of wagons coming into Fort Hindman from Pine Bluff. William would not ask a white man, civilian or soldier, which wagons had just arrived, and no black men were close to the pair. Jesús looked around searching for his cousins and their freight wagon, but neither Quinn brother was to be seen. Jesús realized that William was waiting for him to take the lead, so he walked towards a teamster who was leading a brace of mules towards the creek.

"Say there, Señor, where's the wagons that just rolled in from Pine Bluff?"

The middle-aged man stopped and looked at the pair, and spat tobacco juice on the ground. Then he walked on by them without replying.

Jesús rubbed his jaw and shrugged at the sling holding his musket on his shoulder. Jesús, with William a step behind him, approached a second teamster, this time one who was sitting on a wagon tongue working on a harness strap.

In reply to Jesús's question, the man pointed down the line of wagons without comment. Jesús nodded and the duo walked further along the row of big wagons. They stopped in front of a blue painted wagon where an older man was leaning against a wheel.

Jesús spoke up, "We're looking for Colonel Garland's crate from the mercantile store in Pine Bluff. Is this the wagon?"

The man nodded and led them to the back of the wagon.

"You got something to show me that I'm supposed to let you have the colonel's crate?"

William stepped forward, took off his battered hat, and pulled the folded pass from inside the crown, and without speaking handed it to the wagon man. The man read it, nodded, and pointed at a large wooden crate near the front of the wagon bed. Jesús raised a foot to step up onto the wagon, but stopped when the teamster said, "Private, you got a nigger right there. Getting that crate out of the wagon is work for his kind, unless you Mex fellers do things different."

Jesús was taken aback by the man's words and attitude, but put his foot down on the ground and stood still while William hauled himself up onto the wagon and manhandled the crate to the back of the wagon bed. Then William dropped down with a grunt, and stooping down, got his shoulder lower than the floor of the wagon bed, and pulled the large wooden box onto his shoulder. William took a step away from the wagon, but then his shoe slipped in a muddy hoof print. He leaned sideways and the crate began to slide from his shoulder. Jesús instinctively jumped towards William and reached out with both arms to grab the crate and stop its fall. But Jesús's musket, which was slung over one shoulder, slid down his arm and knocked against the wooden crate. The musket nearly tripped Jesús, who stumbled against William, interfering with his effort to regain control of the wooden crate.

William held on for an instant, then dropped to one knee for balance before the crate fell the last foot to the ground, landing on one corner and emitting the unmistakable sound of something inside breaking. William immediately uttered, "Oh Lawdy, I's in for a bad day now."

Jesús pulled his musket back onto his shoulder and put a hand on William's shoulder. "Don't fret, William. I will explain to the colonel it weren't your fault. These things happen, that's all." William looked at Jesús and shook his head from side to side. Then he stooped to pick up the crate and with unexpected strength, lifted it to his shoulder and started walking away.

Jesús and William had not walked far back towards their camp when the path took them directly behind a trench where sweating men were shoveling dirt and dragging logs. A sergeant stepped onto the path and held up his hand for the pair to stop. William did and left the crate on his shoulder, but dropped his eyes to the ground, not looking at the sergeant.

"Private, what are you and this nigger doing at my trench? I need two more men to replace them what got too sick last night to work today."

Jesús stammered, then said, "William, show the man our pass." Then to the sergeant, he said, "Sergeant, we'd be obliged if you would stand aside. You see, we're on a detail for Colonel Garland of the Sixth Texas Regiment to bring this here box of necessaries to his headquarters." Then he spoke again to William, "Show him the pass, William."

Without looking up, William said, "The wagon man kept the pass."

At that the sergeant grinned, revealing several missing teeth, and said, "Well, since you boys got no pass, and I got two shovels that is idle, I reckon the nigger will set down that box, and you will lay aside your Enfield, and you both will spend the rest of the day helping my boys finish this trench. I'll have you back to your camp by supper time and you can tell them other beaners and niggers that you been working hard the whole day long with your Arkansas betters."

Jesús hesitated, then took a step to move past the sergeant, but the man shifted over to block him. Jesús stopped, looked back at William, shrugged, and said, "Guess we're gonna dig a while, William."

The sergeant smirked and turned away to call for someone to bring two shovels. Before he turned back, he felt a wasp sting in his side. Starting to slap at it, he felt his hand pulled away, and heard a whisper at his ear, "Sergeant, I done told you that me and William is on a detail for our colonel. Now you can walk away and go back to watching your men work, or you can walk in front of me with my knife pricking your ribs, and ask Colonel Garland yourself if he would like us to dig your trench all afternoon."

The Arkansas sergeant stepped away and turned as Private McDonald lowered his musket towards him. "I don't know your name, you damned greaser, but I ain't done with you." Then he turned and stomped towards his work party.

William looked at Jesús and they both nearly smiled as they continued their trek back to Colonel Garland's headquarters. The colonel was still seated at his fold-up camp desk when William gently lowered the box to the ground.

"Well, fetch a pry bar and open it, William. Don't waste time, I'm eager to see the new dinnerware. They are hand-painted with our new national banner on every plate and cup. They shall be used by General Churchill himself soon enough." Looking up at William, "As they eat your biscuits off them too, I might add."

"Yas, suh. Ugh, Colonel, Sah, dey's sumten you needs to know 'bout dem plates."

"What, William, what might that be?" Then the colonel glanced down at the crate and saw the mud splashed up on one corner of the box. "Dear me. Don't tell me the damned teamsters dropped my crate loading it. Don't tell me they broke my new dinnerware. No, don't tell me that, William, don't you dare tell me that."

"Well, suh, no dey didn't drops it dat we's saw." William swallowed, raised up his head and squared his shoulders, then said, "Sah, it slipped a mite off my shoulder, and well sah, de corner, it hits de ground afore I could stops it."

Colonel Garland carefully set down the paper he had been reading, and looked sternly at William. "Get the pry bar, William, it's time to see what damage you have done. While you open the crate, I shall consider how many strokes each broken piece will cost you."

"Yas, suh."

Private McDonald had been listening without thought of interfering, when he heard himself say, "Colonel, sir, William didn't quite tell you the truth. You see, sir, it was my musket. It slid off my shoulder and tangled my feet, and I... I stumbled against William and that caused the box to fall. It weren't William, it was me."

Colonel Garland looked at Jesús, then at William, and asked, "That so, William?"

"Yah, suh. I reckons it was."

"My, my. I got a Mescan private in my regiment who is standing before me willing to take punishment for my clumsy nigger. You know that's what you are doing, Private? Well, let me be straight with you. Your confession won't keep the lash off William's back, but it will cost you two bits out of your pay for every broken plate and cup in that box. Captain Garland, you will oversee the unpacking and make a note for the paymaster of how much to deduct from the private's pay. Now, Private, you may resume your duty post."

Endless hours passed before Jesús was finally relieved by the next guard detail. Marching back to their tents, he decided that the next time Company K was due to stand guard at headquarters, he would instead fall out for sick call and take his chances with the surgeons. Any poison they might force on him for an imagined ailment would go down easier than the morning that had just passed.

That night, long after midnight, Jesús felt a hand shaking him from his sleep. Looking down at his feet, he saw a dark face motioning him to come out of the tent. Jesús threw off his blanket and crawled out of the tent, shivering as he turned to the side, unbuttoned his trousers, and began urinating in the mud. When he was through and buttoning his fly, he looked at the man who had awakened him. It was not William, but was another black man who Jesús had seen working around the regimental headquarters tents.

"Is you Mastah, I means, Private McDonald?" Jesús nodded, and the man held out a hand and Jesús took it and shook it. "Thank you for standin' up fer William. That's from me and the other cooks and drivers. William, he asks me to come finds you and to tells you that you best watch out now that you done got the eye of the big mastah. And William, he say to steer clear of the fort an' them Arkansas fellers, too. He say your knife and that red scarf is gonna make you a target for that sergeant one night. William, he say, stick with your partners. Day and night."

"You tell William that I will be careful and I will stick with my pards. And thanks for warning me."

"I's do that." Then the man held out a cloth poke sack. Jesús took it, and the man stepped back into the darkness and was gone. Jesús pulled the draw string open, reached in and pulled out a fresh biscuit, grunted and grinned, ate the biscuit, then returned to his blankets and soundly slept the last few hours until dawn.

The next day and during the next week Company K resumed working on the trench line beyond the fort. Jesús left his scarf rolled up in his knapsack in the tent, kept his head down and even borrowed a kepi instead of wearing his distinctive tall slouch hat. He didn't volunteer to fill canteens at the creek or bring armloads of firewood to the camp, and he did not wander far from his tent after the work shifts ended each day. But he did stick with his pards and he wore his belt knife.

The three men were silent and still, sitting around the dying embers of the campfire. Each was thinking about his wife and children, and not feeling obliged to share his thoughts with the other two. One man picked up a stick and stirred the fire, tossing the small branch onto the coals. Flames quickly flared up, reflecting off the dark faces of the trio. The oldest of the three softly started humming the tune to a favorite hymn, one which had given comfort to him over the years since he was a boy.

Another of the trio stayed in his reverie for another minute, then started singing the old song:

"Jesus walked --------------------this lonesome valley,
He had to walk ------------------it by himself.
Oh, nobody else----------------could walk it for him;
He had to walk------------------it by himself"

By the end of the first verse the last man had joined in, and their low voices carried in the night air into the tents of the officers who slept just a few feet away. Captain Garland heard their singing and it tore his thoughts away from his own wife and infant child who he would not see on Christmas morning. He fell asleep still listening and wondering why the headquarters servants were singing about lonesome valleys instead of singing about the joyous birth of Christ on this Christmas Eve of 1862.

answer, Jesús continued, "And I been thinking about your sister, Susan. You reckon she would mind if I sent her a letter?"

"Here," Gill said tossing Jesús a hard yellow ball of fried cornbread. "And, no, I reckon Susan wouldn't mind if you sent her a letter. It's not like you two ain't been introduced. But don't you go writin' about things a girl like Susan shouldn't oughta be hearing. You know what I'm getting at."

Now grinning broadly, Jesús replied, "Yes sir, Brother Bain, I surely won't go offending the sensibilities of your sweet sister Susan."

Gill was about to sternly tell Jesús he wasn't joking when a loud crash and a vibrating thud off to their left caused all six men to look, then duck. Realizing that they were under artillery fire, Gill joined the other NCO's shouting for the men to fall to the bottom of their rifle pits.

"Git down, dammit!"

"Cannon fire! Eat dirt, boys."

More crashes came as the gunboats in the Arkansas River found the range. Exploding shells began to replace the solid shot of the first rounds. Hearing shrapnel ricocheting off trees encouraged the men to hug the bottoms of the rifle pits. The noise was deafening and the Texans quickly learned that the earth did truly shake from the explosions.

For all its terror, the first wave of firing from the gunboats on the river harmed few men in the mile-long line of rifle pits. A private, who was cooking lumpy dough wrapped around his bayonet over a tiny campfire on the back edge of his hole, stabbed himself in the leg falling backwards when the first shell exploded nearby. Another man was grazed in the jaw with a piece of iron shrapnel and was holding his hand to the wound that left his cheek flapping and bleeding. A man slow to reach the bottom of his rifle pit had a piece of pine wood jutting from his shoulder, the head log of their rifle pit having been splintered by an exploding shell. A few other men were wounded, but no one had been killed or dismembered. The steady barrage of cannon fire continued for two hours, then with darkness, died away.

The men of the Sixth Texas were left alone in the forward rifle pits until morning. By eight o'clock, with the sun burning through the mist, the shelling resumed and steadily increased in volume. Sergeant O'Donoghue ran towards Gill's rifle pit and leapt into it as a round exploded several yards away. He landed at one end, next to a pile of excrement where an impromptu sink had been used by two or three men during the night. O'Donoghue pulled his hand from the filth, and wiped it on his trousers.

"You damned animals. Grab your gear and crawl out of here. We're moving to the trenches by the fort. The scouts say there's a whole Yankee army comin' through the woods. They'll roll over us if we stay out here."

Having delivered his message to Corporal Gill, Sergeant O'Donoghue climbed out, and hunched over, ran towards the next rifle pit.

Corporal Gill was the last man to leave the hole, staring after Sergeant O'Donoghue, wondering if he himself was brave enough to move across the line while under artillery fire. With no answer, Gill started crawling until he was some distance from their original position. Then he stood in a crouch, collected the men in his squad, and moved quickly back towards the protection of the main trenches.

"Which way?" Gill asked the lieutenant as the men of the second platoon tumbled into the deep trench, grateful to have earth again between them and the exploding cannon shells.

"Go that way, past the first platoon and stop when you reach the boys from the 24th. Spread 'em out, but don't leave a big gap in the line. Watch for Sergeant Degas. Until he gets there, you take the left post. Who knows when they'll come, but keep the boys ready."

With that the lieutenant left to search for the captain. Gill moved his platoon down the muddy trench until he reached the end of the Twenty-fourth Regiment and where he stopped and positioned his men. The huge cannons on the Union gunboats continued to lob shells into the Confederate defensive positions. The trench protecting the soldiers in the Sixth Texas was well within their range and patiently the gunboats' cannons refined their range until the exploding shells had the trench line bracketed.

"Down, men, for God's sake, keep down!" Sergeant O'Donoghue called over and over as he crawled on his belly along the back of the trench. He saw that many of his men were curled into balls against the bottom of the trench wall, had their eyes clenched tightly shut and held their hands over their ears. Others were sitting with their backs to the trench wall, eyes glazed over, staring at the opposite wall a few feet away. Some were praying out loud and a few of the younger teenage soldiers were crying and calling for their mothers. O'Donoghue could offer no help to any of them, other than his repeated mantra to keep down. He was scared too. Even in Mexico he had never been in a lengthy artillery barrage, and the constant noise and vibrations when shells hit and exploded nearby were unnerving him.

O'Donoghue reached the last of the Company K men, and looked up to watch a young private in the next company climb up on the back of their trench, stand tall, and bark like a dog at the enemy hidden in the woods in front of them. He jumped back down after a few barks and howls, but not before a Yankee sharpshooter grazed his leg with a minie bullet.

Without warning, a cannon shell landed in the midst of Company I which was next in the trench alongside Company K. Simultaneously three things happened to Sergeant O'Donoghue. He felt the concussion as the shell exploded; he heard the incredibly loud crack of the explosion; and he saw a red mist fill the trench ahead of him. In another instant he saw men writhing in the smoke. O'Donoghue couldn't tell how many men were dead or hurt. He watched one man sitting against the trench wall, holding his hands around the bleeding stumps of both his legs. Another man had been torn in half by the exploding shell and his belt now lay loose on the trench floor, separated from his shredded torso and missing legs. Barking Private Hampton and Sergeant Robert Chalk were thrown from the trench, both men bruised, cut, and scraped, but both were able to crawl back into the ditch. Other men were now moving in the smoke, trying to help their company pards.

The artillery shells finally stopped falling. Within a minute, shaken sergeants and lieutenants were moving in the trench urging their men to find their weapons, clean off the dirt and take their positions along the trench wall facing the Union infantry. The men in Company I may have been slower than most in responding to their leaders, as they left seven dead and wounded men on the trench floor, all victims of the single exploding shell from the gunboat in the river.

Sergeant Degas made his way along the trench trying to assure the men in his charge that the worst was over. He repeated over and over that it would soon be their turn to cut down the Yanks who were about to enter the killing field they had cleared of brush with their axes. But his gruff manner did little to diminish the men's fears, except perhaps for Private McDonald, who alone seemed unfazed by the cannon barrage. Jesús was leaning against the trench wall standing on the firing step, his musket laid on the dirt under the head log. Bain was next to him.

"Hey, Bain, I figured it out."

"You figured what out, Jesse?"

"I figured out we need a mascot. A dog. You know, a mutt to march with us, and lick his balls and beg for food we ain't got while we're sitting around the campfire."

"Jesse, you are something else. Every Yankee in Arkansas is about to come out of those trees right at you and me, and you're thinking about getting a puppy. Besides, an hour ago your mind was on my sister. Which is it you want, a puppy or my sister? Nah, forget I said that. Would you mind ever so much just thinking about the damyankees for a bit. Is your musket loaded? I don't see a cap on it."

"Sure Bain."

"Sure you're thinking about Yankees, or sure your musket's loaded?"

"Well, both I reckon."

"That's real good, 'cause here they come."

The edge of the woods across the field had suddenly blossomed blue. Several red and white striped banners unfurled over the blue line, and drum beats became audible. When the Federal line of infantry was clear of the woods, the Confederate colonels up and down the line ordered their regiments to open fire. Musket fire from the trenches shrouded the men in thick white smoke. The Federals marched forward and Gill could see men dropping, and even saw a large blue regimental flag dip low almost to the ground, before being pulled upright again. About half way across the field, the Union soldiers started going to ground, seeking cover in the shallow dips or behind brush and stumps. Just going prone took most of them out of the Rebs' line of sight as the southerners in the trench were firing from nearly ground level.

Gill could also again hear the Union artillery shells from the gunboats as they fired at Fort Hindman itself, trying to silence the big cannons there. But the explosions barely registered, Gill's whole focus was on the infantry coming towards them. The 1,500 riflemen in the Texas brigade were trying very hard to put forth a curtain of lead that would stop the Federal assault.

Captain McAllister appeared near Gill, pulled him down from the firing step.

"Where's Sergeant O'Donoghue?"

"I don't know, Captain. Ain't seen him since he we left the rifle pits. But I saw Sergeant Degas off that way," Gill answered pointing to his right.

"How are your platoon's cartridges holding out?"

"We ain't been fighting that long, so most of the men probably still have plenty."

"Good enough. Get your boys and fall in behind the first platoon when they come by. We've been ordered down to the left where the general's thinking Billy might move around our flank. Seems them Arkansas boys out past the trench need some Texas backbone."

"Captain, that's likely to be out where the ditch is real shallow. Ain't been dug deep at all yet. Hardly any cover, and it's flat as a pancake out that way. It's gonna be hot."

Captain McAllister looked sternly at Corporal Gill and said, "I ain't your pal, Corporal, just because I overlooked the ghost bushwhacker on the march, so beware what you say." Then the captain continued, "Bring your platoon, Mr. Gill. We're about to see who's got grit. And keep an eye for Sergeant O'Donoghue."

Company K moved past the other two regiments in Garland's Brigade. Then they were in the half-finished section of the trench and found themselves unprotected and still in the killing zone of the Federal infantry whose firing had not lessened.

"Go prone, Boys!" Captain McAllister yelled as Federal bullets hummed by.

"Now crawl, dammit. No need to get knocked over in our first tussle."

Crawling on all fours to shorten their silhouettes, and with rifles slung on their backs, Company K moved to the left while under fire. One man's rump was nicked by a bullet when he rose too high, and he lurched forward knocking into the man ahead of him, yelping and cursing. The others hunkered down further and kept moving as fast as they could. Finally they reached the end of line, where the Federals were not yet firing.

"Here, lads, form up here." Captain McAllister rose, stopped and pointed out to his NCO's where the colonel had directed his company, beyond the point where the half-dug trench ended.

"Company, kneel! Keep low!"

There were six companies, two pulled from each regiment in Garland's brigade. They were stretched out in a single rank in the shallow, partly dug ditch that bent backwards in a bow, over 300 rifles waiting nervously for the expected assault.

Soon Captain McAllister could see movement in the tree line, affirming that the Federals were seeking to turn the flank of the Rebs. Wisely, the blue troops were keeping well inside the cover of the trees, but their movement was plain enough to a man who had spent a decade searching the brush for Comanche ambushes.

Having decided the Union infantry had faced about, and were ready to leave the protection of the trees about two hundred yards away, Captain McAllister called out, "Company, rise! Fire by file. Ready, aim...Fire!"

Sergeant O'Donoghue, now at the right end of the company line, suddenly realized that the men were in a single rank, not the double files that they had always drilled in when learning and practicing to fire by file. "Johnson, that's you, Boy, fire NOW!" Johnson jerked the trigger, whooped, and dropped the butt of his Enfield into the dirt to reload. Man by man the rest of the company fired one at a time in a rolling volley that lasted almost a minute. Then each man continued to load and fire without further orders.

Captain McAllister's command to fire had coincided with the first rank of the Federals stepping into the open. The rolling fire had an impact, as Gill saw several blue coated soldiers fall or stumble backwards. All along the hillside, the six companies continued shooting.

The Federals quickly disappeared in the smoke of the Confederates' firing as they moved back into the trees, the regiment's colonel having learned rather abruptly that their flanking movement had been expected. He withdrew his regiment further back into the forest and ordered two companies to deploy at the edge of the tree line as skirmishers. Then he sent a runner to his brigade commander, politely suggesting that all four regiments in the brigade might be needed to complete his orders to find and turn the Rebs' flank.

Seeing the puffs of smoke of the new Yankee skirmish line, Captain McAllister ordered his men to cease firing and lie down as flat as they could and ignore the skirmishers. Several minutes passed and the slow skirmish fire from the tree line didn't appear to cause any casualties in Gill's platoon, but he wanted to be sure.

Crawling, Gill moved by each man until he found Jesús, stone still, his eyes shut. Gill reached out and shook Jesús's foot. "Jesse, you OK?"

Jesús's foot jerked, and he raised his head up as he turned to see who was behind him. Suddenly Jesús's hat jumped on his head, a little cloud of dust flying off it. Jesús ducked his head again as he said, "Dang it, Bain, I told you I weren't going to offend your sister. Why you trying to get me kilt, reaching out and grabbing me like that?"

"Jesse, you were sleeping. You were sleeping during our first battle. Sleeping! How can you do that? How can you just shut your eyes and sleep when we're all being shot at? There's men out there trying to kill you. And me. How can you sleep?"

" Well, heck, Bain, I didn't sleep at all last night in that danged cold hole. I just sat and shook, and there wasn't even room to lie down. I never slept a wink. And the sun sure does feel warm out here."

"Yea, I know. But just stay awake, alright? And take off that scarf. It's so red it looks like someone done cut your throat. And it makes you noticeable."

" Sure, Bain. Wide awake, ready to shoot me some bluebellies. But I'm keeping my scarf on. It is my luck. *Mi madre* made it for me and told me to keep it on and the Lord will protect me."

"Well, keep down, and you might want to take off that damned sombrero. It's a sure 'nuff target. Reckon those boys in the woods never seen a hat quite so tall. It's like shootin' at a foot high ant hill."

"Aw, Bain, there you go to meddlin' again. It's just a bit high," Jesús muttered in a hurt voice. But he took off his tall black sombrero and set it beside him just the same, not noticing the new bullet hole at the top of the hat's crown.

The wait ended with a line of blue coated soldiers coming into view from the edge of the woods barely a hundred yards distant. They advanced slowly behind their skirmishers and used what cover was available as they moved forward.

"Company, rise! Independent fire! Choose your targets. Aim at their belts, boys," yelled Captain McAllister. Each man began the methodical process of aiming, firing, and loading. Over and over, each man dropped the butt of his Enfield to the ground, pulled a paper cartridge from his cartridge box, bit off the folded end, poured powder into his musket's barrel, pushed the lead minie bullet into the barrel, pulled the ramrod from under the barrel, rammed the bullet to the bottom of the barrel, returned the rammer to its slot under the barrel, and finally grabbed a priming cap in the pouch on his belt and put it on the firing cone. Only then did a soldier hoist the nine pound weapon to his shoulder, pull back the hammer, take quick aim at a spot of blue and squeeze the trigger. The white smoke from their muskets hid the Federal soldiers as often as not, causing most of the firing to be made blind.

Four times the Federal infantry started forward, advancing into the heavy fire from the defenders. Four times the blue lines refused to close the gap, unwilling to continue forward.

During the fighting Sergeant O'Donoghue had rejoined the company and now paced back and forth behind the single line cautioning the men to stand firm, aim low, and keep their wits. Gill had returned to his post at the end of the platoon and begun shooting. After firing only a few rounds, Gill noticed his Enfield's barrel was growing too hot to touch without singeing his fingers. Then he forgot the quick pain and just loaded and fired, loaded and fired, without thought. As he was groping in his pockets for one more cartridge, Gill felt a hand on his shoulder and turned to see Sergeant O'Donoghue loudly telling him to cease firing. Gill looked to his right and saw that the other men were reloading but not raising their weapons to their shoulders.

Jesús yelled, "Why we stoppin'? *Los soldados azure*, they're still down there."

Gill shrugged his shoulders as he realized the Federals were no longer firing at them. Then he heard a loud "Cease Firing!" command from Captain McAllister. Without further orders, Gill and the others moved their muskets to their shoulders and stood waiting. Gill looked sideways, saw Jesús raising his canteen and swallowing a long drink, and he did the same. When he

34

lowered his canteen, Gill saw a Yankee officer walking towards them with a handkerchief on the end of his sword held high. Colonel Deshler, a twenty-nine year old West Point graduate who commanded the second brigade of Texans, moved out to meet him.

The two men stood not far in front, close enough for Gill to hear their palaver.

"Colonel, your general has surrendered the fort. It is over. Look around. You must order your men to ground their arms."

"No, sir, I will not. And your men are still moving towards us. You, sir, will order them to halt where they are, or I will instead order another volley on them."

"Colonel, sir, please...."

"Order your men to halt where they are, or we will fire upon them. By damn, sir, I do not jest."

With a hard look into the Texan's eyes, the Federal colonel turned and called, "Battalion, halt! Captains, hold your companies where they are. No further movement forward."

Then looking back at his opponent in gray, the northerner said, "My men will not advance further until you disarm your men. It is over, sir."

"Colonel, while your order to your men was prudent, I remain committed to my orders to hold this line. I am not accustomed to yielding to tyrants, and I do not intend to succumb to your trickery. I shall not disarm my troops without the direct order of General Churchill himself. But I will grant you the time to withdraw your men and return to your boats, or we will re-engage our fire."

With a deep sigh, the Union colonel said, "Allow me ten minutes, sir, to send a courier to fetch your general." With that, he summoned a lieutenant to whom he handed a hastily scribbled note. The Union colonel then turned, paced back to the front rank of his men, and ordered them to hold their muskets at the ready, but not to fire.

Lieutenant Henry Burns was behind the other men in Company K when the firing stopped. When he saw the Union officers begin to approach, he quickly reached out and patted the two men directly in front of him on their shoulders. With his finger to his lips in a sign to remain quiet, he started walking backwards, motioning for the two men to follow him. They looked at each other and simultaneously turned and followed the lieutenant, moving to the rear. When the trio was twenty yards back, they reached a few bushes to crouch behind. Burns leaned in close to the other two men and said, "I just know them Yank officers are coming up to tell us it's over, that the fort is lost, and for us to surrender. I'm not going to a Yankee prison, and I need you to go with me back to Texas."

The two privates nodded and the three stood and in a stooped-over run, they fled. If they had looked around they would have seen other lone men and small groups moving quickly back into the trees as they were doing. Altogether, within just a few minutes hundreds of the five thousand defenders of Arkansas Post abandoned their regiments and ran for the woods and swamp rather than wait for a formal surrender.

After half an hour, as the two rows of soldiers separated by only a few yards stood and stared at each other, a mixed party of blue and gray officers walked into view from the far side of the slope that hid the fort. Among them was General Churchill. He called for Colonel Deshler, as well as all the company commanders, to attend him. There he quietly affirmed to them that the fort's artillery had been battered into submission by the heavy cannonade from the Yankee ironclads, that the Yankee infantry far outnumbered them, and Fort Hindman was now in Federal hands. In spite of the fact that the Texans were still holding their end of the defensive line, the surrender of all their forces was real.

The captains absorbed this news, saluted the general, and moved towards their waiting commands. As soon as McAllister was close enough to be heard he called the company to attention.

"Men...some damned coward has raised the white flag." Gill and O'Donoghue looked quickly at each other, then stared past the captain at the Federal soldiers across the way. They were moving forward with bayonets fixed and muskets lowered.

"I am shamed as a man and shamed as your captain to give this order in our first contact with the enemy, but..." Captain McAllister paused, turned and stared for a long second at the line of blue coated soldiers who were almost upon them, then squared his shoulders, looked straight ahead, and with all the dignity he could muster, ordered, "Company, Ground... Arms." Gill hesitated, as did many of the men, then knelt on one knee, laid his musket on the ground and stood to attention.

Captain McAllister then directed the first sergeant to have any wounded men pulled from the line. The captain, along with other company and regimental commanders, made a special effort to ignore the sight of many men stepping back and turning to run towards the woods before the Federals reached them. He didn't mind if a smaller company surrendered, and devoutly wished he could have run for the woods too. After a dramatic pause, Captain McAllister turned to confront their captors and with a force betraying his anger, plunged the end of his sword into the earth, leaving it shaking while he and Company K awaited their fate as prisoners of war.

Chapter 4

Last Two Weeks in January 1863,
Union Riverboat John J. Roe, on the Mississippi River
42 Men Present for Duty

C orporal Gill tried to shift from one haunch to the other, but the men on either side were scrunched in so close to him that movement was nearly impossible. While the left side of his rump was aching from the long hours of sitting, Gill reflected that at least he was inside and there was some amount of body warmth from the men packed in around him. His thoughts went to the unfortunate men crowded onto the deck of the steamship John J Roe, men who had little protection from the freezing rain and must be suffering terribly without blankets or overcoats. It was not yet dawn of the first night on the crowded transport ships. The new prisoners had been suffering from the frigid air and snow since before dusk when the long lines of men had sullenly shuffled onto the big paddle-wheelers. With the enlisted men and the officers intentionally separated as soon as they had surrendered, the non-commissioned officers were sought out by the young privates seeking answers and assurances of their safety.

"Corporal Gill?" Bain looked around to see the broad face of Private Gustav Marquerd just inches from his own. He was younger than Bain, and Bain had been surprised when the two Marquerd brothers had enlisted in the Alamo Rifles. The Marquerd spread was a good piece to the north of San

38

Antonio, and not many German homesteads willingly gave up two healthy sons whose labor was needed all the time and whose guns were needed when the Comanche threatened. Besides, the family had only been in Texas a few years, and both boys were born in Germany. It seemed to Bain that the new German immigrants generally held no strong feelings about the politics of states' rights. Moreover, the tradition of slave trading was not part of their European culture, and if anything, the more vocal Germans tended to question the Christian basis for such commerce. In fact many German farmers would not even contract for the labor of skilled black men held in bondage, betraying a stubbornness that did not endear them to their neighbors who profited from renting the services of slaves. Bain didn't know if the Marquerd brothers even understood the concept of a state seceding from the Union. But the Marquerd father, himself a veteran of the Prussian army, had relented to the recruiters and allowed his sons to enlist. Both Gustav and Edward were small in stature and had turned out to be dependable, if not enthusiastic soldiers.

"Yea, Gus, what's wrong? Is my elbow poking you in the ribs too hard? Can't help it much if it is, since we're crammed in here like steers in a chute. Have you seen your brother since we got shoved onto this boat?"

"*Nein*, Corporal, it is not your elbow, and I did see Edward. I think he is against the wall and not in the snow. I am only asking if you know where we are going on this freezing river. What will the Yankees do with us? Will we be put to work in a prison? And I am thinking if we might be offered a chance to buy our release. That is, if our families would send money. I think my mother would ask my father to do that."

"Well now, Gus, I don't rightly know where we are going, except up river, where it ain't going to be any warmer. I reckon it will be a prison somewhere, and danged if I know if we will be put to work. I hope so, myself. I sure wouldn't want to spend the rest of this war doin' nuthin' but settin' and waitin' for it to end. But it sure looks like we won't be in the fight again. Seems one battle is all we're going to get. Maybe we should be grateful for that."

"Corporal, I will not be sad about that. The fighting was not ... what I am thinking it would be. I was....fearful I would die. I do not wish to be in a dirt trench again. I do not wish to be shot at again. Do you think the Yankee officers will allow my father to pay to have me let go? I have heard of such arrangements between generals before we crossed the ocean. It would be a civilized thing, I think. "

"Gus, I don't know how the generals fight wars in Europe. But I don't think the Yankee generals are going to send letters to all our families offering to send us home for fifty dollars a head. They have gone to considerable trouble to get us on this damned boat. I just can't see them letting us go for money. Heck, the Yankee states are afloat in money. Nope, I do think we are bound for a long stay in prison. As long as this war lasts."

"Then I will offer prayers for a short war. Perhaps when we get off this boat and into a warm prison with dry blankets, you will teach me what reasons we became soldiers to march so far, to work so hard with shovels, and then to shoot at men who are not Comanche. I will like to learn why we did this."

"That's a tall order, Gus, but I imagine we'll have time to consider those questions. But danged if I know the answers. Maybe we can figure 'em out together."

Gill was still pondering the hours right after the mass surrender. First the men had been inspected by Yankee generals and colonels who had slowly ridden their horses up and down the long lines of Confederates. Gill remembered one colonel who peered straight at him over the tops of his reading spectacles, then looked down at the crumpled paper in his hand, as if checking off that Gill was where he was supposed to be. It was a humiliating feeling to be examined like he was a steer in a herd. Gill wouldn't have been surprised if the colonel had dismounted and ordered Gill to open his mouth so he could inspect his teeth.

Later in the afternoon, some Federal guards had pestered the captives near them to partake in a singing match. Gill hadn't known what to make of this effort to start a friendly competition after a morning of earnestly trying to kill each other. He figured maybe the Yankee guards were just as homesick as he was and just as tired of being soldiers as he already was. After all, they were mostly all young and not but a year or two past their school days, and they all were a long ways from home and families. Perhaps they thought they could erase the horror of the morning by reverting to the harmless experience of singing like they were schoolboys again. Whatever the motivation, the Yank guards had started off with a lusty version of "The Star Spangled Banner," to which a group of Texans had countered with "The Girl I Left Behind Me." The two songs broke the ice, and the guards then sang "Hail Columbia, Happy Land." While the words to this popular patriotic song riled up some of the POWs, others including Gill, were saddened by the poignancy of its lyrics. Not to be outdone by northern sentimentality, the Confederates then sang "The Bonnie Blue Flag" and "Dixie" with unabashed gusto. At point, a Federal colonel with great drooping mustaches had stepped up and ordered the serenading to stop.

Bain rubbed his bare elbow, exposed and raw from the holes in his jacket and shirt. While the afternoon after the surrender of Fort Hindman had included the unexpected rations and singing, he still had been in shock. In the long hours of marching through Texas and Arkansas he often thought about the unknown dangers ahead, wondering if he would be wounded or killed. But he never even considered that his first battle would end in the surrender and capture of his whole regiment and brigade, and certainly not the whole Confederate army. Gill thought he would never come to grips with how that happened, how some high ranking officer had panicked and waved a white handkerchief, causing the fearful men in his command to toss down their muskets; the sight of others giving up causing the capitulation of company after company and regiment after regiment, as the plague of surrender swept down the mile-long trench.

Gill had heard during the long afternoon and night of their capture that Deshler's brigade of Texans were the last to stop fighting, but he also had heard that Colonel Garland, his regimental commander, was one of those being cursed for first waving the white handkerchief. Gill had also heard it was a chaplain from another brigade, but he doubted he would ever learn what the real facts were. Whoever started the panic, the outcome was the same: 4,000 Confederate soldiers were being transported up the river to POW camps in northern states. Gill didn't know that the defenders of Fort Hindman had faced an army of nearly 32,000 Federals, and the loss of the fort was pretty much assured from the moment the battle started.

Gill looked up to see young Benjamin Quinn standing in front him, feet planted awkwardly among the legs of other men who glared up at him.

One of the men, Private Bernard Anderson, gruffly muttered, "Move on, nigger, you smell like mule dung."

Even though Anderson was a large man, Quinn ignored him and asked Gill, "Bain, have you seen Cap'n McAllister? I needs him to write Pap about the wagon. Pap ain't gonna take kindly to us losin' the red wagon and the mules. Don't see that we'll ever lay eyes on 'em agin."

"I said move, nigger. Now do it, 'fore I toss your black ass in the river. Why you on this damn boat anywise? You ain't no soljer."

Quinn still said nothing but moved away from the man, and Gill got up and followed him. When they reached the rail, Quinn said, "I knows we don't carry no rifles, but me and Matt, we're free men, and we wear gray coats just like you do. The Yankee officer, he said 'cause we're Negroes, we could put on the blue coats and drive the red wagon for them. But we both said, 'Naw, sir, we're teamsters fo' the Sixth. We goin' where the Alamo Rifles are goin'."

"Ben, you know we're going to prison? We're being taken somewhere up north to sit out the rest of the war like drunk cowboys in the jailhouse, if we don't all freeze to death on this boat first. You know that? You don't have to be here. You can just tell the Yankees you'll drive for them. You don't have to be freezing here with us."

"Bain, I know you're just tryin' to look out for me and Matt. But we're from San Antone too. Our daddies be friends. Hell, Jesús is our cousin. He's kin! How can you say we could turncoat on you?"

Gill reached out and patted Ben's shoulder and said, "Never mind what I said, Ben. I weren't thinking straight. But you listen to me now. I haven't seen Captain McAllister. He may not be on this boat. And I already heard that the Yanks are going to take the officers to their own camp. Our sergeants will be in charge once we land. If we ever get a chance, I'll write a letter to your pap about the wagon and us getting captured and you and Matt staying with the boys from San Antone. But he's going to hear it anyway, because the news of us surrendering back at the fort will be in the newspapers back home. It'll be big news. For now, you get with Matt and you two stay together and stay close to your cousin Jesse or me. That man you were standing over is one of ours, and he ain't a real friendly feller, and there's a lot more like him on this boat, especially towards colored folk."

"Bain, I seen plenty of his kind. I know not to rile up white men. Me and Matt, we born free men, but we know we ain't free like you free. We been takin' the red wagon to the coast long enough to know a black man hold his tongue and nod his head iffin' he don't want big trouble, even if he's a born free man."

"Good enough, Ben. You best find Matt now and you two find a corner somewhere and try to stay warm."

The journey upriver took twelve days during which the winter weather never abated. Several men died on the open deck of the boat. The snow and freezing temperatures were simply too harsh for men who were already sick or of fragile health.

"Jesse, get up and help me here," Gill nudged his friend Jesús McDonald, and watched him slowly uncurl from his cramped position that had his legs half wrapped around a barrel. "Come on. You grab Walter's legs and I'll get his arms." Jesús had been fitfully sleeping in spite of the cold, and he was surprised to see another Company K man, Walter Sweigart, dead and propped up against a crate.

"Aw, Bain, do we have to touch him? Can't he just set there?"

"Sorry, Jesse, but he can't. We got living men who need that spot by the crate. It blocks some of the wind, so grab hold." Jesús took a deep breath and bent to the task. The two young men carried their expired friend to the rail of the boat and laid him on the deck.

"Bain, you think Walter would mind if I borrow his jacket?" Jesús's teeth were chattering, and he was shivering.

Corporal Gill looked at his friend, "Naw, Jesse, I don't think Walter would mind at all. He was always willing to help out a friend. And I bet his jacket will fit right over the top of yours. Let's pull it off before he gets any stiffer. And pull your mama's scarf up over your ears."

Twice the boats had already put in to shore to allow the dead to be buried, but they didn't know how long before it would be before the next burial party could go ashore. The two young men removed the dead man's coat with some difficulty and Private McDonald gratefully put it on. Walter's skin was already turning a pale blue and was disturbing to those men who had no choice but to remain near him.

Once a day the prisoners were fed hard crackers and a thin soup that had been half warmed on the stoves in the galleys. While the prisoners quickly ate what little was offered, few guessed that the poor fare given them on the steamboats would be better and more plentiful than what they would receive during their coming internment.

On the fifth day out, the weather warmed a bit, but snow still blanketed the Missouri shoreline. The John J Roe was only a few yards from the bank, having stopped to load firewood onto the deck of the steamship. Gill and most of Company K were on the open deck watching the work crew hauling the wood across the plank bridge from the shore to the boat.

"Bain, look yonder! Look!" Jesús was excitedly pounding Gill on the back as they both watched a group of six young ladies stroll down from the road to the edge of the water. The young women were each carrying a straw basket, and the Confederates on the deck were hoping the baskets might contain fried chicken, meat pies, or cookies, gifts that would cheer the prisoners. Their hopes were bolstered as the women daintily made their way as close to the shore as they could, and then started pulling out what was hidden under the linen napkin covers. Jesús and several others were beside themselves, already tasting what they knew would be fine delicacies, when the first snowball flew towards them, hurled by a blonde girl in a blue calico dress. The snowball hit McDonald square in the chest, and his jaw dropped, leaving the normally glib young soldier speechless. His surprise changed to glee as all the young women threw snowball after snowball at the prisoners, laughing and calling out to them.

James Kincaid, a private in Company G, was standing on the other side of McDonald from Corporal Gill, and called back at the girls. Kincaid was a tall handsome man of twenty years who had been more depressed than most of the men about their new status as prisoners. Any talk of parole or exchange just worsened his mood, as he firmly believed that the northern generals had no need or intention to send southern prisoners back before the war was over. Seeing the teenage girls laughing and flirting with the men on the boat snapped something in Kincaid, and while waving to the Missouri girls, he said, "I'd rather be dead than stay a captive another minute." With that Kincaid vaulted himself over the rail of the steamboat, landing in the water just a foot or two from the bank. Kincaid was thrashing in the frigid water trying to find his footing while several Union guards, who had been watching the young ladies with equal pleasure, quickly raised their Springfield muskets and fired at Kincaid. Two bullets zipped into the water near him, but one bullet hit him in the shoulder and another entered his chest.

Most of the gaggle of girls on shore turned and ran for home at the first shots, but two held back watching, transfixed by Kincaid who was no longer thrashing about, but from whom a circle of dark blood was spreading in the water. Then, quickly, the blonde girl who had thrown the first snowball pulled her friend into the water where they waded the two steps to Kincaid, and each lifting one arm, they dragged the half-floating soldier to the shore. There with his head bobbing and hidden by their loose wet skirts, the girls somehow managed to pull him out of the water. With sobs and shouts at the guards, they laid Kincaid on his back in the snow. Kincaid's eyes were already glossed over, and only God knew if he was aware of his pretty rescuers, the girls whose teenage frivolity had inadvertently driven him to leap to the freedom of the hereafter. One of the girls took the linen napkin from a basket and placed it over Kincaid's face. Then without a look back, they stood and arm in arm walked back to the road and out of sight.

The next day the John J Roe inexplicably began to drift sideways towards the west bank of the river where a slight bend left a short cliff that was not yet undercut and was almost as tall as the hurricane deck of the steamboat. The prisoners who were crowded on the deck nearest the pilot house could hear the captain and the pilot yelling at each other, and any who looked could see the pilot excitedly pointing towards the embankment while the captain continued to hold the wheel steady. The Confederates were eagerly watching the shore grow closer and closer, until the top of the embankment was just a few feet away and a few feet below them. As quickly and as silently as startled deer, several prisoners bounded over the rail, landed on the bank, and scuttled away into the brush. The corner of the cabin wall prevented the nearest guards from seeing that small section of the deck rail, so the escape was successful. Within seconds the river boat found its forward line again and quickly slid back into the current in the middle of the river. Those who witnessed this event never learned if the boat's captain was a loyal southern man, or simply a clumsy one.

That night, Private McDonald found Corporal Gill sitting against the wall of the cabin brooding over his bad luck in not being able to jump ship with the others that afternoon. "Bain, did you hear about them boys in Company G of the 15th Regiment?"

"No, Jesse, I ain't. They planning to jump off the boat too? If so, they better be real careful now."

"Heck, no, Bain, it's better'n that. They done got away 'fore we ever got on the boat."

"You mean they deserted during the fight back at the fort? You mean they run off during the shooting? Or did the whole company slip away while we were waiting there at the end before we gave up our guns?"

"Nah, not that. Well, sort of, maybe. What I hear is that Company G was sent out as skirmishers on the very end of the trench line to keep the Yanks from wading the creek and flanking us. Then when the shootin' stopped and they saw all the white flag ruckus and us'ns laying down our muskets, they just kind of melted down into the brush and waded that creek themselves and never did get caught."

"Don't mean they got away though," said Bain.

"Well, it does mean they ain't freezing on this damned boat headin' upriver to a Yankee prison."

"That's a fact. Maybe someday we'll meet them boys in a saloon back in Texas."

"Well, if we do, they owe us a *cerveza* for not rescuin' us."

"Yea, sure. Jesse. Now leave me alone and let me just go back to sittin' and thinkin' how you and me might get off this tub. Why don't you find your cousins Matt and Ben and see how they're doing. You can cheer them up with your stories."

Unknown to Corporal Gill and the other enlisted men who were living on the open deck of the John J Roe, others were successfully pondering the same challenge of how to escape the boat. Colonel Majors was a Confederate staff officer and shared a tiny stateroom with three other officers. Colonel Majors was a man of means, both clever and with a wallet full of Yankee dollars. During the early days of the river voyage, he had befriended a porter on the boat, and with an ample bribe had managed to purchase a Union captain's frock coat, kepi, and navy blue trousers. The next day when the steamship was again docked to take on provisions, Majors had simply put on the Federal officer uniform and strolled up to the sentry at the gang plank, saluted him, and disappeared into the crowd on the busy pier, not to be seen again. But Corporal Gill was not so well heeled, enterprising or audacious, and he and Jesús remained on the cold deck of the John J Roe and shivered through more days and nights.

Shortly before the small fleet of steamboats left the shoreline of Missouri to head further north up the Mississippi River, they were moored off shore at the village of Cape Girardeau, once again waiting while more fuel wood was loaded aboard. Gill, McDonald, and several others were leaning over the rail enjoying what warmth the afternoon sun brought. Gill heard a shout and looked to his right. Near the shoreline a young black man was waving his arm in greeting. Impulsively, Jesús waved back.

The black man yelled, "Is you mons soljers goin' to fight the 'cesh?"

"No, *Señor*, we are the 'cesh!" called back McDonald.

"You mean you all is 'cesh from down da riber? You not be soljers from up da riber? Dat mon, he gots the blue coat on," pointing toward a Federal guard wearing a blue great coat.

"That's right. We are prisoners of these here damyankees who done caught us with our drawers down."

The black man in his ragged clothes considered that for a short moment, then jumped, lifting both feet off the ground, twirled in the air and ran off.

"Dang it all, Jesse, I believe you done scared that feller plum out of his wits."

"Maybe he never saw such a handsome man and is off to tell his mammy about me."

Within minutes the young man was back with two other black men and two black women. The first man with great animation pointed at Gill and McDonald and then at their guards. Then the next man started mimicking a marching soldier and pointed an imaginary gun at the third man who put his hands high in the air, loudly laughing. The two women pranced around in circles, dancing and whooping, stopping only to wriggle their backsides towards the boat. Meanwhile, the three men went down on all fours, and pawed at the snow with their hands and feet, snorting, howling, and pretending to be bulls or mad dogs or some sort of fierce imagined animal.

"Maybe you 'cesh now feel da whip!" one woman shouted at the prisoners.

46

"You be sayin' Massah to da mon in da blue coats now, yessee you be!"

"Here, boy, put da black on dese boots," shouted the first man holding out his bony bare foot and guffawing at his own joke.

The joy of the five black men and women was so clear that the all the Confederates at the rail were taken back. Few of them had been around many Negroes, free or slave, and those few had been house servants or laborers, always reserved and deferring to any white men.

"Those bucks must be chawin' loco weed," one private muttered. "They would do well by a whuppin'."

Corporal Gill was still watching the antics of the five, and as their boat started moving again, he replied, "Well, that may be, but we're the ones who have been shot at, rounded up like cattle, and are headed up river to a prison, and they're the ones dancing on the shore. Maybe their sun is just now rising and our day is getting on towards dusk."

Chapter 5

February 1863, Camp Butler, near Springfield, Illinois
39 Men Present for Duty

The boats finally docked. The enlisted men were led off the transport boats and loaded onto train cattle cars. They were packed in tightly, nearly too tight to sit, and the floor planks of the cattle cars were covered in manure and stank of urine. This last leg of the trip took a long day, and they finally off-loaded at an old army training camp near Springfield, Illinois. It was called Camp Butler and had been converted to a prison to house the huge numbers of Confederate soldiers who had been captured over the past year in the western theater of the still-young war. Corporal Gill and his companions soon learned Camp Butler was already brimming with sullen gaunt soldiers.

The Texas prisoners had been in camp for only a day and were standing in line to receive a tin plate of beans. Private McDonald, with hands thrust into his pants pockets and head down in the cold wind, was wearing his mother's wool scarf.

"You, yea, you, Mex Boy! Fall out of line and come here!" The order was given by a tall corporal who was pacing up and down the line of Confederates. His words were directed to Jesús, who dutifully stepped out of the food line and stood before the Union corporal.

"What's that thing on your head, boy? Is that a hat or a chicken coop?"

48

McDonald stammered it was a hat and kept his eyes down.

"Is that a Mex hat, boy? I heared the Mex wear them tall hats so they can hide stolen chickens on top of their heads. Is that what you do, boy?"

"No, Corporal, I have never been a chicken thief."

"I bet. What's that wrapped around your neck? Looks to me like something you stole."

"No, Corporal, that is a gift from my mother. She made it for me before I joined up."

"Joined up? You mean this rabble is something you joined up? Don't look like nuthin' but outlaws and ruffians to me. Hand me that gift from your mama. Take it off from around your scrawny neck."

McDonald stiffened, "Corporal, the scarf is a gift from *mi madre*. It is mine."

In answer, the Union guard swung his rifle butt around and drove it deep into Private McDonald's stomach. As he doubled over in pain, the corporal brought the hardwood butt up under McDonald's jaw, lifting him up before he crumpled to the ground. Then the corporal reached over and pulled the scarf from around the stricken man's neck.

"Reckon your *madre* just made a gift to Corporal Jones, boy. You be sure and thank her for me."

With that the corporal draped the red scarf around his neck and moved on down the line, leaving Gill to help Jesús to his feet. Neither man said anything, but both looked sullenly after the guard who was easy to recognize even from a distance with the colorful scarf around his neck.

The days at Camp Butler were slow, cold, and repetitive. There was no work for most of the prisoners, little food, few blankets, and the shelters were overcrowded and dilapidated. The guards were quick to anger and punishments were frequent and brutal. Any infraction could result in being clubbed with a rifle butt. Time crawled, and men died at a rate that reflected the conditions of the prison.

"Sergeant Chalk, are you sure about this? I mean, that's Bill in there and he ain't alive, and the rats done chewed on his face and his fingers, and you'll be pushed up against him for no telling how long. All manner of things can go wrong, and you'd be buried alive or die of starvation before the ground ever thaws, lying there next to Bill." The young private was sincerely scared for his friend and was nervous about his own role in the escape attempt.

"I'm gonna do it, and it will work. It's so cold Bill's body is frozen solid, and there's enough room in there for me. Besides, it'll be black in the coffin so I won't be studying on Bill's missing nose." Sergeant Robert Chalk was

49

talking bravely, but he shivered anyway as he assured his friends the plan would work.

"When you boys get me into the Dead House, I'll just pop out of the coffin, put the lid back on, and be off like a weasel once it gets dark. There ain't no moon, and I'll be miles down the river by sunup. They won't even know I'm gone. You just got to be sure you don't hammer in those nails, but push them easy-like into these here holes we drilled out. I'll be holding tight on to that rope handle we put under the lid. I'll make sure the top don't slip around while you're taking me and old frozen Bill to the Dead House."

"Robert, once we leave Bill's casket in the Dead House, we won't be able to check on you. We'll be inside the fence, and you'll be outside, all on your own. If that coffin lid gets stuck, well, you're going to be frozen Bill's partner 'til the Kingdom comes."

The three men were part of a detail that worked building wooden coffins for the steady trickle of prisoners who succumbed to the cold and illnesses that plagued the prisoners. The camp cemetery was outside the walls. In the midst of winter when the snows came and the ground was too frozen to dig graves, caskets containing the remains of recently departed prisoners were routinely stored for several days in the Dead House, a shack on the edge of the cemetery. Sergeant Chalk had recognized the opportunity for a resolute man to manage an escape, but now that it was the moment to climb into the casket with frozen Bill, he was wavering.

After pausing for several long seconds, Sergeant Chalk swallowed the bile in his mouth, handed the glass whiskey bottle of water he was holding to one of his friends, and stepped onto a hardtack box and into the casket, wedging himself in next to the corpse of Bill Rodgers.

"See there, boys, there's room enough for Bill and me," the sergeant said, even though in fact, Chalk was startled at how tight he and the corpse were pushed together.

"Hand me that water bottle, and ease the lid on and slide those nails through the holes. Now don't you fellers dawdle around. You load me 'n Bill onto the cart and get us to the Dead House fast as you can. Bill was a fine soldier, but I don't cotton to the prospect of spending an extra night with him." With that, Sergeant Robert Chalk smiled a thin smile to his friends, and told them, "See you fellers back in Texas."

The two soldiers followed Chalk's instructions and shoved the six nails through the pre-drilled holes. They hoped the coffin lid was snug enough not to move around when they loaded the casket onto the cart and pulled it to the Dead House. Straining with effort, they quickly set the coffin onto the back of the hand cart and set off for the front gate to the camp.

50

Within minutes, the two men were at the edge of the deadline and waved to the guards in the tower over the gate. One of the guards slung his rifle, came down the ladder, cracked open the gate, and approached the cart. The snow and ice was a slush that crunched under his boots.

"Where's your sergeant? You two always have your sergeant with you. He die off? He the one in the box today?" the corporal asked, chuckling to himself.

"Just one casket?" he then asked the pair without waiting for an answer about their missing sergeant.

"Yes, Corporal, that's all today. The poor soul inside ain't Sergeant Chalk, it's Bill Rodgers, Company F of the Sixth Texas. He done crossed over last night in his sleep."

The Union soldier grunted. "Then where is your Sergeant Chalk?"

The other prisoner gulped and quickly said, "He's down at the sinks. Has been half the morning. Has the loose bowels today and told us to go on without him. He said didn't want to shit frozen turds all down the road."

The guard laughed at the joke and accepted the probable truth to the answer. Walking up to the cart, he pulled his bayonet from its scabbard and poked at the wooden casket. One of the biggest fears that surfaced during the prisoners' planning was that the guards would discover the casket lid was not tightly nailed down. Before they loaded frozen Bill into the casket, they had tested to see if Sergeant Chalk could hold the lid in place using the rope handle under the lid. It seemed to work, but that didn't make the moment any easier. Next the guard tried to push the edge of the lid sideways but couldn't move it. Finally, he slipped the tip of his bayonet into the seam between the lid and the top edge of the casket, and pried up. The two prisoners pulling the cart swallowed hard but didn't say a thing. The lid didn't move.

"All right, you men can take Bill Rodgers on down to the Dead House. I reckon he'll sleep well enough there for a few nights until this weather breaks and you can plant him."

The guard stepped to the side of the road and the two prisoners slowly pulled the cart through the gate. The Dead House was a quarter of a mile from the gate and by the time the pair reached it, Sergeant Chalk had been in the casket for well over an hour. They pulled the casket off the cart and set it on the ground. The guard, who had followed the cart from the gate, leaned against the side of the cart and yawned. Chalk's two friends opened the door to the shack and again lifted the casket, struggling with the weight of the two men inside.

51

"You boys seem to be working purty hard to lift old Bill Rogers. He must have had some meat on his bones, not like most of you scarecrows."

"Yessir, Bill was a tall one and liked his rations, and everybody else's too."

After just a few steps they set the casket on top of one they had brought in the day before. As they turned to leave, they heard a muffled voice from within the casket. They couldn't understand what the voice was saying, but it sounded agitated. One man immediately thumped his palm hard on the lid, urgently trying to signal to the live man in the box that they were not alone.

The guard heard the thump and called out, "Hurry up in there. Them dead men don't care how straight you stack 'em up. Get out here and let's get going. My toes are starting to freeze."

The two men looked at each other, shrugged, and left the building. They closed the door, and pulled the cart back to the confines of Camp Butler, leaving their friend Sergeant Robert Chalk in the Dead House. When Sergeant Chalk was noted as absent during the next morning roll call, neither man so much as blinked, and they were not in the work detail that returned a week later to bury the three caskets.

"Corporal Gill, come walk with me." The invitation was offered by Sergeant O'Donoghue, who as the ranking non-commissioned officer of Company K, was still responsible for the welfare of his men. His task was nearly impossible, but he was a conscientious man and tried to do his duty.

Gill had been squatting near Jesús and a couple of other men, none doing anything but staring at the ground. Gill nodded, stood and moved off with Sergeant O'Donoghue, as they joined many other men in slowly walking the long loop around the perimeter of the prison yard.

O'Donoghue spoke first, "Tell me about those Marquerd boys. How're they doing?"

"Reckon they're doing as good as any of us, Sergeant," Gill replied. "They ain't eating enough. Their clothes are half rotted off, and they need blankets. Gustav says his teeth are all loose and his bowels are looser than his teeth." Gill managed a weak grin. "Nothin' out of the ordinary."

"Hrrmmph," O'Donoghue grunted. "I hear they've talked to a guard, asking to see a Yankee officer."

"Well, hell," Gill uttered more to himself than his sergeant. "Sergeant, you know those boys ain't been in Texas, ain't been in America, all that long. They were born in Germany somewhere. On the boat right after the surrender, Gustav asked me if their daddy could buy his and Edward's way out of prison. May be Gustav's really trying to do that. Don't reckon it's gonna work though."

O'Donoghue answered, "I also heard the Yankees are going around to each company trying to recruit men. They're saying that a man won't have to fight his own pards. That if he joins their army, he'll be sent out west to go fight the Sioux Indians. They say the Sioux been raising hell up in the state of Minnesota, purty much like the Comanch' been doing in Texas."

"Sergeant, the way things are here, fighting Sioux don't sound like such a bad way to spend out the rest of the war. At least if an injun gets his paws on you and starts cutting and gouging, you know it's because he's a heathen devil. Here, well, here the hurtin's being done by white men. White men who steal the blanket from a freezing man and dump the food off the plate of a starving man. All just to keep us in our place." Gill and O'Donoghue walked on without further words for a long time.

"Damned if I could put on a blue coat now, after what I seen here," Gill finally said softly.

"You talk to those Marquerd boys, then. See if they're really meaning to put on the blue to get out of here. Let me know."

"Yes, Sergeant, I'll do that. I wonder if more of our boys are thinking that ways."

"I don't know, Bain, but it's our job to keep the company together. Someday the war will end, or they might exchange us for Yankee prisoners anytime. If that happens, I sure don't want to fess up that any of our boys crossed over to the enemy. And they are the enemy now. After this place, how can they be anything else? Men don't do this to other men without becoming enemies."

The pair walked further along and finally Gill said, "Sergeant, Jesse McDonald told me once that his Mexican grandma had been a captive of the Ute Injuns for a spell when she was a little young'un. She learned some of their lingo and told Jesse that the word they call the Comanche means, 'those who will be my enemy forever.' Wish I knew that word, because I bet it sounds a lot like 'Yankee.'"

This time Sergeant O'Donoghue smiled grimly and nodded.

The sound of the musket was so close that both men jumped and jerked their heads towards the watchtower at the top of the wall. Gill saw the white smoke from the just fired weapon before he looked down. There lay a youngster, a boy of no more than sixteen or seventeen, eyes wide open in death as blood flowed out the wound in his chest. He was just a foot or two on the other side of the single strand of telegraph wire that marked the border of the prisoners' allowed turf. Just inside the wire the dirt was beaten down smooth and the walkway sunken a few inches below the dirt on either side. This was the perimeter path that hundreds of men walked every day in their boredom and yearning for a sense of freedom. But one step or even a stumble to the other side of the wire could cause a guard to fire. Gill and Donoghue didn't know if the young soldier had stumbled or intentionally crossed the deadline, but he was surely now dead.

Gill looked up again at the watchtower where the guard was now visible since the white smoke from his musket barrel had dissipated. Gill and the prison guard's eyes locked. The guard was wearing a great coat and kepi, with a red and brown striped scarf wrapped around his neck. He smiled at Gill and patted the stock of his musket. Then he slowly and deliberately pulled a fresh paper cartridge from his cartridge box and held it up for all to see. Then, before he bit off the end of the cartridge, he pointed his finger straight at Corporal Gill, and clearly said, "Bang, you're dead."

Soon a pair of guards came to pull the corpse out of the prohibited area next to the wall. They left the body lying across the path and ordered the next two southerners that approached to drag the remains to the store room where a dozen prisoners worked every day making wooden caskets.

Gill and O'Donoghue were standing further back, near a lean-to where more men were huddled together. Gill was mentally shaken by the guard's words and was physically shaking from the bone-chilling wind. He finally looked at Sergeant O'Donoghue and said, "That man truly scares me. He needs killin'."

Corporal Ezekial Jones walked into the barracks taking off his great coat and scarf as he approached his bunk and the stove. He walked with a slight limp. He sneered at the two privates who were warming their hands over the stove, nudging them aside as he put out his own hands towards the hot coals.

"Shot a Reb an hour ago," he announced to the pair. "The boy tripped and stumbled into the dead-zone. Got to his knees before I could knock him back down."

After a pause, one of the privates asked, "Zeke, don't that bother you none? Shooting a feller like that?"

"Corporal Jones to you. He was over the line. He could have escaped. It's why we're here - to stop any thought of escape. There are thousands of them Reb prisoners and just one regiment of us guards. Ten of them for every one of us. Don't you ever forget them odds."

"Sure, Zeke, we know that, but they're weak 'cause they're starving, and we have all the guns."

"Damn right, and we best use our guns as often as we can to keep reminding those Secesh scum where they are and that they got no hope. No sir, I'm not about to risk my hide again by being nice to them Reb trash. They got lucky with me once, and I ain't about to let that happen again."

Corporal Jones had been wounded in one leg at the battle of Shiloh several months before. The fact he had been hit by a stray bullet while hiding behind a tree was never noted by superiors, as the woods had been full of scared men trying to hide or run. The wound had been painful, the battlefield surgery to pull out the bullet even more painful, and his recovery long. The wound still ached, especially during the cold spells, even though his limp lessened each week. Jones' one constant fear was that he would be sent back to his old Ohio regiment once he was deemed fit for campaign duty. He made a point to rub at his wound and exaggerate his limp whenever the company officers or the regimental surgeon were around, but Jones was too dull to understand his clumsy subterfuge only made those men joke about him during their evening bull sessions.

Nonetheless, Ezekial Jones was a valued guard because of his instinctive brutality. The numbers of prisoners was astonishing to most of the officers stationed at Camp Butler. By early February, 1863, nearly four thousand Confederate soldiers captured at the battles of Shiloh, Fort Donelson, Arkansas Post, and even the recent battle at Stone's River, Tennessee, were confined in Camp Butler. The extremely crowded conditions left the officers of the single guard regiment always slightly nervous about the prospect of riots or a mass breakout. Harsh punishments by the guards were seen by many as critical to keeping the morale of the prisoners broken, and it seemed to work.

In mid-March the Marquerd brothers joined seven friends from Company K and one hundred and three other men from the Sixth Texas regiment in formation at the main gate. Nearly one-fourth of Company K and over three-fourths of Company I, who were mostly recent German immigrants, were in the formation. There, in front of a silent crowd of several hundred prisoners, they took the oath of allegiance to the United States of America. Then they were marched out of Camp Butler to serve as galvanized privates in the Union army. The men of Company K never learned if the Marquerd brothers spent the rest of the war fighting Sioux Indians or fighting Confederates. But those men who made it back to San Antonio after the war learned that the Marquerd ranch had been burned out, their cattle confiscated for the war effort, and the family driven north by the provost guard shortly after the list of men who had galvanized was published in the San Antonio newspaper.

"Bain, Cousin Matt found me this morning, and it don't look good for Cousin Ben," Private McDonald said to Corporal Gill as they did their daily walk around the prison yard just inside the deadline wire. Bain and Jesús knew the Quinn brothers had been assigned to the barracks building nearest the slush pool where urine from the sinks drained and the solid filth was taken in buckets by the Negroes when the sinks trench began to overflow. That dilapidated structure had no bunks and was home to the few dozen black teamsters, cooks, and body servants who had come to the prison camp with the white Confederates.

"What do you mean, Jesse?" asked Gill.

"Matthew told me that his brother has the pestilence. He's caught the small pox and they took him to the pox house yesterday."

"I'm going to get out. I ain't staying in this pig pen no longer. I'm going over that wall tonight." The speaker was Private James French, who was thirty-three and older than most of the men. It was late March, but the weather was still cold. French was talking to two other men of the Sixth Texas in the dark corner of a crowded canvas covered hut.

"What happens to us if we do get over without getting shot? What then?" asked John Alexander who was considering going with French.

"We run, then we hide, then we steal clothes and food and start walking south, I reckon," replied French.

"If I get out, I'm not headed back to Texas. I'll be going somewhere west where the war ain't reached," said the third man.

"Right, we can't go back to San Antonio. The provost guard would just send us back to the fighting with some other regiment," Alexander said.

"Well, you boys do what you gotta do. Me, I'll work my way back to Texas and take my chances in another outfit. I don't care about the war, but San Antone is home where my family is and where I'm going to live after the war, so if I have to put on a new uniform when I get back, that's what I'll do. Maybe they'll put me in an outfit that don't leave Texas. Maybe they'll put me in one of them regiments that are guarding the forts down near Galveston."

"James, you are a God fearing man, and I admire you, but once this filthy uniform is off my back, there won't never be another one on me."

"Boys, none of that matters until we are over the wall and far away from here. Do either of you know how far north we are and how to find the big river we come up? Reckon if we can get that far, we can sort out things then. How's that sound?" the third man said.

The next night the three men crouched next to the wall of a barracks, staring at the tall log fence some fifty yards away on the other side of the deadline.

"John, you go first, and kneel down on all fours next to the wall. I'm gonna run to ya and step on your back and jump up to grab the top of the logs. I'll hook a leg over and git sideways and reach down and pull you up, and then we'll both pull up John."

"Them's tall logs, James. You sure you can bounce off me and git to the top?"

"Don't know 'til we try, do we? And we can't dig under the wall and we can't gnaw through it. How else we gonna make it to the other side?"

"I dunno. How about a rope made out of jackets and trousers?"

"Only spare clothes in this place are on the corpses, and I ain't takin' the clothes off a dead man to make a rope."

"Me neither. I reckon your climbing idea is good as any. When do we go? We need a dark night and we need a long night to git a far piece down the road from here by sun-up."

"And we need a couple of days to stash some hardcrackers so we won't starve the first couple days on the outside."

Four nights later the three men, with hardcrackers stuffed in pockets, made good their escape.

Private William Oliphant was leaning against the wall of the barracks building. It was midmorning and cold enough that the seventeen year old private from Company G was shivering and had both hands crammed into the pockets of his torn trousers. His chin was tucked into the collar of his jacket, and he was staring at the ground trying to not think about home and a warm bowl of thick beef and potato stew. Oliphant was unaware of the Federal officer who walked by just a few feet in front of him until the officer had passed, stopped, turned, and stepped back to stand close to the young prisoner.

"Private, you did not salute. Didn't you 'Sech learn enough from your traitorous officers to know that privates salute officers? Especially officers in the real army. Now stand to attention and salute me, damn you!" The Union officer was short, portly, and red-faced. His breath smelled of whiskey. He wore a well cut dark blue wool overcoat, a fur cap with earflaps, and leather gloves. No insignia was visible on his coat or cap.

Oliphant cut his eyes towards the Union officer, took in his appearance, and said, "Go to Hell. It's too cold to take my hands out of my pockets, unless you're offering me your bottle."

The officer started to speak, then turned and stalked off. Within minutes a pair of armed guards approached Oliphant with bayonets fixed on their muskets. One of the guards lowered his weapon and pricked Oliphant in the ribs with his bayonet while the other stood back with his musket pointed at Oliphant's chest.

"The doc says you volunteered for a special duty. Inside, where it's warm," said the smiling guard who was pricking Oliphant's ribcage. "Let's go."

The trio made their way to a dilapidated wooden building in the far corner of the camp near the sinks. Oliphant had heard the building called the pox house and knew that bodies were removed from it almost every day. The guards nudged him forward to step inside. There stood the Union officer just inside the open door.

"Don't speak, you little piece of rat scat. I don't even want to know your name. I am Dr. Emory Merrifield, the camp surgeon, and I have selected you to work as nurse to your fellow prisoners who are afflicted with small pox. You will remain here until the pox takes you, or I decide you have learned to salute like a soldier. That means every time I enter this godforsaken room of infested men, you will rise and salute me."

Oliphant, horrified at where he was and what the doctor was saying, but striving to appear unaffected, gamely replied, "I don't know nuthin' about nursing sick men, but it's warm in here, and I reckon I can help out some. Who's in charge in here to tell me what to do?"

"Why, you are in charge now, Private. Do whatever you like to comfort these men. Food will be brought, and there is a slop bucket in the corner. There's a little hole in the floor where you can empty the bucket when it's full. I will look in each day to receive your salute and observe the pace at which these men die. And to see when the first mark of the pestilence appears on your young cheeks. I suggest you salute me now, or I might not return at all."

Oliphant, by now numb, raised his right hand to his eyebrow and scratched it in what might be considered a salute. The doctor nodded and left. Oliphant's anger remained, but he soon mentally shrugged to himself, and started doing what he could to comfort the sick men.

The number of men in the shack changed as men died and newly infected men were brought in. Oliphant learned their names and spoke softly to them as he wiped the hard weeping blisters on their brows with a wet cloth.

During Oliphant's second day in the pox house, Benjamin Quinn was carried in by two other black men. Oliphant had him placed on a bunk with a white man who was too delirious in his fever to know a Negro was now sharing his blanket.

"You a Texan?" Benjamin Quinn asked as Oliphant spread a filthy scrap of blanket over him.

"Yea, Company G, Sixth Texas," Oliphant replied, "You?"

"I'm a teamster with Company K of the Sixth," Quinn answered, "Am I bad? Is this pox goin' to kill me?"

"Dunno. Maybe. I ain't been in here long enough to see if everyone with the pox blisters dies or not. Don't know if you niggers die faster than us white men. How long you been ailing?"

"Been hurtin' in the back and joints for a few days now, but was feeling better today, then the blisters started poppin' out on my face. I don't want to die like this."

"Reckon not," was all Oliphant could bring himself to say.

Oliphant fed those too weak to lift a spoon and took the slop bucket from bed to bed and emptied it often. The doctor appeared every day for a few minutes and stood near the door while guards carried out the corpses of any stricken men who had died since the doctor's last visit. Oliphant grudgingly saluted him each day and cursed him loudly as soon as he left. The men who still had the strength enjoyed the colorful language their young nurse used and valued his attempts to wipe their faces and care for them.

Some of the men grew no worse, but others died. Some of the deceased men's faces were so covered in the moist pox blisters that they were not recognizable, so Oliphant wrote their names on slips of paper and pinned them to the men's jackets or shirts. He had no way of knowing if anyone in the burial parties took note of the identification papers and passed the information along.

When the young black man died five days later, Oliphant remembered that the body was a teamster named Ben from the same regiment he was in, but he couldn't remember his last name or company. So Oliphant wrote "Teamster Ben – 6 T X" on a scrap of paper and stuck it in a button hole of the dead boy's shirt.

Matthew Quinn had been there when his brother's face broke out in small pox blisters. He had watched in agony as Ben was carried to the pox house and disappeared inside. He had taken to spending all day near the building and was there when a single Union guard dragged a limp body by its feet out of the building, the head banging on each of the three steps.

Matthew saw that the body was a Negro and ran to see if it was his brother. The sight overwhelmed him. The corpse's face was covered in boils, even the eyelids a mass of overlapping pustules forcing the eyes shut, lips and tongue swollen with pestilence, blood and pus leaking from the nose. Matthew Quinn fell away from his brother's remains, howling and wailing, unable to force himself to follow the guard as he dragged away Ben's body.

Because the corpse was a Negro, its diseased features so terrible to behold, and something no one wanted to touch, the prisoners in the burial detail didn't bother with a wooden casket. They simply used their feet to roll the body into a shallow trench and covered it with a few inches of soil and left as quickly as they could.

On the eleventh day, Dr. Merrifield regretfully noted that Oliphant was still healthy and showing no signs of being infected with small pox. In the early afternoon the teenage Rebel was abruptly ordered out the pox house by guards.

He immediately joined the other healthy prisoners as they were lining up in formation near the gate. They were being exchanged. Their nine and a half weeks in Camp Butler were over. But it was a smaller group that gathered by the gate, as hundreds of men had died during the sixty-seven days in the camp, including fifty-five men from the Sixth Texas who had died of exposure or illness. Or maybe it was fifty-six, since no one knew if Sergeant Chalk was above ground or still in the coffin with the remains of Bill Rodgers.

Part 2

Chapter 6

Jesús literally bit his tongue rather than tell Bain that his feet hurt, that he wasn't used to such marching since their time at Camp Butler had not required any daily exercise involving marching. In fact, Jesús was feeling an enthusiasm that had left him after the surrender at Fort Hindman. Not that the future looked particularly rosy, but it sure looked better than what they had been enduring, having spent a hard two months of winter in the north, a winter wholly unlike any south Texas winter.

Finally, the heavy breathing of the men in the column and the silence became too much and Jesús blurted, "Bain, where we goin'? They takin' us to Canada? I heard of Canada at *la escuela*. You was there, you know 'bout Canada. Canada is full of soldiers in red coats who shoot 'mericans in blue coats. Why they takin' us to Canada? They gonna give us red coats so we can shoot the Yankee guards? I know one I'm ready to shoot. He's wearing my red scarf. But, I don't speak no Canada-ish. Where we goin', Bain?"

"Jesse, we're going to the railway siding. They're going to put us on a train and send us back home. Or somewhere. And you knew that. You were just carrying on 'bout Canada to hear yourself jabber. Blathering like a sheep, that's all you're doing."

"Ba-a-a-a-a, Ba-a-a-a-a," came from somewhere forward in the company column.

"No, I ain't blathering like no sheep. I'm roarin' like *el tigre!* R-r-r-r-r-R! A freed tiger! A tiger not in no cage no more," Jesús responded, not a bit taken back.

"Silence in the ranks!" came the call from Sergeant Degas who was just behind Corporal Gill and had heard the whole exchange. For his part, Degas was just damned glad to be marching away from Camp Butler and towards anything but being a prisoner of war. That was a sentiment shared by every man in the regimental column, regardless of rank. It had not been a pleasant two months for any man.

The railway siding was muddy and filthy with the droppings of the thousands of cattle which had been unloaded there over the past few months. Without any pause, the prisoners were marched up to the side of the train and ordered to climb into cattle cars. Men helped each other into the wide doors, and many men weakened by illness were lifted up and settled against the rough board walls. The cars stank and the floor was spotted with cow patties. The Texas soldiers were pushed into each car until there was barely room for men to sit. When the doors were shut and locked, the train jerked a few times as the couplings between the cars engaged, and then they were moving. No food, water, or honey buckets had been loaded into any of the cars.

The first day went uneventfully as the train travelled east through Illinois. The men soon grew weary of trying to gaze through the cracks between the wooden slats to watch the countryside roll by. Most simply sat down on the crowded floor and tried to roll with the bumps as the train lurched along the uneven tracks. Late in the afternoon they stopped at a rural station so the prisoners could relieve themselves and eat cold rations of boiled beef and hard crackers that had been set out for them. Since the men had no plates or eating utensils, they formed a line and each man reached into the greasy water in the beef pot and fished out a chunk of cold meat and then grabbed a few hard crackers in his other hand. Within half an hour, the time needed for the wood tender to be reloaded, the Texans were pushed back into the cattle cars. Some had been able to gulp down a dipper of water from a large barrel, but many of them re-boarded the train without drinking anything.

The train rolled through the night and around midmorning stopped again. By now the prisoners were in Indiana, headed towards Ohio, although none of them realized their direction of travel during the long cold night.

"Jesse, can you see out between those boards?" asked Corporal Gill.

"Well, yea, I reckon I could, Bain, if I was to turn around and press my face up close. But that ain't on my list of chores to git done before daylight today. The milkin' can wait, too. I'm sleepin' in today, if that's alright with you and the Almighty." Private McDonald was half-lying down, contorted into a curve, trying to fit into what space there was on the crowded floor.

"It ain't alright. I know you slept all night 'cause you snored and passed gas for hours. So twist your head around and look outside and tell us what direction we're going."

Jesús did that, pushing his eye to the crack between the slats, and said, "Well the sun is comin' up in generally the direction we're headed, but it's off to the right a good piece."

"You sure the sun ain't off to our left? If we're headed south, the sun oughta be to our left."

"Well, Bain, I do know my right from my left, and the sun is risin' to our right."

"Damn, that means we're headed east. What's east of where we was in Illinois?"

No one within ear shot of Gill knew that answer, but most assumed reasonably, but mistakenly, that they were headed generally south. The train kept rolling through the long day. Men who had to answer nature's call made their way to the rear of the car where two low boards had been pulled away, allowing the prisoners to relieve themselves without further fouling the crowded cattle car. They stopped once for wood to be loaded onto the tender and water to be added to the engine's boiler. The doors to the prisoners' cars were unlocked and pulled open, letting badly needed fresh air in. But the southerners were not allowed out of the cars. A bucket of water and a crate of hard crackers were manhandled into each car before the heavy doors were shut and secured again.

In four days of nearly non-stop rolling through the days and nights the train of Texas prisoners passed through Illinois, Indiana, Ohio, New York, Pennsylvania, and Maryland. In Baltimore, the Texans were ushered off the train and marched to a wharf where they were crowded onto a steamship. From there they made another all night trip down Chesapeake Bay and finally up the James River to reach City Point, Virginia, where they unceremoniously disembarked.

64

Chapter 7

Late April 1863, Near Richmond, Virginia
28 Men Present for Duty

"Fall in, dammit! Corporals set the line on me! Where are you, Corporal Gill? I need you here. Now!" shouted Sergeant Degas as the men of Company K straggled down the gangplank and started to mill around on the wharf.

Gill moved as quickly as his stiff legs allowed and set himself near the sergeant marking the spot for one end of the company formation. With more shouting from the regimental sergeant major and the company sergeants, all nine companies of the Sixth Texas were soon in a ragged formation with their backs to the river.

"Battalion...Attention!" came the command as a major in a clean gray frock coat and a gold trimmed kepi rode to the front of the formation. The major was slim and sat very erect in his saddle, easily handling the reins with one hand. The left sleeve of his frock coat was folded up to the elbow, as his lower arm had been amputated.

After walking his horse from one end of the formation to the other and returning to the center of the line, he finally spoke in a loud voice, "You men are blessed to be back in the bosom of the Confederacy in the Commonwealth of Virginia. You are still a long march from Texas, but for now, your assignment is here. Your services are needed here, near Richmond. I am Major Wilkerson of the Army of Northern Virginia, and I am

65

your new commander until your captured Texas officers arrive. Whenever that may be." The major's tone was just short of openly scornful as he looked at the four hundred men in front of him.

"You do not look like soldiers and you did not do your duty as soldiers in Arkansas." The major paused, then continued, "Regardless of the shame you brought upon yourselves and your state, you have been exchanged for Yankee prisoners captured by the Army of Northern Virginia during our victorious winter campaign. While we whipped a whole Yankee army at Fredericksburg and captured thousands of their soldiers, you surrendered en mass and gave up a key river fortification to the enemy with barely a fight. That was a disgusting episode that will NOT be forgotten, will NOT be forgiven, and certainly will NOT be repeated while you are serving in the army commanded by General Lee, and in a regiment which I command.

"Soon you will be issued uniforms and weapons. Then, the entire body of exchanged prisoners from the Arkansas debacle will be used to protect the capital city of Richmond. Your service here will free up troops who have already demonstrated their valor and steadfastness to join General Lee's army in the field."

This comment caused scarcely contained growls and murmurs of protest from many of the men facing the major. Ignoring the reaction of the Texans to his last statement, the major continued, "Perhaps in the future, should Mr. Lincoln's army not quit the field first, you might ably acquit yourselves in battle and earn the privilege of serving in General Lee's army. But not now. For now, you will be garrisoned around Richmond to deter any desperate Yankee raids or efforts to surprise us."

The major paused a moment to allow his comments to sink in before he concluded, "Since there are no lieutenants and captains available to assume command of each of your companies, your sergeants will continue to maintain the discipline and order of each company as they did while you were imprisoned."

With that welcome home speech, the entire regiment was marched to a railway siding where, once again they were ordered into a train, this time in passenger cars, not cattle cars.

"Bain, I don't like that major. Don't like him at all. You could sure tell we was salt in his coffee. He thinks his lost arm gives him the go-ahead to as much as call us cowards. And what's a 'dee-bacle' anyway?" Jesús asked as the two men sat in the luxury of the wooden benches in the rail car.

"No need for us to like him, Jesse. We just have to follow his orders for a spell 'til Colonel Garland and the rest of our officers catch up with us.

Meantime, you keep your mouth shut and your head down. Let the sergeants take care of things with these Virginia roosters."

It was a week later and the Sixth Texas had spent the last four days protecting a crossroads between Petersburg and Richmond. Company K and three other companies were deployed to either side of the intersection, on both sides of a log barricade that blocked the road. Sergeant O'Donaghue took the opportunity to refresh the company's memory of operating as a moving skirmish line. Gill often saw Major Wilkerson during the four days, as the Virginian was either very diligent in his temporary assignment as the Sixth Texas' commanding officer, or he was very disdainful of the Texans' abilities should the Federals appear. Either way, he often appeared behind Company K when they were deployed and questioned the NCO's about their positions and what they would do if attacked from one direction or another.

After another week, word came down that the threat of a Union cavalry raid on Richmond had passed as Lee's army had whipped the Yanks again at a place called Chancellorsville, not too far from Richmond. Within two days the Texans were marched back to the railway yards where to their surprise, they were ordered to turn in the old smoothbore muskets they had been issued. The muskets were staying in Richmond to be available for the home guard should the capital be threatened again. But the Texans were headed elsewhere, unarmed.

Under the close watch of their sergeants, the men of the Sixth Texas once again boarded a train, this time many of the men riding on open flat cars. The train was headed to central Tennessee where the entire group of exchanged Texas prisoners was being assigned to the Army of Tennessee under the command of General Braxton Bragg. Major Wilkerson did not make a farewell speech to the Texans, but he did watch the train chugging away while he sat on his horse and wondered how those frontier boys would do when they were called on to hold the line.

Chapter 8

Early May 1863, Middle Tennessee
27 Men Present for Duty

Private McDonald was kneeling by the smoking fire, stirring his cornmeal mush into the black grease in the skillet. He looked up at Corporal Gill. "Bain, what do you mean, 'Nobody wants us'?"

Sipping his coffee from the dented tin cup, Bain answered, "Why, Jesse, I reckon I mean just that. Ever damned general in the whole damned army thinks we're cowards 'cause of our surrendering back in Arkansas. And take that mess off the fire before it burns."

"But you know that ain't so. We didn't give it up. No ways," Jesús answered as he pulled his hot skillet off the fire. The cornmeal had turned yellow-gray except where it was singed black around the edges, and it was gooey in the middle. That didn't stop Jesús from digging at it with his spoon, and swallowing a mouthful of crumbly mush.

"Maybe not, but there's sure enough word going around that Colonel Garland held up the white flag before anybody else did."

"Why that's just plum crazy. *Caramba*, Bain, we were the last bunch firing. When we stopped, there weren't no more shooting."

" Well, maybe somebody's got it in for Colonel Garland, or maybe them other colonels are just better at pointing their fingers towards the other guy. Don't matter now."

"I bet it matters to Colonel Garland. Who's gonna trust him now?"

Tossing the dregs of his coffee onto the ground, Bain sighed and said, "Jesse, that ain't our worry. Our job now is to show General Cleburne we ain't no cowards."

"*Sí*, I suppose so. But I wonder if this General Cleburne will ever let us fight. He may make us baggage train guards 'til it's over."

"I wouldn't count on it. These new uniforms are plum too purty to waste on wagon guards," Gill replied as he brushed a glob of mud off his sleeve. He was quite taken with his new blue trimmed jacket and gray trousers. Back home on the ranch, he had never owned any clothing with colored trim on the cuffs and collar and shiny brass buttons. His homespun shirts, pants, and coats had been plain brown and worn until he outgrew them. He'd seen the fancy-dans in San Antonio strutting around the square and lounging in front of the *cantinas* wearing jackets with such stylish adornments, but he'd never thought a poor private in the army would rate such a coat. Officers, maybe, but not privates like Jesse and the rest, and not himself, corporal or not. Even the uniforms they had been issued in Texas and Arkansas had been devoid of any color but brown or gray. The new suit only itched a little bit and he knew after a few weeks of wear he'd not notice the scratchy cloth. By then lice would likely be making themselves to home in the seams and he'd forget anything else about the new uniform.

Returning his thoughts to Jesse's comment, "Maybe that wouldn't be so bad. Say, Jesse, speaking of wagons, I ain't seen your cousin Matt since we got on the train outta prison camp. What became of him after his brother died?"

"Bain, I don't understand that boy. The Yanks done gave him another chance to sign on as a teamster instead of getting' on the train with us. He told the lieutenant who was tryin' to get our coloreds that he was stickin' with his kin and goin' back to Texas. But we ain't in Texas, and Matt's done been put back on a wagon in our supply train. I ain't seen him since we was around Richmond."

Sergeant Degas was kneeling by an open crate, and looked up at Lieutenant Garza. "What the hell kind of guns are these?" he asked as he lifted one from the box and passed it over to Garza. The weapon was shorter than their Enfields had been, and rust speckled the barrel.

69

Garza hefted the musket and looked into the barrel to make sure he could see the grooves of the rifling. "Hmm. The quartermaster tells me they're from Austria. That's somewhere in Europe. It seems light though. I reckon the men will be thankful for that. They said the bullets are smaller too. Wonder if they will go as far? Soon as you get these things issued out, have a couple of smart fellers take theirs apart and let me know if they think these guns will hold up. And get some of the boys to see how straight they shoot."

Lieutenant Joseph Garza wasn't near as concerned about the new rifles as he was about his new role as the commander of Company K. Captain McAllister had taken ill during the winter as a POW at Camp Chase, and once they had been exchanged for Federal prisoners, McAllister had been sent back to Texas to recover. That left First Lieutenant Garza as the officer in command of McAllister's company. With only one battle and one winter behind them, the reality of ever-changing names and faces in command had not yet affected Company K.

Garza knew most of the men by name but was worried that some of them might not cotton to a Hispanic officer leading them. He knew a few of the older men had fought during the long fracas between the US and the Mexican armies not long over ten years ago. He also knew some of the men had lost fathers and uncles at the Alamo and in the massacre of 400 Texian prisoners at Goliad twenty-five years ago. Garza hoped that he had earned the respect of the company during the months of training at Victoria and at Arkansas Post. He'd not faltered during the battle and had stood with his platoon during the firefight before the mass surrender. Still, Garza was comforted to know that a handful of his soldiers were from Tejano families, Hispanics whose loyalty had come down with Texas rather than Mexico.

Sergeant Degas, who had come to Bexar County from the French Creole country of south Louisiana, was still inspecting the Austrian rifles and the black leather accouterments that the quartermaster left on the company street. The green painted wooden cases of ammunition for the muskets were stacked with the arms. Degas pried open a box and pulled out a pack of ten paper cartridges. The printing on the wrapper was not in English or French, so he supposed it must be Austrian. He popped the wax-covered paper wrapping open and pulled out a cartridge. He twisted the lead bullet out of the cartridge and poured a bit of gun powder into his palm. It didn't seem damp or clumped together, and that relieved him since the ammunition had crossed the Atlantic Ocean. The cone-shaped lead bullet seemed smaller than the Enfield bullets, but not so much as to be a concern. It was still a big chunk of metal that would do a man serious harm. Degas slid the bullet into his vest pocket and let the powder and paper wrapper fall to the ground.

"Corporal Gill! Fetch your squad over here. It's time to get these weapons issued. A soldier ain't a soldier 'til he's gripping a loaded musket."

"Men," Lieutenant Garza began, "General Cleburne figures there ain't enough of us to fight as a regiment no more, so he has put us with the *hombres* from two other Texas outfits. From today on we are Company K of the Sixth and Tenth and Fifteenth Consolidated Regiment."

The men of the Alamo Rifles shifted about in their two ranks, looking at each other and at their lieutenant. Corporal Gill spoke up quickly, voicing the question most of the men were wondering about, "Sir, are you going to still be our company commander? And what about us corporals and sergeants? Seems to me that a combined company is going to have a mite too many fellers with stripes on their sleeves."

Lieutenant Garza hesitated only an instant before he replied, "You are right, Corporal Gill. The senior officer among the three captains will lead the new Company K. Since I'm only a lieutenant, I'll be transferred out, maybe back across the Mississippi, if I'm lucky. Captain Houston from the 15th regiment will assume command of Company K tomorrow. Lieutenant Navarro will stay as first lieutenant and Lieutenant Hawkins from the 10th regiment will serve as second lieutenant. There's rumor that Sergeant O'Donoghue is to be promoted to sergeant major of the regiment. I don't know who Captain Houston has in mind for Orderly Sergeant."

This speech was far more information than Lieutenant Garza, or any other company officer, normally shared with his enlisted troops, but Garza thought this consolidation of companies was a mistake, and he wanted his men to understand. He didn't mind the prospect of being transferred closer to home, maybe even to serve in Texas, but he was leery that the men who had fought together in battle and endured the privations of prison camp together were being mixed up with two other companies.

Garza continued, "It's the way of the army, gentlemen. No recruits from Texas are apt to reach us this far from home, and the high command figures one big regiment of Texans will fight better than three little' uns."

Chapter 9

Late June 1863, Liberty Gap, Central Tennessee
26 Men Present for Duty

Lieutenant Navarro led the company column up the dirt road, thinking that the hills of central Tennessee looked much like the hills of Arkansas. The trees were tall, the slopes steep, and the grass was still slick from the morning rain. All of it left him yearning for the sight of cactus, sand, and mesquite. Bell Buckle was the name of the nearest little town, and the name reminded Navarro of Christmas, *Navidad* to his family, and the ringing of church bells to celebrate. *"Feliz Navidad* – Merry Christmas." Maybe this war would end by Christmas, but right now it was June and they were being put on the picket line of the Army of Tennessee. They were relieving some troops from Arkansas who had been skirmishing all morning.

The last of the ten companies in the new 6th-10th-15th Consolidated Regiment, Co. K was slogging through the mud churned up by the 700 men in the other nine companies. In the especially muddy bottom of the swale between two slopes, Company K was the last to execute the maneuvers that resulted in a regimental battle line, a long line two ranks deep, and 370 men long. Then the left wing of the regiment deployed as skirmishers, while the right wing remained in the swale as the ready reserve, able to provide quick reinforcements if needed.

As corporal of the second platoon of Co. K, Bain Gill was again the last man on the far left end of the entire regimental skirmish line. Second Sergeant Degas and Second Lieutenant Hawkins were somewhere behind him, but Gill was the man whose job it was to keep the platoon as straight as the terrain and cover allowed. Gill had to make sure that his platoon did not drift forward, leaving behind the flank protection provided by the next regiment to their left. It was altogether more responsibility than Gill preferred, especially when the Yanks' fire became brisk.

"Braden, get on your knee and get your damned head back behind that tree. Use your cover. Kneel down before you look out!" Adam and Martin Braden were twenty-one year old twins who looked enough alike that Gill had given up wondering which one he was talking to, even though it didn't matter most of the time. At that moment he was just glad that both twins had a sharp eye and were fair shots. But this one, Gill thought, was likely to get himself killed if he didn't start minding his business.

"Shoot from the other side of the tree so your whole head ain't sticking out like a damned turtle."

Gill tried to see through the brush to the next man in line, who he thought should be Jesse, but he couldn't see anyone. A bullet snapped a branch off above Gill's head, and he instinctively ducked and brought his Austrian rifle to his shoulder. If he could see any patch of blue, he'd pull the trigger and move a few feet over to his right to get away from the tell-tale white smoke of his firing.

"Corporal Gill, let's move the men forward a few yards and see if we can persuade the Billies to retire further up the slope." That was Second Lieutenant Hawkins, who Gill considered a steady officer, but too aggressive in his idea of how to maintain a skirmish line. The space to their front looked more open, with fewer boulders and trees than where they were now and the Yankee fire had not lessened any. Gill didn't see how risking their necks advancing in a thin skirmish line without flank protection was going to cause the Yanks to fall back. But he replied with a "Yes sir," and called to Braden to pass the word to advance.

Skirmishing in rough terrain was tricky business. Sight was so restricted that the opposing lines sometimes bent like snakes and the distance between enemies was only a few yards. A man could quickly find himself isolated and captured. In fact, taking prisoners on the skirmish line was the main method used by both armies to gather information about who was fighting them. The simple rule when a gray skirmisher saw a solid line of blue coats coming forward was "Shoot, Shout, and Skedaddle." But when you only saw one or two blue coats at a time, you couldn't just take off running. That was cowardly and might open just the hole the enemy was probing for. A man had to stay put and trust his pards were alert, each pair taking care of the area facing them. Moreover, the corporal and sergeant on the end of the line also had to constantly watch for a flanking attack that could scoop up a whole company of skirmishers, the enemy working down the line gobbling up one or two men at a time.

The drill manual teaches that advancing in a skirmish line is done by partners in alternating fashion, so the man to the rear always has a loaded musket covering the man up front who may need quick help. Gill hollered to Braden that he was moving forward and to hold his position. While skirmish drill had been well rehearsed back in Texas, the drills had been nearly a year ago, and a lot of hard times had befallen the Alamo Rifles since then.

Gill ran to the nearest tree in front of him, noting puffs of white smoke ahead as he finally dropped behind the tree trunk. He looked to his right and saw a big rock that should protect Braden, so he waved him up. Gill then looked to his left and saw two blue coats moving towards them on Company K's exposed flank, no more than fifty yards away. Damn. Before he raised his weapon to aim, he glanced back and saw that Sergeant Degas had also seen the threat and was at the ready. Gill fired. He then reloaded as quickly as he could, and then nodded to Degas that he was ready. Degas moved to his left and quickly rose and fired. Within a second, Gill saw white smoke of answering fire and this time heard a soft "thunk" as a bullet hit his tree trunk. Gill chanced a glance to his right and saw that Braden was intently staring to their front, doing his job of covering what was now Gill's right flank. Beyond Degas, behind them and off to the left, Gill thought he could see movement in the trees. Maybe the boys in the next regiment were moving up too.

Gill held still until Degas nodded that he was loaded again, then he took a quick look around the left side of the tree trunk. He saw what might be a black hat, with a spot of bright metal catching the sunlight. Gill immediately pulled his head back and aimed his musket around the other side of the tree trunk, found the black patch again in his sight, and fired a foot below it.

Degas called a brief "Good Mon," just as Gill heard firing from Braden's position. Gill looked that way and caught a glimpse of Jesse's tall black *sombrero* moving forward. Gill still worried about Jesse, but right now he was just glad to see him. Lieutenant Hawkins' voice came from behind, calling to the entire platoon to hold their ground, that Company C was moving up to support them. Gill figured that meant the fight was growing hot all along the slope and Captain Houston must have sent word back that the Yanks could be pushing for a breakthrough. It was hard enough to tell what was actually happening in the thick brush to their immediate front. There was no way to know where the Federal commander on the far side of the crest would concentrate his troops for a determined attack.

Gill gave an audible sigh of relief when he turned and confirmed that the noise was several men moving his way from behind, wearing gray jackets. Lieutenant Hawkins was with them, and quietly gave orders for Gill and Degas to move the platoon to their right and make way for Company C to take over the end of their regimental line. Company K was not yet relieved, but the additional company would lessen the gaps between riflemen.

With the increased firepower facing them, the Union skirmishers soon pulled back up the hill, but continued a sporadic fire from the cover of the rocks on the crest of the ridge. Around mid-afternoon, a brigade from Mississippi came out to relieve the three Texas regiments. Soon those companies were finding their way into a skirmish line behind the Texas troops, waiting until the order filtered down the line for Churchill's Texas Brigade to withdraw.

"Hey Bain," Jesús crawled over to Corporal Gill and pointed down the hill to the new regiment. "Ain't them *soldados* back behind us the same ones what was giving us a hard time about Arkansas Post? Ain't they the ones who was hollering, 'We don't want you here if you can't see a Yank without holding up your shirt to him?'"

"Yea," one of the Braden boys crouched down near Gill added, "They's the ones alright. I heard one call out, 'Lie down now, I'm about to pop a cap! Don't pull off your shirt, it won't hurt you.'"

Corporal Gill looked for a moment at the Mississippi troops down the hill, then smiled to himself. The Yanks on the crest were still firing their muskets in a desultory manner, so Gill decided a little payback just might work. "Grab up some little rocks, fellers, but stay down. We're gonna help them Yanks a little bit." Then Corporal Gill, at that instant more of a twenty-year-old adolescent than seasoned corporal, swiftly let fly a flat pebble that sailed low over the head of a Mississippi private, causing him to drop face first onto the hillside thinking the pebble was a minie ball from the Yanks on the hillcrest. Within seconds Gill's whole platoon was furtively, but gleefully, chunking small pebbles just over the heads of the Mississippi troops, who kept their heads so low in the grass that Lieutenant Navarro observed later that their mustaches took root and began to grow.

During the late afternoon another thunderstorm rolled through, dousing the men and making the seven mile march back down the muddy road even more miserable. But the spirits in Co. K were high from the joy of throwing rocks like youngsters and pulling a fast one on the Mississippi troops. More importantly, the regiment had fought a hot skirmish without any serious wounds or deaths, and more than one soldier loudly told his pards of the dead Yankee left on the hillside, killed by the speaker himself. No one could contradict these braggarts since any bodies would still be in the contested ground between the foes, or would have been pulled back by their company mates. Regardless of the facts, the whole company wanted to believe they had inflicted casualties on the enemy. The memories of the freezing river trip to prison camp, the months of imprisonment and the indignities hurled at them during the long train ride back to City Point, Virginia had left them all eager to show they could fight.

Chapter 10

"Texas cavalry on the right, Texas cavalry on the left, A Texas battery in the center, and all supported by Texas infantry. Who dare come against us?" Colonel Mills, commanding the consolidated 6th-10th-15th Texas Infantry, was justly proud of the Texans' combined arms that protected Bethpage Bridge over the Elk River.

They were ordered to remain until the last of General Bragg's army crossed with all their supplies. Corporal Gill, who was standing close enough to hear his colonel's confident words, thought he might be a bit hasty. After all, the Texans were two miles from the safety of the Elk River and the Union troops were closing in on the bridge, aware that it was a key crossing point. There were a lot of Yankees coming their way, and the quickly assembled Texas legion of one artillery battery, two cavalry regiments and one consolidated infantry regiment were not going to hold back a division of Union infantry.

As Gill pondered the colonel's confidence, an eruption of grass and dirt exploded to their left where several hundred cavalrymen of the Eighth Texas Cavalry regiment were sitting on their mounts in line of battle. Gill heard the explosion as more artillery shells struck near the cavalry. Being at the left end of the infantry regiment, Gill was able to hear the frightened squeals of several injured horses and could even see one rear up and fall backwards as his rider was thrown off. He heard the command for the troopers to dismount and for the horses to be led back behind the formation. Within a few minutes Union skirmishers appeared from under the trees to their front, and the dismounted cavalry threw out an answering line of skirmishers. Gill knew cavalrymen preferred to remain mounted, but he figured they also understood that while mounted in a skirmish line they were tall, wide targets for the opposing skirmishers. The fact that southern cavalrymen had to replace their own mounts when they were lost, and that there were not any replacement horses available, also led Gill to believe the boys out front were glad enough to be on foot this time.

Just then Colonel Mills shouted, "What the hell are Young's cavalry doing over there? Dammit, I didn't order them to charge! Damn fools."

Gill strained a look to his far right, and was able to see clods of mud and grass being thrown up by horses' hooves and hear shouts as the Eleventh Texas cavalry on the right flank of the Texan infantry charged obliquely towards the advancing Yankee skirmishers.

"Eyes to the front, men," Sergeant Degas reminded Gill and the others who were rubber-necking trying to watch the cavalry charge. It wasn't often that they were in a position to see cavalry thundering forward, brandishing pistols and shotguns, whooping like Comanches. It was an impressive sight, something the veteran infantry would not forget. Most of the infantry flinched when their own artillery began to fire in support of the cavalry charge on one flank and the skirmishing dismounted cavalry on the other flank. The infantry had yet to fire and Gill was happy to watch.

The cavalry charge ended as the blue skirmish line hustled back into the trees where the cavalry would not follow. The bugles called for the mounted cavalry to retire and reform, their job done, but at what cost Gill had no idea. More bugles recalled the dismounted cavalry, who then quickly remounted and moved off. The artillery battery limbers came rumbling forward and quickly the four cannons were hitched and the order came for the 6th-10th-15th Regiment to execute a right face, and off they went towards the bridge, their covering job done, and feeling an urgency to reach the bridge and cross the river before they were caught in the Yankees' net.

"Hey Bain, what're them fellers doing under the bridge?" Jesús asked as they marched towards the wooden bridge, ignoring the heavy rain and mud. Gill had his head down watching the moving feet of the man in front of him and was deep in a daydream about his dry bed at home when Jesse's voice made him snap his head up.

"Danged if I know, Jesse."

Sergeant Degas, who was marching behind Gill, provided the answer, "They're tying on barrels of gun powder to blow the whole thing up once we all get across."

Gill now looked to both sides of the road and saw the cavalry waiting on their horses, ready to harass and delay any Yankees one more time as the infantry crossed the river.

"I reckon we should be glad those horse-boys are watching over us," remarked one of the Braden boys. "I sure hope they don't get caught or blown up on the bridge."

Frankly, Gill wasn't giving any thought about the cavalry's safety. Hell, they had horses, didn't they? He was tired, had only his own legs to keep him moving, and badly wanted to have the river between him and anyone wearing blue. It was with great satisfaction that Gill crossed the bridge. Ten minutes later, he hardly noticed the noise of the explosion behind him as the bridge piers were blasted into pieces and the wooden planks of the roadway collapsed into the rain-swollen Elk River.

Chapter 11

Early September 1863, Chickamauga Creek, Georgia
23 Men Present for Duty

Day 1

The three regiments in the brigade had been moving since the courier from General Cleburne had reined in his lathered horse and handed the folded paper to General Deshler. No one had said so, but Corporal Gill suspected that the past month of marching without much fighting was about to end.

"Bain, it ain't right, it just ain't right," moaned Jesús. "We shoulda had time to take off our trousers and shoes 'fore we crossed that creek. *Caramba*, it had a foot of mud on the bottom. Now Jake's gonna have to go barefoot or hop along on one foot. It was bad enough the water was so deep we got our private parts wet. A snappin' turtle mighta bit me on my manhood. But it just warn't right that Jake had to lose a shoe when we all coulda hung 'em around our necks. It warn't right."

"Hush up, Jesse. Now ain't the time." Gill had a deep affection for Jesús, but his questions and groaning did stretch Gill's patience. Crossing the waist deep creek had been rushed and more than one soldier had slipped and dropped his cartridge box that they all were holding high over their heads. Wet cartridges aside, Gill figured the haste driving their officers was justified this time. The sound of guns was clear, and even Jesse wouldn't want to be caught by surprise with his shoes dangling around his neck.

The sun was edging downward and unknown to the enlisted men, the brigade had orders to move towards the extreme right behind the first Confederate line. Gill and all the men in the regiment soon saw that this was no skirmish. They had marched past other columns of soldiers moving away from them and were in sight of other regiments marching in their direction. Gill had given up trying to count how many flags he had seen, but from the colors and designs he could see, it looked to Gill like the whole army must have converged on this spot. Gill figured it all meant that General Bragg had chosen this patch of Georgia, if they were still in Georgia, to push back at the Yankees who were driving them south.

"By Company Into Line!" shouted Captain Houston. From his position as corporal at the back of the company Gill had to hustle while urging the men in his platoon to look sharp. As soon as they had formed their company line at the end of the column of ten such company lines, the colonel ordered the companies to form a single long formation. Each company did a quick left half-wheel followed by a short dash to fill in the long spaces between the guides who had set the forward position of the regiment's battle line. Gill dared a quick glance to his right and saw their line stretched over the slope out of sight. Next came the order came to, "Fix...Bayonets!" Even as the slower men were still attaching the long blades to the muzzles of their muskets, the regiment was ordered forward.

Gill saw that their regiment was going to pass through the line of gray clad soldiers to their front, so he had expected the shouted order to collapse each company line into short columns as they interpenetrated the ranks of the regiment which they were relieving. There was no waiting in reserve this day. As soon they cleared the other regiment's position, the Texans quickly reformed their own regimental battle line.

Sliding his Austrian musket up to rest on his shoulder on the order to "Right shoulder shift, Arms," Gill looked to his right to be sure his platoon was not lagging or surging ahead of the others. Then his attention was all to the front where he suddenly saw a cloud of white smoke appear in the midst of the long dark shadow he had thought to be brush in the twilight, but now instantly understood was the enemy. Gill heard the whining of minie balls passing over their heads and a metal on metal ding, followed by a single grunt.

"Bain, Bain, they killed my bayonet! They done shot it in two!" Jesús called loudly enough to be heard by the whole platoon.

"Battalion, Halt! Fire by Battalion! Ready, Aim, Fire!"

No sooner had the smoke emerged from the muzzles of the 700 muskets, than the command "Charge, Bayonets!" was shouted by the Colonel and echoed by every officer. Lowering their muskets into a two-hundred yard long hedgerow of bristling points of steel, the 6th-10th-15th Consolidated Texas regiment stepped forward, muskets unloaded, but ready to use their bayonets like the long spears of the ancient hoplites. Corporal Gill had no such romantic thoughts as he walked forward through their own musket smoke that still hung low over the ground. His only conscious thoughts were worries that his platoon might falter if men were shot and fell or just stumbled in the fading light.

"Bain, I'm chargin' with a stub!" Jesús yelled.

"Shut up, Jesse!" Gill replied.

The dim light was accented by small fires here and there across the field they were crossing. Gill knew that muzzle blasts would sometimes, but not usually, ignite any dry grass or brush. The number of fires told him this pasture had already been the site of some serious fighting. Gill and the others also had to step over or around wounded or dead men who they often didn't see until they were right upon them. It was unnerving and soon caused their straight formation to bend and separate here and there.

"Battalion, Halt! Kneel, Load!"

The orders came quickly, and Gill reached for a cartridge while looking to his right and calling encouragements to his boys to be quick. Loading while kneeling was slower than loading while standing, and the fixed bayonets made use of the ramrod awkward. In seconds the order came for volleying by company followed by independent fire. Company K rose and on the command of Captain Houston fired a volley. Then each man began to load and fire without commands.

Gill noted that one man in his platoon had fallen backwards, but he had no time to note if the man was badly wounded or worse. He did hear Sergeant Degas growling at the men in the rear rank to stay close behind the front rank, and heard the sergeant shout profanities at a young private who stepped backwards. The sergeants were directly behind their men to hold them firm in the line, to prevent their succumbing to the normal urge to run from the terrifying noise and being fired upon while standing elbow-to-elbow. Gill held no doubts that his sergeants would use deadly force to stop the first man who tried to break ranks and run to the rear.

As Gill loaded and fired he noted the smoke was so thick that he could no longer see where he was shooting. They were simply firing into a wall of white fog. The enemy's incoming fire was lessening, causing the colonels to think the Federals opposite them were running low on ammunition or were moving back, so the regiment was ordered to again charge with their bayonets lowered. The entire regiment, actually, the whole brigade of three regiments, stepped forward.

For the first time the Texans let loose the high-pitched yipping, yelps, low-pitched barks and howls that were already part of the folklore of the war – the Rebel yell. After moving forward for several minutes without ever seeing the enemy, the brigade halted, and the men were ordered to kneel while skirmishers were sent forward to search for the Federal infantry. Meanwhile, couriers moved back and forth sorting out just where the brigade was in relation to the rest of the General Cleburne's division.

Night

It was dark and a line of sentries from Company C had been sent forward to cover the front of the regiment. Gill had gathered Jesús and the rest of his section in a small circle behind a fallen tree trunk and let them know that at midnight they would relieve Company C and to try to sleep until then. Degas had also sent three men to the rear with all their empty canteens. They had crossed a big creek back there somewhere, and the sergeant knew tomorrow was likely to be another long dry day.

It was cold and getting colder, and the moans and cries from the many wounded men in the field between them and the Federals were eerie and played on the men's nerves. No fires were lit for fear of drawing the attention of Federal sharpshooters, so no coffee was brewed to ease the tension felt by everyone. A few men nibbled on hard crackers, yet no one felt much hunger even though they had marched through the midday meal time. But fatigue was setting in as well, and one by one the young soldiers fell asleep, all sleeping on their backs, with loaded muskets cradled in their arms and leather accouterments still on.

Gill just sat and reflected that their first big battle since Arkansas Post had so far been a whole different beast than had been the defense of the river fort nine months earlier. He wondered once again, as he had at Arkansas Post, if he had killed another man during the fighting. Probably best he didn't know, and Gill honestly hoped he would never see someone fall to one of his aimed shots.

Word had also drifted through the regiment that the other consolidated Texas regiment in their brigade, also veterans of Arkansas Post, had captured not one, but two Yankee regimental flags. Gill figured that was big news and should go far in redeeming the reputation of the recent POW's who had not been wanted by any general but Pat Cleburne. A regiment's

83

flag was sacred, a prize above other prizes and something to be protected at all costs. Gill wondered just how the fellows in their sister regiment had managed to snatch two such treasures during the day's fighting. He envied them for their success, but also felt a tug of anxiety guessing at the human cost of their triumph. How many lives is a piece of blue cloth worth? Gill shook his head clear of those thoughts and closed his own eyes.

"Get up, Jesse, come on, wake up." Jesús opened his eyes and blinked at Gill who was still leaning over him with a hand on his shoulder trying to shake him awake.

"Bain, my friend, I reckon I won't ever get used to your smelly breath in my face hollerin' at me to wake up. Even *mi padre* after a long night of *tequila* ain't so abrupt as you are. And I was still dreaming a sweet dream of romance and wet kisses. But now I can't remember if the kisses were coming from a puppy or a girl named Susan."

"Jesse...well, never mind. Just get up and fall in. We're moving out to the sentry line now. And it was a puppy. My sister don't do such things. Even in dreams. Especially with you. And if you keep mixing her up with a danged puppy, I'll take back my permission for you to write to her."

Bain was still kneeling over Jesús when Sergeant Degas stepped next to them and growled in a low voice, "Corporal Gill, them damnyankees are close enough to us to spit. So if you and your young friend would be so kind as to shut the hell up, I'd be grateful."

Gill swallowed hard and ducked his head knowing the sergeant was right. Jesús was still grinning as the company moved out into the dark towards their sentry posts.

Bain had just crawled up to the position held by four privates. All four of the men were hunkered down behind logs or pressed into shallow swales, trying to stay alert and watch the dark field for movement. He could clearly hear the moans and whimpering of a wounded man not far away to their front

"Bain," Private Jake Spencer whispered in a low hiss, "That feller sounds like he's hurtin' somethin' awful. He really does sound bad. Reckon I might slide out there to see if there's anything we can do for him?" Spencer was a gaunt mild mannered young man who was the son of a circuit preacher.

Bain considered the whispered question for a moment, thinking that Jake's request would require him to seek out the sergeant, who would then have to clear it with the lieutenant, who probably would want to get the captain's permission. Then Captain Houston might even ask the major. Gill wondered if he should he just say no; or was this a time when a good corporal might better seek forgiveness and forego the request for permission. The poor man was right in front of them and he did indeed sound pitiful, and no doubt his cries of pain were disturbing the platoon, if not the whole company.

"Jake," Bain whispered back to Spencer, "How are your feet doing? You wearing one shoe, or did you take it off too since you lost the other in the creek?"

"Aw, I reckon they're well enough. I took off the other shoe. Didn't feel right hobblin' around just wearin' one. You know I never wore shoes except on Sunday back home. Getting a mite cold, though. My toes might be blue plumb through by dawn. But what about that poor soul out there? Can me and Tom go real quiet like and try to ease his pain?"

"Well...Jake, it could be that the feller making that pitiful noise is going to pass sometime soon. I reckon it wouldn't hurt if you had a look at his shoes to see if you might squeeze your old horny heels into them after he's gone. Might be though that he ain't on the edge of life at all, and would be grateful for your Christian charity in offering him a swallow of water. Might even be you could persuade him to swap his shoes for a chaw if you got any. It don't seem like he's going to be walking far even if he's breathing come dawn."

"Sure thing, Bain. That's some powerful good thinking, and brotherly too. And I got some chaw. Come on Tom, let's go."

"You still got a belt knife, Jake? Take mine if you don't."

"Got one, Bain. Thanks for offering. We'll be slithering out there now. Don't shoot us comin' back."

"Mind your canteen don't knock around on the rocks, Jake. No need to draw the attention of some Yank sentry."

"Sure thing, Bain."

As two men crawled forward, Gill watched the soles of their feet disappear among the tall grass and listened for any sign of trouble.

As Gill waited with the two remaining men at the post, he heard random sounds out of the darkness, but nothing he could pinpoint to Jake and Tom's mercy mission. Then the sound of shuffling and grunting came clearly to him, so Bain and others raised their muskets, ready to shoot. Just as Gill was about to call out softly for Jake, he heard his own name in a hoarse whisper from beyond his sight.

"Bain, it's us. We got us a Yank prisoner, so don't shoot."

Jake's head appeared as he crawled forward. Then Tom's face popped out of the dark and finally, the top of the head of a third man. The two rescuers

85

each had one arm hooked around the armpits of the unconscious man as they dragged him through the grass.

As the trio came over the protecting log, Jake Spencer whispered, "He was moaning and groaning when we got to him, but when we started to drag him back, he passed out."

Gil knelt close and could see the wounded man's head was matted with clotted blood. He also saw the man was young and wearing the single bar of a first lieutenant on his shoulder boards.

Gill whispered, "Dang it, Jake, what're we gonna do with a Yankee lieutenant? Even one that's barely old enough to shave. Ain't there enough dead Yankees out here in the dark without bringing a dying one into our lines? Hell, he's head shot and if he ain't dead yet, he soon will be."

Just then Lieutenant Navarro crawled over from the sentry post to their left to see what the noise and movement was, and took in the situation without questions. He stared in the moonlight at the wounded officer, and then at Jake's bare feet.

Also in a hoarse whisper, Navarro quietly said, "Corporal Gill, you might as well finish what you have started. Have those two privates carry this unfortunate lieutenant to the rear. Maybe they can find a surgeon. And since he won't be needing his shoes, why don't you have Private Spencer try them on. Looks like they might fit well enough. It's a cold night."

Privates Spencer and Doyle finally set down their charge to rest a moment. They were behind a small cabin and leaned the wounded lieutenant against the log wall. They had walked quietly away from the sentry post and on past the rest of the regiment without being stopped or even questioned. It was so dark that the NCO's and officers who might have seen them would have assumed they were carrying one of their own wounded back for medical treatment.

"Tom, I'm whipped. I don't know how far we've carried this feller, but I know he's been eating more rations than we have."

"Yup, I'm thinking the same. And I'm real cold."

"Yea, boy, even with the shoes, my toes are just brittle as stones. Feels like a mesquite thorn is going up one heel ever time it hits the ground. I sure could use a little warmth."

"Jake, I'm going to build a fire. Just a little one. We're hidden from any Yankees behind this cabin and we can shield the light between us and the lieutenant. Besides, with the light from a fire we can see to bandage his wound."

"That's fine with me, Tom. You scrounge up a little wood and I'll get my tender box."

Soon the two men had a tiny fire blazing next to the log wall and they huddled around it. Some heat reflected off the cabin and Jake wriggled his toes gratefully near the flames while Tom turned his attention to the unconscious officer.

Private Doyle probed his fingers around the man's bloody head and found that the man's wound was caused by a glancing strike, most likely from a spent bullet, causing profuse bleeding, and probably a terrible head-ache if he ever woke up. But Doyle did not feel any pieces of metal when he rinsed the wound with a little water from his canteen. The matted blood still made the fellow look mutilated, but both privates thought the wound might not kill him.

After covering the man's wound with a dirty handkerchief Doyle had in his pocket, the two men sat silently feeding the fire one stick at a time until they ran out of twigs and the fire burned down to ashes. By then they were less cold and their captive was still breathing.

"What now, Jake? We going to keep looking for a surgeon?" Tom finally asked. Spencer was still wearing the young lieutenant's shoes, leaving him in a pair of socks with a hole in each heel. The man was still unconscious, but groaned and jerked his arms or legs from time to time.

Spencer answered, "I think it's time we left this man here and get back to our outfit. Bain and the lieutenant would be mighty roused if we ain't back when they move out, and that could be before daylight. If he dies, at least we got him off the field and warmed him up a bit and washed out his wound. I imagine that's as good as a surgeon would've done. Somebody will find him when it gets light, stone dead or breathing. I don't reckon he's going to jump up and make off back to the Yankee lines. It's either a grave or prison camp for him. I'll just give him a short prayer, and then we git." It never occurred to either of them to rifle through the man's pockets for valuables or to learn his name.

Doyle didn't argue, and after Spencer asked the Lord to look after the unfortunate man, the two privates made their way back to the regiment, never learning the fate of the man they rescued and nursed, and whose shoes they stole.

Day 2

Deshler's brigade was on the move not long after dawn, moving even further to the right as General Cleburne's division supported the assault

87

being made on the center of the Federal position The brigade was marching in the open under the fire of Union artillery emplaced on the hills behind their infantry. The effect of the cannonade was not severe, but men died as random shells exploded near them or solid shot plowed into a line of unlucky men. Company K was spared the shock of any sudden deaths or limbs torn asunder, but several men would long remember the pine tree that fell from the sky without warning when a cannon shell severed a tree trunk forty feet up from the ground. With the noise of the battle and the shelling, the men didn't notice that the tree had been struck until the top half of the pine crashed down and the trunk landed only a few feet in front of the first platoon. The branches exploded as they struck the earth, showering the men with pine cones, pine needles and shards of wood and bark. One man's arm was broken and another had a gash across his cheek, but remarkably, no one fell and the company kept moving forward.

"Bain, if that tree had fallen on us like that, I'd have wet my pants," uttered Jesús as the company leaned forward, hats pulled low, muskets on their shoulders, hurrying to reach a place where the hail of bullets might lessen.

"Jesse, there you go again," said Gill, "Worrying about the wrong damned thing. How many pine trees do you think are ever going to fall out of the sky like that? Not one more, that's how many. But I promise if we get through this field without being shot dead, I'll worry about pine trees from the sky then."

The banter between the friends belied the seriousness of their situation. The Union line was thick with riflemen and artillery which were uphill and well entrenched behind logs and earth works that the northern soldiers had spent the previous night constructing. The task of Cleburne's Division to take those works and push back the Yankees was overly optimistic, if not foolhardy. Nonetheless, Deshler's Brigade had orders to relieve a brigade that had taken heavy casualties in its failed attempt to break the Federal line.

"Company, Halt! Prone!" called Captain Houston echoing Colonel Mills orders, "Independent Fire!"

Jesús had been lying on his stomach to shoot and rolling over onto his back to load his musket. He was glad the new Austrian musket was shorter than his British Enfield had been back in Arkansas, because the shorter barrel made it easier to ram down the cartridge without rising up for leverage. Then he hollered to Corporal Gill.

"Bain, Bain, I cut my hand. I done rammed my hand right down on the jagged edge of my own bayonet nub. I been stabbed by own my stub."

"I don't care, Jesse. Bleed if you have to, but load and shoot, dammit, bleed, load, and shoot," Bain replied.

McDonald did just that, and had fired enough times that the grit in the musket barrel was beginning to make it hard to push the lead bullet all the way down the barrel. As Jesús concentrated on loading his next round, he heard George Cagle giving commands to himself.

"Cagle's Battery, make ready...Load, Take aim, Fire!" At that Cagle pulled the trigger to an old smoothbore musket, set it aside and pulled another musket to his side. Jesús then saw that there was a pile of muskets next to Cagle.

"Bain, Bain, where are you, Bain?" Jesús shouted over the firing din.

"Jesse, I'm over here. What's wrong, you hit? You all right?" Corporal Gill rolled over the few times it took him to reach Jesús, cussing as he rolled when a few dry sticker burrs speared him in the neck.

" Bain, lookee yonder at old George. Where'd he git all them muskets?"

" Jesse, dammit! Just load and shoot. And bleed if you have to. How's your hand? You didn't notice George has been collecting dropped muskets all morning. He looked like a danged pack mule by the time we got here."

"Well he don't seem to be shootin' any faster than the rest of us. *Caramba*, totin' all those guns don't make any sense a'tall. The man has lost his brains. And my hand ain't bleedin' no more. But I don't trust that stub."

At noon, under a hot sun, the regiment was still prone occupying the same hill, loading and firing, Corporal Gill grabbed for a cartridge from his leather box and his scrabbling fingers came up empty. Gill knew he had not been rushing his pace of loading and firing, as he had kept checking on Jesús and the other privates. As he lay still to listen for the frequency of muzzle blasts, he suddenly realized that all of Company K must be about out of cartridges and were conserving their rounds. He glanced towards the rear, wondering if the captain had noticed, and he saw a courier moving fast and low to reach the regimental flag where Colonel Mills would be. Figuring the message might mean a shift in their position, Gill did a fast count of his platoon and took a quick sip from his canteen. A minute or two later Sergeant Degas crawled over to him.

"Corporal Gill, make sure each man is loaded. But stay down!"

"Sergeant, we been pulling cartridges from the dead and wounded for a spell now. Don't know how many the boys got. We're nigh on out, Sergeant."

"I know that, Gill. Of course I know that. So does the colonel. And so do the damyankees if they got any ears at all. They know we've been here all morning and gotta be about out of lead. So, we ain't gonna charge, but they damsure just might. The colonel says we will hold our ground and meet any attack with the bayonet. Now get your boys ready, Corporal!"

Gill looked to the front through the smoke and had a brief clear vision of hundreds of screaming Yanks charging right at his platoon. He shivered and then started crawling from man to man to make sure each one got his bayonet locked onto his musket barrel. Those without bayonets, and there were several who had tossed them aside as unwanted extra weight, would have to use their rifle butts as clubs; and Private McDonald would have to make do with his stub. Then Lieutenant Navarro plopped down next to Gill. His face was black with powder grime and he looked excited.

"Corporal Gill, we are retiring twenty yards to the rear, beyond the crest, on the backside of this accursed hill. Out of sight of these *Yanqui* devils. Keep your men low and dress your line on the sergeants when you get there. I am told there will be ammunition boxes waiting us. Be sure each man grabs at least two new packs. I want every man to have twenty rounds." With that the junior officer rose and crab-walked on bent knees to the first platoon, his sheaved sword sticking out behind him like a stiff tail.

"Bain, I just saw the colonel git on his horse and ride like thunder. I don't reckon he's runnin' off, but I do wonder what he's about."

Gill gaped at his friend Jesús for the thousandth time since they had left home, and shook his head once more.

"Jesse, you got no more business wondering what a colonel is about than a ...Oh' never mind, maybe he's gone to tell the general we're tuckered out and need water. Maybe he had to relieve his bowels. Maybe he's gone to get a bucket of beer for every man."

"I dunno, Bain. I'm thinking that maybe the colonel was called for new orders. May just be that we are about to go get shot at some more."

"Well, until somebody tells us different, I'm just fine waiting right here where no Yankee boy can see us. We done lost three good fellas today. Company K is going to be mighty short after this fight."

Once again Lieutenant Navarro duck-walked towards Corporal Gill and plopped down next to him.

"Mr. Gill, it appears our good Colonel Mills is now in command of the brigade. Word is that General Deshler was hit by a cannon ball and died about an hour ago. They say he was actually down on all fours looking under the smoke and a round ball took him square in the chest and just tore him apart."

"Lieutenant, I am sorry to hear that. But at least it wasn't a gut shot. Least it was quick. Why you tellin' me this right now?"

"Because, my good Corporal, the first sergeant is missing. I fear he may have been killed or perhaps captured earlier today when he was sent to find the next regiment. Now I have other things to do. You are now to find the second sergeant and let him know, and remind him to squash any rumors about losing the general. We will NOT be retiring."

"Yes, sir," With that the lieutenant waddled off to the right, while Gill moved on his hands and knees to the left searching for a sergeant.

The soldiers of the 6th-10th-15th Texas Consolidated Regiment held their position and the expected Federal attack never materialized. Lt. Colonel Anderson, now commanding the regiment in Colonel Mills absence, sent forward as skirmishers the four companies who had been on the far left. Those companies had not had a clear line of sight to fire, so each man still had full cartridge box. The fire from these 250 rifles persuaded the Union commanders to stay behind their barricades until ammunition boxes could be sent forward and the rest of the regiment resupplied with cartridges.

The day was not over for Company K, as a gap had developed and was being exploited by Union skirmishers to the right of the Texas Brigade. Lieutenant Navarro appeared behind Corporal Gill relaying orders for the company to join Companies G and H and move to the right to repulse the advancing Yankee skirmishers.

Once again, Gill's platoon dispersed into a thin skirmish line and began seeking targets as blue jacketed figures darted from tree to rock, coming slowly towards them. Gill was relieved that they only faced skirmishers and not a determined attack by a formed regiment. After using up most of his new supply of cartridges, Gill saw the men in front of him begin to move back towards the woods, having found their way blocked by the three Texas companies. With that, Gill slid down behind the boulder he was using as cover, and took a long drink of warm water from his tin canteen. He had survived the first major battle of the many the consolidated Texas regiments would fight during the next eighteen months.

Chapter 12

Mid-November 1863, South of Chattanooga, Tennessee
20 Men Present for Duty

Day 1

In the cold dawn light Lieutenant Navarro squatted down by Corporal Gill's camp fire and settled his tin cup into the ashes on the edge of the glowing coals. Then he poured some water from his canteen to fill the half empty cup, stretching last night's coffee dregs into another cup of diluted, but hot brew. Only then did he look over at Gill and nod.

"How did the picket line go last night, Bain? You boys hear anything unusual? You were pretty far down the side of the ridge. I reckon if any Yanks had been sniffin' around, you'd of heard them."

"Quiet, Lieutenant. It was quiet. But any Yank scouts would have had to sneak past our skirmish line at the foot of the ridge, so I'm not surprised it was quiet. But it was chilly. We sure could have used this little campfire last night."

"Don't doubt it," Navarro replied as he reached for his tin cup and then settled back on his haunches. "I'm here to pass along word that we're getting a new brigade commander. It's been nearly two months since General Deshler was killed at Chickamauga, and the big bugs finally turned us over to the command of General James A. Smith. He's a West Pointer and hails from Tennessee, and the Seventh Texas is coming into the brigade with him. The Arkansas boys are being pulled out, so we're going to be an all-Texas brigade now. Three regiments, all Texans."

"But fighting under the orders of a Tennessean. Can't we grow no good generals in Texas? But I don't see how it's gonna make any difference to our boys. Don't think any of them have ever spoken to any of our other brigade commanders. But it's good to know we'll be all Texans now. I'll let the boys know that."

With only a nod in reply, Lieutenant Navarro rose and moved off to another camp fire to continue spreading the news of this most recent reorganization. As Gill was sipping his own steaming coffee, Private McDonald plopped down next to the fire and began stirring the coals around with a stick.

"Bain, how long you reckon we are going to sit up here on this ridge? It seems like we done been here all winter and it's only November. Seems like we're growing roots here. Not that I'm complaining. Watchin' Yanks from up here is better than marching, and marching 's better than getting shot at, so we're two steps up the ladder from Hades. But I'm wondering if we're gonna spend *Navidad* up here starin' down at them fellers in that town."

Corporal Gill looked over at his friend Jesús and smiled. "Jesse, it's been two months of comfort and relaxation, and here you are belly-aching like we're back in prison camp. How would you rather we spend the time since that big fight in Georgia? Would you rather we were cutting down trees to build another damned fort on the banks of the river off yonder?" Bain pointed to the north where in the distance and far below them a narrow slice of the wide Tennessee River was visible as it wound its way around the town of Chattanooga.

"Last time we done that, look what happened. We got sent up river on the freezing deck of a boat and spent three hungry months as prisoners. No, sir. I'll enjoy life right here for as long as General Bragg wants us to stay on top of this ridge. It may feel like we're up in the clouds and the wind might blow and it might even snow before we git, but I'm a happy soljer to just set here. We got good rations, we got tents, we got firewood and blankets. And like you say, we ain't getting shot at."

"Bain, *mi amigo*, it may be I'm just wondering how long this good time will last. Word is that a new general done showed up down in that town, and he's the one who whipped General Johnson out west last year, and he's the one who captured Vicksburg and two other forts here in Tennessee, and now he's here to whip and capture us."

"Jesse, I heard about General Grant too. Word's going all through the camps that he's a real fire breather. But I heard he's a drunkard too. Likes his whiskey. And just look out there. Heck, we're up here on top of the tallest mountains there is, and they's down there staring straight up at us. You can't march up this mountain, you gotta climb it. You gotta sling your rifle and pull yourself up from tree to tree. We could roll big rocks down this mountain and stop them boys from comin' up without ever firing a shot. Nope. That army down in town ain't going to chase us off this hill. We'll move from here when that General Grant gets tired of seeing us up here and decides to go back up that river so he can come at us some other way. Then we'll march off to find another place to face 'em down like we did in September. We'll be fighting again, but it won't be up here. Nope. Up here we're just going to enjoy the view. And we got us a new brigade general too. Brigadier General J.A. Smith, a West Point man from Tennessee, used to be Colonel of the Fifth Confederate Regiment.

"That so? I wondered why you were talking to Lieutenant Navarro."

"Yup, our lieutenant was playing messenger boy this morning. And did you turn in that busted bayonet for a new one yet? You might want a whole one 'fore we all go home. You can't even cook a hunk of beef with that little piece you got left."

"Bain, you know me. I was the first man to the quartermaster once we quit marchin'. I held out the bayonet stub in my left hand and held out my right hand for a new one."

"And you got one, right?"

"Well, not right then, no. The sergeant said he didn't have none that fit our foreign rifles, I'd have to wait 'til we got resupplied with a new shipment of rifles and bayonets."

"That ain't real likely to happen any time soon," Bain said.

"*Sí*, that's what I figured, too. So I stole one in another camp. It fits fine," Jesús said with his usual grin. Then his visage went solemn and he paused before blurting out. "Bain, how come our company is called the Alamo Rifles?"

"Well, I imagine it's because we're from San Antone where the Alamo sets. And don't forget that big ruckus in front of the Alamo to get the old army to turn over all the guns and supplies to us Texans back just before the war started."

Jesús grunted, then said, "You ever think it's not right for us *Tejanos* to be in this army? I mean, I got Mexican blood and so does Lieutenant Navarro. Our people was on the outside of the Alamo trying to get in. Santa Anna's side, not Travis'. And that guard corporal back at the prison, he

94

spotted me as *Mexicano* right off, and then started that talk about *mi madre*. He made me so mad, I almost jumped him. And then they woulda shot me or hung me. But, what I mean is, Lieutenant Navarro and me, and the other *Tejanos...*, a lot of the men don't see us as real Texans. They act like it was us that marched with Santa Anna, and it was us that kilt those men at Goliad and the Alamo. Bain, that was over twenty-five years ago. Me and Lieutenant Navarro, we wasn't even borned yet when all that fightin' was going on back home."

"Jesse, I just don't know. Can't account for some men's thinking. You stood in line firing and getting shot at in every scrape we been in, and Lieutenant Navarro, he's done his part too. There ain't a *Tejano* in our company that's a shirker. Can't say that for some of them Dutchmen or Scotch boys. Some of them is worthless. But I reckon the truth is they look whiter than you and the lieutenant and, face it, none of their kin were in Santy Anna's army, but some of yours were. It don't have to be you, iffin' your daddy or uncle was there. That's enough for some of these crackers."

"Bain you know *mi padre* is a Scotchman. He just had the eye for *mi madre's fandango* dancin'. If it weren't for her beggin' him to lite out 'til Santa Anna moved on, he might have been with Travis and them others in the Alamo."

"Yup, and you'd a had another *padre* and wouldn't be sitting on this ridge top in Tennessee. You'd probably be throwing slop to the hogs out back of some *cantina*," Bain said with grin to show his friend he was joking.

"But like you said, Bain, my uncle, he did join up with Santa Anna, and he did fight against you Texicans."

"Jesse, also like I said, you ain't him. Which side a man picks in a war sometimes just depends on who is standing right there in front of him with a musket sayin' come with me, we're gonna make you a soljer. Look at them Marquerd boys and all them other Germans from Company I who switched sides back at the prison camp. They only joined us last year 'cause ever one else was signing up. Heck, they was scared not to join, scared their girls would shame them, or scared their pa's barn might get burned down."

"I reckon you're right, Bain."

"I am on this one. But don't you go and ever tell one of the boys that your Uncle Juan was at the Alamo on the Mexican side. That might be pushing your luck. After a little whiskey, you might find yourself on the wrong end of a Bowie knife, even if that fight at the Alamo is long gone and best forgotten."

"*Sí*, you mean, *los Tejanos sangrientes* – the bloody Texans. Long memories, short fuses, sharp knives. But tell me the truth, *mi amigo* Bain, didn't you ever holler, 'Remember the Alamo!' when you was a little *muchacho* playin' with stick guns?"

In reply Corporal Gill picked up a stick of firewood and pointed it like a musket at Jesús. With laughter in his voice Gill said, "Damn right I did. Remember the Alamo, you little peon! Now grab your skillet and git that fat back sizzling while we still got time to eat."

Day 2

The next morning the order came for Cleburne's whole division to pack their knapsacks and cook three days rations. They were being sent eastward. However, the march only lasted as far as Chickamauga Station before orders came instructing Cleburne to return his division to Missionary Ridge. General Bragg had become alarmed that his army overlooking Chattanooga was now outnumbered and was vulnerable to attack on both flanks. Missionary Ridge was truly high and steep, and Bragg had deployed three lines of defenses: The first near the foot of the ridge, the second half way up the steep incline, and the main line along the crest of the ridge. Regardless, Bragg was properly concerned that both ends of his defensive line were susceptible to flanking movements. Thus, he ordered Cleburne's Division to reinforce the right end of his line which was dominated by a hill through which a railway tunnel had been excavated – Tunnel Hill.

Panting for breath, with his musket bouncing on his right shoulder, Private Jesús McDonald used his right hand to hold onto his tall hat since his musket barrel kept hitting his hat brim. Jesús knew if his hat fell to the ground he would never recover his beloved *sombrero*, as Company K and the whole regiment was moving at the double quick along the dirt road in the late afternoon.

"Bain, when we going to stop? My shoe's untied."

"Shut up, Jesse. Don't you dare drop out to tie your shoe. Just shut up and keep up."

After moving at the quick pace for nearly a mile, the Texas Confederates crossed a railroad track and passed the dark entrance to a tunnel into which the iron rails disappeared. Finally the regiment slowed down and began to move uphill through brush and trees. Soon they reached the crest of the hill and were ordered to stack arms and rest. The soldiers quickly sat or lay down on the leaf covered ground and pulled long swigs of water from their canteens. It was almost dark and the men sensed the night would be active.

Night

Sergeant Degas made his way slowly across the hillside. Although the moon was nearly full when the evening started, the night had quickly gotten so dark he couldn't see his hands before him. But Degas knew the pitch black darkness would lighten soon. He looked up at the moon and saw the tiny bright sliver was already growing as the lunar eclipse began to ebb. Degas had heard of such occurrences but couldn't rightly actually remember ever being in such a thing before tonight. Well, he thought, this war was bringing one new thing after another to him and the others.

"Who's there? Is it a bear in the night?" came the call from near the dark shadow of stacked logs.

"It's Sergeant Degas, and keep your voice down, you damned fool. You want to catch a Yankee sharpshooter's bullet?" answered the sergeant.

"Aw, Sergeant, we've been swinging axes, crashing down trees, and dragging tree trunks all over this hillside. Don't you think the Yankees know where we are by now? And it's too dark to see anybody to shoot at."

"McDonald, you are close to being insubordinate, and I might decide to kick your backside."

Out of the deeper darkness Bain Gill spoke up, "Don't be hasty, Sarge. We're all here for the same reason. No call to threaten Jesse for just being friendly."

Degas walked towards the voice and spoke intensely, "Oh, I hear Corporal Gill as well. Corporal Gill, you and me will have a private talk soon. You must be taught to keep out of my business."

"Looking forward to it, Sergeant," came the reply.

Without further comment Degas stepped towards the line of logs stacked two and three high in a makeshift barricade. This short fence would serve as their defensive line should the Federals attack their position on the north side of Tunnel Hill.

"That's enough logs for now. That's high enough to shoot behind. Now get your boys out front and start hacking down the brush so's you can see the Yanks before they are on top of us. You can cut more logs after the firing lanes are cleared."

"Yessir, Sergeant. We were just aiming to do that, weren't we, Jesse?"

"You bet, Bain. Come on, Antonio, grab your knife and let's go cut down some brush."

Sergeant Degas made his way further along the hillside stopping when he reached the last of Company K's men. The log barricade stretched far enough to give all sixty riflemen of the combined company enough room to kneel and shoot. Degas saw Sergeant Walker of the 15th regiment talking to some of his men. Degas just nodded and moved by them. The sergeants in each of the three regiments that had been consolidated into one regiment had come to an informal structure where each NCO was responsible only for the men in his original regiment. This arrangement meant each company really operated as three platoons, one from each regiment, and each run by their original sergeant, rather than the two platoons that Hardee's drill manual dictated. Not by the book, but it was working.

Next, Degas, who had commandeered a detail of six privates, headed up over the crest of the hill to see if the wagons carrying the ammunition boxes had arrived from the division wagon yard. He sensed they were going to need a lot of cartridges in the day ahead.

Next to the wagons a group of officers were clustered together looking at a map by the light of a lantern held by a lieutenant. Degas saw that three of the officers were generals and heard one who spoke with a mild Irish accent say, "Yes, General Smith, that is exactly what I mean. The line of logs is too far down the slope. You must be closer to Swett's Battery to support them. Where you are now will also expose your men to the battery's fire when the Yanks get close. You must move up the hill. I want the 6th-10th-15th Regiment to build another line of works fifty yards nearer to the crest of the hill. Anchor their left on Swett's Battery. Angle the line to the north east until you touch the left end of the Seventh Regiment. Do you understand me?"

Degas saw their new brigade commander, General Smith, nod and heard him answer, "Yes sir, General Cleburne, I do. There is not much time left to dawn. With your permission, I will return to my brigade now."

Cleburne nodded and returned his attention to the other officers. Degas hurried along the line of wagons until he found the proper one and signed for three crates of cartridges, 3,000 rounds to be held in reserve for the company should the expected battle consume the forty rounds each man had now. With two men carrying each crate, the detail returned to where he had last seen Co. K, but they had already shifted up the hillside and were busy felling more trees to construct a new defensive line. As the last company in the regiment, Company K was next to Swett's battery of four Napoleon 12-pound smoothbore cannons. Degas has a bad feeling about being so close to the cannons because any counter-battery artillery fire from the Federals would very likely also hit them. With that discomforting thought, Sergeant Degas directed a squad of men with shovels to start digging a trench right behind the logs, throwing the dirt onto the logs for more protection. The night passed slowly as the men of Cleburne's Division prepared for the expected attack.

Day 3

Dawn brought the unmistakable sound of musket fire as the Union divisions began their attack on Missionary Ridge and Tunnel Hill. The skirmishers from the 6th-10th-15th Texas Infantry held their position for a short time as the Federal skirmish line felt out their opponents and then doubled the number of skirmishers that were leading the Federal assault. Soon Captain Foster withdrew his Texans up the hill, firing from behind trees and rocks as they retired to the main line of defense near the hill's crest.

A half hour later, Private McDonald pulled the trigger of his rifle and stared through the white smoke that was hanging low in the air, making it difficult to see their targets down the hillside. "Bain, Bain, do you see that? Do you see where them Yankees are now? They're hiding behind our logs! OUR logs! *Caramba!* That ain't right. Ain't right at all." Jesús pulled another cartridge from his cap box and bit off the end. "We cut those logs," he added as he poured the powder down the barrel. "We dragged those logs," he said while ramming the lead minie ball down the barrel to rest on top of the powder. "We stacked those logs," he said while he put a priming cap on the cone of the barrel. "Those ain't your logs to hide behind!" Jesús finally shouted towards the Federals as he brought up his rifle, perhaps aimed or maybe just pointed downhill, and squeezed off one more round before ducking back down behind his own protecting logs.

Sergeant Degas was right behind Jesús but never heard his ranting. It was not just the noise of the men in front of him shooting, the cannons to their right blasting, the whizzing of minie balls sailing by overhead, or the thunking sounds of bullets hitting their log wall. It was that his attention just then was on the crews of the four artillery pieces that were aligned next to Company K. The guns were positioned almost hub to hub just below the crest of the ridge, and they had been firing continuously for nearly an hour. Their canister shells were very effectively doing bloody work, spraying out hundreds of lead balls with every round. Degas didn't see how any Yankees could move up the steep slope under such fire. Yet, the crews of the cannons kept being hit by enemy rifle fire. They were being wounded and killed at a rate that may soon silence one or more of the pieces when too few artillerymen remained to serve all four cannons. Even as the infantry sergeant watched, an artillery officer jerked and dropped to the ground. Degas looked back to his own men and then looked towards the battery again. The officer was being dragged backwards out of the way and leaned against a tree.

As if someone was reading Sergeant Degas's thoughts, he felt a tap on his shoulder and turned to see Lieutenant Navarro who bent forward and shouted into his ear, "Henri, look behind us."

Degas turned and looked uphill behind Navarro. Standing not five yards behind them was the same general who had been studying the map last night. Degas recognized him as General Cleburne and felt a flash of admiration for any leader who could stand so stoically while bullets flew by. Then Navarro continued, "That there is General Cleburne. He just told me personally to pull a dozen men from our logs to help man the cannons over there," pointing to Swett's Battery." Navarro continued, "You get every second man from your platoon. Tell them to leave their muskets and double-quick to me. I'll be with the battery's officer to see where he wants our boys. Do you understand?"

"Yes sir, Lieutenant. I don't like it. Our boys ain't never drilled as an artillery crew. They won't know what to do."

"I know that, but just get them moving. They will learn quickly today. You stay here and keep the rest of our boys firing, and keep them down behind those logs. Send Corporal Gill to me."

Within minutes Corporal Gill led the dozen soldiers, feeling naked without their muskets, the few yards to Lieutenant Navarro who was talking not to an officer, but to a sweating artillery corporal. Gill approached the pair and saluted and heard the corporal saying, "They'll have to do. Send four of them over the crest to the ammunition caissons. They will carry the rounds to the pieces. Send two more to each of the four guns. Report to the corporal of each gun. You won't find a sergeant still standing."

Navarro assigned his dozen men as directed by the artillery corporal. The riflemen were quickly put to work swabbing out the smoking barrels with water after each piece fired and then ramming fresh canister rounds down the steaming tubes. It was hot and energetic work that required concentration, even though these tasks required less skill than those performed by the crewmen who cleaned the firing vents, punctured the powder bags at the base of the barrels, and lastly inserted new priming rods that touched off the powder when the cord was pulled.

Gill was handling a long handled swab and was so engrossed in his efforts that he also didn't notice the whizzing of incoming minie balls until Private Jerre Gordon fell against Gill's shoulder. "Careful, dammit, Jerre!"

Gill shouted, then he saw that Private Gordon had been shot in the head as his body slid the rest of the way to the ground. Gill didn't have time to feel remorse, only to stoop over and grab his comrade's wrists to pull the corpse away from the cannon so others wouldn't stumble over it as they kept cleansing and loading the Napoleon.

"Cease fire!" came the order from the artillery corporal. Gill's ears were ringing so loud from the repeated firing of the battery that he didn't hear and continued plunging his rammer down the cannon's barrel until Lieutenant Navarro shook his shoulder and pointed to the corporal who was now commanding the battery. The man drew his hand across his neck indicating to the crews to stop their loading procedures. Black-faced with soot from his work, Gill leaned against one wheel of the cannon and turned to look around.

What he saw was the rest of the 6th-10th-15th Texas Consolidated Regiment climbing over the log wall and, with bayonets fixed and screaming like Indians, charging down the slope. Gill caught a glimpse of Captain Houston waving his sword urging the men onward. Then he even saw Colonel Mills doing the same thing further down the slope. Gill still had his eye on the colonel when Mills jerked backwards and fell to the ground.

Private McDonald jumped down from the topmost pine log and whooped loudly as he started running and sliding down the steep slope. He had left his tall slouch hat behind the log wall and was among the front runners in the company and his attention was focused ahead, searching for blue coated *soldados*. He stumbled and regained his feet. He kept moving recklessly downhill while trying to keep his musket leveled and pointed ahead. He could now see Yankees turning and plunging downhill trying to stay ahead of the screaming mob of Confederates. Jesús moved past a big boulder and to his right saw a Union soldier just a few yards away raising his musket, not at Jesús, but uphill, not yet having seen Jesús emerge from around the boulder. Jesús, still moving, swiveled his Austrian musket towards the enemy soldier and pulled the trigger. The bullet hit the man and he toppled over. Jesús did not pause, but kept sliding and leaping downhill, now with an unloaded weapon, but one that was still capped with two feet of pointed steel.

The Union corporal didn't at all like how this morning was unfolding. Since dawn his regiment had been marching towards the sounds of the battle on the hillside. They had crossed a big stream and moved uphill, all while catching glimpses of wounded men moving back downhill and soon the sight of dead men lying where they fell. This was bad business. The regiment had moved from a marching column into a long battle line as soon as they left the road. Now they were beginning to hear the whine of bullets passing overhead and the corporal saw the first man in his company stumble and fall, clutching his stomach. The rear rank man stepped over the prostrate soldier as the regiment moved on up the steep incline.

Soon they broke out of the thick brush into an area where freshly cut stubs of small trees and brush were protruding from the ground. This area was more open, exposing the regiment as they stepped forward, and the sound of the rifle bullets passing by was augmented now by the booms of cannons being fired towards them.

Without warning, four men to the right of the corporal fell as the canister balls cut a swathe out of the long line of Ohioans. The corporal didn't even notice the warm wetness on his upper thigh until he had taken another step. Then he stopped and put a hand to the spot and felt not the sticky flow of his fresh blood, but the warmth of his own urine as his bladder released. Fearing for his life, and seeing the deaths of the men next to him as an opportunity to stay where was, he dropped his musket, fell to the ground and held his thigh, keeping his head low to avoid locking eyes with any officer.

The regiment moved past him, men shuffling to their right to close the gap left by the casualties. After a moment, the corporal chanced a look up the hill and saw the regiment moving through more trees, and then as if by order, many of the ragged line of men turned back down hill and started leaping and stumbling towards him. A few dropped their weapons and others took a few steps and then stopped behind trees to aim and shoot uphill before resuming their retreat. The corporal rose and leaving his musket on the ground, joined the soldiers fleeing down the hill. He had taken only a few steps when his right leg collapsed under him and he fell and rolled a few feet before being stopped by a freshly cut stump of a small tree.

The corporal was conscious and had the wits to pop two buttons of his fatigue blouse and pull out his scarf and wrap it around his bleeding wound. Just as he was trying to stand, he saw two young men in drab uniforms bounding down the hill straight towards him. Rather than risk being shot again in flight, he stayed still and held his wounded leg that was now hurting so bad he didn't have to exaggerate his loud groans.

Jesús had run further down the hill and finally stopped and leaned against a tree trunk to catch his breath. As soon as he stopped, Private Leon Fremon stumbled to his knees close to the tree. Jesús reached out and grabbed his elbow, asking, "Leon, you hit? You okay?" Private Fremon was eighteen, skinny with blonde shaggy hair and had a wisp of beard just starting to grow, yet he was a combat veteran.

"Yea, Jesse, I'm good. Let's go. Them Yanks are runnin' like sheep."

"Sure thing, Leon," and the two men resumed sliding and leaping downhill side by side.

Within seconds, the two young men in gray saw a line of blue-coated bodies lying in the leaves directly in front of them. Near the bodies was a Yankee who was sitting and holding his leg as he loudly moaned. The man looked up to see the pair of Rebs and let go of his leg and raised both arms in surrender. The two young men slid to a stop in front of him. The Federal soldier had no way of knowing that neither held a loaded musket, but both were pointing their bayonets just a few feet from his chest. The Yankee uttered, "Don't shoot me, boys! I'm hurt bad. Gonna bleed out. Let me just sit here and meet my maker."

Jesús's attention was focused beyond where they stood, looking for any enemy who may be a threat. But when he heard the man speak, Jesús's head jerked down to stare hard at their captive. He looked at the corporal's stripes of rank on his sleeves. Then he looked at the man's face, and finally, he looked down at the wound, and saw the red and brown striped knitted scarf.

"Oh, *mi madre*," Jesús whispered to himself. Without thought or warning, Jesús thrust his bayonet down hard, pushing the point through the man's flesh and impaling him on the leaves. Leaving his musket quivering upright with the point of the bayonet buried in the ground, Jesús reached out with one hand and shoved the corporal hard down on his back. Next he lifted the soldier's right leg and with his other hand Jesús unwrapped the scarf his mother had given him nearly two years before as the new recruits left San Antonio. "This is mine, you *Yanqui* piece of *caca*. You forgot to give it back to me before we left Camp Butler."

Jesús then picked up the nearest Springfield, saying as he pointed the barrel at the corporal's chest, "This is for the boy you killed at the dead-line."

As Jesús was about to squeeze the trigger, Leon reached over and knocked the gun barrel sideways, saying, "Jesus, Jesse, no more."

Leon's shove of the barrel pushed the bullet to the side enough that it just grazed the corporal's ribs, but still embedded a scrap of blue cloth in this third wound. Satisfied with his retribution, Jesús dropped the Yankee musket, grasped and jerked his own musket upward, freeing the bayonet and causing blood to start gurgling out of the wound on top of the Ohioan's left thigh.

With fresh blood splattered over both their trousers, the two teenagers stepped over the sobbing man and continued downhill while Jesús tucked his scarf inside his jacket.

Corporal Gill helped load the Napoleon and then stood to the side of the wheel out of the way while the battery pieces held their fire. They watched the infantrymen of the Texas Brigade return up the hill and slowly resumed their positions behind the logs. Gill saw Jesús and Leon Fremon walking together up the hill and waved to them, but they both were looking down as they climbed the slope.

Lieutenant Navarro stepped in front of Gill and said, "Corporal Gill, I trust you have been enjoying your lessons as an artilleryman?"

"Lieutenant, sir, I'd prefer to return to the company. All us boys would."

"First, Corporal, a casualty report?"

"Huh, I.... Private Gordon is dead, sir. I, huh, don't know about the others. Sir."

"You will be pleased to learn, Corporal, that Private Gordon is your only fatality. Private Hoever is wounded in the arm, but it is only a flesh wound. The others are uninjured."

"Huh, thank you, sir. Can we go back to Company K now?"

"Soon, Corporal. I have been told that half of Swett's Battery is being moved further to the right where the range is greater and they are needed. The battery's crew will remain here to work the two guns remaining. But until the pieces actually depart our patch of ground, you are to remain here just in case the Yanks come up the hill again."

"Yessir. Sir, did we push them off this hill? I saw the regiment climb the logs and charge downhill. Did we do it? I saw Jesse and Leon and some others coming back just now."

"Yes, Corporal, your comrades did their duty. We pushed the blue bellies that were threatening this battery off the hill and out of sight. We captured a few too, and perhaps a regimental flag as well. All in all, not a bad effort."

"We lose many men this morning? I mean in my platoon?"

"Unknown, Corporal. The butcher's bill of your boys is for you to add up when you return. But be prepared. The Yanks will try us again. The day is yet young."

"Yes sir." Within a few minutes two of the Napoleons were hitched to their limbers and they rolled over the crest out of sight. Without further orders, Gill gathered the Sixth Texas men and moved them back to the log breastworks.

"Hey, Jesse, how did the fight go while we were at the battery? Are the boys okay?"

Jesús looked up at Bain from his seat leaning against the logs. "Yea, Bain. We pushed them off the hill."

Gill noted that Jesse was speaking softly and his tone was like nothing Bain had heard from Jesús before. "I saw you and Leon and the others charging down the hill. Did everyone come back?"

"Doan know, Bain. I...I don't know. Bain, I tried to kill him. Leon stopped me"

"Of course you tried to kill them, Jesse. That's why we're here. Did you notice they're trying to kill us too?

"No, no, Bain. It was the guard. The corporal from Camp Butler." Without another word, Jesús slid his hand between the buttons of jacket and pulled out his red and brown scarf.

"Holy cow, Jesse! It was him? Honest? Looks like you done just fine, Jesse. Got your scarf back and that pig...is he dead?"

"No. We left him calling for his *madre*. But he won't be running for a spell."

At that moment, they both heard Captain Houston bellowing, "Here they come again, boys. Independent fire. Knock them back down that hill."

McDonald and Gill both picked up their muskets and fired a round into the smoke. A few seconds later the ground shook as the two Napoleons to their right fired simultaneously, hurling more canister down on the unfortunate regiment from Illinois that was now trying to reach the crest.

More spots of unmoving blue began to be visible down the slope as more and more Federal soldiers fell from the combined musket and canister fire. A second and then a third regiment had been committed to this one section of the assault. The three regiments of the Texas Brigade fired without let up, Company K using the fresh ammunition packs that Sergeant Degas's detail had carried to the position shortly before dawn, now over eight hours ago.

At nearly 3:00 pm, Captain Houston gave a surprising command, "Company K, rise. Right face! Into a nice march column, boys. Be quick about it."

Then they moved to the right along with the rest of the regiment. "Company, Front!" The men turned and faced downhill, now back in a long line of two ranks. "We are going through the gap in the logs, gentlemen, in a column of companies. We will be behind the Seventh Texas. When we pass through the gap we will form a battalion line and move downhill in an orderly fashion, sweeping the Yanks before us. Fix Bayonets!"

Company K stood in place for a few minutes wondering what was happening in front of them. Finally Captain Houston realized far too many Confederates were trying to squeeze through the short gap in the log wall and in the confusion their path was blocked. Without further hesitation, Houston ordered his company, "At the right oblique! Forward, March!" The captain moved his company to the piled logs and urged them to climb straight over. Once on the other side, he tried to gather them back into a formation, but each man simply took off down the hill as he cleared the logs. Other companies were doing the same, and the intermixed mob of shouting Texans charged downhill a second time in three hours.

When the order came from Captain Houston to climb the log pile, Lieutenant Navarro took a step back, unbuckled his sword belt holding his sheathed sword and leaned the belt and sword against a tree. He never said if he was trying to ease his climb by removing the encumbrance that might get tangled in his legs, or if he foresaw he might be captured and did not want to lose his sword. Whatever his thoughts were, he left the expensive sword behind and simply picked up a big rock in his throwing hand and joined his men racing down the hill, hollering like a madman.

Captain Houston remained standing on top of the logs, waving his sword encouraging his company to climb over quickly. While men were still moving past him, a bullet hit his thigh. Houston instinctively thought one of his men had struck him with a steel ramrod until he looked down to see the blood as his leg gave way under his weight. Two musicians who were waiting several yards behind the log wall saw Houston fall and hustled forward with a litter. They quickly loaded him on and jogged over the crest towards the brigade field hospital.

Houston had to wait his turn, but soon he was lifted to the operating table. The surgeon walked up, wiping his hands on his bloody apron. First, he cut open Houston's trouser leg and, with a grunt, stuck his index finger into the wound. The captain gasped and cursed but didn't faint. The doctor then put his other index finger through the exit wound at the back of Houston's leg and pushed both fingers deeper into the wound until his fingertips touched. Satisfied that the bullet had missed both bone and artery, and that his probing had not found any cloth scraps, he pulled out his fingers, directed his orderly to wrap the wound tightly, and moved on to his next patient. The captain was carried to an ambulance and told to stay in the back with three other wounded men.

Gill and McDonald stayed close together as Jesús instinctively retraced his path from the first downhill charge. He had to see if the Union corporal had indeed bled out or if he was still holding on. If he was still breathing, Jesús had decided he would somehow drag him back up the hill as a prisoner. He now admitted to himself that Leon had been right in knocking his gun aside, preventing Jesús from murdering the man, but Jesús was still intent on completing his revenge by capturing the sadistic guard. Jesús recognized the big boulder where he had first fired his musket, and he ignored the body of the soldier he had felled there. The two Rebs then both ducked as a minie ball careened off the boulder and whistled by them. They both dropped to a knee and scanned the trees ahead of them for movement or telltale blue. Seeing the dark back of a man moving downhill before them, they both rose and resumed their descent. Coming out of a tree line to the edge of the small pasture where Privates McDonald and Fremon had seen the row of dead soldiers and encountered the Camp Butler guard, Jesús pulled up and grabbed Bain by his arm.

"Here, Bain. He was here."

"Who, Jesse? No one here but dead men, let's keep moving!"

Gill was right in that the Union corporal with the bayonet wound in his leg was not sitting there, nor was he a corpse in the row of men who had died from the cannon fire. Jesús figured he had been helped down the hill by other Yankees in their retreat.

Gill looked around and saw several Confederates, some still whooping and bounding downhill, but most moving purposefully now, searching ahead for targets. The pair went forward and into more trees. Just yards ahead they saw a handful of Rebel soldiers shouting and aiming their weapons at a trio of Yanks, one who was holding a blue regimental flag.

"Gonna die for that flag, boy?"

Hearing the taunt, one of the men, a bearded sergeant, abruptly raised and fired his musket, hitting one Reb in the arm. The sergeant was immediately shot down, his defiance prompting the Texans to leap the final yards. With muskets extended, they lunged forward, driving bayonets into the chests of both remaining Union soldiers. One bayonet pierced the silk banner before skewering the private holding the flag.

A corporal then tore the silk flag loose and quickly rolled it, tied the ends together and hung it over his shoulder like a thin blanket roll. Then the group moved further down to the foot of the ridge. More Rebs were moving across the large field between the hill and the creek, but they were opposed by a growing blue line across the creek and the attacking Southerners were taking casualties.

A lieutenant who Gill recognized said, "This is far enough, boys. We ain't going to push them back any further. I say they are done for the day. Let's get back up the hill to our logs."

The corporal wearing the blue silk banner nodded and said, "Lieutenant, that sounds fine to me. I'm ready to personally hand this trophy to General Smith."

"Doubt you will get to do that, Jacob," said the lieutenant. "Ain't you heard that Colonel Granbury's been our brigade commander for, oh, two, three hours now. General Smith got hit during our first downhill run. Now we are Granbury's Brigade."

With that news, the men moved back uphill, confident that the day had been won and there would be celebrations in the evening. They also expected that they would work to improve their defensive positions, bury their dead, and the generals would shift regiments and batteries about to be ready if the Yankees resumed their attack at dawn tomorrow.

Night

"Bain, somebody's lying to us. Somebody's lyin'. There ain't no way the whole rest of the army's been pushed off this mountain. You was there too. You saw how we run the whole danged bunch of 'em down the hill and across the creek. We herded them like we do the longhorns back home. Bain, we even got their flags," Jesús exclaimed to his friend.

"Yea, Jesse, we did all that. Four Yankee flags brought back by just our regiment. Ain't that something. But I only know what I've been told, and that's that we are moving out, *pronto*. The lieutenant says we're the only division in the whole army that ain't skedaddled already,"

"*Caramba*! When we gonna not be the last men fightin' before something bad happens. It happened in Arkansas and now it's happening in Tennessee. If we march back into Georgia, I bet us Texans will be the last men fightin' there too.

"Ain't that why we marched all the ways from San Antone, Jesse? To be the last men standing?"

As Corporal Gill spoke, Second Lieutenant Navarro approached with the news that Captain Houston had been wounded during the afternoon battle and the company was now under the command of First Lieutenant Davenport of the 15th Texas, Mulling over this news that the command of the consolidated company was now in the hands of yet another officer they did not know well, Gill and McDonald joined the rest of the surviving eighteen men from San Antonio to be issued fresh packages of cartridges,

108

refill their canteens, and file by a wooden crate to pick up handfuls of hard crackers to stuff in their haversacks. Then the company joined the regiment, and the regiment joined the rest of the brigade on the road south, moving away from Chattanooga.

It was dark and cold when Jesús spoke as they were marching, "Bain, how am I going to get my knapsack back? I left mine back behind that log wall. Nobody told me we was about to march off."

"Damn, Jesse, didn't you hear the sergeant hollering for everybody to grab their kit?"

"I didn't hear nobody hollering, or maybe everybody was hollering. Heck, I don't know. All I do know is when I came back from clearing my bowels, you was hurryin' me to fetch my rifle and 'couter up. You didn't say nuthin' about my knapsack. Now I guess it's going to lie behind that log fence 'til some farm boy finds it."

"So now it's my fault you're marching without a blanket and whatever you had stuffed in that rat nest you been carrying."

"I didn't mean it's your fault, Bain. But, where am I going to find a blanket?" Then Jesús visibly brightened as he remembered his long lost scarf that was still tucked into his jacket. "But today wasn't so bad after all. You and me are both still alive and ain't shot up, and I would've traded my knapsack for *mi madre's* scarf anyways."

Chapter 13

Late November 1863, North Georgia
18 Men Present for Duty

"**B**ain, are we ever going to get to march in the daylight again? This marching by moonlight is about to make me start hootin' like an owl. We been marching all night. And I'm still shivering from wadin' that creek. We didn't get near long enough by the fire to dry out our trousers 'fore we were marching again. I don't know why we can't just cross over creeks on bridges like regular people do."

"Jesse, if you start hooting like an owl, I swear I'll shoot you myself. And if you don't quit your bellyaching I might just shoot you anyway."

"Aw Bain, you know I'm just griping to take my mind off my worries."

"Worries, what worries? You are a pampered private in the best fed, best dressed, best equipped army to just get kicked out of Tennessee. Now you are in the best fed, best dressed, best equipped army in Georgia. At least I think we are still in Georgia."

"Georgia, Tennessee, Arkansas, they all look the same to me. Trees, muddy roads, and freezing creeks. And no bridges."

About that time, the sound of shoes on boards was audible as the regiment's march took the lead companies over the first of the two bridges that spanned Chickamauga Creek at Ringgold Gap.

Ringgold Gap lay just a mile or so beyond the train station. Both a road and a train track ran next to Chickamauga Creek as it flowed through the gap. On the south side of the gap Taylor's Ridge loomed tall and steep. Just north of the gap White Oak Ridge was covered with pine trees and brush, making the location a suitable place for Cleburne's Division to delay the advancing Union army. General Bragg had said Cleburne only need hold out for a few hours to give the Army of Tennessee's wagon train, the highly vulnerable tail of the army, time enough to extricate itself from threat of capture by the pursuing federals. So Cleburne himself had ridden back in the moonlight to scout the gap and the ridges. He figured Ringgold Gap would do nicely, but he worried about how long his one division might hold on against far greater numbers of Federals who would be chasing Bragg's mangled army.

General Hiram Granbury was a lean, very tall, and handsome man in his early thirties. It seemed to the regimental officers in the Texas Brigade that he was everywhere at once. Granbury was excited about leading the brigade in battle, but worried that two of his regiments were commanded by newly promoted officers, as he himself had been. So he worked with a sense of urgency to position his three regiments to the north of Ringgold Gap to put forth maximum firepower, and to keep a mobile reserve to respond to any breakthroughs by the Federals.

The 460 riflemen in the Consolidated 6th-10th-15th Regiment were now under the temporary command of Captain Kennard, after Colonel Mills was wounded at Tunnel Hill. The regiment was deployed in line of battle just north of the gap at the foot of White Oak Ridge, but far enough back in the tree line to benefit from the cover. To their right the brigade's largest regiment, the Consolidated 17th-18th-24th-25th Texas Regiment, with nearly 600 men, extended the line and protected the right flank. The small Seventh Texas Regiment, now only fielding about 160 riflemen, was held back on top of the ridge in reserve.

A brigade of four regiments of Arkansas troops was positioned in the gap itself. The gap was so narrow that the Arkansas regiments had to deploy in four lines, one regiment behind the next. Alongside the Arkansas regiments, straddling the road and next to the railroad tracks, were two Napoleon cannons hidden behind a cut brush barricade at the most narrow point in the gap. Two more brigades of soldiers from Alabama, Tennessee, and Mississippi were in reserve near the two bridges that spanned the swiftly flowing serpentine creek.

What Corporal Gill and the others in Company K did not know was that their regiment was stationed at the absolute rear of the entire Army of

111

Tennessee. They were put there when General Bragg turned to General Cleburne to fend off the Union pursuit, and General Cleburne selected the Texas Brigade to bear the brunt of the inevitable Yankee assault. General Granbury picked his two consolidated regiments to hold the tree line with a thousand riflemen, keeping the Federals in the open field, and not allowing them to flank the Confederate defenses. It was a tall order, required by the desperate need to save the army's supply train.

Corporal Gill knelt behind the pine tree and looked to his left. It was almost light enough to make out the shapes of the soldiers in that direction.

"Corporal Gill, I remind you that you are the last man in our regiment and you must watch your flank. Our flank. You must be alert and give us time to face about if we are attacked from that way," Sergeant Degas said as he knelt by Gill.

"Sure, Sergeant, but won't there be another outfit between us and the gap? There's a lot of space between me and there," replied Gill.

"Arkansas boys. Joshes, you call them, I believe. Some of the same men who were captured at Arkansas Post with us are coming up from the gap now," Degas answered.

Within minutes of the first direct morning sunlight reaching the field to their front, Federal soldiers became visible on the road approaching the gap. Two hundred Kentucky cavalrymen wearing gray came thundering into the gap in a hasty withdrawal from their initial skirmishing position a mile up the road towards Chattanooga. They had been the bait to draw the Federal advance party into the range of Lieutenant Goldwaithe's two hidden Napoleon cannons. As the cavalry troops were passed through the barrier of brush across the road, General Cleburne himself met them and ordered them to dismount and join the defenders to his right. "We are going to salivate those men when they get close," yelled the excited general.

The Federal company leading the way down the road came within two hundred yards of the Confederates invisible behind the brush barricade and the trees on the hillside. Finally, General Cleburne who was intently marking the Union advance coming straight towards them stood straight up, turned to Lieutenant Goldwaithe and shouted, "Now, Lieutenant, give it to them NOW!"

Immediately, the two cannons hidden in the gap roared together. Gill jumped, almost dropping his musket. By looking to his far left he could see that the front of the Union column had been hit dead-on and men were writhing on the road while others lay still. Almost immediately, companies from the regiments further back in the Federal column started peeling out of line and sending skirmishers across the field toward the wood line where the Texans were hidden.

Gill knew to wait until he heard the order to open fire, and he hoped his platoon would likewise hold until the Yanks were too close to miss. Gill waited and nervously rubbed his thumb on the top of the gun's wooden stock. He waited and kept waiting and wanted to shout the order to fire himself. But he waited a little longer until the advancing Union skirmishers were within one hundred yards, when Lieutenant Davenport finally relayed Captain Kennard's order to fire a single volley by the whole regiment. The company commanders in the middle of the battle line heard and repeated the order more quickly than did the officers on each end of the regiment. Therefore, the resulting volley wasn't a single coordinated blast. Rather, the regiment's first fire was a rolling volley starting in the center of the regiment, moving out both directions. Even if not a simultaneous opening volley, over 450 riflemen fired well-aimed first shots from cover, without a screen of smoke obscuring their targets.

The staggered nature of the volley gave the Federal skirmishers in front of Company K just enough time to drop to their bellies as the Confederate riflemen on the wood's edge pulled triggers. The shock of Company K's opening volley was thus diluted, but still had the effect of stopping the skirmishers' progress well into the middle of the field.

By the time Gill and his platoon had reloaded and been given the command for independent fire, reinforcing lines of Federals were rapidly moving up behind the prone skirmishers. Gill intuitively shifted his aim to this new target, since the reinforcements were shoulder to shoulder, making them easier to hit. As Gill reloaded he glanced to either side. To his right, he could see a few of his men and they appeared calm enough as they bit off the ends of the cartridges and went through the routine of loading. To his left, he could see a few Arkansas soldiers firing obliquely to their left, doing what they could to slow the Federal advance down the road. Gill again heard the cannons, recognizing the odd sound of canister pellets ricocheting off rocks as they bounced on towards the Yanks. Gill realized he was very glad he was leaning against a wide tree trunk, hidden except for the few seconds it took him to fire each round.

Gill was kneeling now behind the tree, methodically, but not hastily, loading his musket. None of the men knew how long they might stay here, and none wanted to empty their cartridge boxes before they or the Yanks withdrew. Gill heard his name being called and looked to his right.

"Bain, them boys on your other side. Where they from?" Jesús called to Bain from behind the boulder he was using for cover.

"Arkansas, Jesse. Part of the bunch that got captured with us."

Jesús heard his friend's reply, dropped to the ground, and crawled to Gill's position.

"Dammit, Jesse, this tree ain't big enough for both of us, git back to your rock."

" Bain, if we're going to be fightin' long next to them Arkansas boys, I need you to watch my back if we get to mingling with them."

"What're you talking about? If we get mixed up with them, we'll all be watching for Yankees."

"Yea, sure, but one of them fellers has me in his sights. A sergeant, skinny man with a missing front tooth. Clean shaved. Mean bastard."

"Hell, Jesse, that's half the sergeants in this army."

"May be, but this one, he has call to shoot me if he sees me when we're in a scrape."

Bain looked at his friend and saw he was serious. "What'd you do, whip out your knife on this sergeant?"

"Somethin' like that. I'll tell you all about it later." With that, Jesús dropped back to the ground and crawled back to his protecting boulder and resumed firing and loading and firing. Corporal Gill pondered his friend's odd request as he bit off the end of another paper cartridge. He looked to his left, could only see a few of the Arkansas boys, and none of them were wearing three stripes, Then Gill forgot about Jesse and concentrated on the enemy across the field.

As the morning sun rose, the 6th-10th-15th Texas continued to put forth a steady stream of musket fire, holding off the Yanks. Lieutenant Davenport was standing on a boulder where he could see the Federals adding even more brigades to the attack, moving regiments to the Confederates' right flank. Davenport knew the other large consolidated regiment in the Texas Brigade was next to them, but that was the end of their line. He knew the two regiments would not be able to stop the Federal flanking attack if more Union regiments kept being fed into the assault. Even further up the hill, Colonel Granbury had reached the same conclusion and ordered his small reserve regiment, the Seventh Texas, to shift forward to extend the brigade's defensive line.

General Polk, whose brigade had been held back behind the ridge, had ridden forward, realized how tenuous the Texans' position was, and ordered his lead regiments to immediately support them. Polk's first regiment deployed from column into line, firing even as they made the swift formation change among the trees on the crest of the ridge. The Federals had advanced up the ridge so far that when Polk's men started firing they were no more than twenty yards from their enemy. In places, the hidden ravines along the ridge worked to the advantage of the Confederate regiments, whose men were uphill and able to rain enfilading fire down on the climbing Federals who were caught in the ravines between the protruding fingers of high ground along the ridge. By 10:00 am, three Confederate brigades were engaged, with only one brigade in reserve, down in the gap.

By 11:00 am, the last Confederate brigade, led by General Lowrey, had also moved up Taylor's Ridge and added its weight to the defense of the Rebel's flank along the crest of the ridge. Meanwhile, Polk's brigade had pushed the northerners completely off their part of the ridge and, with Granbury's Texans, were ready to press a counterattack across the field. Captain Kennard gave the command for the whole regiment to fix bayonets in preparation for the expected order to charge. However, Cleburne wisely kept all his troops within the woods, not letting them venture into the field, knowing his task was only to delay the enemy, not to avenge the debacle at Missionary Ridge.

By noon, the Federals had finally brought up an artillery battery to duel with Lieutenant Goldwaithe's pair of Napoleon cannons. As the six Union cannons began to batter the Confederate positions, a courier delivered word from General Bragg that the army's wagon train was now far enough away for Cleburne to disengage. Cleburne had the brush screen in the gap pulled back into place, masking their movement, and ordered each brigade to quietly pull back one regiment at a time, until the ridge and gap were empty again.

General Joseph Hooker, the Federal commanding officer, chose not to press another attack. Instead he sat on a barrel at the train depot that had become his headquarters and had a hot cup of tea, waiting for General Grant to arrive. Without further bloodshed, both armies fell to the chores of recovery from the battle for Chattanooga, which ended with Cleburne's successful defense of Ringgold Gap and Taylor's Ridge.

Part 3

Chapter 14

January 1864, Winter Camp Near Dalton, Georgia
17 Men Present for Duty

"Dammit, Bain, how the hell do I know how far it is to old Woodrow out there?" asked an exasperated Private McDonald. "It's a fer piece distant, that's how far it is. I can barely see him."

"Jesse, let's do this one more time. Hold out your arm and turn your thumb sideways, and put it next to Woodrow. Now who is taller, Woodrow or your thumb?" Corporal Gill was determined that his friend, and all the other men in his platoon were going to master this simple technique for estimating how far an enemy line was from their own position.

"Come on, Jesse, which is taller, your thumbnail or Woodrow?"

Jesse squinted along his arm, holding one eye shut, and muttered, "Well, Woodrow is about half as high as my thumbnail, I reckon. But he's wearin' a tall hat."

"Forget about the hat. Yankees wear hats too. So how far away is that? What did the sergeant say about how far away a man is if he is as tall as your thumbnail?"

"Bain, you know I got no head for cypherin'."

"This ain't cyphering, Jesse. It's just remembering. What did Sergeant Degas say if a man is as tall as your thumbnail?"

"Yea, Jesús, what is it?" Private San Miguel added just to goad his friend along.

"You shut up, Andrew, you don't remember any more'n I do." Jesús paused, looked up to the sky for divine guidance, and finally blurted out, "It's *tres*, ugh, 300 feet to a thumbnail. That's what the Sergeant said. 300."

"Danged if you ain't right, Jesse," Gill said. "Now if a man 300 feet away is thumbnail high, how far is a man only half a thumbnail high?"

"Bain, you said no cypherin'. Besides, I'm getting all mixed up with thumbnails and men and hats or no hats. And I quit school ten years back to work cows."

Corporal Gill rolled his eyes, and then looked Jesús square in the face. "Jesse, you ain't dumb. Look, General Cleburne, he's trying to keep us from wasting our bullets shooting too high or too low. And the more Yankees we shoot when they are only thumbnail high, the fewer Yankees are going to shoot at us when they are a whole lot closer and we are great big targets. So, forget cyphering, and just remember thumbnail high is 300 feet and you aim at the man's waist belt. If he is only half a thumbnail high, he's more like 600 feet away, so you aim where his neck grows out of his chest. Now, say that back to me."

"OK, Bain, one thumbnail high, I shoot his belt buckle..."

At which point Private San Miguel injected, *"Sí,* you shoot at his *cajones."*

"Shut up, Andrew, we gotta aim higher than the *cajones,* we gotta shoot him in the belt, where his guts are, not down where his brains are."

That brought a gruff laugh from most of the men circled around, since the Anglo men from San Antonio had all heard enough jokes and saloon talk spoken in the Tex-Mex mix of rough Spanish and English to follow the thread of the Hispanic privates' exchange. Even Corporal Gill had to smile as Jesús continued, "And iffin' he's only part of a thumbnail high, I shoot him in the neck. *Sí?"*

"Sí, my friend. That's right." Bain looked around at the small group of men gathered around him and spoke loudly enough for all to hear him, "Tomorrow the whole regiment is going to be shooting at some old wagon tarps that the teamsters are going to paint up like Yanks. When it's Company K's turn, I want you boys to remember this stuff. It ain't just for fun. It may be what saves our skins in the next big fight. Thumbnail high man, shoot at his waist belt. Part of a thumbnail high, shoot at his neck. Not his balls." That brought another laugh and Gill hoped the humor would aid the men's memory when it counted.

Private San Miguel spoke up this time. "What if they's moving towards us, Bain? Usually they ain't really standing still out there."

"If they are advancing towards us, and getting bigger and bigger, hold your rifle at the top of their jacket and squeeze your trigger. Don't hold out your thumb checking how high they are every time you load. Just do it once before our first volley."

"Can't we just listen to you or the sergeant, Bain? Can't you tell us how high to aim?"

"Boys, we'll be doing that, but you know how loud it gets, and me and Degas might be gut shot ourselves and not able to do nothin' but bleed out and die." Bain tried to grin at his dark humor, but instead, he and the men around him all got tight lipped as they thought about being gut shot. It was their worse fear. To break the sudden quiet, Bain quickly followed with, "Besides, every man of you grew up with a rifle in the family, and most of you done shot game for the supper pot, and will again after this war, so knowing how to figure how far away that big old buck is, will make you a better provider when we get home."

"Or how far away that Comanche is..." muttered Private San Miguel. Everyone in the platoon knew that San Miguel's family had been burned out and his sisters kidnapped by Comanche raiders before the war.

"But right now it ain't deer bucks or Injun bucks, it's Yankee bucks that we're shootin'," Jesús quipped, not wanting Andrew to start brooding again over his sisters' fate.

Bain dismissed his platoon, waved for Private Woodrow Sheppard to come in, and then returned to the log hut he shared with half a dozen men.

The next day the whole regiment remained in formation after the morning parade and marched the short distance to the new shooting range cobbled together by the ordnance sergeant with the grudging assistance of the teamsters. Two hundred yards away the teamsters had set up long six-foot high panels of canvas. This canvas screen was held in place with tent poles and ropes and was twenty yards long with crude outlines of men painted on it. Each company was to take a turn firing a single company volley at the canvas. After each volley the teamsters would go count the bullet holes in the canvas and paint an "X" over all the holes.

Each of the ten companies had over forty riflemen firing, and many men were calling bets to soldiers in other companies, each sure they would put dozens of holes in the canvas when their company fired their volley. The contest was creating a stir among the officers as well, with the lieutenant colonel soon holding two fistfuls of Confederate bills and his aide writing a long list of bets made by proud officers. The colonel had even put forth a keg of whiskey to the company that put the most holes in the canvas.

Company A was to shoot first, and its members rather casually stepped up to the line and fired a volley when ordered by their captain. In truth, the volley was ragged because many of the men took an extra second to aim their muskets. Then the teamsters went out to count the holes. Soon the teamster sergeant painted a large number on a board and held it up for the men to read from 200 yards away.

"7"

"Seven?" Nah, that ain't right!" cried out Company A's first sergeant. The men in the other companies hooted and hollered while Company B marched up to the firing line, did a crisp "Front" and came to attention in two ranks facing the canvas screen two hundred yards away. Their volley was sharp, sounding as one giant muzzle blast. The men in Company B then let go a loud Indian shout, putting an exclamation point on what they were confident would be a high score.

The sign held up by the teamster sergeant read, "9." More catcalls and shouts of disbelief followed.

And so it continued until Company K, last of the ten companies, marched forward. The highest score among the nine companies that had fired was a "19." That was Company G and they had fifty-eight men firing.

Sergeant Degas glared at Corporal Gill, who in turn looked down the front rank and glared at Private McDonald. Private McDonald, who was having a good time and was looking around instead of focusing to his front, saw his friend's grimace, so he flashed a big smile and pointed with his left hand at his neck.

Gill nodded as he heard the captain giving the commands, "Load!" The men pulled paper cartridges from their leather cartridge boxes, bit off the ends, carefully poured powder down the barrels, and even more carefully used their steel ramrods to plunge the lead bullets to the base of the barrels. Then each man put a copper priming cap on the firing cone and came to the ready position.

"Aim...Fire!"

Since nine companies had already fired at the canvas screen and it was perforated with dozens of holes, it took longer for the teamsters to find and count the new bullet holes in the canvas. The delay in tallying Company K's score was also because Teamster Quinn was busy behind the canvas screen furtively poking small round holes through the canvas, with a leather punch, having promised the teamster sergeant a bribe of a substantial share of the whiskey keg prize. The bribe was guaranteed by Private McDonald's belt knife wrapped in his red and brown scarf, which the sergeant thought may be worth more than the whiskey promised to him. The sergeant was fully aware that the whiskey was not yet in his possession, but the knife and scarf were, so he delayed painting a number on the last board while he considered how thirsty he really was. Finally, with Teamster Quinn talking about Sergeant Degas' history as a Creole thug with a habit of revenge when he lost a game of chance, the sergeant painted a number and held it up.

"20"

The groan from the men in Company G was audible to the whole regiment. The shout from Company K quickly drowned out all others as they realized the whiskey keg prize was coming their way. Matthew Quinn and his sergeant passed out before midnight beneath a wagon, while several of the men in Company K wondered why their share of the keg seemed so small.

It was cold and damp. The regiment had spent the morning drilling and the afternoon cutting small tree trunks to finish their winter huts. The three men were silent and still, all three wrapped in blankets, sitting around the dying embers of the campfire. Each was thinking about home and not feeling obliged to share his thoughts with the other two. One man picked up a stick and stirred the fire, tossing the small branch onto the coals. Flames quickly flared up, reflecting off the solemn faces of the trio. The oldest of the three softly started humming the tune to a favorite hymn, one which had given comfort to him over the years since he was a boy. Another of the trio stayed in his reverie for another minute, then started singing the old song:

> "We have to walk ----------------this lonesome valley,
> We have to walk ------------------it by ourselves.
> Oh, nobody else------------------can walk it for us;
> We have to walk------------------it by ourselves"

By the end of the verse the last man had joined in, and their low voices carried in the night air into Sergeant Degas's tent which was just a few feet away. The Creole Sergeant heard their singing and it jerked his thoughts away from Julianne, the French prostitute in New Orleans who he hoped to marry someday. He fell asleep still listening and wondering why his men were singing about walking lonesome valleys when they were crowded into winter quarters on a flat plain in Georgia.

Throughout the winter months General Cleburne continued to keep his division busy with drill, including more time on the shooting ranges. Even though there were complaints from the ordnance officers about the heavy use of cartridges, each regiment kept practicing firing at distances out to 200 yards until the percentage of "hits" on targets rose considerably from the miserable ten percent seen the first time most companies went to the shooting range. Shooting practice also expanded to platoon level sessions at the ranges. Soldiers shot at individual targets drawn on upended planks stuck in the ground down-range, and saw for themselves how good or bad their aim was. Most of the men tried to improve their marksmanship, but some just went through the motions, especially those near-sighted men who saw the distant plank targets as fuzzy blurred shapes.

The imported Austrian rifle muskets issued to the consolidated regiments in the Texas Brigade had fixed sights, with no rear sight adjustments possible when shooting at distant targets. That was unlike the imported British Enfield weapons and the American made Springfield muskets which were in use by many other regiments in the Army of Tennessee. Therefore, the Texans practiced firing at the "belt buckle" middle of the planks, as well as chest high near the top of the plank. With many men it didn't seem to make any difference where they were told to aim at the varying distances, their targets continued to reflect random strikes. Some men blamed the foreign weapons, others blamed their poor eyesight, and often even the wind was vilified as the cause for clean targets. However, on the whole, the target practice seemed to help the confidence of most riflemen as the targets sprouted ever more holes as the winter weeks passed.

Chapter 15

Late February 1864, North Georgia
17 Men Present for Duty

"Step up there, boys. Step up," Lieutenant Navarro repeated over and over as the men in his company boarded the train. Most of the men wore knapsacks and all carried their rifled-muskets, making it awkward to climb the high steps onto the passenger car and then wedge themselves through the door.

Sergeant Degas and Private Bernard Anderson were already seated on the bench across from the empty seats that Gill and McDonald slid onto. Wearing the knapsacks caused all the men to sit up on the edge of the seats, with muskets held upright between their knees, and the knees of each man knocking against those of the man across from him. Soldiers were packed into the car until finally the aisle was filled with men who stood and leaned against the end of the seats or found a way to sit on the wooden floor. Bayonet scabbards stuck out at odd angles as men shifted them around searching for comfort on the hard benches, causing other men to growl when their neighbor's scabbard poked them.

"Sergeant, where we going?" asked Private McDonald as soon as he sat.

Sergeant Degas just stared at McDonald, not answering him. Private Anderson was a tall burly man with a thick beard and spoke when he saw

Degas was going to remain silent, "You don't need to know, you little Mex. You just go where you're told."

Corporal Gill tensed, not knowing how his friend might react to Anderson's words and was not surprised when Private McDonald replied in a low voice in Spanish, *"Recuerde el alamo, you cerdo peludo."*

Degas, who had picked up some of the language from his Creole family and learned more in south Texas, looked sharply at McDonald, then nudged Private Anderson in the arm.

"You know what this here private done said to you, Anderson?"

"Nah, I don't, but I don't care what no Mex says in that gibberish. Besides, this little beaner ain't brave enough to badmouth me none."

Degas looked sidelong at Anderson, turned up one side of his mouth, nodded, and looked out the window as the train lurched into motion.

Corporal Gill remained uneasy as the time passed, but Jesús went to sleep with his head on Gill's shoulder swaying back and forth with the train's motion, while Anderson also slept with his head thrown back and snoring.

Degas caught Gill's eye and quietly asked, "Corporal Gill, do you know what your little friend told Private Anderson?"

Gill shook his head no, but thought he had an idea from the one word he had understood.

"The little man said, 'Remember the Alamo, you hairy pig.'"

Gill shrugged his shoulders in reply and Degas continued, "I hear some things about the little man. Things like a sergeant in Govan's brigade is hoping to catch him alone. I believe a knife was involved back in Arkansas. Things like he found the Yankee guard who stole his scarf in Camp Butler, and the little man put a bayonet through him when he tried to surrender."

Gill shrugged again as Jesús drooled onto his coat.

Degas concluded, "He's a fighter, the little man, but his friend should perhaps teach him the value of a closed mouth."

Gill nodded.

The train rumbled along, the tracks rough and at places in such need of repairs that the engineer slowed the train to a crawl to avoid derailing. As they approached a trestle bridge over a deep ravine, the engineer pulled the lanyard to sound the steam whistle and leaned back on the brake lever. The train ground to a stop just short of the bridge. The engineer and fireman both climbed to the ground and walked along the track to study the bridge. Two of Granbury's staff officers joined them. The train engineer pointed at the bridge where a wide gap in the timber cross-ties was visible and the ends of the steel rails were separated. One officer walked slowly out onto the bridge looking down between the heavy timbers. The other officer slid

125

down the ravine slope and climbed onto one of the trestles looking for broken timbers below the gap, trying to gauge the extent of the problem. Colonel Granbury approached the edge of the ravine, looked at the bridge, and then looked at the engineer with a raised eyebrow.

"This sort of problem ain't so rare. That thar is why we keep some square-cut timbers, spikes, and tools on the flat car," the engineer informed the growing cluster of officers. "I reckon you fellers could slide in a couple of new cross ties and brace thangs up under thar. Elsewise, we're gonna have ta back up a pretty fer piece, and I don't rightly know when the next train's gonna come up behind us. Ain't no telegraph line along this track for a good ways. Yessir, the best thang would be for you fellers to git to it and shore up this here bridge."

Granbury nodded, and his chief of staff took over. He directed other officers to gather work parties and detailed a regiment to establish a picket line around the whole train.

Sergeant Degas and the other Company K NCO's got their men out of the car and lined up to help with the bridge repair work. Soon they had pulled several long timbers off the rail car and carried them down the ravine. Then the men were directed to climb onto the trestle timbers under the gap so they could wedge and hammer braces into place where the falling cross ties had damaged a couple of horizontal beams. Since most of the younger men in Company K had grown up around San Antonio, they had missed the boyhood adventures of climbing tall pines and oaks. Regardless, several men from Company K were ordered onto the underside of the trestle bridge to work on the repairs. A few of them were reluctant to stand on the beams and inch their way forward, balanced on the narrow timbers, holding onto the timbers above them.

"Keep moving there, James," Corporal Gill called softly to the private who had stopped and was clinging to an upright timber. "You need to swing around that post you're holding and keep going forward."

"Bain, I ain't never done anything like this. I never been higher than a horse. It's a long way down."

"Don't look down then. Just look forward."

"I have to look at my feet, Bain, when I step around this post. I have to."

"Then focus on the beam and move your front foot around to it, now."

Private James Miller did what the corporal told him, and then swiftly brought his other foot around. He was now past the first vertical beam and moved forward, slowly walking the beam with his arms raised and both hands holding another horizontal beam that was a foot over his head. Since he was the first of four men headed to the same damaged area, Miller had a rope tied around his waist. The other end was held by Sergeant Degas on the ground. When the work team reached their destination, Degas planned to tie the rope to the end of the timber that came off the train so the four men could haul it up to be used as a new brace. Private Anderson was behind Miller, and Private William Potter was next. Bringing up the rear was Private McDonald, who was also wearing a rope to attach to the other end of the new timber. Corporal Gill held the end of McDonald's rope.

When the work party had reached a spot under the gap in the cross-ties, they had to start moving upward on the beams that were angled as cross braces. Private Miller negotiated the first beam by straddling it and inching upwards. He finally had to kneel on the beam, and then stand stooped over holding tightly onto the next horizontal beam. Then he pulled himself up and hooked a leg over the same beam he was holding onto. Finally, he swung his torso up and straddled the horizontal beam. He smiled down and waved to the men on the ground. It had been awkward, but Private Miller was confident in his technique now and kept going up the next diagonal beam.

Meanwhile, Private Anderson who was still standing at the base of the first angled timber had watched in near terror. Anderson was not a small limber man, and he had no climbing experience. But he considered himself brave, so in his blustering way he had pushed into the group that was going to scale the bridge. No one tried to stop him. Now he was under the middle of the bridge, twenty or more feet off the ground, standing on a narrow beam, with no way to go back past the two men behind him, and too frightened of falling to climb further up.

Degas called to him, "Bernard, you must move up!" In reply, Anderson shook his head sideways and shut his eyes.

"Bernard, open your eyes! You are tall and strong and you can sit on the beam and pull yourself along. Start now!" Degas was sympathetic to the private's fear of heights, but he also was becoming impatient as Private Anderson remained frozen in place. "Move, dammit! Move!" Anderson didn't move or open his eyes.

"Bain, drop your end of the rope, I'm going to coil it up here," Jesús called down to Corporal Gill. Gill did as his friend directed and Jesús pulled up the rope, coiling it as he went. Then he moved up to the back of Private Potter, warned him to hold tight to the beam above them with both hands, and deftly swiveled past him, holding onto Potter as he stepped around him to stand again on the beam, now in front of Potter and near Anderson. Jesús moved the few steps on the beam that took him next to Anderson who towered nearly a foot over McDonald's head.

"You hairy pig, open your eyes and look at me," McDonald spoke softly but firmly to Anderson, this time in clear English. Anderson looked down at him, eyes round.

"I'm going to tie the rope around your chest and then we will lower you to the ground. Do you understand?" Anderson nodded.

"Good. Now hold onto my jacket with your left hand so I can use both hands to put the rope around you." Anderson slowly reached out with one large hand and grasped the front of McDonald's coat. Jesús deftly put the rope around the big man's chest, tied a bowline knot, cinched it tight, let out six or eight feet of loose rope to dangle between Anderson and him, and then wrapped the coil once around the diagonal beam above them.

"Let go of my jacket now. You are going to sit on the edge of this timber, and then I'm going to ease you down to the ground." Anderson nodded at McDonald and released his hard grip on McDonald's jacket. The smaller man quickly sat down on the beam, slipped the loose end of the rope around his back, and held it with one hand. With his other hand Jesús reached up to grab the waist of Anderson's trousers, and without hesitation yanked the still standing man off the timber, saying in clear English, "Remember the Alamo, Hairy Pig."

Although Anderson was falling through the air and not running in the dust like a steer back home, McDonald was particularly pleased to see how the hairy pig bounced like a steer which had hit the end of the rope when his cow pony braced all four legs and slid to a halt, jerking the steer off its feet, legs flailing in the air, eyes wide in terror and snot flying. Jesús watched Anderson dangle six feet below him, limbs jerking and snot dribbling down his chin. McDonald regretted he couldn't let the hairy pig fall the rest of the way as he slowly let out the rope cinched around the beam that was holding Anderson in place, gently lowering him the final fifteen feet to the ground. Then he waved at Degas and Gill and the crowd that had gathered to watch.

Degas looked at Gill and said, "I think the little man did not make a friend, although he may have saved a life." Gill shrugged and went to untie the end of the rope from around Anderson's chest.

The bridge repair was completed without further mishap and the train continued its journey into Alabama. The entire division was in route to Mobile to protect the Confederate arsenal there from the threat of a Union raid. However, before the train reached Selma, a telegraph message reached General Cleburne at a station stop that the Union forces had changed directions, and his division was to return back to Dalton. The men were glad to reverse their path and looked forward to another few days of leisurely riding the rails.

"Jesse, you got a piece of paper?" asked Private Martin Braden.

"Maybe I do, Marty. What for?" replied Private McDonald.

"So as I can write my name and outfit on it and toss it out the window in the next town to some purty young lady."

"Paper don't throw so good, Marty."

"Aw, I know that. I got this here chunk of brick that I'm going to wrap the paper around. Look here, I even got some twine. A bunch of the fellers are doing it already, and some of them girls even waved at the boys hanging out those windows, smilin' like we're their beau's already."

"Alright, Marty, here's a piece," Jesús said as he dug into his jacket pocket. But I ain't doin' it."

"How come, Jesse? You always got something to say. I bet you'd write a fine note and get two or three Alabamy girls to write back to you.

"I ain't doin' it, 'cause of Sweet Susan Gill back home. I been writin' her."

"No fooling, Jesse? You mean Bain's sister? You're writing to Bain's little sister?"

"Sí. Susan Gill is who I'm going to court when we get home."

Private Braden took this news with consternation, as he had been thinking lately of writing to Bain's sister himself. He immediately started worrying that Jesse or Bain would tell Susan that he had been eager to write notes to girls unmet and fling the notes off a moving train. Such wanton behavior towards the young women of Alabama might not sit well with Susan. But Martin quickly dropped that line of thought and wrote his note. After all, he was here and Susan Gill was not, but those Alabama girls were.

Chapter 16

Corporal Gill was sitting next to the fire rubbing wood ash on the barrel of his musket in an effort to slow the ongoing creep of rust. When he finished with the musket barrel he planned to work a while on the bayonet, and if time allowed he even hoped to brighten his tarnished tin canteen. Gill figured he spent most of his free time either hunting lice and plucking them from his shirt or scouring the metal parts of his kit. Gill was looking down at his musket barrel when he felt someone sit down beside him.

"Bain, Bain, did you hear?"

"Did I hear what, Jesse?"

"Did you hear that Sergeant Chalk is back? You know, the sergeant in Company F that got buried alive back at Camp Butler."

Gill glanced over at Jesús, "Naw, Jesse, I ain't heard that. But if the man was buried alive, how'd he get to Georgia? He tunnel all this way like a prairie dog?"

"No, Bain. No, he weren't really buried alive, but he did spend a night in a pine box with a dead man."

"You mean the feller that crawled into a casket with a corpse, then waited until dark and climbed out and disappeared?"

"That's the one, Bain, that's the very one. And he's back, right over yonder in Company F's camp."

"Damned nice of him to rejoin us after all this time."

"Yea, I thought about that, too. Don't know if I'd been so eager to put on another uniform. But he's a sergeant, and sergeants see things different from regular men, I reckon,"

"Well, it's always nice to have another good sergeant around. Elsewise, who would tell us what to do every day? But now that you gave me the good news about Sergeant Chalk risin' from the grave, let me tell you about our new general."

"Oh, Bain, don't go tellin' me we they done shipped off General Cleburne to win the war somewheres else. Who we got now?"

Bain handed Jesús his grit-covered rag, "Here, Jesse, how about putting some fresh ash on that cloth patch. I ain't quite done yet."

As he did so, Jesse said, "Sure, Bain, but now you tell me who our new general is."

Bain took back the cloth and began scrubbing the metal lock-plate on his musket. "There's not a different general, Jesse, and it ain't General Cleburne I'm talking about. It's General Granbury. He's not a colonel no more, he's our brigadier general."

Jesús had settled in by the embers of the fire and was poking around in the ashes with a stick. He didn't reply to Corporal Gill's news.

"Ain't you goin' to say somethin' Jesse? I mean about the new General Granbury?"

Jesús looked straight at Gill and said, "No, I ain't, Bain. I got nothing to say about that."

"How come, Jesse? You told me the other night you thought Colonel Granbury actually knew his head from his backside. I figured his being promoted would please you."

"No, it don't, Bain. It don't because a good general is more likely to be called on to put his men in where things are hot. Who held their end of that ridge back in Chattanooga while the rest of the whole danged army run off back to Georgia? Then who was it that held that gap and ridge so the wagon train could get over all those bridges after we got run off the mountain? It was Cleburne and Granbury. It was us. It was you and me and the rest of our *amigos*. Making Granbury a general just shows me we ain't done yet. Next time General Bragg puts the whole danged army in a bee hive, he's gonna send a courier to General Cleburne with a message that says, 'General Cleburne, at your earliest convenience, would you please take your division and save our asses.' And General Cleburne will ride over to General

131

Granbury and say, 'General Granbury would you please take your Texans and go whip 50,000 Yankees so as the rest of the army can...can ex-tri-cate itself from the big damn mess General Bragg done put us in. Again.'"

Bain stared at Jesús and said, "I didn't know you fretted over such high matters."

"Bain, you know ever man in this army frets over what the generals do. Ever *hombre* here can see that we had the Yanks whipped down at Chickymauga Creek last year, and then General Bragg let 'em get back to Chattanooga to hole up. Then for two months he let that whipped army lick its wounds and rest up. And then, by God, if he didn't just let 'em climb like squirrels up the steepest ridge in Tennessee and run off his whole army, exceptin' us. Yup, I fret over high matters."

"Well, I suppose you're telling it straight. But it still seems to me that Colonel Granbury rightly earned his promotion to General Granbury. Lieutenant Navarro told me Granbury was all over the hillside back at that last fight. He made sure every hole got plugged in time. "

Gill continued, "And now, now if half what I hear is true, there's a helluva lot more Yanks facing us, than us facing them. I think I'm glad our brigade is led by General Granbury and he's takin' orders from General Cleburne. Them two are smart, and they'll take care of us."

Jesús kept poking the ashes with his stick, silent, and lost in his thoughts. He looked up to see his cousin Matt approaching, carrying a big cloth sack.

"*Ola*, Jesús, I been looking for you, Cousin," Matt said as he plopped down next to Jesús.

"*Ola* to you too, Cousin Matt. What's in the sack, and why ain't you back with the wagon train?" Jesús asked.

"Some cookin' pans and other things I grabbed up before I left the wagons," Matt said as he patted the sack. He continued, "We got more teamsters than we got livestock, since some yellin' artillery colonel took away most of the horses. Then a yellin' sergeant come and took away a bunch of us to dig earthworks and cut down trees. I said to myself that I only left Texas to drive a wagon, and since I'm a free man, and not a field hand, I'll find my cousin and his outfit an' cook for 'em. So I walked the other way, got me some pots, and come straight here."

Jesús liked his cousin and felt sorry for him since his brother had died of small pox at prison camp. But Jesús wasn't sure how Matt's offer to become a cook would set with Lieutenant Navarro, so he took Matt to the lieutenant. Navarro liked the idea, so he went to Captain Davenport, who went to the battalion adjutant with the transfer request. Not wanting to turn away a proven hand, the adjutant walked over to the brigade headquarters with

Quinn in tow, and put in the request to the brigade adjutant. The brigade adjutant questioned Matthew Quinn about his status as a free-born man, and his experience as a teamster. He finally told Quinn he was more needed at Granbury's headquarters, both caring for the wagon stock, and taking over the assistant cook duties from another black man who had become too sick to work.

The word went back down the line and finally reached Private McDonald the next day. McDonald thought that was a fine idea, because his cousin would be safe with the headquarters wagon, and his aunt might not lose both her sons in the war. As a bonus, now Jesús would know someone in the general's camp, and he might overhear interesting news, a commodity that was always high on McDonald's list to be bartered for hot coffee or food he himself hadn't had to cook.

Chapter 17

"Again? No, Bain, not again! I'm just now beginning to get used to those hillbillies from the Tenth Regiment. Why is it again that they are movin' out on their own? And if they can, why can't we just be us again? Just us in the Sixth Texas, and them boys in the Fifteenth Texas on their own?"

"Jesse, it's because there're as many of them in the Tenth as us and the Fifteenth boys put together. And if we was separated from the Fifteenth, neither of us would have a regiment big enough to spit at."

Gill wasn't too sure he agreed with that reasoning, but he knew it was not for corporals or privates to second guess the thinking of the generals. Besides, he and his platoon were fond of both General Granbury and General Cleburne. One upside was that the ten companies from the Sixth Texas were being consolidated into six companies, while the men from the Fifteenth Texas would now combine to form just four companies. Gill was already wondering where Company K would land. Which company would they now be combined with, and who would be the officers and NCO's? Gill was still loathe to lose his corporal's stripes and equally sure he wanted to stay with his friends from Bexar County and not be transferred to another company as a surplus corporal. When Gill was being honest with himself, he understood that the one thing that had made the past two years bearable was the bonds he had made with the other men in Company K. There certainly had been a steady stream of men dying in camp or left behind in hospitals sick and dying from disease, and a few had died from battle wounds. Plus there were the few deserters who slunk away in the night, and men continued to be transferred to other duties. But, the core of his platoon, men who had come with him the long distance from the frontier of Texas, they had become important to Gill. Maybe not like his own brothers back at home, but closer than anyone else in his life. And he did not want to walk away from them until they all went home together.

"Corporal Gill, round up the rest of your men and fall in at the head of the company street," called Sergeant Degas to Gill. "We're about to hear from the colonel how the companies are going to be combined."

Captain Rhoades Fisher of Company G of the Sixth Texas Infantry stood before the nearly 300 men in the Sixth and Fifteenth Texas regiments. Fisher, as the senior captain, was the newly appointed commander of the downsized 6th-15th Texas Consolidated Regiment.

"Bain, Bain, look at me, Bain!" Private McDonald hoarsely whispered to Corporal Gill, who with a sigh turned his head towards Jesús who was standing one man away from Gill.

"Bain, that ain't no colonel up there, it's just the captain from Company G. Why ain't we got a colonel no more? Ain't had one the whole danged winter, since Colonel Mills got shot. Ain't we good enough for a colonel? Why we got to have another danged ole captain out front when them other regiments, they got colonels!"

"Shut up, Jesse. I don't know. Maybe all the colonels got kilt. Just shut up and listen."

At that, Sergeant Degas whacked Corporal Gill in the back of his head and muttered, "Quiet in the ranks! Eyes to the front, Corporal Gill." Gill glared with squinted eyes another second at Jesse, then looked back to the front as he knew he should have been doing.

With the men of the Tenth Texas now departed to their own new campground, the combined 6th-15th Texas Company K was half the size it had been yesterday, with thirty-three men standing in the two ranks today. Being the last company at the end of the long regimental formation, Gill strained to hear Captain Fisher, but only heard bits and pieces. He finally got the gist that the Sixth and Fifteenth regiments would be split apart, with the Sixth Texas combining their ten companies into six new companies, while the Fifteenth Texas would collapse down to four new companies. Company K of the Sixth Texas was being aligned with Company A, and would now be at the front of the regimental formation, rather than at the back. Gill still wondered about his corporal's status, and figured he'd quickly learn if his rank was changing. Once Captain Fisher finished his first speech as the regiment's commander, he dismissed the men to sort out their new company organizations.

Company K was now placed under the command of Captain Simon Longnecker of Company A of the Sixth Texas. Second Lieutenant Navarro was promoted to First Lieutenant of the new company, which pleased Corporal Gill for he liked and respected Navarro. Their old first sergeant, Thomas Copeland, had been captured at Chickamauga, one of the men taken while on a scouting patrol beyond their lines. Gill had hoped that Sergeant Copeland's misfortune would open up a sergeant's spot for him. That didn't happen, as there was already a sergeant in Company A, Rayferd McGrew, who assumed the first sergeant's rank. Meanwhile, Sergeant Degas, remained as the combined company's second sergeant.

Gill's fear that he might be a surplus corporal turned out to be needless, as he was named the new combined company's second corporal. He would keep his position at the back end of the company, where the short privates fell into formation. That was OK with Gill, since his handful of Hispanic friends from Bexar County were generally shorter than the Anglos. Most of his former platoon members from Company K would still be under his tiny sphere of influence. That was important to Gill since he knew each one's abilities, who could be trusted to complete or lead work details, and most importantly, who would keep his wits under fire in a skirmish line. The original Company K of the Sixth Texas was now down to only seventeen men, and even when in formation with the nineteen men of Company A, the new combined company barely had thirty riflemen, half what Company K of the Consolidated 6th-10th-15th Texas had the previous fall during the battles in northern Georgia and southern Tennessee.

Chapter 18

Late March 1864, Winter Camp near Dalton, Georgia
17 Men Present for Duty

Snow had been coming down since before dawn. Now at midmorning, the ground was glistening white, even the mud holes and wagon wheel ruts having frozen over and coated with three inches of powdery snow. It was a serene scene that belied the sullen mood of Cleburne's Division. Every man in the division knew what was going to happen this morning, pastoral snow or not, and not one of them was happy about it, and not one of them wanted to watch it. But the whole point of the thing was to make an example in front of all the men in the division, all 5,000 of them. So, the Consolidated 6th-15th Texas Regiment was in its place in the brigade formation, flanked to either side by the other Texas regiments in Granbury's Brigade. Their brigade formed just one side of the huge hollow three-sided square, with two other brigades comprising the opposite side and the bottom of the giant square. The fourth brigade was pulled back a few yards leaving a gap wide enough for a wagon to pass through.

Private McDonald was wearing a Federal overcoat he had somehow acquired, and his red scarf was wrapped around his neck and ears. His slouch hat was pulled low over his eyes and the snow was beginning to stick to the hat's brim and McDonald's shoulders. The entire division was standing at attention, and many of the men were feeling the cold in their toes and beginning to shiver.

Corporal Gill was daydreaming, thinking of how warm San Antonio was this time of year, when he heard General Granbury's adjutant shout, "Brigade, Rear Ranks to the Rear in Open Order, Ten Paces Back! March!" This was an uncommon order in that the men in the rear rank normally only stepped back four paces when muskets were inspected each morning. But the sergeants and lieutenants were on their toes and quickly oversaw their men stepping back the extra six steps.

Gill heard Jesús wondering out loud why he had been told to separate so far from the front rank, when Gill first heard the slow drum beat and the creak of wagon wheels. It took a while, but eventually the slow procession passed in front of Gill, making its deliberate way down each side of the giant square. The wagon moved first past the front ranks, then wove its way into the open space behind the front rank, so it also passed directly in front of the rear rank troops. The procession was led by a captain in a dress coat with gold trim reaching up each sleeve and the fine dark gray wool trimmed in blue. The captain wore a dark red sash under his sword belt and marched with all the dignity he could muster. Behind the captain, the single drummer beat a slow cadence for the infantry company that followed him. The sergeants of the company were grim and kept their eyes straight ahead. Some of the privates looked equally grim and some appeared scared and nervous, shifting their eyes from side to side, seeking assurance that was not there.

Behind the marching soldiers an open supply wagon rolled along pulled by four mules. The wagon driver was a black man wearing a ragged gray uniform jacket and kepi, and for once was not berating his mules with his normal string of curses. In the back of the wagon rode just one man, kneeling, facing backwards, hands tied behind his back. He wore a uniform jacket, and snow was also gathering on his shoulders and hair. He had been riding silently and sullenly in the wagon bed, but while in front of Granbury's Brigade, the lone prisoner looked up and around, and started calling out to the men in the ranks as he was driven past them.

"Boys, I just did what you all want to do. I just went home to my family. My God, my wife is sick, my children are starving, there weren't nobody else to bring in the crops."

He paused a few seconds, then began again pleading, "Boys, I was comin' back. I weren't gonna leave you for good. I was comin' back when things got better at home. I wasn't leaving my pards, no sir, I was plannin' to come back and do my part."

Then his anger showed through and he shouted, "Many a man is still out there, doin' just what I done. Doing what you want to do. Can't a man take care of his family?"

Finally, he passed beyond Gill's vision, but he still could hear the man trying to explain his flight to the thousands who had not snuck away on a moonless night, the thousands who every day put duty and loyalty above their concerns for their wives and children, and those who maybe were just too scared to run.

After an endless time, the wagon and its escort had filed past every man in Cleburne's Division. The prisoner was quiet again, head down, chin on his chest, tears freezing on his cheeks. Finally, the wagon moved into the center of the hollow square and stopped next to an open grave and open wooden coffin. The deserter was sobbing, repeating over and over, "I only done what you all want to do. I only went home to my family. I only went home to my family. "

The escort company had been marched ten yards away from the coffin and stood at attention. The prisoner was lifted out of the wagon and stood up in front of the coffin. Silent guards remained standing on either side of him .

A colonel from General Cleburne's headquarters walked into the middle of the square and faced the prisoner. He opened a stiff cardboard folder and loudly read the charge of desertion with which the man had been charged. He then read the findings of the court martial judges, they being officers from every brigade in the division. Finally, the colonel read the sentence of death by firing squad. He then instructed the captain to proceed.

The captain saluted the colonel and nodded towards a chaplain dressed in black, but whose shoulders were now a white cape of snow. The man of God approached the prisoner and spoke quietly to him. The chaplain opened his Bible to a dog-eared page and, without looking at the words, in a strong voice reaching across the snow-covered parade ground, he recited the 23rd Psalm to the deserter and to the 5,000 men in Cleburne's Division. If every soldier in the division could not hear the chaplain, every soldier could hear the hoarse male voices of hundreds of men who spontaneously joined the pastor in reciting the scripture that was familiar to many of them.

The soft rumble of "Amen" that punctuated the chaplain's closing of his Bible did not come from just hundreds of somber men, but by thousands of soldiers uttering the single word to themselves. The chaplain withdrew as the captain then walked up to the condemned man. Without hesitation he put a black scarf around the man's eyes and quickly walked back to his company, now aligned in a single rank.

139

Snow swirled around the prisoner, his executioners, and the long lines of men who were unwilling witnesses. Most of the men were fighting conflicting emotions about their love and worry for their own families and their duty to their company pards, on whose loyalty their chances of survival lay. The entire setting was becoming ever whiter and quieter as the snow kept falling and muffled the shifting of feet and the coughs and sniffs of the men who couldn't hold back. Jesús and Bain caught each other's eye, and each thought the other's jaw was clinched tightly.

The captain commanding the company drew his pistol and held it at shoulder height, pointed up. "Company, Ready...Aim...Fire!"

Twelve muskets went off, shattering the silence. The deserter fell to his knees, and moaning loudly fell to his side, but he continued to thrash and groan wordlessly, clearly not dead, but now bleeding and in pain.

"Company, Load," came the order from their captain, not shouting, but not speaking softly either.

"Ready," up came the muskets a second time..."Aim," the muskets went up further, the gun stocks nestled into the shoulders of the men, and ... "Fire!"

This time the prisoner jerked as the bullets drove into his side and back, and he sunk further into the snow, much more blood flowing from a dozen holes, and forming a pool of red that quickly crystalized around and under his body.

The captain walked slowly to the prostrate form, cocked his pistol as he pointed it, and fired a final bullet into the back of the deserter's head. The captain holstered his pistol, marched back to his company and led them in single file out of the square. Quickly, but not in obvious haste, two black body servants appeared, picked up the limp body and gently laid it in the open casket. Then two more slaves carried out the casket lid, set it in place and hammered six nails into place. The four black men picked up ropes that had been pre-positioned under the casket. Together they lifted the casket and carried it the few steps to the open hole and using the ropes lowered it into the grave. The head of the coffin was lowered faster than the foot, and those men who were close enough could hear the body sliding forward and a soft thud as the corpse's head bumped into the end of the wooden box.

The four slaves picked up shovels and slowly began to toss spade loads of hard dirt clods onto the casket, each of the first dozen helpings of dirt landing almost rhythmically and loudly on the wood until the top was completely covered. While the four black men continued to fill in the grave, orders were given and each side of the huge square of silent men began to move away. Major Fisher led his regiment back to their camp, dismissed the men without further comment, and retired to his tent even though it was not yet noon.

"Jesse, you ain't said a word for an hour since we got back to camp," Corporal Gill said to his friend while they were both on their homemade bunks. "That ain't like you. Were you asleep on your feet out there?"

Jesús remained silent, lying still as a stone, hands laced behind his head, staring at the branches and dried out foliage in the roof above their heads.

"Jesse, you there? You all right?" Gill said, trying once more to draw out his friend, since when Jesús got quiet, Bain worried about him.

Finally Jesús spoke, "Nah, Bain, I ain't all right. This ain't all right. This morning was not all right. This whole danged war ain't all right. Look what we done this morning. We stood there at attention while a man was gunned down by his own, just for goin' home to take care of his family. No, it ain't all right at all."

Gill didn't respond for a spell, but finally offered the obvious, "Jesse, you and I know that poor soul might have been me or you just as easy. Granted, we ain't got wives and young'uns back home, but if our ma's wrote they needed us, I reckon we'd both lite out for home. But that don't make it right. Maybe what we saw this morning weren't right either, but sometimes a man's gotta choose. And it's a devil's choice to choose between your family and your country, your kin and your pards. It ain't an easy choice for any man."

Jesse lay still a minute more, then rose from his bunk, looked down at Gill, and said, "Bain, if *mi madre* ever does write such a letter to me, 'course she can't read or write, but I reckon she could get my sister to write one... but if she begged me to come home, and you wake up some morning and I ain't here... well, you just know I didn't run 'cause I was scared. Sure, I'm scared ever time a bullet comes our way, but I ain't run yet from no Yankee bullet. But I might just run home if they call for me. *Mi familia,* after all."

Private McDonald then brushed aside the canvas flap that covered the opening to their log hut, took two steps and was hit in the back of his head by a well thrown and hard packed snowball. Jesús gasped, took a quick look around to see Private Hawkins grin and dart behind another log hut. Jesús then yelled for Bain to come help him, scooped up snow and mashed it into a firm ball, and began stalking his friend Ambrose Hawkins.

Gill took a moment to put on his jacket, snatched up his hat, and reached the company street to see a quickly forming line of soldiers, each cradling several snowballs in the crook of one arm, while each palmed a snowy missile in their throwing hand. Then Gill heard Sergeant Degas holler to him.

"Corporal Gill, if you please, come take command of this squad of Texas grenadiers and move them towards the sound of the guns. It appears we have taken the fight to the men of Mississippi. Best arm yourself with a few grenades first. I'll be along with reinforcements as quickly as I can." With that Degas smiled the only smile Gill had seen on the older man's countenance in nearly two years, and with a bounding step Degas turned and moved down the snowy street to find more troops to uphold the honor of Texas.

As Gill stooped over to scoop up snow for his ammo supply, he shook his head in wonder at the sergeant's sudden joyful demeanor. Then Gill joined his squad of snowball grenadiers and marched them off to find their Mississippi targets. Before they had turned the first corner Privates McDonald and Hawkins fell in with them along with several others. At the next intersection of company streets, Gill halted his formation, saw a band of soldiers marching past whose uniform jackets were a different shade of gray and trimmed in black. Gill figured if they weren't Mississippians, they weren't Texans either, if that really mattered.

"Grenadiers, Ready, Aim, Throw!" Gill ordered and his troops hurled their white grenades, landing an exploding enfilading strike on the column of "invaders." The "Mississippians," who turned out to be Alabamians, immediately launched their own volley of snowballs at the Texans. As the two lines stood and exchanged volleys of snowballs, more and more men joined both formations until the lines were as long as regiments. Gill looked around to see Major Fisher standing in the line a few men down, throwing snowballs as fast as he could, as privates kept handing him fresh ammunition.

Gill's attention was diverted when a bugle sounded and then a drum roll cut in on the bugle. Gill couldn't see it, but men from every brigade in the division were piling out their log huts and joining in the escalating snowball battle, forming companies and even regiments to advance upon their neighbors. Impromptu companies were commanded by NCOs like Gill, and officers were as often in the ranks as they were commanding groups of snowball grenadiers. Whether leading or standing between privates, the officers quickly began to attract far more snowballs than did the enlisted men, although sergeants became particular targets for many a private delighted with the chance for a little payback.

For over an hour tens of thousands of snowballs were thrown, until the men finally began to tire and retreat to their campfires and cabins. Some men sported bruises from rocks hidden within snowballs, this occurrence seemingly more a danger to sergeants than anyone else. As Gill's formation was about to abandon the cause, word came flying like lightning through the ranks that General Cleburne himself had been engaged in the fight, and had now ordered barrels of whiskey opened so every man could have a swig to celebrate what came to be known throughout the Army of Tennessee as the Great Dalton Snowball Fight. Little was said or remembered about the snowball battle occurring on the same day as the only execution of a deserter from Cleburne's Division during the entire war.

Few ever gave thought to just who threw the first snowball, although a good detective might have traced the flash point of the snowball fight to a few junior officers on General Cleburne's staff, who perhaps were acting on a "suggestion" from those of too dignified a rank to consider such a diversion.

Chapter 19

Early May 1864, Dug Gap, Georgia
17 Men Present for Duty

"Bain, see them *caballos* over yonder under the trees?"

"Sure, Jesse, I see the horses. I reckon there's cavalry men up on the ridge fightin' on foot."

The men in Granbury's Brigade had been moving uphill at a quick-time march for over an hour, and had halted at a pass called Dug Gap. While the men in the four regiments sprawled on the side of the dirt road and were gasping to catch their breath, General Granbury had ridden ahead searching for General Cleburne to learn how his men were to be deployed.

"Bain, ain't we goin' up that ridge too?"

"Looks like it. Don't know why else we came all this way so fast. I imagine the Yanks are fightin' their way up the other side."

"Wouldn't you rather ride than run up that hill? I ain't been on the back of a horse for going on two years. Why don't we volunteer to go ahead of the others on them ponies?"

"Jesse, we don't know where we're going, and we can't steal the cavalry's mounts."

"Bain, I'm doin' it. I'm going to ride up that slope and find out where the genr'l wants us."

"Jesse, you can't do that. You ain't no courier or nothin' like that."

"Bain, thinking like that is why you got stripes and I don't. See you at the top of the hill."

With those words Jesús slung his musket and trotted to the line of tethered horses. Without hesitation he approached a small bay mare, slipped her reins off the tether line, and bounded into the saddle. He was galloping up the slope of the ridge when a lieutenant saw him and hollered. The other men in the brigade saw Private McDonald wave his hat back at them as he rode up the hill. Spontaneously, two dozen more men in Granbury's Brigade bolted to follow his example, grabbing horses off the line and trailing Jesús up the slope. Lieutenants and captains were yelling threats, but their curses were quickly lost in the third rush of men who ran to the last of the tethered horses, mounted, and headed up hill at a gallop. Corporal Gill was still staring where his friend Jesús had ridden out of sight, not quite believing what he had just witnessed.

Within a few minutes of leaving the gap as the sounds of the battle grew louder, Private McDonald neared the first crest along the ridge. There he saw a mounted sergeant holding a big blue flag with a white circle in its center. At least a dozen riders were gathered together, and Jesús recognized the trim bearded figure of General Cleburne talking to another well-dressed officer who wore a pointed beard on his chin. Jesús rode directly to them, pulled up within a few feet of the pair, dismounted and saluted.

"General Cleburne, I am Private McDonald of the Sixth Texas of Granbury's Brigade, and I have ridden up this here hill as fast as this mare could run. I am here to fight Yankees. Where, sir, am I most needed?"

General Hardee simply sat and gaped at Private McDonald. General Cleburne tried to speak, but his intended rebuke caught in his throat, and within seconds the high ranking officers and their escorts were laughing out loud. By this time the front riders among the other sixty or seventy mounted infantrymen were almost to the command group.

General Hardee finally spoke first, "Private, it appears your impetuous spirit has infected a goodly number of your friends. General Cleburne can point you all to where the sounds of the guns is the loudest. But I do believe it would be best if you now tie off your mounts and proceed on foot. And I expect the owners of those horses, who are presently engaged just over the crest, will be glad you brought their mounts all the way up here. I'm told that a true cavalryman never likes to walk further than he has to. Are you, by chance, accompanied by any officers, or perhaps a sergeant, or even a corporal?"

Jesús replied that he hadn't actually waited to see who was riding with him.

General Cleburne directed a lieutenant on his staff to accompany the reinforcements to a place along the military crest of the ridge where he wanted them to deploy in a skirmish line and engage the enemy. Some quarter hour later, the forward elements of Granbury's Brigade arrived on foot and joined their hasty brethren in the defense of Rocky Ridge.

When Corporal Gill eventually recognized Jesús's tall hat among the boulders, he worked his way to him.

"Jesse, what in the hell have you done? You led the thievin' of a whole herd of horses and ignored Captain Longnecker's orders."

Jesús looked at Bain, looked down the slope, and swung around to sit with his back against the boulder, fully hidden from the Federals' position down the steep slope of the ridge.

"Bain, I didn't steal no horse, I just brought it back to its owner. And Captain Longnecker didn't order me not to ride up here. Besides, I done talked to General Cleburne hisself about it."

"Jesse, don't you go to lyin' to me."

Jesús winked at Bain, and without another word, turned back around, and resumed peering over the rock in search of a target. The defense of Rocky Face Ridge at Dug Gap continued through the day and was successful in holding the Federals at bay.

Granbury's Brigade was withdrawn off the ridge at dusk and spent half the night marching south. At dawn they were moving again, following the guides who had been sent to show the first elements of the army where the next defensive line would be made.

Chapter 20

Late May 1864, North of Atlanta, Georgia
17 Men Present for Duty

Corporal Gill noticed that even the most vigorous men in his platoon were beginning to slow their pace climbing up and down the steep hills as they moved from one ridge line to another. It was hot and humid and the undergrowth had been getting thicker. Some of the men had been munching hardtack since morning, but all were growing hungry, as well as being tired. Bain looked back at the column and caught Jesús's eye. Jesús looked back at him without any of his normal good humored banter or even a nod.

Lieutenant Navarro was marching near Gill with his sword slung over his shoulder. Gill asked him, "Lieutenant, how many days now have we been marching and fighting without a real rest?"

"Hmmm, seems like we ain't stopped since that day Private McDonald joined the cavalry and became General Cleburne's personal savior. That was two or three weeks ago, if my diary ain't lying to me."

Gill replied, "Your diary? When do you have time to write in a diary? Why you doing that anyway? Who's going to want to read about this damned war? Who's going to care what we've been doing?"

"Bain, I don't know. I just know it helps me get through the night to write down what we're doing. I think we're seeing things and doing things that we might want to remember someday."

"I ain't too sure about that, sir. Seems to me like it's all marching and being cold and wet, that is if we ain't hot and hungry. Don't see much that would interest any normal person."

"We'll see, Corporal, we'll see."

"Well, you, me, and the boys first got to see things through to the other side of all this marching and killing before we see if anyone cares what we done when we get home, " Bain replied as they both kept marching, having used up what talking energy either man had.

Soon the order came to file into the woods to the north of the road and construct a new defensive line. The few wagons that accompanied Granbury's Brigade carried the only shovels and axes that the quartermaster had been able to keep for the recurring pioneer work the brigade was called on to do. There were never enough tools and many men used their bayonets and belt knives instead. While axes were needed to fell trees for the log barricades, firing lanes were cleared of brush with knives and dirt loosened for trenches with bayonets and the loose soil slung out with tin plates or fry pans.

"Dammit, Bain, where does it say on my enlistment papers that I got to dig to China once a week? Where does it say that?" Jesús muttered as the two men knelt in the shallow trench trying to scoop dirt up.

"Tell you what, Jesse, Bain retorted, "You put up your plate and just go hide somewhere. Maybe go find your cousin Matt back at the general's wagon and trade family stories. When the Yanks come, you come on back and stand tall behind the trench when you fire at them. Then I'll get to tell your mama that I planted you in Georgia. Would that make you happy?"

"Well, to tell you the truth, Bain, the hidin' and visitin' Cousin Matt part sounds just fine. The standin' and getting' shot part don't sound so good. So I reckon I'll just keep usin' this plate for dirt work a bit longer."

The 6th-15th Texas Consolidated Regiment stayed in their new breastworks through most of the night. It was another night of no campfires to cook their meager rations because at dusk it started raining hard while the rations were being issued. Some men tried to chew the grisly beef raw, others put it in their haversacks hoping there would be an opportunity to boil or fry the meat before it spoiled. Others just tossed it, knowing from experience that the heat and humidity this time of year would turn the beef rancid in just a few hours. The rain continued through the night preventing anyone from sleeping much, although many men wrapped blankets over their heads and curled up under trees to try. It was a night of sharing the last of their hardtack and parched corn.

With dawn came a clear sky and the men were pleased that no order had reached them to move again. Blankets were draped over fences and hung from branches to dry them out.

"My Lord," muttered Captain Longnecker to Lieutenant Navarro as they walked towards the campfire of Bain's platoon. "If you fellers don't look like you're decorating camp for a barn-raising dance, I don't know what."

"Not a barn raising, Captain, but a *fandango*. A Mexican dance. All that's lacking are paper streamers, *mariachis*, and a dozen *señoritas*," replied a smiling Navarro. Their attention had been drawn to the several brightly striped blankets that the men from San Antonio had drying in the sun. All the blankets had been sent from home after their release from the prisoner of war camp the prior year. More than a few wives, mothers and grandmothers, Mexican and Anglo, had been so relieved to learn their husbands, sons and grandsons had survived, that they sent blankets off other children's beds to their soldiers. The result was indeed a very colorful patch of forest for the few hours the blankets hung to dry.

Finally, around midmorning, Captain Longnecker told First Sergeant McGrew to form the company. The regiment was issued additional packs of cartridges and the word quickly spread that today would likely bring another fight, as they were going to provide infantry support to an artillery battery that was already engaged. To the relief of the men in Company K, the artillery was never attacked, so the 6th-15th regiment was never called forward. They spent the six hours in reserve behind the cannons, listening to the sounds of the battle, but never seeing the enemy. Jesús took at least two naps, each time indignant at being awakened by those who couldn't bear to let a sleeping man lie when they couldn't sleep themselves.

"Corporal Gill," Sergeant Degas said loudly to get Gill's attention.

Gill looked around at Degas as he gummed a piece of hardtack. "Yea, Sergeant?"

"I've been watching Private San Miguel. He's looking pale and his hand is shaking some. May be fever. May be he's just wore out. You make sure he gets water and a cracker. Then keep your eye on him if we get into it. And if we have to move back fast, be sure he don't get left behind. We need ever rifle now."

Gill said, "I'll do that. Don't need to lose Andrew. We've been a long ways together."

At that moment bugles sounded and the men knew what was coming, so they pulled each other to their feet. As quickly as the column reformed they were stepping off at the double time. Within half an hour, now panting for breath, they turned off the road and moved fifty yards into the dense foliage

149

and halted on the top of a slight slope. Musket fire could be heard all across the front, but not a soul could be seen. Skirmishers were sent out further down the slope another twenty yards to the edge of a steep ravine. It was close to 4:00 pm and the skirmishers stared down the incline into shadows where the sounds of movement became louder and louder.

Without warning, a voice called up from the bottom of the ravine, "Don't shoot, we's with Genrul Kelley. You men up there hold your fire 'til we'uns git on past your line." With many such calls for caution, men dressed in drab browns and grays became appearing far down in the hollow. Most carried shotguns or smoothbore muskets and they were pulling themselves up as quickly as they could, using saplings as handholds. These men were part of Brigadier Kelley's cavalry division and had been fighting dismounted in the thick woods, making the oncoming Federals fight for every yard. The cavalrymen moved through the skirmish line, and as soon as they cleared the skirmishers, they turned toward their own left, hurrying to reach the far right flank of Granbury's regiments.

Even as the last of the Kelley's troopers were still climbing in front of the friendly skirmishers, Union soldiers began firing from the bottom of the ravine. Without orders, the skirmishers on the lip of the ravine began shooting at the puffs of white smoke coming from the dark cover at the bottom of the gully. Within a minute the ravine was wholly shrouded with the acrid white smoke from hundreds of weapons firing. The Confederate skirmishers were well protected by trees and did not need to expose themselves to shoot or reload. But the Federals were pressing forward and upwards and were unable to move quickly.

Dozens of men were hit by Rebel fire and dropped, sliding or rolling a few feet back down the steep slope until tree trunks or rocks halted them. The Federal fire was slow in coming as each man who started climbing up had to use one hand to hold onto limbs and tree trunks while the other hand gripped his musket. Officers were no better off, since their swords, whether sheaved or held, continued to get caught in the thick vines and foliage. Regardless of their heavy casualties, an entire Indiana regiment was pushing to scale the side of the ravine and the Texas skirmish line couldn't load and shoot fast enough to stop their advance.

Degas, Gill, and the rest of Company K waited twenty yards back, still able to clearly see the backs of their regiment's skirmishers. Gill glanced sidelong at Private San Miguel, who was staring downslope as intently as the others. The Federal soldiers in the ravine were shooting at such a high elevation at the skirmish line above them that the men in the main line of the 6th-15th Texas further back were not taking any casualties from bullets passing through the skirmish line. Instead, leaves and twigs from high in the trees began to float down on them while they waited for the skirmish line to withdraw.

"Bain, here come our boys back!" Private McDonald needlessly yelled as the skirmishers turned and ran to rejoin the regiment. As Jesús shouted, a Federal captain appeared on the lip of the ravine. He turned to urge his men on and fell backwards, torn by half a dozen minie balls. A whole line of Union troops took his place, and the front rank of the entire 6th-15th regiment fired on command, dropping all the visible Union soldiers. Seconds later another cluster of Federals appeared a bare twenty yards away and the Texans' rear rank fired, again obliterating the leading wave of men.

The one-sided fight continued long enough for the muskets of the Texans to begin fouling, making it harder and harder for the soldiers to ram home the next bullet. Men started stepping back of the firing line to pour canteen water down the barrels of their weapons, watching the steam swirl out of the metal tubes. When the weapons were upended, a foul black liquid came out as the gunpowder residue dirtied the water. Usually the water dissolved enough of the black grit for the men to resume shoving lead bullets to the bottom of the barrels.

Private Bernard Anderson had just stepped back to his place in the second rank of the formation, his musket cleaned and reloaded. He was leveling it towards the enemy when he saw the tip of a royal blue flag appear near the top of the ravine. He shifted his aim to his left and waited for the flag bearer to appear under the rising blue banner. When the man's head and shoulders were fully visible, Anderson squeezed the trigger. The smoke from his barrel dissipated, letting Anderson see the body of the man supine on the ground. In those few seconds a sergeant had stooped and pulled the flag staff free from his friend's grip. No sooner had the Indiana sergeant held the regimental flag erect than he too was shot, mortally wounded, and so released the flag to fall again. A third Union man knelt by the flag, laid his musket on the leaves and hoisted the blue flag up, running forward and waving the pole side to side, trying to rally the other men forward to their regimental colors. After only a few steps, this man also fell backwards, the victim of his own act of bravery. This time the flag remained on the ground for a minute or two as the concentrated firing of the Confederate infantry had cleared the area around the flag of any standing Yanks.

The flag lay only a scant ten yards from the gray soldiers and Private Miller started to set down his musket so he could run out and retrieve the trophy. But before he could take a step a Union corporal let his own musket fall and dashed towards his fallen regimental colors. Several Texans were aiming their weapons and saw the unarmed corporal running towards the flag. As they were about to shoot, Sergeant Degas impulsively shouted loud enough to be heard by the every man in the company, "Hold your fire! That man is too brave to kill! Let him live!"

Degas expected to see the Yank fall any second, but the men did as he ordered, and without firing they all watched the corporal reach the flag, stoop and pick it up, and scuttle back to the lip of the ravine where he dropped from sight, still carrying the blue flag.

Eventually, the charge of the Indiana brigade played out, the Federals never able to reach the Texans' battle line. The Union soldiers had been so close once they gained the top of the ravine, that any shot they fired had an excellent chance of striking the Confederate line. The 6th-15th Regiment took casualties, as they had stood for an hour in an elbow-to-elbow formation, without any cover because there had been no time to even gather fallen wood for protection.

It grew dark and a new skirmish line took position at the drop-off of the ravine which now was littered with the corpses of Union soldiers. The Reb soldiers went through every haversack among the fallen Yanks, looking for anything to eat.

"General Cleburne, sir, the hillside is still littered with Yankees too scared to move, or too wounded to move. What's more, I don't know if every Yankee regiment has withdrawn from the woods to our front. If we don't see to it ourselves, come first light, we may be in a pile of trouble." General Granbury told his division commander. "I request permission to move my men down the hill to take prisoners and clear the area."

"As you will, General," replied Cleburne. "But do not advance further. You will have no flank support, and even in the dark your men will be in grave danger. And do not set your pickets in the bottom of that ravine. Send them up the other side to the next ridge top when you are done. They'll buy us some time if General Sherman decides to continue the assault here."

"Fix bayonets!" came the order from Major Fisher. In every company of the 6th-15th regiment, along with all but one other regiment in Granbury's brigade, those men who still carried bayonets locked them onto the muzzles of their muskets.

"Charge bayonets! March!" came the next order, and nearly a thousand Texas Confederates moved together down the steep hillside. It was so dark under the trees that, even with moonlight, many men tripped over fallen soldiers. There was sporadic firing as nervous men fired at sounds and shadows, but there was no resistance among the Federal soldiers who remained in the area. By the time the Texans had reached the bottom of the several ravines and swales that marked the dense landscape, they had captured scores of Federal troops, rifled through their belongings, taking any food or money, and escorted them to the rear of the Confederate lines.

It was the morning after the Federal assault near Mr. Pickett's grist mill. The trio of generals had walked several yards down the slope in front of the line held by Granbury's Texans the previous day. The ground was a nightmare of dead soldiers in blue, scores of men lay in every direction from where the generals stood and surveyed the result of the futile charges.

"General Hood," spoke General Johnston, the commanding general of the Army of Tennessee to his corps commander, "From this day forth, these men will not be known as Granbury's Brigade, but as Johnston's Brigade. The state of Texas should be proud of her sons today."

General Hood nodded sagely in agreement, even though he would have preferred that his corps had been more aggressive in yesterday's battle. General John B. Hood was not a man who enjoyed fighting a defensive battle. Still, there was no doubt that Cleburne's division had once again fought like cornered bears, ferociously hurling back Mr. Lincoln's hounds, savagely torn and bloodied. Hood continued this line of silent reflection, thinking that perhaps next time General Sherman won't be so quick to attack, and Hood himself will be allowed to unleash his own dogs of war to find the vulnerable flank of the massive Federal army facing them..

Private McDonald lifted the body by the feet while Corporal Gill gripped the dead man's jacket. "Bain, you remember that first night on the boat back in Arkansas? When we was captured and headed north to prison camp? You remember you and me carryin' poor old frozen Walter Sweigert?"

"Yea, and you got his jacket to keep from freezing yourself."

"Yea, but that's not what I was thinkin'. I'm thinkin' how that was the first time I'd ever touched a dead man. It sure bothered me then. Now dead'uns seem to turn up ever day. Ours, theirs, even the poor folks who live where we're warrin'. And, I was thinkin' about how bad I wanted to kill Yankees back then. I was thinkin' about all these poor dead souls we sent to their maker yesterday. I was thinkin' how they kept on comin' up out of the ravine. How they didn't quit. How those men kept pickin' up their blue flag knowin' we were just gonna shoot 'em down like dogs."

153

"Yea, Jesse, they did that. They sure enough did that."

Jesús shifted his grip as they prepared to toss the body into the long shallow trench that had been dug earlier in the morning. "Bain, could we do that? Could we just keep comin' on like that? I don't know if I could."

The two men swung the body backwards, then flung it forwards onto dozens of other corpses that already filled the trench. Bain stood looking at the mass grave and shook his head. "Jesse, I hope we could. Lord above, I hope we ain't ever ordered to do that, but yea, I know you would keep goin' forward, and I think I would. I reckon most ever man in our outfit would keep goin'. The shirkers and skunks have all slunk out by now. We're better off without 'em, and yea, we'd do it if we're ordered to. God help us, we'd do it. Now let's go get one more of these boys. They're starting to get too stiff to carry."

"And real ripe. They're getting' real ripe. Some of 'm are already bloatin' and are gonna start poppin' in this heat," Jesús added.

Private Hawkins knelt by the dead man. He pulled the corpse's jacket around to straighten it so he could grab the cartridge box strap that crossed the dead man's chest and provided a convenient handle for dragging the body. The man's ruined head was not something Hawkins wanted to look at, and the young Reb pondered that a whole lot of the dead Yanks who littered the area around the ravine had bloody head wounds. Hawkins figured that the range was so close that it was easy to hit targets as they first appeared climbing the last few steps up to the top of the ravine. Crazy war.

When Hawkins wrapped his hand around the leather strap across the dead man's chest, his knuckles felt something hard inside the jacket, so he wormed his hand past the buttons and pulled out a flat glass bottle from the inside pocket of the jacket. Hawkins saw the brown liquid nearly filled the bottle, so he tucked it into his haversack, and gave the corpse a silent thanks. Next he quickly turned the man's trouser pockets inside out searching for any loose coins or maybe a good pocket knife. Finding the pockets empty, Hawkins then sliced the strap of the man's haversack, pulled it free, and quickly dumped out the contents on the ground. He found some broken pieces of hardtack and a stained envelope. He popped a piece of hardtack into his mouth and left the envelope unopened on the ground. Then, with effort, he dragged the body to the mass grave.

First Sergeant McGrew called Sergeant Degas and the corporals to him and excitedly, but softly, said, "Men, my cousin Mordecai in the 24th just come running to tell me that they was out as skirmishers all night on the next ridge over and come on six big piles of new rubber blankets the Yanks left behind. He thinks they were about to be issued to one of those regiments we tore up so bad yesterday. Those men we're planting this morning. Seems the good Lord's been bringing the rains down on our enemies too, but they got a quartermaster department that works better than our'n does.

You men get a detail out there fast as you can and collect one of them rubber blankets for ever' man in the company. Go now 'fore the word spreads all over the brigade."

Hearing such news was enough for Degas and Gill to pull four men from burial duties and personally lead them almost at a run over the ridges and ravines in search of the treasured rubberized canvas blankets. No such articles were produced in the south and the Confederate who could secure one from a captured or dead enemy soldier was considered a lucky man. To discover enough new ones for the taking to provide rain protection to every man in Company A/K was a godsend.

Chapter 21

Early June 1864, Near Atlanta, Georgia
17 Men Present for Duty

The company had been standing in formation for several minutes without knowing why. They hadn't been ordered to put on their knapsacks, so they knew they weren't about to move again. Lieutenant Navarro finally approached the company accompanied by two men wearing civilian clothes, each carrying a sack. The white man stood quietly with his canvas satchel slung over his shoulder and the black slave set his tall lumpy burlap bag on the ground, turned and walked back to the supply wagons.

Lieutenant Navarro began with ceremony, "Sergeants, please distribute two of the fruit in this sack to each man. Gentlemen, you are about to receive two tomato fruits from the state of Florida. If you have never eaten a tomato before today, get ready for a treat. General Johnston has observed that scurvy has afflicted many of you men throughout the army. The doctors have told him that limes and tomatoes will serve as medicine to improve your condition. The British navy eats little green limes to cure and prevent scurvy, but little green limes don't grow in the Confederacy, so General Johnston has found big red tomatoes for you. Eat both of your tomatoes today, and perhaps more will be provided later.

The lieutenant continued, "This here is Mr. Jacob Britton. He is from Gonzales, back home in Texas. Some of you boys might remember that Gonzales was the town where one little cannon started a great big war when some fellows waved a flag that said, "Come and Take It." That was thirty years back before most of us were born. But that war ended with *Generalissimo Santa Anna* handing Texas to General Sam Houston. And look where that got us. Here we stand a thousand miles from home fighting for Texas's freedom again."

Gill and McDonald looked at each other, each wondering just what the lieutenant was getting at.

"But that's old history. Mr. Britton came all the way from Gonzales to tell you how things are going back home. And, oh, yes, he brought a mail packet. Some of you men are about to learn if the crops got planted this spring back on your farms and if you still got any hogs in the pen. And don't neglect to eat your tomatoes."

With those words the lieutenant stood aside for Mr. Britton to step forward and start calling out names of soldiers for whom he had letters. The officers had already pulled their mail from the stack, and had also removed letters addressed to men who had died of sickness, been killed in battle, or deserted. Every man in the company formation was now fully alert, listening for his name. Those who stepped up to accept mail were immediately dismissed and the disappointed group of men, including Ambrose Hawkins, who remained in the formation after the last letter was given over, were quickly dismissed to go brood over why no one had written to them. Private McDonald was as eager to find out what was in Corporal Gill's letter as he was his own mail.

"Bain, did you get a letter? I know you did. Did Susan write? Did she ask about me?"

"Jesse, I ain't read it all yet. I barely even opened it. Go read your own letter."

"I will, Bain, I will. But as soon as you read it, you gotta tell me what your sister said."

"Wait a minute. Here it is, right here at the bottom of the page. It says, 'If that McDonald boy asks about me, tell him he needs to bathe and remove the lice from his hair before he mentions my name, because I will not be seen with young men who are covered with grime and infested with critters.'"

"She said what? She said that? She said I'm dirty? She said I've got lice? She said I'm infested?" Jesús asked as he scratched at his scalp.

157

Bain looked up at his friend with a solemn face and said, "Yea, Jesse, she sure 'nuf did. It's writ right here. You look." Bain handed the letter to Jesús and pointed to the bottom few lines on the page.

"Now, Bain, I don't read so good, but let me see." Jesús studied the letter, moving his head back and forth as he worked on the three lines of script.

"Bain, that ain't what it says."

"You sure, Jesse? Sure looked like it to me. Dirt and lice. Grime and critters."

Jesús kept reading, his lips moving as he reread each word. Then a smile replaced his frown, and he looked up at Bain.

"She says she will be glad to receive me when we get home. She says she hopes I'm well." Jesús was now grinning from ear to ear.

"Bain, you are nothin' but a skunk," Jesús said as he handed the letter back. "Now I'm going to go read what Pa has to say about the ranch. See if we still have any cows. Or hogs in the pen."

"Don't forget to eat your tomatoes," Bain said as Jesús walked away, "We don't want to disappoint General Johnston after he went to all that trouble to send to Florida for them."

McDonald took a big juicy bite of a tomato as he walked past Sergeant Degas who was sitting on a log with an opened envelope and a letter in his lap. With both hands Degas was holding a large sheet of heavy paper that he was studying intently. Jesús knew better than to interrupt the sergeant's reverie, but he changed his walking direction so he could pass behind the sergeant and look over his shoulder. What Jesús saw made him stop, stare, and say without thinking, "Sergeant, that lady is nekkid as a jaybird! *Madre de Dios*, she is...beautiful. Who likes you good enough to send you such a drawing?"

Sergeant Degas hastily refolded the paper, stood up, and took a step to put his face very close to McDonald. "That's not your concern, Private. You did not see any drawing and you will not speak of my letter to anyone. Now go away. Quickly."

The Army of Tennessee was making a defensive line northwest of Atlanta, and Sherman's army was once again working to outflank the smaller Confederate army. The general engagement along the Marietta line had already lasted several days, with Federal probes and sometimes determined attacks first by one division or corps, then another, as Sherman endeavored to uncover and exploit any fatal weakness.

Since their stand near Pickett's Mill, Granbury's Brigade had been marching from one area to another, providing the second line of defense for other divisions. The intermittent heavy rains had continued for nearly a week. There were no tents for the troops when they stopped late in the day or well after dusk, so the men just sought out places under low hanging branches and tried to sleep a few hours. Rations reached them some nights and did not some nights. A gnawing hunger remained the standard condition for the troops.

Corporal Gill and Private McDonald were both leaning against the trunk of the same pine tree, wrapped in their new rubber blankets with their hats pulled low over their brows.

"Bain, what time is it?"

"Jesse, I imagine it's about two in the morning."

"Nah, Bain, that can't be. That's what you said last time I asked."

"And that's what I'll say next time you ask. Now let me try to sleep."

"I been trying to sleep and I ain't nodded off yet. I think it's this new blanket. I been under it since we sat down soaked to the bone, and now I ain't been this dry in two weeks. Is this a magic blanket? What's this slick black stuff anyway?"

"Jesse, that's Mr. Goodyear's patented vulcanized rubber. That's what it is."

"Bain, I didn't understand a word you said, and how you know such a thing, anyways?"

"Back at the prison, there was one guard, an old fellow, must have been forty or forty-five. Gray beard. One day when it was snowing real heavy he was on duty outside the carpenter's shed, standing there in the snow all morning, and he told me about it. The old fellow liked to talk. He told me that talking kept his mind off the unpleasantness around him. Sort of like you. Said before the war he used to work in a factory up east that made rubber shoes. He said Mr. Goodyear was a scientist who was half crazy and kept making new things out of rubber. Said he's dead now. But they still use his recipe to turn rubber tree sap into waterproof paint. They mix the sap with kerosene and sulfur or vulcan or something, heat it up and paint it on a piece of canvas."

" Ain't that something. I don't know about you, but I'm feeling mighty grateful to Mr. Goodyear just now. Bless his dead crazy bones. Wonder why nobody makes these rubber blankets in Texas or Louisiana or somewhere besides up east? And what's patented?"

"Reckon we can't get rubber through the Yankees' blockade, and all our factories are making muskets and cannons. I don't know what patented is. But that's what the old graybeard called his rubber blanket. His had a slit in the middle and he wore it like a poncho, like you Mexicans do."

"*Sì*, our *serapes*. We've always been smarter than you *gringos*."

"Yea, if you're so smart how come you're sitting outside in the rain for the hundredth night and you're a thousand miles from home? Home where there's a hot bowl of beans on the fire."

"All that wishin' about home don't matter, Bain. All that matters is this here rubberized blanket."

"Sure, Jesse, that's right, we're here in the dark, hunkered down in the rain, hungry, and all that matters to you is our new rubber blankets."

"You think about it Bain, you're good at thinking. Come morning you'll be agreein' with me that the rubber blanket was what mattered most when you was cold and wet."

"Next you'll be saying we're fighting this war, killing men we never even met, good men mostly, I imagine, all for a rubber blanket."

"I don't know about that part, Bain, but we sure ran like Texas jackrabbits to fetch these rubber blankets when Sergeant McGrew told you about them. Seems to me that maybe we killed a whole lot of Yanks that day just so we could steal their rubber blankets. And their food, and their shoes, and their muskets. I ain't stole a dead man's letters from home yet, but if your sister don't write me again real soon, I may start stealin' Yankee lovey letters too."

With those final words, both men may have nodded off to sleep for an hour or two.

Before dawn the regiment was on the march again.

"Rain, Bain, rain. When is this rain gonna stop? I'm drowning standing straight up. My feet are in mud up to my knees and I'm about to croak like a frog."

"Just shut up and march, Jesse. Shut up and march."

Company A/K was now marching as the first company in the consolidated regiment. Gill still was at the back of the company, with the other fourteen privates who comprised the depleted ranks of Company K just in front of him. Shortly after the reconsolidation of Companies A and K, First Sergeant McGrew and Second Sergeant Degas had come to an informal agreement that Degas ran the Company K half of the company, while McGrew handled the men from Company A. Gill was glad of the arrangement because having de facto command of Company K had made Degas a little less angry most of the time. The only officer left from Company K was Lieutenant Navarro, and he was willing to let Degas operate without much interference from above.

The four regiments in the brigade marched until mid-morning when they were ordered off the road into a meadow. It had stopped raining and the sun was out. The entire 6th–15th Texas Consolidated Regiment was ordered to deploy as skirmishers ahead of the rest of Granbury's command while the other regiments stacked arms and took a rest break in the field.

Unless they were defending breastworks where good stout logs protected them, Gill much preferred skirmish fighting to standing in the regimental battle line as they had at Chickamauga. Having room to move about and the ability to find cover was the style of fighting that made most sense to Gill. Sometimes he wondered why the generals still ordered their men to stand elbow-to-elbow trading volleys or worse, ordered them to march forward elbow-to-elbow, not able to load after the first volley, but taking casualties with every step. Gill knew from the fights at Tunnel Hill and Ringgold Gap that it wasn't all that hard to hit advancing enemy when they were jammed in right next to each other. Sometimes it was even downright hard to miss. On the other side of the coin, Gill also was aware of the comfort he took in knowing his comrades were so close they were touching sleeves. Gill certainly wasn't a general, and he acknowledged he didn't know himself how he would get enough riflemen close enough together to overwhelm a position if the men weren't packed in close. But they sure made easy targets.

The regimental skirmish line was comprised of just under 300 men and stretched nearly 300 yards. As Company A/K made their way forward, Gill continuously swiveled his head to left and right. He kept looking to his right to make sure Hawkins, Jesús, and Miller were on line with him, and he kept snatching glances to his left to be sure he was staying abreast and not getting ahead or behind the second company. The brush at the edge of the field soon gave way to larger trees, and within minutes the right wing of the regiment was working its way down a gully where a creek was flowing fast, swollen from the ongoing rains.

"Ambrose, you go first through the creek. Be careful with your feet, and keep your musket up high. And watch your cartridge box don't go under water, too," Bain needlessly cautioned. Hawkins waded into the running water and it quickly reached his knees, but he was across before it went higher. Hawkins climbed a few steps up and leaned against a tree to look over the top of the gully.

Gill crossed quickly and looked to see if Jesús and Miller had made it over. He looked just in time to see Miller take his first step out of the creek, while Jesús knelt behind a tree. Without warning, Private Miller fell backwards, dropping his rifle and limply splashing into the creek. Private

McDonald looked on, frozen in place by the unexpected sight of Miller lying on his back in the creek, his face under water and blood flowing from the hole in his neck, swirling pink in the current.

Gill bent low and ran towards Miller's body, as Hawkins and McDonald fired, both seeing the same small cloud of white smoke ahead of them. Then the popping of muskets sounded up and down the line as men reacted to the first shots. Gill dropped his musket on the bank of the creek, grabbed Miller's shoulders and pulled him up on the wet leaves. The wound had already quit pumping blood out, and Gill saw Miller was gone. With a silent curse, Gill retrieved his weapon and moved quickly back to his position. When he got there, Degas was behind a rock gazing towards the trees to their front, and gave Gill a questioning look. Gill shook his head sideways, and pointed at his own neck. Degas nodded and moved back, letting Gill resume his work.

Gill waited where he was, not seeing any more puffs of smoke to their front as the initial flurry of shooting stopped. Soon Gill saw the second company was moving forward, so he waved his men to resume their advance. He watched Jesús splash into the creek at a run, pumping his legs as hard as could in the moving water for the four steps it took him to cross. McDonald climbed out and reached Miller's body, pausing to touch Miller on the forehead and make the sign of the cross on his own chest, while he quietly asked the Blessed Virgin to look out for Miller's departed soul.

The entire regimental skirmish line moved past the meandering creek and continued without opposition until they reached the edge of the woods. Facing them was a field with a road and fence on the far side about a hundred yards away. Here the regiment stopped, every man finding good cover, kneeling or lying down to lessen their chance of being seen.

Across the field that was planted with knee high oats, Company D of the 42nd Ohio Volunteer Infantry made their way through the gap in the fence and reformed inside the trees. A shallow swale on their side of the field had masked the Federal company's final withdrawal from their skirmish assignment. Their captain reported that Reb skirmishers had crossed the little creek and probably were holding the far woods line.

After an hour, Major Fisher ordered a few scouts to move to the top of the rise in the middle of the field and stay hidden there, with orders to quickly retire without firing if the Yanks entered the field. Fisher was hoping he might get an unexpected volley into the enemy as they crested the rise. Gill was hoping even one blue coat would show himself, so he could avenge Miller.

An hour before dusk, with no activity in the field, Captain Longnecker sent a canteen detail back to the creek. Corporal Gill, Private Fremon, and Private McDonald went on the detail. After filling the Company K men's canteens in the creek, Gill directed Fremon to carry all of the canteens back while he and McDonald stayed behind to bury Miller's body.

Miller was still laid out on the creek bank, and as the two men approached they saw a large green snapping turtle edging his way towards the corpse, following the trail of dried blood.

"Bain, would you look at that. Old Cooter is goin' to pay his respects to James," Jesús said.

"More likely Old Cooter is working his way over to taste on James' himself," countered Gill.

As soon as they reached the turtle, walking up behind it, Jesús bent down and picked up the round creature by its tail.

"Bain, this ole boy is just the size to make us a fine soup tonight. I bet some of the fellers got onions and maybe a tater or two."

Gill was suddenly angry at his friend and said, "Jesse, poor James is right there in front of us laid out cold as stone, and you're messing with a damn turtle."

McDonald's countenance immediately turned serious as he said, "Ah, Bain, you know I'm frettin' about James; he was *mi amigo* too. But he ain't the first and won't be the last of us to be laid out 'fore we get home. Maybe I latched onto Old Cooter to brush aside how glad I am that it ain't me layin' there cold as stone. Or you."

Gill, embarrassed by his friend's sudden sincerity, interrupted to say, "Well, you can't boil water, how you gonna make a turtle soup?"

Jesus replied, "'Cause it's true that when I was a *muchacho* we caught snappers out of Salado Creek and *mi madre* made some fine soup. I bet I can do it." With those words, Jesús opened up his haversack and stuffed the turtle in, head first.

"And if I'm too tired to cook turtle, I can always let him loose in Bernard's blanket after he goes to sleep."

Corporal Gill had no reply to that, so without more talking the two friends lifted the corpse and carried it up the slope further from the creek. Using their bayonets and hands, they dug a grave two feet deep. Gill reached into Miller's jacket and checked the pocket where he found a folded letter which he tucked away in his own pocket. They then wrapped Miller's new rubber blanket around him, covering his head, but leaving his feet sticking out, and gently laid him in the ground. After shoving the loose soil over the body, the pair worked another ten minutes gathering large rocks to cover

163

the grave, hoping the stones would prevent animals from digging up the body. Neither man offered to pray over the grave, but they stood silently for a few seconds before picking up their muskets, and Miller's, and returning to the skirmish line. Jesús's haversack was heavy on his hip, and soon a green head appeared under the edge of the flap, but the turtle was too big to force its way past the buckled flap.

Neither side moved from their positions on the edges of the woods until dark, when the 6th-15th Texas was relieved by the 24th-25th Texas Consolidated Regiment. The men of the 6th-15th were granted a few hours of sleep and a cold ration issue before the brigade moved on again, once more withdrawing out of General Sherman's net that stretched beyond both of the Confederate flanks.

Jesús's snapping turtle finally pushed its way out of the haversack shortly after the company returned to camp, having eaten the only food in the sack, a small wild onion and half a piece of hardtack, and then relieved itself before leaving its temporary quarters. If Jesús ever noticed the waste left behind by the turtle, he never said anything, but he complained about the leather buckle strap the turtle had chewed through and the loss of a fine supper of turtle soup.

Chapter 22

Mid June 1864, North of Atlanta, Georgia
16 Men Present for Duty

During nearly a month of daily engagements, General Johnson had been slowly retiring the entire Army of Tennessee towards Atlanta under the pressure of the Union army. General Sherman had learned through many brutal bloody frontal assaults that the Rebs could be tough nuts to crack if allowed the time to build entrenched breastworks, and General Johnston's army had become very adept at doing just that. Yet, regardless of their successes in holding the massive Union army at bay until their flanks were overwhelmingly threatened, the men in the ranks were stretched to their physical limits as they continued to fight, withdraw, and build new defensive positions time after time.

Today General Johnston was worried about Pine Mountain. He had been informed by General Hardee that it created an untenable salient that might be the focus of a new Federal attack. Therefore, during the evening of June 13th, Johnson asked that General Hardee join him in a personal visit to the entrenchments on the crest of Pine Mountain the next morning. Hardee in turn asked Division Commander General Polk to accompany them.

The crest of Pine Mountain was barely 300 feet above the valley it faced, and it was much more a ridge than a mountain. The slope had been clear-cut of timber allowing the Floridians who manned the breastworks on the crest an open field of fire should the Federals attack them. The crest created a rough semi-circle that jutted out towards the valley, making it an admirable observation point; but it was also a point that could be attacked from three sides. On the morning of June 14th, the Rebs on Pine Mountain were able to see several Union artillery batteries as they rolled into position across the valley below..

General Johnston stood behind the log works and held his binoculars to his eyes, noting the enemy artillery on the far ridge and thought that Hardee's concerns about the position being vulnerable to attack were well founded. Next to Johnston, Generals Hardee and Polk were likewise studying the terrain spread out before them.

Johnston turned to Hardee and asked, "Can you hold this salient? Do you have the troops to support it on both flanks?"

Hardee didn't reply immediately as he did a mental tally of the divisions in his corps and thought about where each division was deployed right now, and how badly they were needed where they were. Polk, who thought his division might be the one ordered to reinforce Pine Mountain, was studying the ground to both sides of the crest

Before Hardee could reply, Johnston continued, musing aloud, "Perhaps tonight we should withdraw from here, and let Sherman attack an empty hilltop tomorrow morning."

Colonel Andrew Dilworth, commanding the Fourth Florida Infantry, approached the trio of generals, "Excuse me, General Johnston, but this is no place for you, sir. You and the other generals are in danger here. I implore you to retire now. There are numerous Yankee cannon across that valley and they have a clear view of us up here. Please, sir. Allow me to escort you back to your mounts."

Across the small valley, General Sherman focused his binoculars on the breastworks on the crest of the ridge labeled on the maps as Pine Mountain. Sherman and his IV Corps commander, General Howard, were studying the ridge and trying to gauge the strength of the Confederate defenses before them. General Sherman was staring at the large group of uniformed men he was seeing in his binoculars. Suddenly he realized the group included a trio of officers who were holding their own binoculars towards his position on the edge of the woods.

"My God, but they are cheeky. I do believe that members of the Rebel high command are studying us. General Howard, would you please send a few shells their way to teach those men some caution. We can do without their interest."

As Colonel Dilworth finished begging the generals to leave the exposed hilltop, puffs of smoke began appearing across the valley. An Indiana battery was firing its 3-inch rifled cannons at the breastworks on the crest. The battery's captain didn't intend to do more than make the Rebs on the crest seek cover, so he had ordered a round of solid shot fired from each of the four cannons in his first two sections. Since the solid cannon balls would not explode on contact, the captain did not expect to see any results of his salvo. Regardless, since there were generals observing, he watched the top of Pine Mountain through his binoculars as his artillery pieces fired. He didn't see anything of the first round, but suddenly a tree inside the breastworks visibly shook and he could see large shards of the tree trunk flying outward. Well, the captain thought to himself, we killed a tree. Maybe that will indeed get the Rebs' attention and they will retire from the hill before we lay a real barrage on them.

As Generals Johnston and Hardee acceded to Colonel Dilworth's pleas to move down from the exposed crest, General Polk stood another moment, just looking outward at the fine expansive view. He was carrying two small Bibles in his coat pocket, which he intended to present to Generals Johnston and Hardee when they returned to Johnston's headquarters. He had written an appropriate note to each of his superior officers in the front of the Bibles.

Polk turned and took a step towards the rear of the fortified position, never aware of the solid ball of iron that hit his left arm from the side, ripping it loose from his shoulder. The iron ball then tore into his chest obliquely and exited through his right shoulder and plunged into the trunk of a pine tree behind him. The tree trunk exploded, sending wooden shrapnel into Polk's back. General Leonidas Polk, the "fighting bishop of Louisiana," as well as the man who owned the most slaves in Maury County, Tennessee, was dead.

The Florida troops on the crest of Pine Mountain retired from their breastworks that night. A single bayonet was left stuck in the ground upon which a handwritten note was attached. The note read, "You Yankee sons of bitches have killed our old General Polk." Upon hearing of the note the next day, General Sherman sent a box of good cigars to the Indiana battery captain.

Lieutenant Navarro and Captain Longnecker were gathered in a circle of all the 6th-15th Texas Consolidated Regiment's officers. They surrounded Major Fisher as he told them that they were going to hold the ridge they were on just to the south of the tiny town of Golgotha.

"Men, General Granbury expects the Yankees to come at us right through the crossroads where the village buildings and log church are down yonder. Since there ain't any trees left on this ridge, we're going to pull down the buildings in Golgotha and haul the timbers up here to add to our breastworks."

"You mean all the houses, and the church too?"

"Yup, that's what I mean. We're going to use the Lord's house to protect our skins. 'Cause if we don't, the damyankees will, for sure. Semple's Battery is unlimbering now and will provide us cover in case the Yanks show up before we're through. Now get to it. Captain Longnecker, you go to work on the church."

An hour later Company K was in Golgotha. "Bain, are you sure it's okay for us to be takin' apart a whole church? What about the pulpit?" Jesús asked as the men climbed onto the church's roof.

"No pulpit would mean a shorter sermon."

"No church will mean no sermon. What about the altar? We ain't goin' to bust up the altar, are we?"

"I imagine we're going to take it all, Jesse. A Yank can hide behind an altar just as well as behind a big rock," Bain said.

"Well, it don't seem right. The Blessed Savior ain't goin' to like us rippin' his home down around his cross of salvation. We're not going to use the cross, are we? What kind of church is this anyway?"

"Dammit, Jesse, it's a church made of logs, and if the cross is made of timber, you can bet it's going up the hill," Bain replied in exasperation.

"Well, maybe takin' a stand behind the cross is a good idea. I been saved by the blood of Christ and maybe it is proper to use his sacred cross as a shield. But what I meant, Bain, is this a Catholic church? Or maybe a Methodist one? I don't think I could abide rippin' the roof off a Catholic church. Maybe not even a Methodist church. *Mi madre* wouldn't want me tearin' down a Catholic church. And ain't your ma a Methodist?"

"Yea, she goes to camp meetings when the circuit preacher comes around. But don't worry. I saw a little sign out front that says this is a Baptist Church."

"Oh. As long as it's not a Catholic church. But I don't know any Baptists, so let's go to work."

By nightfall, the church and other structures that comprised Golgotha, Georgia were torn down and all the timbers laid on top of the red dirt piled in front of the trenches that Cleburne's Division dug that afternoon. Around dusk the heavy rains returned as the tired men sat in the new trenches that were quickly becoming quagmires of slushy red mud.

168

Corporal Gill was slowly working his way down the row of the men in his platoon, checking to be sure their muskets were clean and loaded. When he reached Private Hawkins, Gill found him sitting on a log leaning against the back wall of the trench, his musket across his lap, smiling up at Gill.

"Hawkins, are you drunk? You look too damn happy not to be drunk." Gill leaned in closer and got a whiff Private Hawkins' breath. "Boy, you are stone dead drunk. Where in the hell did you find whiskey?"

"Ambrose, answer me. Where'd you get that pop skull? Who gave it to you?"

Gill had a sudden fear the men had found a hidden stash of spirits when they had dismantled Golgatha, and that Private Hawkins would be just one of several men who were already under the effects of the soldiers' favorite pain-killer.

"Corporal Gill," Hawkins said as he gave Gill an exaggerated salute while still sitting, "I must report that a spirit forced these spirits upon me." Then Hawkins giggled.

Gill was getting mad, but it was hard to get mad at Hawkins.

"What damned spirit was that, Ambrose? A spirit down in Golgotha this afternoon?"

"Oh no, Bain, tweren't no spirits in Golgotha. This spirit was back..." Hawkins waved his arm towards the side, "back at Pumpkinvine Creek."

"Pumpkinvine Creek?"

Thinking fast, Gill realized what Hawkins must have done.

"Ambrose, was your spirit wearing a blue coat?"

"He sure was, Bain. A blue ghost."

"Hawkins, are you telling me you stole a bottle of whiskey off a dead Yankee back there where we were burying them fellers a couple of weeks back?"

"No, Bain, no, I didn't steal no whiskey. The spirit, he give it to me, so's this here bottle wouldn't be lost under all them dead bodies." As he spoke Hawkins pulled the nearly empty bottle from under his gum blanket and handed it to Gill.

"Ambrose, have you ever had a drink of whiskey before tonight?"

"Well, sure, Bain, lots of....," at which point Hawkins leaned forward and vomited into the red mud.

Hawkins wiped his chin, and continued, "Well, no, Bain this here is the first whiskey I ever had. Ma don't hold with pa keeping a jug."

Gill stood in the mud, a stream of water coming off the brim of his hat in the pouring rain, and stared at Hawkins, deciding what he should do. The boy had come a long way and done his part in a big handful of fights and never faltered. He wasn't a whiner or a shirker and was as brave as men bigger, older and meaner.

Gill pulled the cork from the bottle, took a little taste of the fiery liquid, capped it and handed it back to Hawkins.

"Thanks, Ambrose. There ain't much left in that bottle. Why don't you see if Jesse wants to finish it?"

At that point, Jesús's arm appeared from the dark at Ambrose's side and freed the bottle from his grasp.

"*Sì*, Bain, *mi amigo*. That's a fine idea. *Muchos gracias*, Ambrose."

Jesús gulped down the last of the liquid in the bottle, and dropped the empty glass into the mud.

Within a minute Private Hawkins was sleeping soundly with his chin on his chest, still balanced on the log, rain running off his hat and rubber blanket. Jesús reached over and pulled Ambrose's musket free and laid it on the ground at the back of the trench, figuring it might rust, but red rust was better than red mud. Moreover, it would give something for Sergeant Degas to yell about tomorrow. Jesús figured that Ambrose deserved some payback for not sharing more of his bottle, even if it was his first one.

Chapter 23

Late June 1864   Closer to Atlanta
16 Men Present for Duty

Company A/K was again on the picket line, strung out on the edge of a woodlot with a large field between them and the Federal pickets. A creek ran through the middle of the field and it was the unofficial border between the pickets. Private Hawkins was leaning against a tree watching the pair of Union soldiers a couple of hundred yards away. Hawkins and the other pickets were more relaxed than normal because an informal "armistice" had been declared by the sergeants of both the Reb and the Yank companies on the picket line. The practical application of the informal armistice meant neither side would shoot at the other on sight, in the hope they might trade goods to the benefit of both. Therefore, Hawkins was eyeing the two Yanks across the field and could see one of them was holding something white. Hawkins hoped it was a newspaper that might be offered up in trade, so he turned and called back to Sergeant Degas.

"Sergeant, I think them Yanks over yonder have a newspaper they may want to barter. You got any flat tobaccy? We might even get some Lincoln coffee if we're lucky."

"Hawkins, hold your voice down, dammit. You want the whole army to hear you. I'll be right back. You keep watching, but don't go calling out."

It was the lure of real coffee, not old news, that stirred the sergeant to go in search of some trade tobacco. Degas had fought all through the war without his cherished strong French coffee, and most of the war without any coffee at all. He was perfectly willing to temporarily forget the prohibition of trade between pickets if he might carry a small sack of coffee back to his campfire. Degas found Private Anderson further down the line and he had a wad of tobacco leaves in his haversack. Degas quickly enlisted his support with a promise of a cup of real coffee.

The two unarmed privates met at the creek and each took a step out into the cool water.

Hawkins spoke first, "I got flat tobacco leaves. You got coffee?"

The Yankee from Indiana replied, "Maybe. How much tobacco?"

"How much coffee? And you got newspapers too, I saw you with them. We'll be wanting those too."

The Union private, who was visibly older and taller than Hawkins, replied, "You're a pushy little Reb, ain't ya? You ever been in a fight, or they just put you out here to watch the blue birds? No matter. I got a whole sack of coffee and two newspapers from Chicago. The papers are only three weeks old."

"Don't you be worried about me. I may be youthful and handsome, but I been a soldier long enough to have done shot my share of blue birds. It ain't been a short war."

Hawkins paused, then got back to business, "I got enough tobaccy to trade for the coffee, the newspapers, and for you to take a packet of letters to put in the mail service for some of our fellers who still got family up north."

"Like I said, you are a pushy piece of cowhide, ain't you. And you are right enough, it ain't been a short war, not short at all." This time the Yank paused, then said, "OK, I'll take your tobacco and your letters, and pass the coffee and the newspapers to you. Deal?"

"Deal."

The exchange was made as both privates stood in the creek, and without a further word or handshake, they both returned to their places on the picket lines to pass along the traded luxuries to their NCO's.

Chapter 24

Independence Day, July 4, 1864, Northwest of Atlanta
16 Men Present for Duty

On the morning of Independence Day Sergeant Degas rousted out his men in the dark and they were marching by dawn.

"Bain, are we going out on the picket line again? How many hundred times have we done that in the last two months?"

"Looks like it, Jesse, don't it. I reckon we didn't get loaded up with fresh ammo packs just to sit in the sunshine."

"I don't mind the picket duty so much, but men get kilt out there. Ever' time we step out I think of burying James and all those other boys we seen shot."

"Well, you be careful, Jesse. You stay behind cover. I promised my sister that I'd look out after you, now that you done stirred her up with your letters."

Jesús grinned his biggest smile, and started humming to himself as he marched.

Granbury's Brigade had spent the last several days in a reserve position. That meant spending long hours manning prepared defensive positions and sleeping with weapons by their sides. Often the brigade was ordered out to immediately march towards the sounds of battle as a mobile body of reinforcements, ready to support other brigades. Sometimes the Texans were ordered to reverse their route of march and return to where they started. Other times they fell out by the side of a road, companies rotating picket duty while the remaining companies tried to sleep. Summer rains continued to plague the ability of both armies to march quickly, as the dirt roads turned into quagmires of deep mud every time a new downpour occurred.

By midmorning the column halted and the entire 6th-15th Consolidated Texas Regiment did a right-face off the muddy road and deployed as skirmishers. As they moved forward they could see other Confederate soldiers hurrying from the woods they were about to enter. Major Fisher halted the regiment and waited for an approaching limping lieutenant to reach them.

"Major," the young officer said, "The Yanks made a strong attack on our picket line and pushed back our vedettes. They came on fast and hit us in our trenches. A few of our boys got captured. The rest of us lit out. We weren't but a couple of companies spread real thin, and they come at us with a regiment."

Major Fisher sent the lieutenant on to the rear, and resumed the advance of the whole regiment. He had Company A/K as the ready reserve company on the right wing, behind the other five combined companies of the old Sixth Texas Regiment which were deployed as skirmishers. One of the four combined companies of the Fifteenth Texas Regiment was held back as the reserve company on the left wing. Within minutes a panting staff officer from General Granbury reached Fisher with orders to retake the trenches that the Federals had just overrun.

Fisher sent runners to each company directing them to fix bayonets and press the enemy aggressively. Fisher left the men in their skirmish lines as they moved through the woods, knowing the skirmishers would draw the attention of the Yanks in the trenches. The skirmishers would also provide cover for the two reserve companies to get close enough for Fisher to personally lead them in a fast assault on the trenches. Fisher counted on their approach from the backside of the earthworks to carry his men straight in among the Federals without having to cross the wall of dirt and logs thrown up to protect the men in the trenches from a frontal attack.

As the reserve companies moved forward with weapons at port arms, muskets held at the ready across each man's chest, Sergeant Degas spoke to the corporal in the first rank of their small company, "Gill, you be ready to get our boys movin' quick and mean. Use the bayonets. Hit 'em hard and ugly. Them blue-backs won't stand and fight when we're pilin' in on 'em using the bayonets. They'll break and run. Don't hold back!"

Gill glanced at Degas and hoped that the sergeant was right as he gripped his musket tighter to keep his hand from shaking. Gill looked across and saw Private Bernard Anderson holding his musket with only his right hand, while with his left hand he loosened his long heavy belt knife in its sheaf. Gill wondered if Anderson would fight as ferociously with the knife as he looked. Gill personally still preferred the idea of his long bayonet on the end of a long musket, especially if that enemy was using his own bayonet.

Major Fisher nodded to Captain Longnecker and the reserve companies on each wing moved up at the double-quick in two ranks, moving fast through their own skirmishers. As they charged towards the trench Gill joined in screaming an undulating high pitched yell. Others in the company barked like fierce dogs or bayed like hounds. The resulting cacophony was the infamous Rebel yell, a sound that had been heard by nervous Federal soldiers for three years and was hard to ignore, even with the sounds of musket fire punctuating the battle.

Gill was moving too fast to stop or look around as he reached the edge of the trench. He leapt down, landing on a Union soldier who was putting a priming cap on the nipple of his musket. Gill's musket came down on top of the man's shoulder, jarring his arm so hard he dropped the priming cap and staggered under Gill's weight. Gill was off balance as well and pulled himself upright to recover, even as the man in front of him swung the butt of his rifle up, trying to hit Gill under the chin. Gill jerked his head back and felt the whoosh of air as the walnut stock of the musket flew just past his face. Instinctively, Gill brought his own musket butt up from near the ground and planted it in squarely in his opponent's crotch. The Union soldier groaned and bent over. Gill pulled back his musket and thrust the bayonet forward into his opponent's stomach. As he had practiced on a burlap bag as a new recruit, Gill twisted his wrists to turn the bayonet blade before he pulled it out. The man before him sunk to the ground, blood flowing from the hole in his blue jacket.

Now Gill looked to his right to see Private Anderson squared off with a Federal corporal whose musket was held low, his bayonet pointing upward at Anderson. The Texan held his big knife forward, moving it back and forth. The corporal lunged, Anderson banged his knife blade off the side of the bayonet in an attempt to parry the thrust, but the bayonet was barely deflected. The point went through Anderson's jacket and imbedded in his beefy upper arm. Even with his arm pierced by the bayonet, Anderson found the strength to swing his knife up backhanded and slice into the soldier's wrist, cutting to the bone. The man let go of his musket as Anderson followed with a quick jab with the point of the blade into his ribcage. The Federal corporal dropped backwards, pulling Anderson's knife with him. Anderson fell to his knees with the Yank's bayonet still in his arm and the musket hanging down. Anderson pulled the bayonet out and sat down holding his hand over his wound.

Private McDonald reached the edge of the trench and immediately fired his musket from the hip without aiming. The muzzle was only two feet from a young Federal private below him in the trench. The Yank wasn't wearing a hat and had thick blonde hair. McDonald's bullet went past his ear, scorching his hair and deafening him. McDonald then jumped feet first into the trench aiming to hit the Yank in the chest with his feet. The man stepped to the side as McDonald leapt and the Texan landed heels first in the dirt and fell backwards. The Yank was swinging his musket butt up for a downward thrust to impale McDonald when Private Leon Fremon shot him in the back. His spine broken, the man pitched forward onto McDonald, his bayonet thrust never delivered.

Fremon slid into the trench next to McDonald, reached down and pulled him up by his jacket collar, saying, "Jesse, you shoulda paid more attention back when we wuz learnin' to shoot at a man's balls."

In less than a minute the first deadly impact of the company was enough to do what Sergeant Degas had hoped. The few Union soldiers who met them were either killed, wounded, or had quickly stepped back with their arms up high in surrender. The defenders to the left and right of the vicious melee backed away or climbed out of the trench and ran for the safety. The men from the 6th-15th's skirmish line reached the trench and accepted the surrender of Federals still there, or shot at the men who were running away.

Gill saw Ambrose Hawkins kneeling next to a prostrate Union soldier, and made his way over to them. The man stretched out on the dirt was a young lieutenant and had been shot in the chest. He was talking to Hawkins and as Gill watched, Hawkins reached over and unbuttoned the man's jacket. The wounded man put a hand into the breast pocket and paused for a few seconds, summoning the strength to continue. Then he pulled his hand out clutching his pocket watch. He dropped the watch on his chest and spoke again to Hawkins who reached out again and pulled the man's ring off. Then Hawkins reached into the outside pocket of the officer's coat and pulled out a small notebook. Hawkins opened it and saw the man's name and hometown in Indiana written on the inside cover. Hawkins collected the watch and ring and put them and the notebook in his own jacket pocket. He then looked up at Gill and said, "I shot the man, Bain. He knows he ain't going to live. He asked if I'll mail these things home to his wife. I'm going to do it."

"That's fine, Ambrose. He was a brave man who stood by his men. You write a note to put with his things and you tell his wife he didn't run. He deserves that."

Lieutenant Navarro was now urging the men to move the corpses out of the trench and for the men to reload and take firing positions in the earthworks, because the Federals were coming again. Just minutes later Gill was looking through the firing gap under the head log and saw blue coated soldiers moving forward. Gill sighed in relief to see it wasn't a solid formation of charging men, but scattered clumps of men who were using cover to stop and fire, rather than making a determined attack. Navarro was beside Gill and, as Gill fired his musket, Navarro spoke what both were thinking.

"I think their colonel ordered them to retake our works, but those men have had enough of us. Keep a fire on them, and they'll back off soon enough."

The enemy's firing did indeed quickly slack off and within an hour the attacking Federals had withdrawn from sight. The 6th-15th Texas stayed in the earthworks through the rest of the afternoon, waiting for another action or for orders to withdraw.

As soon as it was dark the regiment was pulled from the earthworks as the whole army was again retiring to the next line of earthworks, even closer to the city of Atlanta.

Chapter 25

Mid July 1864, Northwest of Atlanta, Georgia
16 Men Present for Duty

Private Anderson stood waist deep in the Chattahoochee River and wriggled his toes in the muddy bottom. It had been two weeks since the bayonet wound in his arm, and Anderson was very relieved that it was healing and had not swollen up and filled with puss. When that happened, the surgeons generally took the arm off, and Anderson still shuddered at that prospect. So even when the wound throbbed and ached, he knew he was lucky.

The entire brigade had been camped along both sides of the river for two days now. Men had a rare chance to leisurely make field repairs to their kits and sew patches on their worn-out clothes. They also took advantage of the sunshine and break from daily marches to wash their clothes in the river. As the warm morning turned into a hot summer afternoon, scores of men pulled off their trousers and shoes and sought comfort in the cool water.

Anderson had a piece of old soap that had been in the bottom of his knapsack for months, and was cheerfully scrubbing his filthy socks. The center seam of Anderson's ankle length drawers had split apart last winter, so he had cut the cloth from the legs into roughly square patches he used for cleaning his musket. He had taken one look at the split seat and crotch of the drawers and tossed them in the fire smoldering in his winter cabin. As soon as the stained flannel started burning and sending foul smoke into the tiny cabin, the other three residents left the inside warmth for the snowy cold outside. Since that time Anderson had simply used the extra-long tail of his shirt to keep his private parts from chaffing during the long marches. Today he was content to let the currents swirling around him work to wash the stiff grime off his shirt tail, since his sense of modesty had not allowed him to enter the river to bathe naked as the day he was borne.

Such misplaced modesty did not affect the other younger soldiers in Company K, who had no soap and no intentions of wasting their time in the river washing dirty socks. Instead they had quickly made a pretense at washing their shirts, drawers, and socks, since Sergeant Degas had made washing a requirement to enter the river. Then they found an overhanging tree a few yards up river that had an old rope tied to an upper branch.

"Remember the Alamo!" shouted Leon Fremon as he leapt off the tree branch, holding onto the rope, swinging out with legs akimbo until he released his hold on the rope, and splashed into the river next to Ambrose Hawkins. Hawkins replied with a lunge to grab Fremon as he surfaced and gasped for air. Fremon went under again with Hawkins on his shoulders and the two wrestled in the water, laughing and shouting. Jesús McDonald was next on the rope and sailed out, let go, and came down nearly on top of the wrestlers, who then turned on McDonald as a new common enemy.

Corporal Gill, wearing his only shirt, had stood in the shallows washing his under-drawers and socks, and then had sat down in the water near the bank, taken off his shirt and was now trying to clean it. He looked up from time to time to watch the three teenagers splashing, shouting, and dunking each other. Degas was sitting near him on a flat rock, his feet dangling in the water, staring at the river full of dirty and happy Texas soldiers.

"Mr. Gill, why are you not enjoying the water, as your comrades are? You are not an old man like me."

"Because I'm a corporal. And it ain't respectable for a corporal to fly through the air showing his manly parts to the world."

"Hmmm. I see. If that is so, you may want to put your shirt back on, as you may need to move soon to save your boys from the sleeping bear they are about to awaken."

Gill looked up to see Hawkins, Fremon, and McDonald, now allies, moving quietly behind Bernard Anderson until they were close enough to spring up from under the water onto his back. The quartet went under the water together amidst frantic splashing. In a few seconds Anderson rose up in the water with Hawkins clinging to his back and Fremon and McDonald each firmly held in a head lock, left and right. While Hawkins hooted and the captives sputtered to be let go, Anderson roared, took a deep breath and went under again. This time he stayed under longer, and when he came up, he still held Jesús on his right and had Hawkins encircled in his left arm. Fremon surfaced a yard away, yelping that he was damaged for life and began moving towards the shore. Then Anderson submerged again and soon popped up, this time gripping an ankle in each hand as he raised his thick arms, pulling up the remaining pair of attackers, who were buoyed by the water, and whose nether parts were even more exposed as each one's free leg flailed about and their heads remained underwater.

Gill who had stood and taken a few steps towards the underwater melee muttered, "Dammit!" just as Degas bellowed in his best command voice, "Anderson, drop those men!"

Anderson looked over at Degas, smiled like a fox, shrugged, let go, and called back to Degas, "Them possums owe me a pair of socks. I dropped mine when they jumped me. I'll take one sock from each of them."

"Fair enough," Degas called back, as the two privates surfaced downstream out of Anderson's reach.

"Ambrose, you and Leon and Jesse, listen to me," Corporal Gill admonished the trio who were fuming over their rough treatment while they dressed. "You had it comin' and got licked fair in a three on one tussle. Let it go now."

"Aw, Bain, I ain't mad about that. I'm mad I only got one sock now. How am I gonna march all day without a sock. I'll get a blister as big as a twenty dollar gold piece."

"You ain't never seen no twenty dollar gold piece. You both might want to cut off a piece of your shirt tails and wrap it around your bare foot. Might help, might not. Next dead Yankee you see, better hope he died with new socks on. You can each take one of them. Hurry up now. Captain's over there talking to Sergeant McGrew. Probably means we're about to move again."

Chapter 26

Mid July 1864, Northwest of Atlanta, Georgia
16 Men Present for Duty

The camp just north of the outskirts of Atlanta was no different from the many other camps that the Texas Brigade had established over the past two months. Since there was a shortage of horses and mules for the supply wagons, many of the supplies had been left in the depot warehouses, including the tents for the troops. However, some extra cooking equipment was available when the supply wagons did catch up to the men, and on those occasions there were usually a few men in each company who would try to make more elaborate meals than skillet fried meat and burnt cornmeal mush.

"I miss Miller. I do miss James," Jesús McDonald said to no one in particular.

"We all miss him," Ambrose Hawkins replied.

"Oh, I know that," McDonald said, "He was a good soldier and our friend. But, dammit, he could cook, too. And you and me burn ever' thing we put on the fire. How am I supposed to know how many coals to put on top of that oven settin' there? How am I supposed to know when to take the oven off the fire? I can't see inside it."

"Well, you might take it out of the coals and open the lid and look inside," Corporal Gill answered.

"Now, Bain, I could do that, yes, I could. But that oven is made of iron, and it's hot. It's too hot to grab onto. And if I use my jacket sleeve to protect my hand, it'll scorch my sleeve black. And then, even if I do that, I'll only see the top of the bread. The crust on top may look just dandy. Smooth, plump, and tan like a *señorita's* backside, but that bread is still gonna be raw in the middle and black on the bottom. Nah, there's just no good reason to go to all that trouble. When it's time to pull it out of the fire, it's time to eat it. However done it is or it ain't."

"Jesse, you don't know nothing about the backsides of *señoritas*. And you better not learn if you plan on sparking my sister when we get home. If we fought the whole war the way you cook, how do you reckon it would be? If the generals just did things by guessing? If they put us in where it was too hot, or didn't pull us out of the fire in time, or pulled us out too soon. If they did that, well, things would just be shot to hell."

Both Jesús and Ambrose looked over at Bain, wondering if he was pulling their leg or not. At that point Lieutenant Navarro approached the fire, his tin cup steaming.

"*Buenos Dias, mi amigos de Bexar,*" Navarro greeted the trio.

"Lieutenant, it's good to see you this morning, too. How about a handful of Jesse's latest baking surprise? We're just about to open up his morning's loaf of bread. If you can stomach bread that looks like a lady's butt on top, a gob of mud in the middle and a burned board on bottom."

"That sounds better than the piece of hardtack I've been dipping into this swamp water. You can roast a sweet potato 'til the roosters crow, and then boil it all morning, and it still resembles coffee no more than McDonald's creation resembles bread. My, but we do sacrifice for the cause, don't we. It will be nice to someday eat a meal cooked by a woman who understands such things."

"Yessir, that is surely the truth," Gill responded. "Now what news brings you to our campfire, sir? It seems every time you come over, it's to tell us we got a new general. Who is it this time? Did General Granbury get promoted already? Or maybe it's General Cleburne?"

"Yes, and No, and No, Corporal Gill. You are a smart *hombre*, for today I do indeed have news of a new general, but it is not our brigade commander or even our division commander. No, this time it is the commander of the whole army."

Quickly, Jesús spoke, "You mean General Johnston? Did he get shot too? Is he sick? What's happened to him?" Johnston was a popular general, and Jesús's questions reflected a concern that would be shared by a great number of the men under his command.

182

"No, Private McDonald, he is not wounded or ill. General Johnston has been relieved by President Davis. We'll be forming up the whole brigade later today for the adjutant to read the official order to us. It seems we have retreated too fast and too far and are now too close to Atlanta. The president fears General Johnston will allow Atlanta to fall into the Yankees' hands. And Atlanta is an important city. Perhaps the most important city left outside of Richmond."

"Hmmmph," Gill grunted. He knew better than to openly criticize the President of the Confederacy in front of an officer, even an officer who was a friend from home who had started the war as a corporal just as Gill had.

Jesús, however, felt no such reluctance to speak his mind.

"Don't see how any other general might of done any better. Ain't we fightin' about twice as many Union men as there are of us? If the president wants us to drive them Lincolnites out of Georgia, he might send General Johnston another army to help us. Thirty thousand more riflemen might make a difference, but there ain't a general nowhere that can do better than General Joe's been doin'. And I know, I been there ever damned step of the way."

"That's quite a speech, Jesús. But I do suggest you don't speak so openly about this particular decision made by Jeff Davis himself. You see, the new commander of the Army of Tennessee is General John Bell Hood."

By evening it seemed that in the camp of every company in every regiment in the whole army, every campfire was surrounded by soldiers weighing the pros and cons of the change in command. Many men were encouraged by General Hood's reputation as a fighter and his experience in the Army of Northern Virginia, learning from Robert E. Lee. Others were not so sure, and many were openly hostile to Hood. They saw his reputation as a fighter as a trait that may well lead him to abandon the successful defensive strategies that had been employed by General Johnston. By now they all realized the value of fighting from behind breastworks and the deadly dangers of assaulting men protected by logs and earthworks. Around every campfire, men were debating.

"I'm sure as I am that I'm a born-again Methodist, Hood is going to attack. He don't care about the numbers. He's goin' to send us out there to whup whatever Yanks is closest. "

"I ain't no damned Bible thumper, but I know we're too damned close to Atlanta not to attack. We got nowhere else to go, and we can't let Sherman have the supplies and ammunition we got in Atlanta."

"May be, but I sure don't want to attack no damyanks behind logs. I say keep on lettin' 'em come to us. We can ring Atlanta with logs and ditches an' hold out forever if we hafta."

"You mean hold out 'til all our food's gone, once the trains can't get in. How long would that take? No more'n a month or two I reckon. Nah, we'll be goin' out to 'em. Hood won't wait."

The men knew the importance of Atlanta since the city was the biggest rail hub south of Richmond, and the supply depots there were critical to keeping the army equipped and fed in the field. They knew they had run out of land, and a battle for Atlanta was just over the horizon, whoever was commanding the army. They knew their war was about to change.

Chapter 27

Late July 1864, On the Outskirts of Atlanta, Georgia
16 Men Present for Duty

"That is one big pile of knapsacks. It's as high as a house," Jesús said. Granbury's Brigade had just halted in a large plowed field. They had been deployed as skirmishers for most of the morning, supporting the flanks of the other brigades in Cleburne's Division. The Texans had seen only light action and only a few men had been wounded and none killed. Shortly before the noon hour they had come upon an immense pile of Federal knapsacks, where an entire regiment had left them. When the whole Union line withdrew under the Confederate attack, the guards detailed to protect the knapsacks ran off too, leaving behind the small mountain of belongings.

Bernard Anderson was already wading into the pile, looking for some secret clue that there was one special knapsack that contained riches beyond what the hundreds of other packs held. Men from every company in the regiment were already pulling packs off the edges of the huge pile of black canvas, and were digging into them. Even though it was in the heat of summer, eager Rebs were slinging wool blankets over their shoulders, and every rubber blanket was quickly claimed. Other contents from the knapsacks were being strewn around the field as men ignored any worn out clothing and kept searching for valuables.

Tin boilers with lids were popular, as were clean socks and shirts. Some men even stole small Bibles, but by far the most prized plunder were the glass daguerreotype photographs of pretty young women, the sweethearts of the Union soldiers. Since most of the young Confederate soldiers had never seen a photograph, the small glass portraits, some of which were tinted with colored paint, were curiosities that every man wanted to take home. That the subjects were attractive young women made the prizes all the more sought after. By the end of the hour the men were allowed to spend rummaging through the knapsacks, all of them had possession of stolen clothes, blankets, cooking ware, and especially the daguerreotypes. Many were putting on the Federal knapsacks to replace their own blanket rolls or worn out backpacks.

When the troops were back in their company formations, ready to march off, Major Fisher ordered the remaining ransacked gear to be collected and piled up again. He then had the pile set on fire, denying the Yanks the chance to reclaim whatever the Texans had not wanted to steal.

"Bain, you see this sweet girl? Look at her. Some Yank is going to be mighty sad that his darlin's picture has been carried off."

Corporal Gill took the leather case with the glass photograph in it as Jesús offered it to him to admire. Gill glanced at the pretty girl in the image, closed the case and dropped it onto the dirt where the next man in the column stepped on it and broke the glass as they marched down the road.

Jesús cried aloud, "Aw Bain, what did you do that for?"

"Are you going to court my sister when we get home? You keep saying you are."

"Why sure, Bain. I aim to approach your sister as soon as we get back."

"Then you don't need no picture of some Yankee girl. My sister Susan don't want no man wooing her if he carried around a picture of some Yankee girl in his time of warring and loneliness.

Jesús let out a loud sigh and said, "Bain, you are a true friend and loyal brother to Susan. You done the right thing. But that sure was a pretty girl whose face you just tossed into the dirt."

By afternoon the 6th-15th Texas was again on the battle-line, this time in a shallow trench dug by a Kentucky cavalry regiment whose men didn't like being ordered off their horses to construct earth works. Therefore, their trench was shallow with the excavated dirt thrown randomly out both sides of the ditch instead of being piled up in front as more cover. The cavalry had soon been sent further forward as dismounted skirmishers and the Texans were working hastily to deepen the shallow trench. There wasn't time to cut tree trunks for head-logs, but the infantrymen still worked with vigor to improve their defensive position.

The noise of the battle was both to their front and right. The armies were engaged near a ridge called Bald Hill very near to Atlanta. General Hood had indeed sought out elements of General Sherman's forces and had attacked with all the troops he could. Both armies had artillery in place and the shelling had become constant.

"Bain, I don't know whether to curl up in the bottom of this hole or to keep digging," Hawkins said to Corporal Gill. "My fingers are getting bloody from the rocks and this tin plate ain't much of a shovel."

"Ambrose, you keep digging. And stop complaining. You've been marching next to Jesse too long. You're beginning to sound like two ears of corn off the same stalk," Gill replied.

Hawkins didn't answer except to stroke his scraggly beard, but he kept digging.

The men from Bexar County were at the right end of the long trench and the troops from the Fifteenth Texas were digging in further down to their left. Company G of the original Fifteenth Texas was down to less than a dozen men and they had been consolidated with two other companies. The shelling from the Union batteries was already a concern to the Texans, but was about to become even worse because a section of twenty-pound rifled Parrot cannons had been unlimbered. These were the largest mobile cannons in either army, and the rifling inside the barrels allowed a good officer to aim with uncanny accuracy.

The Union captain who commanded the battery was standing on top of a limber, which was parked on the crest of a small rise. He was using his binoculars to scan the battlefield before him. The smoke of the mass musket fire and artillery had become a pervasive haze over the whole engagement, but from time to time a gust of wind would clear a patch of terrain of the smoke and the artillery spotters could identify enemy positions. For an instant the captain clearly saw the entrenchments at the point of an angle made in the center of the Confederates' position. He realized that his battery was to the side of those earthworks and his cannons could aim down the length of the exposed Reb defenses. It was a perfect enfilade that artillery officers dream of. He quickly ordered solid shot loaded and loosed his lieutenants and sergeants to begin firing.

Every man in Company A/K ducked in reflex to the sound of the first shot passing close over their heads. The solid ball of iron hit the ground and bounced beyond them, just a few feet in front of their trench. It scared them as all as the men could both hear the shell and feel the air moved by its

187

passing by. The second round went higher over their heads, but still the men began to drop down and press tightly against the dirt floor of the ditch.

Sergeant Degas was still standing behind the trench, calling to his men to keep low, while he kept a watch to their front for any Union infantry attack. The artillery barrage continued dropping round shot near Company A/K, but without causing any injuries. Finally, Captain Longnecker got word from Major Fisher that the regiment had been ordered to retire.

The Texans were not aware that General Hardee was watching from the rear and deemed the position too dangerous because of the enfilading artillery fire. His decision was influenced greatly by the messenger from General Cleburne's staff with the information that all of the men in Company G of the Fifteenth Texas had been killed or wounded by a single Union artillery solid shot. ("That is correct, General Hardee, ALL of the troops in that company were killed or wounded by one round!") The round shot had entered the trench in a flat trajectory at head height and decapitated three men and severely wounded several more before burying itself in the dirt wall of the ditch. The horrific scene had utterly demoralized the troops in sight of the slaughter, and it had been all their officers could do to hold them in position as the Union artillery continued pounding the earthworks from their elevated position on their target's flank.

The same night the Texas Brigade was on the march again. General Hood had reports that the left flank of the Union army was "hanging" loose, without reserves to protect the vulnerable rear areas behind the frontline regiments. Hood decided to send a large part of his forces around that way, marching through the night, and to attack early the next day.

"Bain, I'm tired. I'm so tired I think I'm sleepin' right this minute."

"Shut up, Jesse. Fall out and rest if you have to, but hush up now."

"Can't fall out, Bain. I can't trust you and Ambrose and the others to win the war without me. You know that."

"I know you won't fall out. You don't want to be left out of anything. In fact, why don't you steal another horse and ride ahead to show us the way?"

"Nope, it's too dark. Besides, I'm a man with a sweetheart back home now. No more hastiness for me. I'm sticking with you and even old Degas."

"Sure you are. Now shut up and march."

It was nearly midday before General Hardee was able to attack with most of his corps and, like so many other efforts, the coordination between divisions was poor. Instead of being a single advance, the assault broke into parts and then each of those pieces began to disintegrate into even smaller actions, each fought in ignorance of what was happening to either side.

The 6th-15th Texas moved forward, once again in a wooded area, and once again in a long skirmish line nearly 200 men wide. The skirmishers of the 6th-15th Texas were in front of the Seventh Texas and the 24th-25th Texas Consolidated Regiment as the whole division advanced, seeking to move past the main Federal battle line. Granbury's Texans were to the right of Govan's Arkansas Brigade, and the final brigade of Cleburne's Division, that of General Lowrey, was right behind the Texans. Granbury was ordered to clear the way to their front, moving fast, so that Govan and Lowrey could wheel left and attack the rear of the main Federal battle line once Granbury opened the way.

On the Federal side of the battle, General James McPherson commanded the Army of the Tennessee, one of three small armies that were under the overall command of General Sherman. It was McPherson's men who were trying to stop General Hood's effort to roll up the left flank of the Union forces that threatened Atlanta.

General McPherson had reports from the front delivered to him by couriers, but these short hand-written messages were always slow in coming and were often too far behind real time action to be helpful. In fact, sometimes such messages were dangerously counter-productive if he sent reinforcements or ordered a withdrawal based on reports from excited or frightened front-line officers who could only see a narrow segment of the whole battle. Therefore, General McPherson was like other good generals who most trusted their own reconnaissance, and that meant spending time near the front of the battle.

Sergeant Degas and Lieutenant Navarro were working hard to keep their men moving forward in the skirmish line. The terrain was partly covered in brush and rocks but there were also large open spaces that the skirmishers were reluctant to enter. Still, the whole regimental skirmish line was moving, the pairs of men working together. The front man fired and reloaded in place, while his partner moved up past him to repeat the process. The leapfrogging was slow, but it allowed the men to protect each other while loading and maintain a steady rate of aimed fire.

Navarro was kneeling ten yards behind Gill and the others, working as a spotter, searching and calling out the locations of Union skirmishers who opposed them. Navarro had just alerted Corporal Gill of a puff of smoke to his left, when he did a double-take. Immediately he called out to Gill and tried to get the attention of all of his men who were in sight. Knowing he was endangering himself even more, Navarro stood straight up and called to his men to look to their front right and shoot at the group of horsemen who had just emerged from a woods line a hundred yards away.

Corporal Gill saw the target group and let off a quick shot, calling to the others to fire now, not to wait for their partners to reload. The result was a staccato volley of six or eight muskets. A couple of the horsemen seemed to slump in their saddles, and the whole group of riders immediately turned and re-entered the protection of the trees behind them. With that, the men of Company K reloaded and resumed their leapfrogging advance against the Federal skirmish line.

Several hours later the skirmishers had been recalled and the Texas Brigade advanced all five regiments in a single long battle line, over a thousand rifles strong. When Granbury received the order to advance, the Texans were waiting on the uphill edge of a large sloping field about four hundred yards wide. The enemy was on the far side in unknown strength. When the bugles heralded the order to advance, the men stepped forward shoulder-to-shoulder. As soon as the brigade had stepped out into the open, the Federals on the far side of the field began firing. Almost all of their fire went over the heads of the Rebels. The Union soldiers were at the foot of the long slope and most of them didn't know to lower their aim to accommodate the downhill advance of their targets.

The field was bisected by a split rail fence. By the time the Texans reached the wooden barrier, the brigade line had grown ragged with some companies surging ahead or lagging behind. Seeing that climbing the fence would further disrupt the order of the formation, General Granbury shouted, "Tear down the fence. Don't climb over! Tear it down!"

Captain Longnecker heard the order and called immediately to Private Anderson, "Anderson, knock that fence down!"

Bernard Anderson looked at the fence, slung his rifle on his shoulder, and stepped to an upright post that was leaning sideways. He told Corporal Gill and the others to grab the rails that were slid into holes in the post. "Pull up on the rail, Gill, when I lift the post."

When the big private wrapped his arms around the post and nodded, the men of Company K pulled up the section of fence in front of them, heaving it over. The companies around them followed their lead and within seconds, the whole length of the old fence had been torn down, hardly slowing down the brigade battleline.

As Granbury's Brigade neared the far side of the field, the single regiment of Federals who had been firing at them withdrew. Granbury's regiments kept moving forward. Once again the 6th-15th Texas was advancing under a barrage by Union artillery. The men had enough experience by now to recognize what types of shells were being fired at them. Solid round balls, the shotgun shell-like canister rounds, and the exploding "shrapnel" shells all had distinctly different sounds as they passed over or landed near the men.

Lieutenant Navarro shared a general hatred for all artillery. Round balls were horrifying as they easily took off limbs and heads, while one round of canister hit like a full regimental musket volley. But shrapnel was the rain of death that he feared the most, and Navarro knew they were the target of the exploding shrapnel shells that day. If the Union gunners cut the fuses to the right length, the shrapnel shells exploded in the air above their targets, sending pieces of metal hurling down towards the ground. Along with the rest of the men surging forward, to avoid the danger of the metal shrapnel rain, Navarro instinctively bent forward at the waist to lower his stature.

The shell that exploded directly above the combined Company A/K killed one man and injured four others, including Lieutenant Navarro. Navarro fell as he felt the blow to his right thigh and looked down to see blood. He dropped his sword and put both hands tightly on top of the wound, praying the big artery that ran up his leg had not been cut. If it was, Navarro knew he would die.

He sat on the ground holding his leg and watched his regiment move forward, away from him. He was wondering if he could rise and try to walk, even crawl, back to the surgeons, when a litter carried by four musicians was set down next to him. Navarro felt relief, then intense pain as he was lifted onto the litter. All the time he kept the tight grip with both hands over the wound. He lay half on his side on the litter so he could keep pressure on his thigh. Finally he looked at one of the men carrying him and asked what he was afraid to know.

"Private, how much blood is there? Am I bleeding bad?"

The musician looked at the wound, and replied in his Irish brogue, "Not a drop of the ruby current to be seen, sir."

Navarro thanked God and closed his eyes.

Sometime later Lieutenant Navarro opened his eyes when he was lifted onto a table in a church building. The surgeon was a slight man with his shirt sleeves rolled up and wearing a blood stained apron. He dismissed the musicians to return to their task of carrying wounded soldiers away from the field. He then cut away the trouser cloth around the wound and looked intently at it. Next he ordered four enlisted men to hold down Navarro by each limb as he selected a scalpel to use to probe the wound. He mentioned to the lieutenant that he didn't have any chloroform to put Navarro to sleep, so he would just have to endure it.

The doctor spent no more than a minute digging in the wound, pulling out a patch of dirty jean cloth material that had been pushed in by the shrapnel and the iron shard itself, which had hit Navarro's leg bone and lodged there. After placing the twisted projectile in Navarro's hand, the doctor picked up a threaded needle from the small table behind him, and quickly stitched the wound closed. Without further comment, he sent Navarro off to a space under a tree outside, where it was cooler and the stench was less offensive. Navarro laid there the rest of the afternoon until around dusk when he was loaded on an ambulance wagon with another wounded officer. The two wounded men endured the pain of a long jostling ride into Atlanta where they were carried into a house.

Degas grabbed Corporal Gill by the shoulder as Gill was loading his musket, and shouted in his ear, "Have you seen Lieutenant Navarro?"

Gill shook his head no.

Degas then asked, "How about Captain Longnecker or Sergeant McGrew?

Again Corporal Gill gave a negative head shake. "Sergeant, for a long time I ain't seen no one but you and the boys. I've been doing what you say do, and just trying to keep Jesse, Bernard, and the rest of the San Antone men together. That ain't easy in all these trees and smoke."

Degas nodded and said, "Let's move to the right and try to find McGrew or the captain. I been seeing a lot of men I don't recognize and I'm worried we've drifted away from our regiment."

Gill nodded and immediately moved quickly to a tree further to his right and began to motion for his platoon to shift towards him. Meanwhile, Sergeant Degas moved by Gill so he could lead the small group of men from Bexar County in their quest to rejoin their command.

"Who's you men's captain?" The question came from an officer who emerged from the brush directly in front of Sergeant Degas.

"Captain Longnecker of the 6th-15th Texas Regiment," Degas answered.

The officer who was carrying a sword, but had no sign of rank on his coat, then said, "Is that 6-15 regiment in Cleburne's?"

"That's right. Granbury's Brigade. You know where they are? We seem to have misplaced them."

"Everybody's misplaced right now, Sergeant. If you're in Granbury's that means you're Texans and that's close enough to Arkansas for me. You're Joshes now. I'm pulling you boys into Govan's until we can all get sorted out. You're still fighting under Cleburne's flag, now follow me." The captain turned and went back into the brush without looking back.

192

Degas caught Gill's eye, and motioned with his head for them to follow the officer from Arkansas. As Gill led and the men filed by, Degas counted and found thirteen men were with him, four of them men he didn't recognize. Degas spoke to Private McDonald who was last in the group, "McDonald, you stay in back and make sure no one slips off, even those strangers. Don't shoot them if they try to disappear, but knock them down if you have to. We need them just like that Arkansas officer needs us."

McDonald looked at Degas and repeated, "Arkansas officer? We're fighting with an Arkansas regiment?"

"Yea, that's right. Now get going."

Jesús slowly moved along keeping the last man in their group in sight, slipping behind trees whenever he saw other figures through the haze. As he stepped back into the trail after a few seconds of watching three grey coated men move past on his left, Jesús collided with one of the strangers who had been moving with the Bexar men.

"Get out of my way," the man growled, moving to push past Private McDonald.

Shifting sideways to block the way with his musket held across his chest, Jesús replied, "No, *Señor*, Sergeant Degas said you have joined Company K for the day, *Vamos*, let's go back that way. You and me." The man was both older and taller than McDonald, but looking at the grim visage of the small young man pushing against him, he turned and moved up the trail, closely followed by Jesús.

Soon the pair caught up with the rest of Company K, and took positions on the right end of the group as they all slowly advanced, carefully probing into every patch of brush and ravine looking for the enemy. Degas and Gill were still unable to keep continuous visual contact with other Confederate groups in the smoke and thick woods. One small group would drift ahead of the cloud of Rebs and find themselves without flank support. They would then either hold in place until others joined them or, if under heavy fire, would retire until they met the advance of other Rebel groups.

"What's your name, anyway?" Jesús said to the stranger he had confronted on the path. The two were kneeling on the lip of a small rise, staring across a small patch of open ground, searching for any movement.

"Keenan. My name's Keenan. Charles. Charley," the man said as he spat tobacco into the sand in front of them.

"I'm McDonald. *Jesús*. Jesse to you *gringos*. Pleased to meet you, Charley. Where you from?"

Before Keenan could answer, three men bolted out of the trees across the narrow field, and ran straight at the men from the Sixth Texas. Jesús immediately fired, and one of the men grabbed at his arm, dropped his musket, and held his hand over the wound as the three kept running across the open ground

"Damn, McDonald, you got him," Keenan shouted as he aimed at one of the other men. Then Keenan felt a rough hand on his shoulder and turned to see a sergeant shaking his head sideways.

"Those are our boys. Don't shoot."

Keenan looked forward and as the trio reached the rise where they knelt, he realized the men were wearing dust-covered dark gray jackets, not blue coats. The three men climbed the short slope and dropped down behind McDonald, Keenan, and Sergeant Degas. Degas immediately told the wounded man to move on back to find a surgeon. When one of his comrades rose and started to go with him, Degas reached out and pulled the man backwards, not wanting to let an uninjured rifleman slip away. The man twisted out of Degas' grip, and spun to face him, bringing up his musket in both hands, pointed at the sergeant.

"Don't no man grab onto me, 'specially no damned half-nigger."

Degas dropped his arm and swung up his own musket, and as he did so the other man pulled back the hammer of his musket bringing it to full cock, ready to fire. Degas let his musket fall back to his side, but didn't let go of it or otherwise move.

"You shoot me, you will face a firing squad." Degas said calmly as the other man backed away.

"Not likely. Come on, Cletus, all three of us is going. These ain't our kind."

"No need for a firing squad, Sergeant," Jesús said.

Private McDonald was partly hidden by Degas and as the trio backed away, Jesús pulled his belt knife from its sheaf and hurled it at the man holding the musket. Jesús rarely practiced throwing his knife, and it landed hilt first on the man's chest, not wounding him, but it did cause him to reflexively pull the trigger of his musket as he jerked at the impact of the heavy thrown knife. The lead ball passed by Degas' ear. A second musket blast followed an instant after the first one, and a man fell to the ground where he lay still as a stone.

Degas looked around where McDonald was frozen in place, silent. Next to him, Keenan still sat and was reaching into his cartridge box for a new cartridge. He looked up at Sergeant Degas, shrugged slightly, and said, "That man was overdue. Used to be a sergeant. Moccasin mean, mean even for us Joshes. Got busted for stealin' from his own men. Nobody's gonna miss him."

194

Degas looked at Jesús and said, "Since you still are carrying that knife, you best learn to throw it so the sharp end goes first." With that Degas nodded his thanks.

Jesús grinned, got up and walked the few steps to the dead man. He bent over and picked up his knife and looked at the corpse's face.

"Mother Mary, I know that man. We met back at Arkansas Post. He tried to borrow me one day."

McDonald looked over at Keenan and nodded saying, "You're right, my new friend. He was overdue. You and him was in the same outfit?"

"Yea, Seventh Arkansas. Company D. Part of Govan's Brigade. But that sack of crap ain't been with us long. Captain tole us when that feller lost his stripes for thievin', they booted him over to us 'cause they can't just kick out a good soldier, even a snake like that one. Said we need ever rifle now. Never even learned his name." With that the man leaned over and spit tobacco again. This time it landed on the face of the corpse.

Degas was looking sideways and saw the whole line of Confederates was moving forward. He said, "No matter now. We're moving again." He noted that the wounded man and his last companion had disappeared into brush behind them and gave them no further thought.

Within minutes Degas saw the Arkansas captain through the trees and moved his men closer to him. The captain nodded and pointed for Degas to put his men into line with a dozen others. The captain held them in position for another quarter hour as more soldiers appeared and joined the growing formation. Degas saw a major approach the captain and watched the senior officer gesture with his arms how he wanted the captain to move his group forward.

The captain waved Degas over and told him, "The major says we are on the left flank of one of Govan's regiments, but they're all mixed up like us. He don't really know who is with them. The major thinks our boys got a chance to hit the flank of the Yanks in front of them, off to our right. We're going to get the men moving forward and when you see me wave, we're going to wheel right and smash that flank. You got it?"

"Got it. Let's go," Degas replied.

"Gill, you keep our boys going forward and when you see me wave, you turn 'em right and follow that Josh captain. He thinks we're gonna hit the flank of some Yanks. Go now, I'm gonna make sure these other fellows don't skedaddle on us."

Gill was relieved that for the moment they were not the targets of any musket fire. That made Gill think that maybe Degas was right, that they had an open path to surprise some Yanks. Gill made sure he could see Hawkins and McDonald and was glad when he saw Bernard Anderson close to the other two. Then Gill heard Degas call and looked over to see him waving to his right. Gill hollered for the Company K men to turn right and double quick forward, while he himself ran to take position on the extreme left of his platoon. No one needed to tell them to charge. The whole group of Texans and Arkansas soldiers could now see a few blue coated men firing, not at them, but in another direction. Gill realized they had caught an enemy formation in the flank, and without thought he howled like a hound and the others joined in.

The first Federal soldier to hear the yell to his right, looked up to see a line of running men in ragged clothes coming straight at him, screaming. He dropped his musket, turned and ran. He made it away, but the others in his company were slower, or braver, and they all either went down or dropped their weapons as their position was engulfed by the forty men who smashed into the vulnerable unsupported side of their formation.

Gill saw Bernard Anderson, trailed by Hawkins and McDonald, rush up to a wounded sergeant who was bleeding and kneeling, but still held onto a blue regimental flag. Gill wondered why the banner wasn't at the center of the whole regiment, protected on both sides by several companies of men, but in the same flash he realized the Yanks were as disordered and confused in the thick woods and smoke as the Rebs were.

Regiments meant little in this fight. The advantage went to whatever officer could cobble together a band of riflemen and find an enemy to attack. The weight of numbers often gave way to the shock of surprise and fury of an attack.

Meanwhile, Anderson didn't hit or shoot the wounded sergeant, but put his foot up on the man's shoulder and pushed him over, grabbing the flag staff with one hand as the standard bearer collapsed on the ground. Hawkins and McDonald both moved in front of Anderson to shield him and tried to push him back towards the other Confederates with his trophy. Other men in the charge saw Anderson with the blue flag and cheered as they moved further forward to keep pushing the Federals backwards.

Among the dozen men still advancing were Leon Fremon of Company K and Willy Oliphant from Company G. Quickly the group moved out of sight into more trees where they had seen the last Federals running away. Their initial rush into the trees ended after a moment, and the cluster of men stopped and looked around at each other, all searching for an officer or even a sergeant or corporal to lead them.

Finally, a tall private spoke up, "I think this is far enough. Let's go back." No one disagreed. As the men turned, they heard muskets firing, up close to their right side. Three of the Confederates fell, hit by musket fire that shocked them all.

A voice called out, "You are surrounded, drop your muskets." The tall private bolted back the way they had come, only to take two steps and fall, struck in the back by a minie ball. The other eight Rebs dropped their muskets and raised their arms over their heads. Leon Fremon and Willy Oliphant had become prisoners of war for the second time, neither of them having yet turned nineteen.

Chapter 28

The doctor took Navarro and two wounded captains to a house in Atlanta which he had commandeered as a temporary hospital. Navarro moaned in pain until the doctor gave him more morphine, which he had kept giving to the lieutenant for four days, until his supply ran out. By then the flesh surrounding the wound had become infected and swollen, popping open the stitches, until Navarro thought it looked and smelled like a rank red rose.

The doctor decided that to save the leg he would have to again clean the wound before the infection grew worse. He ordered his large orderly to hold the lieutenant still while he applied a white hot iron rod to the infected thigh, cauterizing the flesh both inside and outside. Navarro fainted from the unbelievable pain since this doctor had no chloroform, but awoke hours later with a scream when the doctor returned to prod the wound with his finger.

The lieutenant sat up and swung his fist at the doctor's head, bouncing a weak blow off his hat. The doc laughed and offered Navarro a bottle of whiskey. Still angry and half-delirious, Navarro took the whiskey bottle and threw it to the floor, smashing it and losing an increasingly rare medicinal tonic, an act which the doctor regretted immediately and the lieutenant regretted later. Navarro lay back down and began to wonder if his war was over and, if so, if he would ever be able to get home to San Antonio.

Two more days passed and Navarro slept. On the second day the doctor and his orderly loaded the other two wounded officers into a carriage and left with them. The Union army had gotten too near to stay any longer.

Navarro woke up to see a small girl sitting in the wooden chair by the dresser swinging her legs and staring at him. "Hello," the young Confederate officer muttered through his cracked lips. Without speaking the girl slid off the chair and ran from the room.

In a few moments a young Negro woman came through the door. Holding a broom, she stood at the foot of the bed, looked at Navarro and said, "Grace said you awake and spoke to her. She was watching you because the doctor feared you might... 'expire' is the word he used. Me, I think it's a mighty hot day to be knockin' on the door to The Promised Land. Anybody cross the river in this heat is more likely to be knockin' at Sam Hill's gate."

Navarro, now fully awake, nodded as he realized the woman speaking to him was extremely pretty. She smelled clean, was short, had slender arms, and a small waist under a full bosom. Her eyes seemed slightly slanted, her mouth was wide over a chin that was firm and protruded just a bit. Her cheeks dimpled when she made the joke about Sam Hill. She had a slender nose that was upturned, and a milk-chocolate face. Her hair was dark and wiry, with a few strands having worked free of the tight yellow turban that covered the top of her head.

Entranced by the fragrance of cleanliness that exuded from her, Navarro finally said, "That's right, I'm still here to endure more of Sam Hill's mischief on this side of the river. Yankee mischief more likely." He continued, "Might you set that broom aside and provide this thirsty living man a sip of the water that must be in that pitcher yonder?"

"I might be doin' that," the woman replied, leaning the broom against the wall. She poured water from the white ceramic pitcher into a small matching glass. Taking the few steps needed to stand next to Navarro, she held the glass out for him. He tried to pull himself up to lean against the headboard of the bed, but as soon as his thigh began to move against the sheet under him, he stiffened and groaned.

"Uh huh. Thought so. Your bandage is stuck to the mattress cover. Your blood and puss done glued you to the bed. Be still now and just hold up your head."

Navarro kept his mouth slightly open as she leaned over him and held the glass next to his lips so he could dip his tongue into the glass. He wiped his parched lips with his wet tongue and held his tongue out again, silently asking for her to move the glass so he could lap some water into his mouth. After two meager efforts, he dropped his head back and looked up at the young woman, who was still leaning forward.

"*Muchos gracias.* Thank you," he said as his gaze drifted from her hand holding the glass to her exposed cleavage above the blousing bodice of her dress. After two seconds of just staring at the caramel colored rounded skin that was lighter than her face, he jerked his gaze up. Instantly contrite and embarrassed, Navarro muttered, "You have lovely eyes," as he quickly looked past her out the window.

"Hmmmph. Those weren't my lovely eyes your own dark eyes was wanderin' around on. These lovely eyes can see you ain't ready to meet the Lord today. Are you Eyetalian?"

"No, *Señorita,* I am Lieutenant *Eugene Javier Navarro,* from *San Antonio de Bexar* in the state of *Tejas. Mi familia* crossed the ocean from *España* before I was borne into the world.

"You a Spaniard then?"

"*Mexicano*, and Texan, and Confederate officer, not a Spaniard."

"Glory, you sure be a passel of things fo' a man who's stuck to his mattress and can't keep from starin' at the bosum of a God fearin' woman. And just so's you know, my gramma crossed the ocean too. But she done it chained and layin' in pain and filth in the wooden belly of a slaver's ship."

"Saucy. I have awakened under the care of a saucy cleaning woman. Does your mistress allow such forward talk from her house servants?"

"Mistress done died tryin' to birth a young'n that died too. Mastah is away with Genrul Hood."

"If your master's gone, who's here with you?"

"Ain't nobody here but you, me and Grace."

"I mean besides me. I'm a guest and I'm stuck to the mattress. Where's the doctor?"

"He left yesterday. He loaded them other two wounded men into a buggy and git."

"But he left you."

"I don't belong to the doctor. I belong to Mastah Walters, an' like I say, he gone with the army. The doctor left you 'cause the buggy was full, and you're just a lieutenant. He said somebody's gotta be left. He tole me to stay with you, long as you breathin'."

"Hmmm. Well, a pox on all doctors. What of General Hood's army? Are they still fighting the Yankees north of town?"

"I hear the guns, but I ain't seen no army, blue or gray. Nobody's tole me what Genrul Hood be doin'. I seen wagons full of womens and furniture out on the streets all goin' away from the sounds, but I would notice an army marchin' through. An' the mastah would be stoppin' in to get his valuables if the Yankees is comin'."

"If General Hood retreats and leaves Atlanta to the Yankees, we've got to leave, too, before they get here. I am not eager to return to another Union prison camp. I have once before enjoyed their hospitality and do not wish to repeat the experience."

"You can't go nowheres. You be stuck to the bed, and too weak to even git out of the bed. You ain't had food in days. An' I ain't goin' nowhere neither. Mastah be comin' back and will take care of me and Grace. An' if he don't come, them Yankees you so scared of, don't scare me none. I'm goin' to open the door wide on the first knock, and let them in. They goin' to make me and my little girl free persons."

"Grace is your daughter? I thought she was Master Walters child."

"Sho' she is, but she's from my loins."

"But, she looks white."

The woman smiled a wry grin and said, "'Yes, don't she. Not just Mastah Walters, but her grampa, and his pa before him, all white men who took a likin' to my gramma's and ma's same 'lovely eyes'" you was feastin' on. That lil' girl come down from three white daddies. She look white, and when she's older, she's gone live white. This war is gone to open doors fo' her, just like I'm gone to open the door to this house to them Yankees. Now you lay there and stay awake while I go fetch you some soup. If you goin' befo' the Yankees git here, you gots to eat."

While he waited Navarro considered his situation for a moment and then fell asleep. He was roused a few minutes later as the woman set a soup bowl on the table next to his bed.

"You can't eat layin' flat. I've loosed the corners of the bed cover, so you use your arms to pull up and sit. The sheet will move with you."

Navarro pressed his arms against the mattress and pushed. His wounded thigh hurt as he moved up, and it remained stuck to the blood-clotted sheet as he fought his way to a sitting position with his back against the headboard.

The woman held out the soup bowl to him, and with beads of new sweat on his forehead, he took it. Then Navarro glanced down and saw to his eternal embarrassment that the cover across his midsection had not moved up. His private parts were no longer private. With both hands holding the steaming soup bowl, he could only mutter, "Ughhh..."

With the same wry smile, the woman reached down and pulled up his cover, saying, "Who you think been carin' for you day and night? You think I been nursin' you with my lovely eyes closed?"

Navarro didn't even try to respond as he spooned the hot soup into his mouth and refused to look up.

The wounded man remained in bed that day and the next, nursed by the young woman with the lovely eyes. Navarro admitted to himself that "for a Negro," she was a handsome woman. When she brought him more food and cleaned his wound the first evening, working together they gently unstuck his backside from the sheet and she managed to slide a fresh sheet under him. Navarro tried to mask his embarrassment of his near nakedness by asking tentative questions about her life in Atlanta. She replied cautiously at first, not with the same wit and candor she exhibited when he first awoke.

When he finished his meal, she changed his bandage, whereupon, instead of leaving, she began asking questions about his family, about life in the army, and how Mexicans were treated in Texas. Navarro began to talk, trying to explain the tenuous relations between white Texans and *Tejanos* like him. He had to explain that *Tejanos* were Mexican families who had sided with the Anglo settlers against the Mexican general *Santa Anna* during the war for Texas' independence over 25 years ago.

Navarro described life on a ranch in Texas, spoke of the longhorn cattle, of six foot long rattlesnakes, of the heat, wind, and dust, and of the constant threat of wild Indians raiding, murdering, and burning out ranches. He spoke of how he and his brother had been sent away from home to be schooled by Catholic priests in a mission, and the austere years of study, farm work, and prayer as a lonely student. The young woman was interested in the priests who taught Navarro. At first, she wouldn't believe that priests couldn't marry and lived celibate lives. She was confused when Navarro tried to explain how Catholics extend their reverence for the blessed Jesus to include the Lord's earthly mother, Mary.

By this time it was near dusk, and still the woman did not leave. She began to tell her own stories. She revisited the day as a child when she was taken from her mother in the slave quarters on the Walter's family's plantation, and sent to learn the work of a house servant, then sent to their city house in Atlanta. She said she was picked because she was short and not strong enough to drag a heavy sack up and down the rows of cotton plants from dawn until dark during the picking season. She spoke of how her sister and younger brother were sold to a neighbor who had bought new acres of bottom land and needed more hands in the fields. She spoke of the stories from the Good Book that she hoped Grace would someday be able to read to her after the war when Negro children would be able to go to school and learn their letters.

By the time the young woman finished telling of her life, it was fully dark. But instead of returning to sleep, Navarro began to tell about the men in his company, those who had joined the army with him back in San Antonio. He spoke of how stupid they all had been to think the war would be a grand adventure. They thought it would be like a hunting expedition, where some days might be uncomfortable and hard, maybe even dangerous, but not too dangerous. It would be a fine journey with friends and fatherly officers. They would get to see the country but still come home after a few months, victorious and heroes. Navarro finally looked straight at the woman and said, "What fools we were."

He found himself speaking about hardships the soldiers made light of with each other, but each of them hated: Trying to sleep through cold rain storms, shivering and shaking with no way to stop; rarely having enough food to fill their bellies; learning to eat badly cooked food every day, or worse, eat raw bacon or rotten beef that would knot up their guts and turn a man's stool into mush that couldn't be controlled. He spoke of men wearing out their shoes and marching barefoot for weeks until a supply wagon reached them; he told how men didn't hesitate to take the shoes from a dead soldier.

Comfortable now in the presence of this quiet young woman, Navarro spoke of how a lieutenant was responsible for what other men did. That he had to make sure the sergeants and corporals took care of the work details and watched over the others. He described how he could not interfere when the sergeants disciplined the men, but he still had to make sure they were firm, but not brutal.

Finally, Navarro talked about his men in battle. He described how some men never shot their muskets and most men never aimed. He spoke of those who faked injuries and others who would quickly "help" a wounded comrade back to the hospital and not return until the fighting was done. He told of those who simply fell to the ground and covered their ears when the shooting wouldn't end or cannon shells began exploding near them.

He did not describe the filth and horror of the battlefields, of friends dying next you, of men and horses blown apart, their offal covering the ground, of the stench that lingered in his clothes. He did not speak of many things that were best left behind, nightmare images that might one day fade, but would be waiting for him in the next battle, and there always seemed to be another battle.

He grew weary of speaking about the army and the war, and asked if she was the only house servant. She told him of Master's man servant, Isaac. Master had taken Isaac with him to the war, and she didn't know if either of them were still alive, but no one had come around to tell her otherwise.

He asked if Isaac was her man, and she said no, but he used to swat her behind and wink at her sometimes. Then she pointed out the window to the backyard where a small stable was in one corner and a white outhouse in the other, both barely visible in the moonlight.

"Isaac was in there one day," she said pointing to the outhouse. "I was in this room cleaning, and saw Isaac bang the door open and bust out, pulling on his braces to hold his britches up. I laughed, thinkin' Mastah had called him fo' he was done, but then I remembered Mastah was gone on his horse. Isaac run into the kitchen and tole me while he was sittin', he felt a sting down under. He jumped up thinking a yella wasp done stung him, and then he seen a big brown spider drop off his man parts. He knowed he been spider bit, and run to the house. He said it burned bad. I told him I ain't treatin' his privates, but I'd make a poultice he could spread on the bite. I done that, and went on 'bout my business.

Next day, Isaac didn't get up from his bed in the stable. He told Mastah that his man sack done swole up like a melon and turned hard. Mastah sent me to fetch the doctor, and he come and looked. Doctor said Isaac's bite was the baddest he ever seen. He said the onliest way to save Isaac is to cut off Isaac's sack befo' the poison spread all over his body. Mastah, he rubbed his chin, then say do it, and Mastah and me hold down Isaac while the doctor used his knife."

Navarro swallowed down bile, relieved the young woman couldn't see his face in the faint glow from the lantern. She said that Isaac recovered, but he never paid no more attention to her

They talked more about things less sad and as the hours passed, the lantern ran out of oil. At last, in the dark when neither of them had any more stories to tell, Navarro reached his hand out to touch her cheek. The young woman did not pull away as she accepted the new intimacy. The touch sparked their awareness of each other's physical closeness, so they talked still more, joining hands at some point until finally, in the last hour before dawn, she joined Navarro in his bed. She was not inexperienced, as her widowed master often summoned her to his bedroom. She willingly helped Navarro through his initial hesitations and clumsiness, until they joined together, passionate, sweating and silent in the dark, in spite of his wounded thigh. He then slept again, and she left his bed and washed herself with water from the pitcher on the dresser.

The woman went down the stairs to the small room in the back of the house which she shared with Grace, but she didn't sleep. She lay next to her daughter and thought about how things were for her in this house. She thought about the many nights in Master's bed, reliving his drunken couplings with her. She thought of the things he demanded of her in bed and elsewhere. Then she thought about the hour with Navarro, how he caressed her face and throat over and over again. Her cheeks dimpled as she remembered how he would not touch her breasts until she placed his hand there herself. How then his hands never seem to leave, stroking in circles around each one and softly squeezing her nipples until she ached. She tore away from those fresh memories when she began to tingle and wanted to touch herself. She drifted into thoughts about the war, about Grace, about Texas, and what would happen when the war ended. Even if she and Grace were free women, what then?

When it was clear to her what she must do in the days ahead, she got up, went to the kitchen and made a large breakfast plate of fried eggs, warm bread, and even jam from the jar she had long kept hidden in the basement. She regretted not having ham or bacon to add to the plate, but still, Sweet Jesus had made this fine morning for her, and the new day offered hopes she had not dared to dream before now. With those comforting thoughts she put the heavy plate on a tray and carried it upstairs to her new man, wondering if rattlesnakes and cows' horns really did grow six foot long in Texas.

Navarro had already used the bedpan before the young woman came in carrying the tray of food. He was back in bed, studying his healing wound, since the bandage had not lasted intact through their predawn encounter. Navarro was thinking of how he had earlier described his infected wound as a rank red rose. Thankfully, the infection was gone, so he wouldn't call the wound rank, but he thought the puckered flesh still resembled a dark red rose.

When the young woman entered the room, Navarro hastily pulled the covers up to his chest. He kept his eyes down as the wooden tray was placed on his lap. He murmured a thank you and began shoveling eggs into his mouth. As he ate, with his mouth still full, he at last looked up at the young woman who was standing patiently by his bed. He started to speak, and had to quickly swallow unchewed bread, before he could blurt out, "I don't know your name."

Once again the dimples appeared and she said, "I wondered what you would call me this morning. Or if you would look me in the face, and not just at my lovely eyes."

Navarro blushed deeply and extended his arms above the breakfast tray. She took his hands in hers and sat next to him on the bed. "My name is Rose."

Navarro and Rose did not touch each other the rest of the day, not even to hold hands for a brief moment. Rose took the food tray back to the kitchen and returned to Navarro's room with Grace. Grace sat in the chair and played with a doll made of burlap cloth and stuffed with straw. She hummed softly to her dolly as her mother sat on another straight chair and opened a small wooden box that sat on the floor. She pulled out a hank of thread and a needle and prepared to mend the tears and holes in Navarro's uniform frock coat. Navarro watched while she threaded the needle, then with his belly full, drifted back into sleep and began to snore. Rose spent much of the morning replacing missing brass military buttons with wooden ones, putting patches inside both sleeves at the elbows and closing the outside holes with tight stitches held in place by the new patches. She repaired split seams in several places around the waist, collar, and sides of the coat.

Soon after she started to work on the young lieutenant's coat, she felt a weight near the bottom hem in the back. She found two pockets in the back tail of the coat, pockets that weren't obvious. She reached to the bottom of one of them and pulled out a small single shot pistol. She quickly and gingerly set it on the bedside table next to Navarro's head. In the other pocket, she found several letters folded together and tied with string, along with a small leather notebook half-filled with hand-written pages. She set these by the pistol on the table. Now, curious what else might be in the coat, she found a chest pocket in the coat's flannel lining. Reaching in, she felt something flat, and brought out a wooden comb with several teeth missing. So, she thought, my lieutenant from Texas cares how his hair looks. She put the comb back, without ever considering that Navarro used the wooden comb not to look well groomed, but to pull lice out of his tangled hair.

As she was finishing her repairs on the coat, Navarro opened his eyes and said, "The sawbones cut my trousers and drawers off when he first worked on me. I am bedbound and without pants. I also don't know where my shirt is."

"I done washed your filthy shirt. I'll brush your coat now that I've put it back together. You look to be 'bout the same around the stomach as Mastah is, so I've taken a pair of wool trousers from his clothes trunk. Got no drawers for you, but Mastah has an old pair of boots, and I darned up some old socks. The boots got a hole in the bottom, an' he was goin' to take them for new soles, but Mastah and the cobbler both went off to the army before he done it. The holes ain't very big yet and I can put some paper in the toes if they be too big. If Mastah misses his old boots or his britches, I tell him you just took them. Might be he will cotton to them being worn now by another Confederate officer, one who was wounded and healin' in his house."

"Rose, you have done me admirably well. I can use my shirt tail for drawers. Most of the men don't wear them no way. And you did comb your hair very nicely this morning."

Her smile returned as Rose accepted the compliments. For the midday meal, she brought up a vegetable stew and bread for all three of them to eat together. Rose knew time was short and she wanted Navarro and Grace to be together all day. She had no doubt Navarro would think about Rose herself when he left them, but she also urgently wanted Navarro to remember her daughter once he rejoined the army.

In the afternoon Navarro wrote a note to his commander, describing what had happened to him. He didn't ask Rose to deliver the message to anyone, but it seemed important to him that he document where he had been. He carefully folded the paper and put it in one of the tail pockets of his mended frock coat.

Late in the afternoon Rose gave Navarro a wooden cane and he slowly pulled himself off the bed and stood. He winced when he put weight on his wounded leg, but he made himself walk, slowly and stiffly at first, leaning heavily on the cane. He made the first hard steps to the door and went into the hall and finally reached the top of the stairs. On the long march back to his bed he put more weight on his bad leg, finding it burned and hurt, but was bearable if he just ignored the pain. He reflected that life, complete with war, injuries, and recovery, just wasn't supposed to be easy. But now there was Rose.

That night Confederate troops marched through Atlanta. Long columns of filthy and weary infantrymen trudged down the main streets. Rose put her little girl to bed and made sure the child was sleeping soundly before she again went to Navarro's bed.

When the urgency of their passion was past, they lay next to each other touching and talked of Navarro leaving the next day to find his regiment. They spoke of what might happen in Atlanta in the coming days and weeks. Navarro promised that when the war ended, he would come back to Atlanta and find her. He would take her and Grace to Texas. Rose promised to stay at this house and, if it was burned, she'd find a way to stay nearby. She would watch and wait for him. She knew people who would help her and

Grace. Somehow they would get by until he came for them. Neither of them spoke of the chance of Navarro being killed before the war ended, or of the hardships that would surely confront Rose and Grace in the times ahead.

Early the next morning, Navarro was up and dressed in Master Walter's trousers and boots and his own clean shirt and mended uniform coat. Rose had failed to persuade him to stay even one more day. He was determined to find his company while they were still around Atlanta. He only wished he had a hat. Rose wished she could give him the blanket off Master's bed, but knew she dare not. He might still appear at the house before the Yankees came and, if he was drinking, he might connect the missing blanket to his dead wife, and grow angry about losing one more memory of her. Rose understood that was natural, but she did not want to suffer a beating for his drunken memory. She had felt his leather belt on her back too often. Never again. She didn't say any of this to Navarro. She was relieved when he never mentioned taking the blanket off the bed with him, and she took solace that it was still summer. Navarro's long wool uniform coat would be ample night cover for several more weeks.

Rose and Grace came into bedroom, Rose holding out a haversack stuffed with bread, hard boiled eggs, and two small apples. She didn't have a canteen to give Navarro, but she had found a hollowed-out gourd in the stable, and she had shaped a piece of a green sapling branch to plug it, and tied a strip of twisted cloth to the neck of the gourd to make a short strap.

Navarro left the little pistol with Rose, loaded with powder and ball, but no way to reload it. He admonished her to keep it in her dress pocket all the time. He made her sit still on the bed and listen while he sternly told her, "When the war ends, times will be hard, even harder than now, and wherever you and Grace are, cruel or drunken men will be nearby. If you ever pull the pistol out to protect yourself, or Grace, let the man get close. If he's a white man, hold your arm out straight, and when the pistol almost touches the man, shoot him in the leg between his knee and waist. He'll go down. Don't kill him, or you will likely be lynched. Woman or not, pretty or not, you would still be a Negro killing a white man and you would receive swift retribution. If your attacker is a Negro, shoot him in the face. No lawman or judge cares if 'a nigger wench shoots a nigger buck', unless he owns one of them. And nobody is going to own you or any man soon enough. In either case, as soon as you shoot, throw the gun down and start screaming, and keep screaming loud and long until someone comes. If no one can see you do it, tear your dress around your 'pretty eyes.' Sob and cry."

Rose stared at Navarro a long time after he finished. His instructions scared her, scared her a lot, but she knew there was truth in his thinking. She finally nodded and put the miniature pistol in her dress pocket, determined it would stay right there until she saw him again. She knew she could use it to protect Grace, and hoped she could to protect herself.

Navarro kept the cane, and with the gourd and new haversack slung over his shoulders, he tenderly made his way down the steep stairs. He went out the front door to the street, turned to his left and started the long walk to rejoin his regiment in defending Atlanta. Rose and Grace stood behind the curtains of an upstairs window and through the narrow gap, watched him until he was out of sight.

Chapter 29

Word reached Granbury's Brigade that a Yankee general had been shot by skirmishers during the fighting near Bald Hill. No one could personally claim credit for the lucky shot that killed the commander of the Army of the Tennessee, General James McPherson, but many of the men of Granbury's Brigade were eager to acknowledge their presence on the skirmish line and their personal high degree of marksmanship. At that time Lieutenant Navarro was still in the house in Atlanta, slumbering through a morphine haze, so he wasn't able to put his recollections of the skirmish that day in the official report of the engagement.

Leon Fremon had seen the other private often enough to know they were in the same regiment. Now, under guard at a train siding, they sat on the ground in a tight group in the midst of scores of other captured Confederates, all encircled by a company of Union soldiers. The young man had said his name was William Oliphant, and he was in Company G. Oliphant, Fremon, and four other men were talking in low voices about their prospects for escape. All six had been captured at Arkansas Post in their very first battle, and they knew they were lucky to have been exchanged after only three months of prison camp. Now, having become prisoners a second time, all of them were willing to take dangerous risks to escape, rather than return to a northern prison.

The man leading the conversation was a sergeant named Westmoreland. He was older, around thirty, and spoke with conviction. "Boys, our only chance will be while we are on the train. And it's got to be while we are still in Georgia. We're going to need luck and a loyal farmer or two along the way to feed us. And we're going to have to stay in the woods and hide out during the days. They are going to send out cavalry to look for us, and we'll be behind the Yankee lines. That means the roads will be thick with Yankee provosts patrolling for deserters and running Rebs like us. And they'll be guarding ever crossroad and village."

A plan quickly took shape as they talked. If the prisoners were loaded onto an open flat car, the plan was straightforward. The six men would simply rush together, push past any guards near them, and jump. But they would have to wait until as near dusk as they dared, and wait until the train was nearly to the top of a long incline and going slow. If the flat car had side rails, they would vault over them as they jumped. Then they would take cover in the forest and divide into pairs. Each two men would head west for three nights and hide during the day. Only after three nights of travel would they turn south to find a way around the Union army.

"What if they put us in a box car?" Oliphant asked the sergeant.

Westmoreland considered the question for a long moment, then said, "William, you seem to be the best talker. Are you a brave man, too?"

"Brave enough, I reckon," Oliphant replied.

"Then once we get in that box car, you watch me. I've already seen they leave one door open a foot or two for light and fresh air. I'll get close to the door where I can see out. You set down right next to the guard they're sure to put in front of the door. When you see me take my hat off and wipe my forehead, you stand up and start up a conversation with the guard. While you're talking and got his attention, I'll ease up next to him, squat down, and stick out my leg behind him. When I do that, you shove him hard right towards the door and he'll trip over my leg and fall out. We all go out right after that guard."

All the men nodded as they considered Westmoreland's plan, and finally Fremon spoke up, "William, we're in the same outfit, and are nearly neighbors back home, you being from Austin town, and me from San Antone. I'll be right by you. If there's two guards by the door, I'll handle the second one as soon as you shove the first one. If need be, I'll wrestle him right out that door and land on top of him when we hit the ground."

211

The other three young privates remained silent but nodded their thanks to Oliphant and Fremon.

In the early afternoon, a train pulled onto the siding and the prisoners were loaded into six box cars. The six Texas prisoners stayed close together as the line of southerners shuffled to the open doorway of the third box car. As soon as they were inside, they spread out, but stalled and let other men pass them so they all remained close to the door. Four Union guards followed the forty prisoners into the car, two shoving their way through to the door on the far side which remained closed and locked from the outside. These two guards leaned against the door and stayed next to each other. The other two pulled the second sliding door to within a foot of closing and took standing positions against the board wall on either side of the door gap. More Union soldiers climbed up to the roof of each car and sat down.

Soon the train rolled onto the main track. The prisoners all found space to sit on the rocking floor of the car or stood, leaning against the walls. It was hot and stuffy. Oliphant sat within a few feet of one of the guards by the open door. Fremon squeezed into a place against the wall on the front side of the open door, standing within a foot of the other guard. Westmoreland sat between Oliphant and the wall. For three hours Westmoreland sat still, watching the countryside go by through the narrow gap in the door. During that time he came to recognize the small jerks when the couplings between cars shifted as the train began to go up inclines. He tried to pay attention to how much the train slowed as the steam engine labored up hills, since he wanted to make their escape when their box car was going as slow as it was going to get.

Finally, Westmoreland figured this was the time, He could see through the gap that the track curved to the left and that train was just starting up a long grade. The hillside had been logged, allowing him to see the long curve of the train tracks, but there was enough brush for immediate cover after they jumped. The sergeant was sitting right behind Oliphant, so instead of taking off his hat to signal him, he extended his leg and nudged the young soldier. Oliphant nodded and stood up. He told the guard by the door that he needed to relieve himself and asked if he could stand in the doorway to do so. The guard grunted and said, "No way, Reb. Just do it in your trousers if you can't hold it."

Oliphant then asked if there was a slop bucket in the car, and the guard shrugged his shoulders. Oliphant hung his head as if in disgust with the guard's answer and started to turn back to sit down again, and saw Westmoreland's leg stuck out behind the guard's feet. Oliphant changed his movement from a turn to a forward push with his shoulder and both arms.

The guard fell back over Westmoreland's legs, bumped his bottom on the edge of the floor right in the open gap, and kept going backward right out of the box car.

Fremon was alert and did his part. The instant the other guard started to raise his musket and turn, Freemon jumped sideways right into him, both of them falling onto the floor in front of the opening in the door. Westmoreland was right there and together the two Texans grabbed the guard and jostled him out the door. Before Westmoreland and Fremon could get up off their knees, the other three men in the conspiracy stepped to the opening in the door and jumped, one after another without hesitation or looking back. Oliphant had fallen to the floor when he shoved the first guard to trip him on Westmoreland's legs. He was now the furthest back from the door and closest to the remaining pair of guards. He had to wait for a precious few more seconds for Westmoreland and Fremon to find their legs and jump. As the sergeant pulled himself up behind Fremon and jumped out the door, Oliphant heard a loud voice behind him, "Move, Reb, and I'll blow a hole in you!"

Oliphant heeded the threat by dropping from his knees to his belly and rolling to the side. The Union soldier who shouted, pulled the trigger of his musket, gouging a long splinter from the wooden floor, but narrowly missing Oliphant and not hitting any other prisoner. Oliphant kept scrambling to put other prisoners between him and the guards by the other door. The guard who fired hit the muzzle of his musket against the roof of the car to be sure the soldiers on the roof understood he needed help. Meanwhile the other guard, now nervous and sweating, held his loaded musket at the ready, knowing if he did shoot he and his mate could quickly be overpowered by the prisoners in the car.

The tense tableau between the prisoners and the guards ended when the train finally stopped and soldiers climbed down from the roof and poked their cocked muskets into the door. All of this took some minutes, as the engineer first had to get the message of the escape, throttle down the engine and bring the train to a slow stop. By this time, it was dusk, and it took the officers of the guard company who had been riding in the caboose several more minutes to enter the box car with a squad of armed troops. It was nearly dark in the closed box car. Oliphant had stayed low and wormed his way to the rear wall, and sat with his head down, shaking and angry that he had not made it out the door. He didn't know if his friends were dead or crippled by the jumps, or moving fast away from the tracks. He only knew he was still a prisoner and had ruined his only chance to escape from a second imprisonment, an imprisonment that this time would last until the war ended. Then it came to him that the two remaining guards might identify him and he might be shot or hanged, especially if the two Yankees who had been pushed off the train had been killed when they fell.

The Union lieutenant climbed into the boxcar, walked to the two guards by the other door and told them to fetch the man who had pushed the first guard off the train. They both hesitated and finally told the officer they didn't see his face and all the prisoners look the same from the back in the weak light. Then the lieutenant shouted for the man who had pushed out the guard to step forward like a man. No one moved and no one turned to look at Oliphant Then the officer shouted that the whole carload of prisoners would be denied all food and water until the guilty man gave himself up. With that the officer left the box car, taking all the guards with him. The open door was pulled shut and the lock bar dropped down on the outside of the car. The officer thought when they stopped at Chattanooga the next day, either the other men would rat out the man, or he would give himself up so the others might be fed and watered.

As the night passed, the other prisoners ignored Oliphant. The next morning the train pulled into the freight yard at Chattanooga, and the six box cars were pulled onto a side track and uncoupled from the engine and caboose. The doors to five of the six box cars were opened and water buckets and crates of hardtack crackers were shoved into each one. The doors were left open and a squad of armed guards took positions on the ground in front of every door. The doors to the car involved in the escape remained closed and locked, as the sun rose and the summer day grew hotter each hour. The temperature in the car rose with the sun and by noon the box car had turned into a suffocating wooden oven.

In the early afternoon an ambulance wagon escorted by two riders approached the boxcars. The lieutenant of the company of guards went to the back of the ambulance to hear what the horseback lieutenant had to say. The guard lieutenant turned to shout orders to his sergeant.

The doors to the last boxcar were pulled open and with loaded muskets aimed, the guards began yelling at the prisoners inside to jump down and form a line. The first prisoners jumped down, but some of the men more fell than jumped. On the ground they all gasped in fresh air. Within a few minutes the thirty-seven men were lined up, some holding others upright. Two guards stood at the back of the ambulance and together they pulled out a litter and set it down so the head of the litter rested on the back of the wagon, putting the man on it in a semi-prone position. The soldier on the litter had one leg in a splint from waist to foot, and his chest and head were

214

encased in bandages. But his eyes were clear, and he nodded to the lieutenant.

The line of prisoners was ordered to slowly walk past the wounded man. When Oliphant realized what was happening, he tried to duck his head and hide under the brim of his hat. He held his breath and clinched his fists when he passed the litter. When he was three steps past the litter, he heard, "That's him. That's him." Oliphant tried to keep shuffling forward, but he was jerked out of the line by a sergeant standing next to the injured man's litter. The injured soldier lifted an arm and pointed, saying, "That's the little pile of dung that pushed me off the train."

Manacles were locked onto Oliphant's wrists and ankles and he was roughly manhandled into the back the wagon that had delivered the crates of hardtack for the prisoners. The other prisoners were ordered back into the box car and the lieutenant reluctantly directed that they be given water and hardtack before the train continued its journey north

Three days later, Private William Oliphant, eighteen years old, a veteran of two years of campaigning, wounded three times, and twice a prisoner of war, stood before the Court Marshal in a small upstairs room in the hotel that was serving as the division's headquarters.

"Private, did you push a guard off the train yesterday?" asked the major leading the questioning.

"No sir. I didn't push nobody. I was sittin' down sleepin' when I heard noise that woke me up. I didn't do nuthin'."

"Private, we have a report here from Lieutenant Clark that Private Mahone, the seriously injured, and now deceased guard, did identify you as the prisoner who pushed him from the train. During his fall he incurred the injuries that led to his death. What do you have to say to that?"

"Nuthin'"

"I see." The major looked at the other two officers sitting to his sides, and they both nodded.

"It is the ruling of this court that the accused, one William Oliphant of Texas, a private in the rebellious armed mob that calls itself the 'Confederacy,' is guilty of murder of Private John Mahone during Oliphant's unsuccessful attempt to escape from the legal custody of the US Army. Therefore, I sentence William Oliphant to be hanged by the neck until dead. The sentence will be carried out tomorrow at the hour of noon.   That is all. This court marshal is adjourned. Return the condemned man to his cell."

"Get up," the sergeant said as he kicked Oliphant in the side. "It's time." Four more guards were waiting in the hall to escort Oliphant out of the city jail. They were speaking to each other and the sergeant in German, laughing at something Oliphant could not understand, but he guessed to be about his eminent death. The sergeant knelt and unlocked the manacles on Oliphant's ankles and then undid the ones on his wrists. Surrounded by the four armed guards, Oliphant walked out into the street. There stood the major who chaired Oliphant's court marshal. He was holding a folded paper, looking very unhappy. The detail stopped in front of the major and the sergeant saluted.

The major returned the salute, then said to the sergeant, "Escort this scum to the train siding where the other captured Rebs are. The commanding general has determined that it is the right of a prisoner of war to attempt escape, even if that means killing a guard to do so. He has overruled my judgment to hang this sorry sonofabitch. Private Oliphant is now going north to Camp Chase where he can rot and starve, damn his black soul. Get him out of my sight."

Chapter 30

"**B**ain, here's how I see it. General Hood done give us a chance to hold onto Atlanta. He saw we weren't gonna beat 'em back by stayin' in our trenches. It was like when we round up them old wild longhorns, we have to leave camp and go out in the thickets after 'em. That's what General Hood done. But it didn't work so good. There's just too many northern boys down here to round 'em up and drive 'em home."

"I'd say you have that one thought out right, Jesse. But you can bet General Hood ain't ready to give up just yet. We'll be hitting on them again soon enough," Gill replied.

"*Si*, I agree. But, now I'm thinking of our *vaquero* days back in *Tejas*. I never thought I'd miss putting a lariat over a pair of real wide horns, or getting' all scratched up pushing through a patch of mesquite, but I do," Jesús answered.

"Don't see why you miss round-up, Jesse. I mean, here we sit around a campfire. We got beef to eat. You got friends who can't get away from your talk. What more?"

"*Caballos.* That's what. Horses. We ain't got horses. Ain't been up on a pony for a year or more."

"Yea, I know. Me too. Besides, we been sittin' here too long, and I'm getting restless."

"No longer, Corporal Gill," said Lieutenant Navarro as he limped up to the campfire. "I have the cure for your restless feet. Gather three more of your *amigos. Vaqueros. Pronto.*"

Within an hour four soldiers who had grown up on ranches in Bexar County were each leading a courier's horse down a wooded path. They were behind a platoon of men from Company C who were led by a local guide.

The guide was a gimp-armed man whose farm had been burned down, his smoke house emptied of a dozen salt cured hams, and his herd of forty cattle taken by a Federal foraging party two days ago. Just before the cattle had been taken, he'd signed a contract to deliver the beeves to General Cleburne's quartermaster. The man had lost the use of his arm in the campaign to Maryland two years before when his Georgia regiment had long delayed the Yanks from crossing a bridge over Antietam Creek. His two sons were still in the army, and he intended to uphold his end of the contract. He had furtively shadowed the Union soldiers for a full day as they drove his cattle back to the Federal lines and finally left the herd in a large field just in front of their forward pickets.

Upon granting the farmer a chance to tell his story, General Cleburne himself had directed that his staff find men and horses to accompany the man to reclaim his cattle.

"Bain, you..."

"Not now, Jesse. Be quiet."

Gill had already shared the plan with each of the other three riders. Each man had his assignment once they found the small herd of beeves.

In a hoarse whisper, Jesús continued, "I just wish I had a pistol. I don't hanker to comin' up on no sentry without I can point somethin' at him."

"Point your knife if you gotta point something."

"And a good lariat. It ain't going to feel right herding cows without a coil of stiff rope in my hand. What am I gonna slap on my saddle to get them doggies moving?

"You ain't going to slap nothing. You're going to ease up on them cows and nudge 'em along quiet like."

"You say that now, but what are you going to say when them cows don't take to being nudged along?"

"Jesse, shut up. You know the plan. Now be quiet."

By midnight the moon was gone and the raiders were close to the place where their guide promised the cattle were held. The riflemen from

218

Company C were split to left and right leaving the four vaqueros in the middle, still leading their horses. The thin skirmish line moved slowly through the woodlot. The lieutenant from Company C saw the clearing ahead and signaled a halt. Jesús took the reins of Gill's horse and the officer and Gill crawled forward to the edge of the meadow. They saw the cattle, most of which were lying down, and did not see any Union pickets on the near side of the field. The lieutenant nodded for Gill to carry on with the plan.

Gill, McDonald, Hawkins, and Anderson led their mounts to the edge of the field and then split, Gill and McDonald going left and Hawkins and Anderson going right. They remained on foot to keep a low profile until they were in position to start moving the cattle. Meanwhile the riflemen took positions on the edge of the woodlot and waited.

The four cowboys knew the cattle could not be driven directly through the woods they had just travelled. They would have to drive the herd down a lane that ran from the field to a road that led away from the Union lines. The bad part was the lane crossed in front of the Yankee pickets for a hundred yards or more before it bent back towards the Confederate lines. The pickets would be firing and Gill and his men would be large and close targets, mounted on the horses.

The plan was for some the Coompany C riflemen to fire ahead of the herd in the general direction of the Union pickets. When the Federal sentries returned fire, other Confederates would fire at their muzzle flashes. It was hoped that the Yankee pickets would not be able to reload before the cattle were driven past. The problem was it was dark and the raiders had no idea how close the Union pickets were stationed, and if they would return fire across the field as hoped. But it was a plan, nonetheless.

Gill hoped their borrowed mounts had been around cattle and wouldn't spook at their smell when they started moving them. Gill and the others had talked about the likelihood they might need to push the herd into a run, a controlled stampede down the lane using the trees on either side of the open lane to funnel the beeves in a tight group running in the right direction. As he and Jesús walked their horses closer to the dark shadows that looked like big half-buried boulders in the meadow, Bain froze when he heard a voice call out, "Halt! Who's out there?"

Instead of trying to fool the man on the picket line with a ruse, Bain quickly put his foot in a stirrup and swung up onto the back of his horse. He bent low over the horse's neck, held the reins with one hand and with his other hand pulled off his wide brimmed hat and clucked his horse forward. He didn't shout or call out to the cattle, but walked his horse towards the nearest ones. He looked over and saw Jesús was doing the same. He couldn't see Anderson and Hawkins in the dark.

By now the sentry had called for the corporal of the guard to come to his post, but he hadn't fired his weapon. Gill was now close to a clump of cows that had lumbered up onto their legs when they saw the horse approaching them, and he hoped the sentry couldn't see Jesús or himself. Most of the cattle were standing with their heads turned watching Gill's horse, and as he got close enough the corporal reached out with his hat and swatted two dark cows on their rumps to get them moving. The second beast mooed at being hit with the hat, but started walking forward. As the slowly moving cattle in front of Gill reached other cows they too started walking in the same direction. Soon a dozen or more cattle were moving down the lane. Gill could now see Jesse off to his left walking behind other cattle bringing the two groups together. Hawkins and Anderson were still invisible in the dark and Gill couldn't hear anything beyond his own horse's sounds and the noise of the cattle directly in front of him.

"Corporal, those cattle are moving. I can see their shadows moving," the excited private said to the corporal of the guard who had joined him.

"I see 'em, Private. And I see a rider out there too," the corporal replied as he raised his musket and fired at the tallest moving shadow he could see in the field. The crack of the musket and the flash of the muzzle blast was all it took to startle the cattle and change their slow walk into an instant run. Immediately the four Texas cowboys bent low in their saddles and whooped at the cows, waving their hats to encourage the cattle to keep running forward. The corporal's single shot had passed over Private Hawkins' head, but was enough to cause several other Union soldiers in the picket line to fire into the field.

Those shots prompted the Confederates in the wood line across the field to fire. Shooting blind in the moonlight in the general direction of the Union sentries, one shot hit a steer in the head, killing it instantly, causing two other running beeves to crash into its falling carcass. Other cattle swerved to either side of the pile and kept going.

Bernard Anderson's horse saw the mass of cattle on the ground when it was scant yards away and instinctively jumped to try to clear the obstacle. The horse's front legs cleared the pile, but with the weight of the heavy man on its back, the gelding's rear legs hit the body of the shot steer and caused the horse to stumble as the front legs hit the ground. Anderson lost a stirrup and his balance in the saddle and fell sideways, hitting the ground hard, knocking him breathless, unable to stand or even crawl.

None of the Rebs' firing hit any of the Union pickets, but did cause them to duck behind trees and stalled the fire of those Federals who had yet to fire. Meanwhile the cattle thundered on through the dark field headed towards the bend in the road. The first beeves sensed or saw the tree line at the end of the field and angled to stay in the roadway and began to slow. Several of the cattle had veered off the track and were lost in the dark back somewhere in the field. The three remaining mounted men from Company K made it to the end of the field and prodded the last cattle near them around the bend.

"Bain, Bain, where's Bernard? You see him? I can't see him anywhere?" Jesús sounded genuinely concerned.

"Jesse, I saw him go down. His mount tried to jump a steer on the ground and Bernard fell off."

"Ah, nah, Bain."

"Maybe he ain't hurt, Jesse. Maybe them boys in Company C will pick him up and bring him back."

"Or maybe Billy Yank will sweep him up when they start chasin' us and these cows. I'm goin' back for him, Bain."

"Jesse, no! You're going to get shot or captured yourself. You do your duty and stick right here behind these beeves."

"Can't do it, Bain. Can't just leave the hairy pig back there." With that Jesús turned his mount and galloped back along the track.

Bain was furious that Jesús left the cattle herd and disobeyed his direct order, all to go back for a man he thought his friend disdained. Bain and Hawkins kept the herd moving. Bain feared he would not see either man again and doubted that the cattle were worth the price they were paying.

Anderson lay on the ground, the shock of his fall keeping him still for a few seconds. The cattle herd and his fellow cowboys were out of sight, but he could still hear them. He couldn't hear or see his horse. Then Anderson heard shouting from across the field and realized the Union pickets were moving in his direction.

Corporal Hagen of Company C had begun pulling his men back from the tree line as soon as the cattle passed by. He didn't see or hear Anderson's fall and his platoon was now many yards back in the trees headed away from the Federal pickets and away from Anderson.

Anderson pulled his legs up under him and knelt upright looking and listening hard across the field. Yup, the Billies were moving his way for sure as they searched the field for wounded men who might be captured and questioned. Like him. Anderson started crawling towards the trees which were ten or fifteen yards off to his left.

221

Anderson heard the horse moving fast and instinctively dropped onto the ground, trying to hide. Then he heard a voice calling, "Bernard, git up off your big arse and git up here behind me! Now, dammit! *Vamos!*" Then Anderson heard two muskets being fired and felt the air move as a bullet passed near him. Needing no further encouragement, Anderson jumped up and ran towards the horse and gratefully grabbed the extended arm that reached out to pull him up behind the saddle.

Another musket flashed as a soldier fired at the dark shadow. Anderson was holding the rider around his waist and felt the man give a little jerk as he flailed the horse with his reins and kicked it with both heels. The horse leapt forward and moved off at a jarring gait. One more shot came from the Union pickets, then the mounted men were around the bend in the dirt road.

"Take the reins, Bernard, *mi amigo*. Hold me up, *por favor.*" Jesús told the man behind him. "I need both hands now." As soon as Anderson grabbed the reins and encircled McDonald's torso with his two arms, he felt the smaller man moving his arms. Jesús put one hand in front of his left shoulder, then seemed to sag in the saddle, his head falling forward and jerking back up as he bounced with the horse's rough trotting gait. Anderson began to feel the warm wetness seeping through his left sleeve and knew Jesús had been shot.

"Stay with me, Little Beaner, you done saved my bacon, and by golly, I ain't going to let you down now. Just stay with me now." Still fearing mounted pursuers, Anderson kept the horse moving as fast as it would, which wasn't very fast with two men on its back.

Within minutes Anderson saw dark shapes moving ahead of him on the track and soon made out the silhouettes of the two riders who were flapping their hats to keep a small herd of cattle moving forward.

"Corporal Gill! Bain!" Gill turned at the call and saw two men riding double on the horse that was now limping on one leg.

"Bernard, good to see you. Jesse looks hurt, what's wrong with him? He shot? He fall? You hurt?"

"Naw, I'm good, but Jesse's shot and bleeding purt bad and passed out. It's his shoulder And this little hoss ain't going to make it with both of us on his back."

"Sure wish I could see his wound better. Can't see nothing in this moonlight. At least Jesse ain't blathering on about how he just rescued you. Get off that pony before he falls on you both. Me and Hawkins got to stay with these beeves another couple of miles. Stay with Jesse, and we'll come back for you soon as we can."

222

Anderson nodded and reined in his horse. He slid off, pulling Jesús with him. He laid the small man on the ground and felt more than saw that Jesús's wound was still bleeding. Not knowing what else to do, Anderson took his jacket off, then pulled his shirt over his head, and put his jacket back on. He pulled Jesús up to a sitting position, holding him up with one hand. With the other, he wrapped his filthy shirt around Jesús's chest and knotted the sleeves right over the wound, hoping it was tight enough to slow or stop the bleeding. The bandaging done, Anderson eased McDonald back to the ground.

By then the cattle herd was gone from sight, leaving the two men alone in the dark. He saw the horse was grazing just a few steps away, so he walked over and pulled the canteen loose from the saddle. He took a long swig and then knelt by Jesús and dribbled some water over the young man's lips. It was still too dark to see much, but he could see Jesús's eyes fluttering when the cool water touched his lips.

Then Bernard heard noises behind them, back down the track. Not knowing if it was just the sound of a possum rooting around, or men easing forward up the road, Anderson pulled McDonald back up and draped both Jesús's arms over his own shoulders and stood up with the wounded man on his back. The jostling and water revived McDonald enough to sense the need to wrap his legs around Anderson's waist. Anderson then grabbed the horses' reins and started walking the way the cattle went, leading the limping horse and carrying his wounded rescuer.

Corporal Gill and Private Hawkins delivered twenty-eight head of cattle to the major commanding the supply train of Cleburne's Division. Then both men turned their mounts around and retraced their path, heading back to look for Anderson and McDonald. No more than three miles out they saw a bear-sized shape slowly moving along the track. A limping horse trailed the beast and stopped to nibble at grass every few steps. Both the beast's heads were hanging low and neither head looked up until the two riders were close enough to speak to the beast. Finally, it was the rear head that was lolling sideways next to the front head that raised its eyes, managed a crooked grin, and spoke.

"The hairy pig done brung me back from the edge of death and carried me a long ways."

Then the front head lifted and spoke, "The little beaner done growed a hunerd pounds heavier since he climbed onto me. Will you please take him now?"

Both riders dismounted quickly and lifted Jesús off Bernard's back. Anderson sunk to the ground and said, "A swig of water, if you please."

After Gill and Hawkins gently put Jesús into Hawkins' saddle, Private Hawkins swung up behind him and without speaking urged his horse into a steady walk, wondering where the division hospital was located.

Gill handed his canteen to Anderson, saying, "I thought Jesse went out to fetch you back. Looks like you took over from him. You hurt?"

"Nah. My back's aching from hauling Jesse half the night, and my shoulder's sore from falling off my horse, but I ain't hurt."

Around midday Private Hawkins returned the three couriers' horses to the general's headquarters, receiving thanks for successfully retaking the cattle herd. Hawkins was oblivious to the glaring stare from the lieutenant whose horse was not delivered back to headquarters. Without his mount the young officer knew he was headed back to his infantry company, and he had rather enjoyed the freedom and status of carrying important messages between the general and his brigade commanders.

Private McDonald was lucky that the bullet had not hit bone or severed an artery, or become infected by a surgeon's dirty sutures. He was also lucky that he was wounded at the beginning of a two-week stretch when Granbury's Brigade was not moving daily. Jesús was able to lie still or sit leaning back against a tree, distracting himself by trying to catch the lice that lived in the seams of his jacket. Meanwhile, the others performed the daily tasks of fetching water and firewood, cooking, polishing muskets, and mending clothes and leather gear. By the time the brigade marched again, Jesús's wound was tender, his shoulder stiff, but healed well enough for him to stay with the company.

Chapter 31

August 31, 1864, near Jonesboro, southwest of Atlanta
13 Men Present for Duty

Granbury's entire brigade had been rousted from their blankets at 10:00 pm the night before, and had marched through the night. They were among the two corps of Hood's army that deployed to attack a segment of Sherman's troops outside of Atlanta near the town of Jonesboro. Major Fisher knew the brigade was at the far left end of the Confederate force, and he was worried because he was the last regiment in the brigade column.

The order came from General Granbury to deploy as skirmishers and seek out the enemy to the north of the road. Once again the regiment formed a thin single line and moved forward. Without warning, firing began from a wooden fence to their front. Two men in Company A/K fell, hit by the hidden Union soldiers' first shots. But the opening salvo was not followed by the expected long pause while the shooters reloaded. Even the breech loading carbines the Union cavalry carried took a few seconds for a man to eject the spent cartridge and pull another one from his cartridge box and slide it into the back of the barrel. Yet this firing continued in a staccato rattling that was unlike what the Reb veterans had heard before.

"Bain, Bain, hear that shootin'? There must be a thousand rifles up there pointed at us!" Jesús called from where he had sought cover behind a small tree trunk.

"I hear it, Jesse. Maybe it ain't a thousand muskets, maybe it is some of those rifles that load a whole bunch of bullets at one time. They gotta slack off soon."

"Move your men, Corporal Gill!" called Sergeant Degas. "We ain't layin' here to trade fire with those fellows. We're going to push them back!"

Gill nodded without looking back at Degas, rose, and yelled for the men to keep moving, leading every other man in the skirmish line forward while the other half covered their partners with loaded muskets. Bain stopped behind a tree, quickly found a target, fired, and began reloading as he watched the back half of their skirmish line move forward past him, leapfrogging again to find cover further forward.

Martin and Adam Braden, as always, were fighting as a team. They had the mysterious connection that twins sometimes exhibit and rarely needed to speak as they moved forward and fought. Although for the past week Martin had been distracted, because he had actually received a letter from a young lady in northern Alabama as a result of the note he had thrown off the train a few months before. The letter that arrived had been folded over and sealed with wax, with his name and regiment written fancifully across the back. It didn't arrive in an envelope, since envelopes were rare in these times of scarcities. But it did carry a faint aroma of rose water, which was the closest thing to perfume that Private Braden had ever smelled. The letter was in the chest pocket of his old jacket, and Martin pulled it out to study it every day at the end of the march. Martin didn't actually reread the letter each day, in fact he had never read it all the way through. Reading was a chore for him and the girl's handwriting was overly decorated with curlicues and big looping vowels that were hard to decipher. None of that mattered though, since Martin didn't expect to ever meet Miss Anna Faye Comer face-to-face. The fact that he had received a letter from a girl and could carry it in his pocket was comfort enough.

Federal trooper John Wilson was a member of the Ninety-second Illinois Mounted Infantry, a regiment in General Kilpatrick's Cavalry Division. The trooper knew he was fortunate to have joined the 92nd, and to have been assigned to Company B in particular, since every man in that company had been issued a new Henry repeating rifle at no cost to the men. Their commander, Captain Amos Henson, was the son of a wealthy owner of a textile mill that had been producing sub-quality wool blankets for the army for the past two years, but continued to charge the Federal government a premium price for every shoddy blanket made. With nearly half a million men in uniform, a steady stream of new blankets was needed, and Henson's Woolen Mill was a prime supplier.

Henson's son, the captain, had seen the Henry rifles in the hands of other companies. He had been mightily impressed and prevailed upon his father for assistance in procuring enough repeaters for his company. With his influential circle of friends engaged in providing the Union army with all sorts of goods and weapons, Captain Henson's father was able to purchase forty of the weapons and fifty thousand brass cartridges. After all, nothing but the best would do for his eldest son. Mr. Henson expected him to succeed him as president of the mill and perhaps even someday run for Congress, with his father's financial backing and his own war record as a fighting officer. Private Wilson knew none of this, he only knew the Henry rifle was the best weapon in the war and he was at this moment in a prime situation to use the repeater to its full advantage.

Trooper Wilson pressed down further into the grass, lying behind a fallen log. He had been there for over an hour and had his canteen and hat laying next to him. He had emptied fifty extra cartridges from his cartridge box into the upturned crown of his hat. If none of the cartridges jammed in the rifle barrel, he could reload a full magazine of seventeen brass cartridges in just seconds.

Wilson peered over the log and saw the first Confederate skirmishers moving his way. He looked to his right, waiting for the lieutenant to give the order to fire. Lieutenant Lozano was a conscientious young man and was waiting for the Reb skirmishers to reach the tree that he had decided was just one hundred yards out, well within the lethal killing field of company's repeating rifles. The lieutenant could not decide if he resented that Captain Wilson had found an urgent need to attend to personal affairs at the telegraph office in the East Point train depot that very day. Lozano knew the captain was overly nervous when the shooting started, and the lieutenant admitted he rather enjoyed commanding the company in combat. Those Henry rifles made it easy to put out a curtain of fire which had protected the company in every engagement so far.

"Fire!" Lozano screamed loud enough for his whole company to hear. Forty repeating rifles began firing as quickly as each man could work the lever behind the trigger of his Henry. During the first fifteen seconds each trooper shot eight or ten bullets towards the Rebs. After that, the rapid firing slacked off slightly as men went through the second half of their first load of cartridges at a slightly slower pace. Enemy targets quickly became rare, since the skirmishers had all gone to ground as soon as the hail of bullets began. Regardless, almost all of the men in the company emptied their rifles before they sank down to reload behind the protection of their fence rails and logs.

"They let up to reload, men. Up now! Move, dammit! Move!" Captain Longnecker was jumping around like a bird on the ground, urging his men forward, wanting them to rise and run towards the enemy. McDonald, the Braden twins, and Gill rose and ran along with a dozen more men from Company K while men of the other nine companies did likewise.

Trooper Wilson finished reloading his Henry, blistering his hands on the hot metal. This time he barely noticed the pain because his view was filled with dozens of Confederates running right towards them. He again raised the repeating rifle to his shoulder and pulled the trigger. As he worked the lever to eject one spent cartridge and push a fresh one into the barrel, he saw the man he aimed at jerk backwards and twist as he fell. Wilson felt elation, then tried to sight in another running man. Wilson kept firing, but before he emptied his rifle a second time, his sergeant yelled at him to run for the bridge. Trooper Wilson quickly complied, and in his haste, left his canteen and hat with the extra ammunition laying by the log.

Private Martin Braden felt the impact of the bullet in his shoulder as he was spun around, falling hard. Within a few seconds Adam was kneeling by him, holding a dirty handkerchief over the entry wound, and patting his pockets looking for something to staunch the blood flow from the exit wound on Martin's back. Adam finally pulled out his shirt tail and with both hands ripped loose a piece of the shirttail and pushed it over the back wound. Then he just sat by Martin, pressing on the wounds trying to stop the bleeding. Martin did not lose consciousness, but his moaning was constant as Adam kept a hard pressure over both the entry and exit wounds. After the Illinois cavalry finally withdrew and Martin was lifted onto a stretcher, he asked his twin brother if his letter from Miss Comer was undamaged.

Trooper Wilson ran, turning back one time to fire three more rounds at the attacking Rebs, before he again turned and ran as fast as he could to cross the stone bridge over the Flint River. Wilson's sergeant and lieutenant were on the far side ordering their company to the left to find cover and resume firing. Wilson had seen a few men fall in the dash across the bridge, and he was eager to reach cover. He had not been aware of any incoming fire landing close to him, and felt excitement rather than fear in this skirmish.

Navarro, Degas, and Gill worked to keep their platoon behind cover as they fired across the narrow river. When they thought the Union fire had lessened to the point they must be pulling men from the firing line to retire, the rapid firing began again. Navarro looked to his right and saw a company from another regiment bunched together in an irregular column running for the bridge, clearly intent on crossing it to further engage the Federals. Navarro saw three men fall as they were hit, but the rest surged past them onto the bridge. Once on the other side, they knelt wherever there was cover and began firing. Right behind them three more clusters of men were running for the bridge and soon most of the Tenth Texas Infantry, now little more than a hundred rifles strong, were across the river. Navarro could see they were taking more casualties as they tried to dislodge the Union cavalrymen. The men in the 6th-15th Regiment held their positions along the banks of the river, most of them firing blindly into the brush away from the end of the bridge, hoping their fire would have some effect on the Federals and encourage them to disengage.

The lieutenant colonel commanding the Tenth Texas realized he could not push the Yanks any further and gave orders for his companies to retire one at a time, but at a double-quick step, back across the bridge.

Granbury was ebullient that his brigade had pushed the opposing Union troops back across the river, but he soon learned that by pursuing the skirmishing dismounted cavalry his regiments had only taken themselves out of the main battle, where they had been sorely missed as the leftmost brigade in the whole Confederate force.

The rest of Hood's two corps had been roughly handled by the Federals. Regardless, he kept the Confederates in place at Jonesboro through the night, expecting them to only be "lightly" attacked the next day. General Hardee, who was in command of the two Confederate corps, ordered Granbury's Texas Brigade and Govan's Arkansas Brigade to march during the night from the extreme left of his force to the extreme right. This was a prudent adjustment, because the far right was where Union divisions were gathering for another push to crush Hood's right flank.

For several hours during the morning, Govan's brigade was the rightmost brigade of the army, and Granbury's brigade was next in line. The men worked during the dark hours before dawn to hastily build breastworks. Being the end of the defensive line, Govan's men dug their trench at a slight angle bent backwards, so the Federals would not have a hanging flank open to attack. By the noon hour, a crow flying over would have a seen a freshly dug trench in a rough bow shape with cut logs and brush piled on the outside of the bend, and the trenches lined with dirty Confederate soldiers from Arkansas and Texas.

Major Fisher was nervous and paced back and forth behind his regiment all morning. He could see beyond their defenses where vague shapes of Federal regiments were massing for an assault. He knew that Govan's brigade was to his right, in front of the growing Federal force. But his regiment's assigned section of breastworks was so long his men were lining the trench wall over a yard apart and were in a single rank. One random artillery shell could create a gap in his regiment that could be fatal if charging Union soldiers reached his earthworks. His men were already stretched way too thinly along the trench to pull any of them back to form a small ready reserve, so he had no way to plug any such hole.

General Hardee had elevated General Cleburne to command his corps for the battle. Therefore, when Govan's messenger reached Cleburne with a dire warning of the massed Federals about to sweep into his open flank, Cleburne was quick to respond by ordering Govan's brigade to pull further back, leaving their freshly built breastworks to better refuse their open flank, and he requested General Hardee to commit two more brigades to the extreme right of the Confederate line of defense. Meanwhile, Govan's repositioning further back put Granbury's Brigade at the salient, the bend in the Confederate line. They could now be attacked on two sides and were still in a thin single rank.

"Corporal Gill, how is the Braden boy doing now his brother is gone with the wounded?" Sergeant Degas asked when the two met as the men worked on the breastworks.

"Well enough. He was shaking and shivering before we moved out last night, but the march calmed him down, I reckon. That is, last night's march and knowing his brother is on a train bound for a real hospital somewhere. And Adam knows Martin didn't have his arm cut off by a sawbones, once they got him back to the hospital tent yesterday. I think Adam was scared of his brother dyin' on him, but Martin was scared of being a one-armed man for the next fifty years. Can't say I disagree with either of them."

"Hmmph, I suppose so. Gill, them bluebellies are going to come at us this afternoon, so you keep a close watch on Adam. Just make sure he remembers he's still a soldier. Don't let him bolt or curl up down in the dirt. One more thing, we're too thin to hold this trench if they charge us hard. We just won't be able to put enough lead out there to make them go to ground.

So you keep one eye on me all the time, and if I signal to you that it's time to git, you get the boys moving fast, real fast. I don't want our whole bunch gobbled up. We ain't going back to no damn prison camp."

"Sergeant, I hear you."

At 4:00 pm the Yanks attacked the end of the line where Govan's Arkansas Brigade was waiting. Private Charley Keenan was now Sergeant Keenan, and he was working hard to make sure his men did not fire at the advancing Yankees until the lieutenant ordered it. He knew the first volley had to be a deadly storm of bullets that would make their attackers hesitate, fearful to go further forwards.

Keenan turned to see the lieutenant standing tall behind them as the regiment waited, the men all on one knee, trying to keep a low profile and afford their officers a better view. The lieutenant was watching the Yanks advance and kept twisting his head to silently plead with the major commanding the small regiment to let them start firing. Finally...

"Now, men! Rise! Aim! Fire!"

Several of the Union company captains saw the formation of Confederates stand up, and immediately ordered their men to drop, to go prone. Sergeants echoed the call and within a second most of the men in the front Federal regiment were lying with faces in the dirt.

At "Fire," the Confederates let off a ragged volley, and only two of the Arkansans in Sergeant Keenan's company had noticed the Yanks dropping down and lowered the aim of their rifles. Similar action in the other companies resulted in the Arkansas regiment's important first volley being wasted as the men shot high over the prone enemy. Instantly, the Union captains were yelling for their men to rise and charge. They came fast and hit the Arkansas line before the men could reload. With no breastworks to slow the charging Yanks and no logs to protect the Arkansans, it was a bloody melee of bayonets and musket butts. Sergeant Keenan's company gave way but did not break and run. On either side of them, men slowly backed up trying to reload or more often, stabbing with bayonets or swinging wildly with their upended muskets.

General Granbury found Major Fisher behind the 6th-15th Regiment and, because of the battle noise, the tall general leaned over so his mouth was next to the major's ear. "Major, General Govan is facing more Yanks than he can hold back. He's starting to give way. If he gives too much more ground, the Federals will be able to turn and hit us from the backside. To prevent that, you are going to pull back your entire regiment in a reverse wheel. Be sure to set your guide far enough back to keep those people off our backs. Understood?"

231

Major Fisher spoke very loudly to the ten captains who had gathered around him, "Gentlemen, the Joshes are having a bad time of it, and the Yanks are going to get around behind us if Govan falls back much further. We are going to wheel back, way back, so we won't present our backs to the Yanks. Captain Longnecker, you set a guide who is far enough back that we won't be flanked."

A moment later, Captain Longnecker yelled into Navarro's ear, "Lieutenant Navarro, you are the guide for the regiment. We are going to wheel backwards to keep the Yanks from getting behind us if the Joshes can't hold. Set your line way back."

Lieutenant Navarro nodded, gripped his sword tighter, and moved off towards the right rear of the company's position. When he thought he had gone far enough, he turned and stood with his sword raised. Captain Longnecker saw him and motioned for Navarro to go further back. When Navarro had reset his position another ten steps back, Longnecker nodded his agreement and the whole regiment left their trench and began moving in a waving line to reset their right flank where Navarro stood. Just as the sergeant set his guide in front of Lieutenant Navarro, Major Fisher arrived and told Navarro to go ten more paces back. Navarro complied and the regiment moved even further back on their hinged refusal of their right flank.

"Bain, did I hear the captain right? Did he just order us out of this trench? Looks to me like we're doing fine right here behind these logs," Jesús asked his friend.

"Let's go, Jesse. Hush up now, we got dangerous work to do. You keep Ambrose and the other boys right next to you as we move back. I don't think we're running. I think we're just going to bend back our line so the Yanks won't get behind us," Gill told him.

As they scrambled out of the trench and reformed with bullets whizzing by them, Jesús muttered a quiet prayer in Spanish. To their right, the smoke was mostly hiding the dire situation of the Arkansas regiment next to them. Govan's whole brigade was being engulfed by overwhelming numbers of blue soldiers, which would surely soon force even the hardest veterans to either choose to die fighting, break and run, or start throwing down their muskets and surrender.

General Hardee was in constant movement behind the defensive works. He had worked his way towards Granbury's Brigade when he saw a gray line moving backwards, the troops having abandoned their earthworks, and seemingly retiring away from the enemy. Hardee didn't hesitate, but rode forward with his staff to rally the faltering line of Texans. General Granbury, who was watching over the difficult movement of the 6th-15th Regiment, saw Hardee and rode quickly to join him. Before Granbury could speak, General Hardee chastised him for the regiment retiring in the face of the enemy without orders.

Granbury sat up tall and stiff in his saddle and, towering over Hardee, indignantly replied, "General, my men never fall back unless ordered back." He then explained the regiment's realignment to protect his brigade's flank since Govan's Brigade was hard pressed and being pushed back. Hardee quickly assured him more brigades were on their way to shore up the right end of the Confederate line and, at Granbury's earliest possible convenience his men must resume their positions behind the breastworks they had just abandoned, even if they have to throw out the Yankees.

The pressure on the 6th-15th Texas was lifted temporarily as the Arkansas Brigade finally capitulated, finding its men surrounded and vastly outgunned. Hundreds of the men and their officers, including General Govan, dropped their weapons and accepted surrender as a better fate than running or dying. Ironically for the Federals, the time it took to accept the ongoing surrenders of so many troops in the smoke and confusion, and to organize their withdrawal from the field as prisoners, stalled their attack. There were more regiments stacked up behind the lead brigades, ready to enter the conflict, but their way was blocked by the new POW's and the regiments that now had to guard them.

The delay gave time for several more Confederate regiments which had been pulled from the other end of the Confederate defenses to form a new battle line, which slowly advanced. The 6th-15th Texas found they could also wheel forward, moving back towards their abandoned breastworks.

"Bain, Bain, there's Yankees in our trench!" yelled Jesús as they advanced, firing as they moved.

"Shut up and shoot!" was all Gill could reply.

The Federal troops who were firing from the trench were only half protected, and their officers knew it would be hard to stop a determined Reb attack to retake their works from the rear. It was now late in the day, and none of the Yanks fancied the idea of holding onto their tenuous success through a long night without better protection than a knee high ditch. The Rebs had piled logs on top of the dirt shoveled from the trench, but they were on the wrong side of the trench to help them survive a long night of sniping or a night bayonet charge. The Union regimental officers were relieved to hear a bugle blowing the notes to recall their brigade. General Sherman had decided that he could not further press his attack in the dark, and he wanted to regroup his far flung divisions.

Shortly after the Union brigades retired, Corporal Gill, Private McDonald and the others returned to "their" ditch and spent half the night trying to sleep, expecting another attack at dawn. The few dead Union soldiers left behind in the ditch were lifted out and added to the logs on top of the breastworks. They had all learned that a corpse could protect them from minie bullets as well as a log could.

Lieutenant John Gibbons hurt. His head hurt, his leg hurt and his ribs hurt. Some would consider Gibbons, who was a lieutenant in Company B of the 6th-15th Texas, to be lucky. Even though he had been wounded by two minie bullets that hit him almost simultaneously, neither had caused his immediate death. One passed through his side, breaking ribs as it tumbled before it exited. The other bullet was a ricochet which had lost much of its velocity when it bounced off a rock and embedded itself in his calf. Gibbons had hit his head on a rock when he fell, and his head still throbbed two days later.

Gibbons shared a seat on the hospital train with a private from his regiment who had been shot in the shoulder. The train was one of the last that the army had been able to pack with wounded soldiers and send down the rails to the hospitals further south, away from General Sherman's army. The train often lurched and bounced as it rolled over rails that were over-used and in dire need of repair.

"Private, were you with us last spring when we rode the train towards Mississippi and had to rebuild a bridge?" Gibbons asked his seatmate, although speaking made the pounding behind his temple even worse. But he felt a need to engage the young man in conversation to buoy both their spirits. While the train was taking the wounded men to safe places where they could recover from their wounds, and maybe even wait out the end of the war, it was also its own little bit of hell. Even if the men with the worst wounds were not loaded onto the train, those who were sprawled or huddled on the benches and floor had been given little treatment, and wounds were already festering and smelling. There were no orderlies or nurses to bring around bed pans or piss buckets and the smell of loose bowels and urine added to the pungency of the air.

"Yessir. I was there. My pards climbed up those wooden trestles like coons. Me, I was on the ground, but my brother went up. He's my twin brother, Adam. He took care of me after I got shot, but they wouldn't let him on the train, and he's back there now. Back with the regiment, while I ride this train to a hospital. We been through ever' day and ever' scrap together. I don't know how he's going to do with me gone."

234

"Private, he will do as any man can in these dark days. He'll march and fight when he's told to, and he'll be glad his twin brother is safe…"

The lieutenant never finished his sentence, for at that instant the locomotive of their train rounded a bend and collided head on with a locomotive traveling in the opposite direction. The noise of the crash was beyond even the sound of battle. The two engines both reared up like rutting bucks, and in a dense cloud of steam, dust, and smoke they crashed sideways to the ground, their iron cattle guards locked together. They crashed onto their fuel tenders, and the wooden and steel cars behind them ploughed forward, buckling, screeching, and being torn apart as each was hit by the car behind, a giant accordion of destruction and death.

The final tally of the dead was only thirty-seven soldiers and six civilians, a number kept low because the second locomotive was pulling a supply train carrying no passengers. Both Lieutenant John Gibbons and Private Martin Braden were among the dead. Having survived being shot on the battlefield, they were crushed and mangled by flying steel and timbers from the disintegrating train cars. The clerks who finally completed the paperwork didn't know whether to record the deaths of the wounded on the train as dying from battle wounds or accidental causes.

Part 4

Chapter 32

September 1864, Southwest of Atlanta
11 Men Present for Duty

As the battle at Jonesboro ended, General Hood finally abandoned Atlanta to General Sherman's armies. When the Rebels left, they destroyed all the supplies that could not be hauled away in their supply wagons. Throughout the night flames from the burning warehouses and the exploding train cars packed with ammunition were visible for miles. The last soldiers of General Hood's army passed through Atlanta, heading southwest, trying not to be shaken by the thousands of civilians fleeing the city, clogging the roads with their overloaded wagons and carts. Few of the men who saw the panic could help but wonder if the loss of Atlanta was also the death of their cause.

General Sherman chose not to press the Confederates after he entered Atlanta on September first. The five-month long Atlanta campaign had exhausted the men and resources of both armies, and each commander was willing to use September to regroup and resupply. For nearly a month the two armies remained very near each other, both behind breastworks and satisfied to do no more than skirmish along the lines of their forward picket posts.

"Bain, you know I'm Catholic. You know I ain't eager to sit for three hours listenin' to a preacherman who ain't even a proper priest," protested Jesús.

"Jesse, it's time for you to get used to it. You know my sister is taken with Methodist-ism. You've seen how she writes about the camp meetings back home. If you are going to court Susan, you best get accustomed to hearing the Word told by Methodist preachers."

"But Bain, now ain't a good time. Look up at the sky. It's goin' to rain. See them dark clouds. We're gonna get drenched, rubber blankets or not," Jesse continued.

"Doesn't matter. We've been wet plenty of times. We've been wet more often than dry for whole weeks. You can do it. And if you want me to keep writing good things about you to Susan, you're going to do it. What can it hurt? It's just words," Bain countered.

Jesús relented, as he intended all along. Both men knew there was no good reason not to sit idly for an afternoon that might otherwise be filled with cleaning muskets, chopping firewood, or some other burdensome duty. The pair joined a crowd of over a hundred other soldiers who had gathered on a hillside between the camps of the 6th-15th Texas and the 17th-18th Texas. First they sang hymns whose lyrics had been set to the melodies of old tavern drinking songs, so un-churched men like most of the soldiers might recognize the tunes, and at least join in singing the short oft repeated chorus of each hymn. They sat through prayers, short and lengthy, and finally the Reverend J.B. McFerrin began his sermon. The good reverend had a high nasal voice, but he could still find a pitch that would reach his whole hillside flock of fledgling Methodists.

The rain started when Reverend McFerrin was only thirty minutes into his message and was warming up to the challenge of confronting so many sinners with the prospect of eternal damnation. McFerrin may have been guilty of embellishing his description of eternal damnation more than the joys of eternal salvation. But he hammered away that only through the blood of Christ for those who might repent and accept the Lamb of God as their savior would that glorious eternal salvation be offered. The thunder and rain became noticable as he was describing the Son of God as a strong manly man, a carpenter by trade.

The pastor paused in his sermon while he and many of his congregants put on rain coats or draped rubber blankets over their heads. The thunder grew closer and the rain grew heavier by the minute, while the chaplain told how one day an angry Jesus man-handled and tossed out of the temple the money changers who were cheating good Jews.

239

Meanwhile soldiers began to abandon the service in search of shelter. Not to be deterred by mere weather, the preacher launched into a tirade about the evil liquor-selling sutlers who followed the Confederate army, and compared them to the evil money changers in the Jewish temple. Then there was a sharp crack of thunder so loud that the preacher thought the heavens had truly burst open so a host of angels might descend upon them. The thunder was accompanied by a simultaneous blindingly bright flash of light as a bolt of lightning hit two tall trees on the ridge top, arced between them and caught on a row of stacked muskets behind the seated soldiers. The electricity visibly arced between the bayonet-capped musket stacks, sizzling, crackling, and popping from stack to stack.

A lieutenant who was walking several yards from the lightning strike was hurled forward a dozen yards, yet landed on his feet, unharmed but shaken. Three men who were standing very close to the musket stacks were killed where they stood, having been caught in the arcing electricity. Others were knocked to the ground, but not fatally injured. McDonald and Gill were sitting under their treasured rubber blankets near the top of the slope at the back of the crowd. Both felt intense pain all over their bodies as the surge of electric current passed through them. Gill later described it as like being whacked with cactus all over his body at the same time, the pain of hundreds and hundreds of sharp thorns searing through him in a flash of burning agony. It lasted only an instant, but both men were overwhelmed by the physical shock.

As soldiers all around were running for cover, or trying to help the fallen, more claps of thunder boomed down on the confused scene as the heavy rain became torrential. Jesús opened his mouth to speak and paused, speechless, when smoke poured out of his mouth. None of the men sitting on the slope for the service were seriously hurt, but most were badly shaken. The grievously injured and dead all had been on the ridge near the musket stacks. The two friends from the plains of Texas, both of whom had endured frightful sudden thunderstorms while working cattle, just sat in the downpour, too numb to move.

Finally, with water pouring off his hat brim and steam coming from his mouth, Jesús stammered, "Bain, I do believe that preacher done persuaded the Lord God Almighty to be a Methodist. Where do I sign on?"

It was barely dawn and the army had not yet begun the day's march. General Cleburne and his escort had ridden ahead of his lead brigade to see how open the road would be that morning and to insure there were flanking skirmishers along both sides of the road.

"Hold here, men," Cleburne said as he reined in his horse. He was looking down at three soldiers who were lingering behind a row of apple trees several yards off the road. At their feet they had spread three rubber blankets, and each blanket was covered with at least a bushel of dark red apples.

Cleburne motioned for two of his escorts to move with pistols cocked to either side of the trio of soldiers and then called, "You men come over here and bring every one of those apples with you. Quickly now! Hop to it, I say! Move!"

The trio took three trips to bring the three piles of apples to the side of the road.

"Where are your accouterments and weapons?" Cleburne brusquely asked them.

"Over yonder, under the trees. We weren't running off. We passed the orchard late yesterday afternoon, and got up early 'nuf to get back and lug these fruit back to our outfit before they march off today. We weren't running."

"What regiment are you?"

"Third Florida, Finley's Brigade, Bate's Division. We weren't running. We were 'bout to take these here apples back to our pards. Didn't get no rations yesterday. We're hungry."

"Yes, neither did my men, and we've all been hungry before. But you well know that foraging means a court marshal. Get your accouterments and weapons, and come back right here," General Cleburne ordered them.

The three Alabamians were quick to return wearing their kits and carrying their muskets.

"Make a stack of those muskets and line up behind the apples," Cleburne said.

At that moment General Granbury rode up ahead of his leading regiment. He took in the scene, but said nothing as he stopped and saluted General Cleburne.

"Good morning, General Granbury. I am peddling apples today."

241

"Yes, sir. And what might I ask, is the price for one of those fine looking apples?" Granbury asked.

"Well that's the beauty of it, Hiram. These fine lads from Bate's Division have gathered all these apples and have charged me nothing for them. Not a single penny. And now, I will give them to you and your men," Cleburne said as he motioned for one of the Florida soldiers to hand General Granbury an apple.

"If the apple meets with your approval, please have your men file by and these good fellows will hand each of them one apple, just one each, mind you, until they are all gone."

They made it through the lead regiment, which was the 6th-15th Texas that day, and through most of the second regiment in the brigade column before the apples were all given out, one per man. General Granbury sat on his horse, beaming, thoroughly enjoying the look on his men's faces as each was handed a red apple.

General Cleburne rode off after leaving instructions for the three men to sling their muskets when they were through issuing the ration of apples, and pointed out a long thick fence rail. "General Granbury, when the apples are depleted, please have the foragers pull that fence rail. If you would be so kind, sir, to provide a guard to accompany these men while they carry that rail, without stopping, for an hour. If they stop to rest, or put it down, start your timepiece over again. A full sixty minutes of carrying the rail. Then they may return to their unit."

"Bain, now ain't this just the way to start a fine morning. I ain't never had such a tasty apple," Jesús said with a full mouth. He even tried to whistle, but just blew out apple scented spittle on Hawkins' back as they marched.

Chapter 33

October 11, 1864, Near Resaca, Georgia
11 Men Present for Duty

General Hood and General Beauregard, who was General Hood's superior, had agreed upon a strategy to draw the Federal army away from Atlanta. Hood's whole force would march north and become a giant raiding party that would disrupt the hundred mile Union supply line from Chattanooga to Atlanta. The two Confederate generals believed that General Sherman would send some, but not all, of his troops to pursue Hood's army, where Hood could then choose a battleground that favored his much depleted force. Until that confrontation, the Rebels would play havoc with the scattered smaller Federal forces that had been garrisoned along the railroads and towns. While Hood's army was only about half the size of Sherman's Union army, each of its divisions greatly outnumbered any of the individual Union garrisons strung out from Atlanta to Chattanooga to protect the continuous flow of supplies Sherman needed.

"General, you can't jump that way. Don't you see my puffball behind that square? Sir," Brigadier General Hiram Granbury politely cautioned Major General Patrick Cleburne. Major Irving Buck, Cleburne's devoted chief of staff, rolled his eyes as Granbury spoke.

"Hiram, I believe I do remember the rules of checkers. I was a fierce player at the hardware store in Helena," replied Cleburne as he moved a red berry diagonally forward to an unoccupied square.

The two generals sat cross-legged in the middle of the dirt road staring at the game while a small crowd of staff officers stood respectfully several feet away watching. The game board was two feet to a side, and each square was scratched in the dirt with leaves marking the alternating dark squares. Cleburne was using red dogwood berries for checkers, while Granbury carefully moved white puff balls.

Cleburne's division was the rearmost division in General Hood's army on the march north from southwest of Atlanta towards the Tennessee border. The three brigades were behind the hundreds of wagons in the supply wagon train making their way north on a single road, and progress was excruciatingly slow. The past month had been one of little activity for Granbury's brigade, beyond manning the breastworks that separated the two opposing armies as they recuperated from the long spring and summer campaign. Neither Cleburne nor Granbury were patient men, and being stuck behind the wagon train as they started the fall campaign was trying to both generals.

"I believe we have skirmished to yet another draw, General," Granbury said as he looked at the two remaining berries and white puffballs within the boundaries of the dirt board.

Cleburne corrected his subordinate, "No skirmish here, Hiram. This has been battle. Eighty percent losses per side. I believe we have upheld our honor and reputation in a way that General Hood would approve."

The off-hand comment made Granbury glance sharply at Cleburne, but he said nothing other than, "Another battle then?"

"No, I don't think so. Two draws gives both our watchful staffs ample ammunition to take to their evening campfires. And I'm restless. Sitting cross legged has cramped my legs."

"Then I know just the cure, if the general is willing to take our competition beyond a game scratched in the dirt," Granbury replied as he stood and held out his arm to help Cleburne up. "I propose a contest of athletic prowess. A race. Our men would enjoy the diversion of seeing which of their generals is most fleet of foot."

"Hiram, I would leave you in the dust, but I can't run a race in these tall boots, and we dare not take them off. It takes me half an hour to get the blasted things back on, and that would be just when the rear of the wagon train finally starts rolling again."

"Then a jumping contest. That we can do in our riding boots."

"Yes, alright, that'll do nicely," Cleburne immediately agreed. "Major Buck, would you hold my coat? And would you draw a line across the road for our leaping point?"

Major Buck took the two generals' coats and handed them back to another officer. He walked twenty paces down the road, picked up a stick, and drew a line in the dirt. Word of the athletic competition instantly spread among the soldiers who lined the sides of the road, most of whom had been idly sitting and waiting, just as their generals had been. The road quickly became crowded with bored soldiers who welcomed the unusual distraction of their generals competing like boys. As Cleburne, being the senior officer, strode up to the line to make his leap, the men began shouting encouragement. Cleburne set boot toes on the line, bent his knees, swung his arms back and forth, and on the third swing forward, he leapt. His boot heels dug into the dust of the road and his bottom plopped down as he fell backwards on his landing. The men yelled and the officers clapped, but everyone knew it wasn't a very long jump.

Hiram Granbury was 6'5" tall and lean. He had taken off his vest, rolled up his shirt sleeves and dropped his suspenders off his shoulders to not constrict his movements. Cleburne had moved off to the side of the road and stood among the soldiers watching as Granbury repeated the same arm swinging routine, and on the fourth swing forward, jumped. Whether by luck or intention Granbury kept his torso going forward so when his boots hit, he fell forward on his face, and not backwards on his bottom. His height and form took him well beyond the marks left in the dirt by the shorter Cleburne's heels. The Texans cheered lustily for Granbury's success, but the men from Arkansas and the other states shouted them down, calling for a second round.

Brigadier General Lowrey stepped up and proclaimed to Generals Cleburne and Granbury, "The men respectfully request that the standing broad jump be supported by a running long jump."

Dusting off their clothes, Granbury and Cleburne both nodded in agreement, and the second contest began. This time Granbury went first, and with his tousled hair sticking out in all directions and long legs and arms churning, he pounded through the loose dust on the road, rather resembling a crane running to lift himself from the shallows. His jump appeared to be respectable. Cleburne followed and clearly he was the faster runner. Not surprisingly, his leap took him a foot or more beyond where Granbury had landed.

"Well, Hiram, I propose we leave today's score deadlocked. What do you think?" Cleburne asked.

"I do believe, sir, that I concur with your suggestion," was Granbury's immediate agreement.

General Lowrey shook both their hands, and stood between them holding up each man's inside arm to signify to the crowd that the contest was a draw. Lowrey then led the troops in three cheers for Granbury's and Cleburne's athletic prowess.

Within an hour the division was moving again, but Cleburne and his men still chaffed at the stop-and-go progress of the long column. Every fifteen minutes or so, the wagons ahead would stop and the men in Cleburne's Division would either stand in the road leaning on the muskets, or without orders would sit in the roadside grass.

On one such stop, an old man, a civilian, was standing next to his horse and pack mule, leaning against a tree. Private McDonald approached him, commenting on his fine horse, but actually wanting to know if the old fellow had any food he might offer a friendly young soldier. The old man had been to the nearby grist mill and was on his way back to his farm when he encountered the lead elements of Hood's army. He moved off to the side of the road, and for the next five or six hours watched the soldiers go by. He told McDonald that, "I didn't know there were this many men in the whole danged world." He never did offer Jesús any food.

Chapter 34

October 12, 1864, Outside of Dalton, Georgia
11 Men Present for Duty

"Ain't we been here before?" Private Anderson asked to no one in particular as the regiment marched in a long column and the outlying buildings of a town could first be seen along the next ridge.

It was Lieutenant Navarro who answered from his position to the side of the formation. Navarro still had a slight limp, but he had no trouble keeping up with the column. "Why, Private Anderson, I do believe you are recognizing the town nearest our winter home. Those buildings are on the edge of Dalton. It seems we have successfully come full circle since we left the comfort of our smoke-filled huts last spring."

It was Sergeant Degas who added what many of the soldiers were thinking, "You mean those of us that are still here come full circle."

Lieutenant Navarro looked over at Degas who was marching next to him, "Yes, Sergeant, we are fewer, but we do carry on, don't we." More quietly Navarro continued, "And the fewer the men, the more they will look to their leaders, including you and me, to remain resolute."

Degas looked at the lieutenant and said, "I do not know that word, res-o-lute. Is it Mexican?"

Navarro replied, "You don't need to know the letters, Sergeant, you only need to be it. You and me, and even Corporal Gill there, we must remain resolute, determined, so our men won't waver because they see that we are unwavering. Regardless who is waiting for us when this war is over, we must be resolute, not faltering."

Degas felt a slight, but undeserved, reproach in Navarro's comments, so he asked just to prod the young officer as he kept walking, "And just who is waiting for you to cause you to remain unwavering, to remain resolute, Lieutenant? You returned from the hospital in Atlanta with new boots and a well-mended uniform coat. Such things don't get done by hospital stewards. Is there now someone waiting for you?"

Navarro was silent for a step or two before he said, "Sergeant, that is not your concern. But perhaps I do have new reason not to falter, not to let my fears be seen."

An hour later Granbury's Brigade was stretched across a field facing the town of Dalton. The men had been hearing the sounds of skirmishing ahead of the brigade, but the scattered shooting had subsided to complete silence. The road was barricaded and the fences across the field were lined with blue soldiers. A trio of Confederate staff officers from General Hood's headquarters had ridden forward to parley with a Union officer.

"Bain, Bain, look at them Yankees," Jesús said.

"Yea, Jesse, there's Yankees over yonder. So what? You've seen lots of Yankees. Hundreds of them. Thousands of them."

"Bain, them were all white Yankees, them over there ain't white."

Jesús was among the hundreds of Texans who were staring across the field at the Federal soldiers who lined the stone fence opposite them and recognizing that they were colored men.

As more and more of the Confederate soldiers saw the black soldiers across the field, a few men began to call out, "Kill 'em all! Kill the niggers!" Instinctively the sergeants growled at their men as the lieutenants and captains barked for silence in the ranks. The open calls subsided, but when all had been quiet for a minute or so and the officers started to relax, a few men in the ranks resumed shouting the epitaphs, yelling again to kill them all, to give no quarter, to take no prisoners. The calls quickly spread up and down the brigade formation. This time the company commanders strode out in front of their men and again demanded quiet in the ranks. Sergeants walked behind the men and whispered threats or cuffed men who were yelling. The shouting died away, but there remained among the long lines of southerners an angry buzz that was almost tangible. It was as if a wasp nest had just been kicked.

Six months earlier Hubbard Pryor wore filthy rags and was on the run from Polk County, Georgia, where he had been a field slave. He escaped the dogs by wading creeks for miles in the dark and climbing trees to hide high in the branches during the days. He made it to Chattanooga, where he enlisted in the United States Colored Infantry, the Forty-fourth Regiment. Now he wore a blue wool uniform coat, trousers, and cap, and carried a Springfield musket. He stood behind a rock fence on the edge of Dalton, Georgia, staring at the long gray line of Confederates. He spoke loudly enough for the men around him to clearly hear, "I'm goan use dis musket. Then I'm goan use de bayonet. I'm not goan back in chains. I'm not goan let de whip scarify my back agin."

"Dat's right, Hub. Dat's right. I be wit ju. Ain't no cracker goan put me back in de cotton rows," responded his messmate Joshua Williams.

"Dem coloreds up to Fo't Pillow, dey gib up unda de white flag, and dey be kilt where de stan'. Not dis brother. No, Lawd, not dis soul," came from a third soldier just a few feet away.

"Easy, there, Men," offered up First Sergeant Smith. "We don't know yet what the colonel is going to do. But you men look out there. There's Rebs as far as we can see. And it's just us over here. There ain't no other regiments here. So stand easy."

"Easy, my black arse," replied Private Joe Jefferson in a low voice as the sergeant walked away. "Easy fo' you, 'cause you be white. You ain't lookin' at no chains or gettin' the bayonet in the belly. Ain't nuthin' easy 'bout this day fo' us what ain't white."

The entire regiment, white and black, kept their eyes on their colonel and the Confederate officers who were still clustered between the two lines of opposing soldiers.

Major Fisher directed his company commanders to gather around him and the sergeant major. They stood in a tight circle ten yards behind the second rank of the 6th-15th Texas Consolidated Regiment.

"Gentlemen, we are about to have a situation here. Those Yanks behind the fence are going to surrender. We have them so outnumbered, their colonel has no real choice," said Major Fisher.

"That's going to be a mite chancy, Major," replied Captain Longnecker. "Those are niggers over there, runaway slaves most likely. You hear how riled up our boys already are just at the sight of them pointing muskets at us."

"I hear them, Simon. That's why I called you all over here. We've got to control our men. They are southern soldiers, not a mob. I will not abide our men committing murder on men who surrender. We will disarm them, but we will not kill them. You think back to Arkansas when we were the men surrendering under the white flag. We shall do no worse than what was done to us. No better, no worse. It's our duty to hold back any men who won't accept a Negro's surrender. You know which men to watch. You know which of your men, even your corporals and sergeants, might "accidentally" let a gun go off and shoot a prisoner. You make sure that doesn't happen. There will be no massacre here by our regiment. Understood?"

With more nods than spoken support for their commanding officer, the company officers returned to their men.

Colonel Lewis Johnson had strong paternal feelings for the Forty-fourth US Colored Infantry. Not only was he the regiment's first and only commander, he was an outspoken and active advocate for a greater combat role for Negro soldiers. The war had already gone on much longer than anyone had first thought it would, and the newspapers from Washington, DC and the other big cities were full of harsh political rhetoric. The draft riots in New York City had been even uglier than the newspapers, with men killed and the army battling mobs in the streets. People were tired of reading casualty lists in the newspapers from a rebellion that would not end.

Colonel Johnson was among those who were eager for the colored regiments to fight, if for no other reason than to absorb some of the casualties. Johnson also was among those who held the opinion that if the war was being fought in large part to appease the abolitionists, then the colored regiments should be actively engaged in the fighting to secure the freedom of their black brethren in the south. Colonel Johnson also believed that since the formation of the regiment six months earlier in Chattanooga, he had demonstrated great competence in the performance of his duties as the regiment's commander. Not only had he insisted that his cadre of non-commissioned officers be diligent in their instruction and drill, he had pressed his company captains to provide instruction in reading and writing to their Negro soldiers. As a result, he now had confidence in their abilities as soldiers and confidence in their trust in him.

Colonel Johnson stood with his adjutant confronting the trio of Confederate officers. "Colonel, General Hood demands the immediate and unconditional surrender of your regiment and any other Yankees that are under your command," stated General Hood's emissary.

"Major, my forces are well entrenched and prepared to defend the good citizens of Dalton from your predations," replied Colonel Johnson.

"Colonel, your forces are a few hundred scared niggers who are nothing but field slaves, and now are fugitives from the law of the sovereign state of Georgia," the major replied.

"Perhaps they were enslaved men six months ago, but now they are soldiers in the United States Army, and they will fight you if I order them to," persisted the Union colonel.

"Colonel, you may have put blue coats on them and taught them to march, but you and I both know you cannot expect them to hold against a division of southern veterans," countered the Confederate major.

"Major, you of all men should know that numbers are not everything in battle. Fortitude, training, and fortifications seem to matter a great deal."

"So does artillery, and you ain't got any, and we do. You also must realize, Colonel, that when our men breach your breastworks, they will go to work with their bayonets and belt knives. I wouldn't be expecting much mercy or quarter given to your troops, white men or niggers," the major observed.

"Yes, well...Major, if I were to order my command to capitulate, do I have General Hood's firm assurance that my troops, all of my troops, Negroes included, will be humanely treated as bonafide prisoners of war?"

"Colonel, I asked that question of General Hood myself before we came out here. Therefore, I can give you General Hood's firm assurance that the niggers under your command will be treated as *bonafide* recovered property, to be legally returned to their rightful owners. Until those owners can be identified, located, and notified, your *Negro* soldiers may be imprisoned or, more likely, they may be organized into work parties alongside other nigger slaves."

"I see. What of my white officers and white non-commissioned officers? I would expect parole for myself and my white staff and company officers, not imprisonment," suggested Colonel Johnson.

The major sighed reluctantly, and said, "General Hood has instructed me to offer paroles to you and the white men in your command, paroles to return north, under the condition you will not pick up arms against the Confederacy for the duration. If you accept these paroles, General Hood was most particular that you understand the generosity behind the offer, and the gravity of the consequences should you or your men return to military duty before southern independence is acknowledged and the hostilities cease."

That brought a snort from Colonel Johnson before he could stop himself. "Major, you have my word on that point. I accept the parole for myself and my officers. But I fear southern independence is not in the cards. You really should allow me to pass along some current newspapers so you might re-evaluate the status of your rebellion."

The major's eyes narrowed, and he curtly told the Union colonel to return to his men and march them out, bayonets unfixed, so the surrender could be consummated.

Colonel Johnson returned to his regiment and gathered his ten company commanders around him. He told them of the offer of parole for the white officers and white sergeants. He told them that the men would very likely be treated harshly, but not murdered, if they surrendered. The ten white captains agreed that surrender was prudent. Colonel Johnson urged the captains to assure the men that they would be treated as prisoners of war, and that their imprisonment would be short. The Rebs were licked and the war was bound to end by Christmas, if not sooner.

The captains did as they were ordered and promised their men that their surrender would be accepted if they did not fight, if they marched out and surrendered as a regiment. The captains stressed that to fight would only bring about the death of all of them, that surrender was honorable and in this situation, the only choice.

Under a large white flag made from a cotton tablecloth, Colonel Lewis Johnson led the Forty-fourth US Colored Infantry Regiment out of their defensive positions, marched them down the road, and halted the column in front of the Confederate troops. He then gave the one word command, "Front!" that turned the long column into a line of two ranks of soldiers facing to the side. The colonel, his voice, breaking with emotion, then gave the command that his regiment knew was coming and that they dreaded to hear for, once done, it would, with finality, put them at the mercy of their enemy. Colonel Johnson said, "Ground, Arms."

Nearly 600 muskets were laid side by side on the road. Then Colonel Johnson ordered, "Unbuckle and drop your accouterments. Keep your haversacks, canteens, and knapsacks. You will need your rations and blankets." The colonel expected his last command to be ignored by the Confederate guards who would surely search through the prisoners' belongings and take any valuables his men might possess, especially from his Negroes. But the Union colonel was wholly unprepared for what happened next.

The first wave of Confederates literally charged the line of prisoners, and when reaching them, many of the Rebels used their rifle butts to knock down black soldiers while other southerners stopped a few feet away and aimed their muskets, covering them while their companions used knives to cut knapsack, canteen, and haversack straps. Knapsacks and haversacks were emptied on the ground and anything of interest was taken by the Confederates. Next, the black prisoners were ordered to take off their jackets, caps, and shoes. If a man was too slow, he was knocked to the ground and his jacket and shoes pulled off. The shoes and jackets were thrown into huge piles. By dusk each of those piles had been picked over by hundreds of Confederate soldiers who took for themselves whatever they needed. Shoes, knapsacks, gum blankets, and wool blankets were quickly dispersed among the southern captors. Company and regimental officers made no effort to stop their men from striking and looting the black prisoners.

The Confederate officers had, however, been ordered to keep the prisoners alive. Officers paced up and down the line. One lieutenant from Alabama could be heard repeatedly warning his men, "Boys, don't shoot the niggers. Don't stab the niggers. They belong to someone, and even one of 'em is worth more than you'll ever be able to repay. They're valuable property, and they are needed to work. So don't shoot 'em, don't bayonet 'em."

"Bain, these poor men look like a flock of sheep that have been rounded up and sheared. No coats, no shoes, no hats. Besides, this reminds me when we was prisoners. I hated it. I don't like thinkin' 'bout it, and seein' these men all beat up don't let me forget we was in their place back in Arkansas," Private McDonald groused as the two friends walked near the colored men. The 6th-15th Texas Consolidated Regiment had been assigned the guard duty, and the whole regiment was strung out surrounding the prisoners in a loose cordon.

The white officers of the 44th US Colored Regiment had been separated from the others and clumped off to the side in a temporary holding area until their parole papers could be completed. With the men of the 6th-15th Texas providing a moving barricade, the Negro soldiers were started forward as a group, not a formation, down the road towards the railroad tracks.

General William Bate was a Tennessee politician and, like Patrick Cleburne, commanded a division in General Hood's army. He had heard of the surrender of an entire regiment of Negro troops at Dalton and had ridden over to see for himself. While he rode, he considered if he might find political benefit from the capture and return of over 500 escaped slaves so close to his home state. What he saw angered him. What he saw was a long straggling column of black men, all without shoes and coats, many without shirts, many bent over, shuffling or limping from being beaten with musket butts an hour before. General Bate spurred his horse forward and reined in alongside Major Fisher who was following the column.

"Major, are you in command of the men guarding these slaves?" asked General Bate.

"Yessir, we are the 6th-15th Texas, Cleburne's Division, Granbury's Brigade."

"Texans, huh. I hear you boys are a rough and tumble bunch of fighters," said Bate.

"General, we've done our part."

"I'm sure you have, Major, I'm sure you have," Bate replied. After riding silently for a few steps, Bate suggested, "Don't you think your boys are letting those niggers mosey down the road mighty slow? Looks to me like they're out for a Sunday stroll. I'd think you'd do the Confederacy a service if you made an example of a few of them. I do believe that would speed up those darkies and remind them that they are back where they belong, back where God intended them to be."

"General, these men have been stripped of their shoes and clothes and beaten. They are headed to work all night tearing up our own railroad tracks. If I push them any faster, they will not be fit to work."

"Well, it's your regiment and your assignment, Major, but I am convinced a lesson made of a few of them would put more energy into the rest."

"General, with all due respect, sir. These prisoners well know the fate of the six wounded and sick men who were in the hospital tent when their regiment surrendered a couple of hours ago."

"And what was that fate, Major?"

"When it was clear they couldn't walk and keep up with the column, they were shot," Major Fisher said.

General Bate took a second look at Major Fisher and said, "My compliments, Major. I confess I misread you."

"No, General, you did not misread me. I tried to stop those executions. There's no honor in putting down sick and injured men. But the guards were from Mississippi and did not know me, and their officers did not care for my interference. Nor do I care for yours, Sir. I respectfully suggest you take up any concerns you have with General Cleburne," Fisher replied. Then he kicked his horse forward.

"That is an insolent young man," General Bate muttered to himself as he turned his mount and rode towards a group of soldiers who were sitting in the shade watching the black prisoners moving away.

"Good afternoon to you good men. You boys Texans?" asked General Bate as he pulled up in front of the soldiers.

"Nah. We're from Mississippi. I got a cousin done went to Texas, though," replied one lean dirty corporal who didn't get up when he spoke to the mounted general.

"Well, you men are almost back in your home state. And you're doing a fine job of clearing out the northern scum that have come down here to turn our niggers against us."

"That's right, Gen'rul."

"Men, you see those niggers on the road? I am dumbstruck that they are being treated like free men, like soldiers. Treated like white men. Why, they ain't nothing but runaway slaves that the Yankees dressed up. And there they go being marched off like real soldiers. And those are Texas soldiers on the guard detail, the same Texans that gave up back in Arkansas and surrendered to the Yanks rather than fight. Just like those niggers there did. Looks to me like those Texans have gone soft."

"That so, Gen'rul?" replied the corporal who had now stood up along with most of his comrades. They all watched one of the prisoners stumble. He was right in front of a guard who reached out and grabbed the prisoner by his elbow, holding him up. Then the guard pulled off his canteen and offered it to the Negro, who took a long swallow before handing it back.

The Mississippians and the general watched until the corporal said, "Nah, Gen'rul, that ain't right a'tall. Sharin' a canteen with a nigger. We'll be seein' to that, won't we, boys?" The group angled down to the road and fell in walking along next to the guard who had offered his canteen to the prisoner.

"Didn't know we had nigger lovers in General Hood's army," the corporal said as he looked at Private San Miguel. "Well, lay me out. Boy, you're African dark yourself. Maybe you should give me that musket you're totin' and join them other darkies in the road."

San Miguel looked at the corporal who had spoken to him, and said nothing.

"Corporal, you seem to have gotten lost. Your regiment is over that way," pointed Lieutenant Navarro as he hurried, still limping, towards the Mississippians, to diffuse the confrontation.

"May be, Corporal, that you best back off," Sergeant Degas said as he moved up behind the Mississippians. "Say any more to my men, and I may be forced to carve on you."

The Mississippi corporal stared hard at the Hispanic lieutenant and looked back to see the Creole sergeant with a knife in his hand and more guards moving up behind him, including a very large, very white private who had unsheathed a very long knife.

"This ain't over," was all he said as he and his companions stepped back a few feet and stood watching the rest of the column pass them.

The black prisoners marched for several hours under the guard of the Texans from Granbury's Brigade. There were more instances of Confederate soldiers berating the prisoners, but none of the southerners were willing to challenge the guards' authority to protect the slowly moving column. By midafternoon the column was strung out in a long line and reached the train track. The 6th-15th Texas was relieved from the guard duty and replaced by a regiment from Tennessee. Crowbars had been collected and under the watchful eyes and loaded muskets of the new guards, the prisoners were told to lever up the steel track rails. The rails were long, heavy, and held in place by steel spikes driven into every wooden crosstie, making the task arduous. But it was the same hard work that the Confederate soldiers themselves had been doing for the past few days. Once each steel rail was pried loose, a gang of men carried it to a bonfire where the rails were heated until they could be bent in a U-shape. The men called them Jeff Davis neckties and Mrs. Lincoln's hairpins.

"Naw, suh. I'm a sahgunt in de fo'dy fo'th US Infan'ry. I ain't no slave no mo'. You pull up yo' own iron rails," the sergeant said to no one in particular. But he was heard by a Confederate private who just days before had learned that his family's house and crops had been burned, the livestock stolen. The destruction of the private's family homestead was done by General Sherman's soldiers, whose supply line the Rebs were now trying to further disrupt. The private took a long few seconds to understand what he heard the black prisoner just say. He saw the other prisoners around the man nodding their heads, one of them letting a long pry bar drop to the ground. The private lifted his musket and pointed it at the prisoner who had identified himself as a sergeant and shot him in the chest. The guard dropped his gun butt to the ground and calmly began to reload his musket. A Confederate lieutenant hurried over with his pistol in hand. He saw the body on the ground and ordered two prisoners to pick it up and toss it in the brush. He looked at the prisoner who was standing near a pry bar that was on the ground.

"Pick it up. Get to work," the lieutenant said pointing with his pistol. The frozen tableau lasted only a brief second. Then the prisoner stooped over and picked up the pry par, and the soldiers of the 44th US Colored Infantry began the strenuous effort of tearing up the train tracks. By the end of the next day, they had destroyed eight miles of track, leaving behind them the ashes from crosstie bonfires and bent, twisted steel rails.

Chapter 35

November 2, 1864, Tuscumbia, Alabama,
Near the Southern Border of Tennessee
11 Men Present for Duty

"**M**an, I'm glad we ain't lifting and hauling steel rails no more," Private Anderson said while he waited in the line behind a wagon. "Muskets weigh a whole lot less than train tracks do."

"Hairy, you were made to lift steel rails. Me, I was made to stroll the plaza in my new uniform, causing all the *señoritas* to blush and flutter their fans when I nod to them," replied Private McDonald.

"Don't call me 'Hairy'," answered Anderson.

"And you better be making eyes at just one *señorita* when we get home, and her name ain't Gonzales or Gomez, it's Gill," added Corporal Gill.

"Bernard, would you rather I call you 'Pig'? And you know I was just funnin', Bain. Since we have been exchanging letters, Sweet Susan Gill owns my heart," retorted McDonald.

"Just make sure your eyes know that when you get around those *señoritas* back in San Antone," concluded Gill.

"Bernard, but not Bernie. Bernie's the undertaker back home, remember? I ain't him."

"Bernard, you will always be 'Hairy,' who carried me all the way home one night."

"Here, you men, move up, quit gabbin' like old women. I ain't got all day," complained the sergeant from the back of the wagon. With that he threw a folded gray jacket at McDonald and in quick succession tossed more jackets at Gill, Anderson, and Hawkins. They all quickly put them on, and looking at one another started laughing and pointing. Hawkins' jacket was huge on his narrow shoulders and nearly reached his knees instead of his waist. Anderson's jacket was so narrow he couldn't even get his second arm into the sleeve. Gill and McDonald's jackets were better, but neither could actually be said to fit. The quartermaster sergeant barked at them to move on to the other wagon to draw their new trousers.

Sergeant Degas was behind Gill and replied, "Not 'til we get jackets that my men can wear. You got more sizes in that pile."

"I said move on, you got jackets. Trade 'em around. And there ain't any jackets big enough for that feller. He better just write home for his family to make him one," said the quartermaster sergeant.

Degas responded by swinging up onto the wagon and started digging through the stack of jackets looking for one big enough for Anderson and one small enough for Hawkins. The quartermaster sergeant turned to push Degas away, but found his arm held tightly in an iron grip. Anderson smiled as he held the man still with one arm and held out his jacket for return with his other hand. Degas quickly found a very small jacket which he tossed down to Private Hawkins, but after rummaging through all the stacks, he confirmed that the quartermaster sergeant had at least been truthful about not having a jacket large enough for Private Anderson.

"Sorry, Bernard. Here's one bigger than the one he gave you, but it's going to be tight. Don't worry about the red trim, you're nigh big as a cannon anyway."

"It'll do," Anderson said as he released the quartermaster.

The men drew new trousers that fit well enough, and moved to the last wagon that was piled high with stiff new shoes, straight from a factory in Mississippi.

"Ain't this just something," Private McDonald said as he held up one of his newly issued shoes. "Look at this new shoe, and look at this one I took off the pile that the colored troops were wearing. Dang if the slaves weren't wearing better shoes than what the army is issuing to us. I think I'll just keep these. At least they're broke in to my feet." With that he went back to the shoe wagon and tossed the new pair back on the pile.

The regiment finished their uniform resupply by pulling new shirts off the back of the last wagon. The shirts were coarse cotton, plain, with no buttons on the sleeve cuffs, but they were clean and like the new jackets

Chapter 36

November 22, 1864,
Near the Tennessee-Alabama Border
11 Men Present for Duty

The snow had fallen all the previous day, but now the clouds were gone. The landscape lay under a white blanket and the stars in the Milky Way seemed close enough to touch. Private McDonald was lying on his back and was shivering, even though he was sandwiched in between Anderson and Hawkins. Jesús was grateful for the shared body heat and shared blankets. The trio had gum blankets and wool blankets over them and beneath them, but the night's cold surpassed any cold the Texans had ever experienced. Even on the nightmare trip on the steamship to prison camp nearly two years ago, a week during which men died of exposure, Jesús was sure the air had never been near this cold. Nor during the most miserable "blue norther" winter storms which sometimes swept down the Texas plains during round-up time, Jesús knew he had never been this cold. He couldn't feel his feet, and his fingers ached with cold even though they had been tucked into his armpits. He somehow inched out from between his friends, making sure he didn't pull the blankets off them. He saw Gill and Degas standing by the fire wrapped in blankets. Jesús stumbled over to them, squatted on his haunches and extended his hands over the fire.

"Not too close, Private," Degas warned. "Your fingers are probably so cold the blood's near frozen. You'll burn your hands and not even feel it 'til they're scorched black."

"Sure, Sergeant," Jesús replied. He was too cold to even consider a wise crack as he raised his hands up a few more inches above the flames. Finally, Jesús said, "I do believe it's so cold the sticks ain't burnin'. Is there coffee or somethin' hot I can put down my frozen throat?"

"Still got some beans we took from the colored yanks. Wanted to heat up some water an hour or two back," Degas answered, "but my canteen was frozen solid. Not just a little bit at the top, but all the way through. Hard as a rock. Couldn't pour a drop."

The brigade surgeon had a thermometer in his kit. He was too cold to sleep, so time and again he checked the temperature by candlelight. When the thermometer indicated it was 0 degrees, the surgeon went to General Granbury's tent and roused his commander. He showed Granbury the thermometer and strongly recommended that the whole brigade be awakened and ordered to spend the rest of the night around their company campfires. The surgeon said he was certain men would freeze to death in their blankets before morning if they stayed on the frozen ground. He opined that even more men would find their toes black and frozen and not able to march

Granbury nodded his head in agreement and summoned his chief of staff to get all the men up. The order went out and soon the company officers and sergeants were kicking men awake and ordering them to move to the fires.

One by one the other eight men from San Antonio got up and found their way to join Degas, McDonald, and Gill at the fire. Men who normally complained about burning eyes stood mutely while the smoke engulfed them whenever more green branches were added to the fires. It was just too cold to joke or complain. For the last four hours of the clear frigid night every campfire in every company in every regiment in Granbury's Brigade was kept burning high and surrounded by men with chattering teeth and near frozen toes and fingers. Blankets and campfires helped, but nothing could keep the cold from finally penetrating through all their clothing. To a man they were miserably cold, but no one froze to death.

November 23 – 25, Southern Tennessee

The army marched sixteen miles on the 23rd and another seventeen miles on the 24th. The weather warmed some but stayed below freezing, and the men suffered, especially in their fingers and toes. During the next two days, the Confederates marched over forty more miles on roads that were alternately frozen hard or were ankle deep, near-frozen mud slush. Finally, they reached Columbia, Tennessee, not far from where the Texans had first joined Cleburne's Division eighteen months earlier. Hood had taken the war back into Tennessee.

November 29, Between Columbia and Springhill, Tennessee

"Bain, ain't that General Hood hollerin' at General Granbury over yonder?" Jesús asked as the company marched towards the group of horsemen who were several yards off the road. "General Granbury don't look too happy, what with General Hood wavin' his arm in his face. How does Hood stay in his saddle when he gets all worked up like that, with just one leg and one good arm, anyway?"

Gill was as interested as McDonald was this time. It wasn't often that corporals and privates marched close by two generals arguing. "Yup, that's Granbury and the army commander, sure 'nuf. Looks like Granbury is getting a bellyful. Don't reckon we'll ever know what they're fussing about."

"Maybe General Hood don't like this road we're on. We're almost marching in circles the way it twists around. Maybe General Hood wants us to march straight through the woods. Maybe he's mad we ain't caught up with the Yanks yet. Maybe he's mad 'cause his bowels are stopped up. Maybe he's mad 'cause his bad arm and missin' leg ache like my shoulder still does when it's cold, which is danged near all the time now days."

By the time McDonald finished his speculations about General Hood's state of mind, the company had marched past the generals. A few minutes later they were ordered to give way on their right so General Hood and his staff could pass them on the narrow road.

What the Texas infantrymen did not realize was that McDonald had been right about General Hood: Hood was indeed angry at the pace of the march caused by the narrow road that was crooked as a snake, and made for slow going. Hood was also mad because his leg stump and ruined arm did hurt. The pain never really went away, and the salutary effects of the laudanum he had taken that morning had worn off, which by itself was enough to further sour his already dour persoality. But mostly, Hood was growing furious that the Federal corps that he was trying to trap between his three corps might get away.

For once his aggressive army maneuvers had worked. Hood had put his 38,000 men between the Union stronghold in Nashville to the north, and the 30,000 Federal soldiers of General Schofield, whose regiments were strung out in a long line along the Columbia Pike. As soon as Cleburne's Division was in position to block the pike, Hood's forces could spring the trap. So, yes, Hood was in an especially foul mood when he learned that Cleburne's troops were still marching along a twisting narrow road in the river bottoms, and not yet deployed across the Columbia Pike. But Hood took solace that there were several hours of daylight left.

General Hood and his staff had by chance encountered General Granbury just as his Texans were finishing a short rest break to eat the last rations they had been issued. Hood exploded in anger to see troops not moving forward, and vigorously made the point to Granbury that he expected results before the sun set.

Granbury, who took pride in his diligence to orders, was now fuming that he had been chastised within sight and hearing of his troops and his staff. When angry, he tended to repeatedly nod his head to one side and the other. For the next hour he looked like a tall stork astride a horse, eyes flashing and head bobbing atop his long neck as he rode back and forth along the brigade column, urging the troops along.

In the middle of the afternoon, Granbury's Brigade finally left the narrow road through the woods and were in sight of the Columbia Pike, which was the major road that connected the area towns. Soon the brigade was deployed in two long battle lines and began a steady advance towards the west. Meanwhile, the other two brigades in Cleburne's Division turned north towards Spring Hill and moved parallel to the pike. These two brigades were charged with insuring that no significant Union force was in the vicinity of Spring Hill. Hood's plan for Cleburne's Division seemed to be working.

Captain Strong was the senior captain among the commanders of the three Union batteries that were unlimbering their guns as rapidly as possible on the low ridge. Through his binoculars he could see the long gray lines moving across the fields diagonally towards the ridge He knew the eighteen cannons could slow or halt the advance, even without infantry support.

General Cleburne held his binoculars to eyes as he groaned and said, "Damn it! Buck, do you see how long that band of smoke is up on that ridge? It's got to be more than one or two batteries. Maybe four. Damn!"

"Not four, General, but certainly two batteries, maybe three," Captain Buck replied.

"And we don't have a single battery close enough to engage them, do we?" Cleburne asked his aide.

"No, sir, we don't. The infantry won't be getting any support from our guns." At that moment a second salvo erupted from the hill, and several explosions of dirt were visible just in front of the Confederate battle lines.

"Bring our boys back, Captain. Get the word to them down there, right now. Put them in the trees along that creek while I send word to General Cheatham. If our boys are going to get ripped up by artillery trying to clear that town of infantry that may not be there, I want our corps commander to order it."

General Cheatham knew Hood's plan was for his corps to do two things. First, he was to clear the town of Spring Hill of any Union troops, or at least hold them there. He had given that job to General Cleburne. Second, he was to put at least one division of infantry across the pike, blocking Schofield's movement north. That was going to be General Bate's responsibility. When Cheatham learned of the presence of both of infantry and artillery around Spring Hill, he decided that his first priority was to attack Spring Hill. Therefore, he ordered Bate's and Brown's Divisions to deploy on either side of Cleburne's Division. Soon, Cheatham's whole corps was poised to attack Spring Hill.

By 5:30 pm, Cleburne wondered why he wasn't hearing the sound of the attack of General Brown's Division, as that was to be Cleburne's signal to launch his division forward. Brown had become aware of Union infantry to the west, on his open flank, and had asked for support from General Forest's cavalry. But Forest had already moved his men further south. Without support on his open flank, and with Union infantry sighted there, Brown refused to attack. What General Brown did not know was his flank was threatened by a single small Federal regiment, which could have been easily swatted aside. By 6:30 pm it was dark, and the attack on Spring Hill by Cheatham's Corps was put off until morning. Cleburne's Division settled in for the night. Granbury's Brigade put its forward picket line along a split rail fence about sixty yards from the Columbia Pike.

All during the afternoon of marching, Jesús could not shake the vivid image of General Granbury being bawled out by General Hood that same morning.

Jesús knew it was none of his concern, but like many of the Texans, he felt a fierce loyalty to his brigade commander and felt an equally fierce dislike for the commanding general of the army. Therefore, after gnawing for hours on his memory of the argument between the generals, as soon as a bivouac had been established and the regiment's picket line set, Private McDonald went searching for his cousin Matthew Quinn. Jesús wanted to find out what his cousin had seen and heard while working around Granbury's headquarters tent in the last few hours.

It was fully dark when Jesús discreetly walked away from his comrades and made his way to the edge of the brigade headquarters camp. McDonald saw two staff officers sitting in front of a tent eating cold rations. He waited next to a wagon until his cousin walked by closely enough to hear Jesús's whisper.

Matt moved over to Jesús and together they slipped further away from the headquarters camp. Jesús immediately asked Matt if he had seen General Granbury that evening. Matt nodded yes, and pulled Jesús even deeper into the dark shadows.

"Jesús, I sure did see the general. Him and General Cleburne both. General Cleburne rode up, and General Granbury almost pulled him off his horse he was so riled. They went into General Granbury's tent. I was behind the tent at the back of the wagon about to unload the general's writing desk and cot. Jesús, I could hear 'em talking. They was trying to keep their voices soft, but they both was so mad they kept talkin' louder and louder.

"What was it, Matt? What had both of 'em steamin'? Was it General Hood? I saw General Granbury getting yelled at by General Hood this morning."

Matthew Quinn looked over his shoulder back at the headquarters camp seeing the two officers still sitting by the wagon. For the first time since he left San Antonio he switched to Spanish as he talked to his cousin in the language their Mexican mothers had taught them. "Jesús, I'm only a driver and a cook, not a soldier, but I could tell they was both mad at General Hood." Quinn leaned in even closer to Jesús and said in a whisper, still in Spanish, "They was talkin' about General Cleburne's idea to give guns to the slaves and turn 'em into soldiers. Get the black men to fight the Yankees in exchange for bein' set free when the war's over. General Cleburne, he said how we're runnin' out of men, an' our only chance is new regiments full of colored troops, like the Yankees have."

Jesús thought that sounded like the best idea he had heard in a long time, but he interrupted Matt to whisper in Spanish, "Matt, that's damned good news, but what about today? What did they say about today?"

In an even lower whisper, Matthew Quinn continued in Spanish, "General Granbury, he said General Hood has gone crazy. He said Hood thinks his generals are scared to fight. Scared to lead their men in a charge. And then General Cleburne told General Granbury not to say such things out loud, even to him. But General Granbury, he said right back that General Hood was going to waste his army away like he done last summer at Atlanta. He said Hood won't stop until he's killed ever man in his army."

Now Jesús interrupted again to say, "Matt, don't you ever repeat that again to anybody, anytime, ever. Them words could get you the whip and even get General Granbury hung."

Quinn nodded in agreement and whispered in English to his cousin to take care of himself tomorrow. With those words the two young men both walked away and returned to their duties.

Captain Richard English rode a mule even though he was a junior member of General Granbury's staff. He and his mule were both tired after the seventeen mile march that day, followed by the maneuvering required once they reached the Columbia Pike. He was leading his mount along a few yards behind the fence, speaking in the dark to the sergeants and corporals of the guard, checking to be sure the sentries were posted all along the brigade's front, before he returned to Granbury's headquarters area.

"Captain, we've been hearing sounds out on the road. Could be Yanks within hollering distance of us. It's so dark, we can't tell just who it is," Corporal Gill said to Captain English.

"Don't worry, Corporal, there ain't anybody but us within a mile around. The Yanks are either holed up in the town two miles that way," English replied, pointing north, "or they're five miles or more that way, bedded down by the pike," he concluded as he pointed south.

"Yes, sir," Gill replied, "but my men are telling me they can hear men coughing and wheels that need greasing out yonder in the dark, where the road is. Just sayin'."

English sighed, "Then it's General Bate's men. I tell you what, Corporal. You pull down a couple of fence rails, and I'll mount up and mosey over there and ease your mind about those noises. If it's anything but Bate's men, it's likely our own supply wagons lost in the dark, or some damned sutler's cart."

Captain English mounted his mule and rode through the fence gap as soon as Gill pulled out the last rail. "Leave those rails down, I'll be back before you know it," he said as his mule quickly disappeared into the dark.

267

Captain English pulled his pistol from its holster and slowly walked his mule forward, stopping every few feet, to listen. The moon hadn't yet risen, and it was pitch black. He could barely see his mule's ears, which he kept watching to see if they were twitching or perked up at some sound English couldn't hear. What English did clearly hear from his right was the sound of a musket hammer being pulled back to full cock, and a whispered voice very close to him saying, "Freeze right there. I can see enough to shoot, and I'm too close to miss."

At first English thought the sound had come from one of Granbury's pickets who must have been posted too far forward in the dark, but the voice had a northern accent, not a Texas drawl. Before he could decide whether to comply, or fire a round from his pistol in the direction of the voice, or jerk hard on the reins and run, English felt a sharp prick in his left side. "Get down off that mule," a second voice whispered as the bayonet was pushed harder against his ribs, cutting through his jacket.

The two voices belonged to a Union corporal and a private in a squad that was providing flank cover to their Ohio regiment which was moving north on the pike. Under strict orders to wrap up any tin cups, coffee pots, and exposed metal and not speak at all, the regiment was just one of dozens that were creeping north along the Columbia Pike. Even the privates had been made aware of the dangerous proximity of the enemy army, and their leaders were desperately trying to squeeze Schofield's whole force out of the trap General Hood had set for them.

Captain English, with a bayonet pricking his ribs, was immediately disarmed, gagged with a filthy handkerchief, prodded towards the road, and his mule taken away. Corporal Gill reported the captain's continued absence on his scouting mission to Lieutenant Navarro when he was relieved two hours after English was swallowed by the dark. Navarro noted it mentally, but knew English was a competent man, and assumed he had simply veered to the side in the dark and returned to the fence further along the picket line, unknown to Corporal Gill. He didn't worry about it or report it to Captain Longnecker. The pickets continued to hear noises in the darkness to their front, but the men on duty in the deep hours of the night were tired and cold, and their alertness dipped as the night progressed. Sounds they should have heard and questioned went unchallenged. Moreover, while the picket line was in position between the road and the camps of Granbury's men, the individual soldiers on duty were spread thin with wide dark gaps between men.

Sometime after midnight, Gill was squatting by the fire in their bivouac some one hundred and fifty yards to the east of the Columbia Pike. He knew he should be sleeping, but his fatigue had given way to his urge for hot coffee, or the roasted sweet potato brew that passed for coffee. Gill was startled when he heard a voice in the dark asking permission to enter camp. Gill grabbed his musket and replied, "Sure, come on in to the fire and warm up." With that he eased back out of the flickering light of the fire and watched as a man in a dark jacket and forage cap and light blue trousers stepped to the fire and stooped over to pick up a glowing twig to light his pipe.

Gill pulled back the hammer of his musket and said, "Ground your musket, Yank, and then raise your hands high. I don't reckon you're going to be smoking that pipe tonight." Gill nudged McDonald and Hawkins awake with his foot, and directed them to take the prisoner back, find Major Fisher, and turn the Yank prisoner over to him.

Major Fisher interviewed the captured soldier and learned that his regiment was moving on the pike. The man had slipped away for a private bowel movement, seen the campfire and assumed it was behind the Federals' line of pickets that were covering their flank. Privates Hawkins and McDonald had waited in the dark out of the flickering fire light while Fisher talked to the Union private. When the captive was led away by guards, Hawkins returned to camp, but McDonald decided he had one more task.

Meanwhile, Major Fisher sent a scribbled message to General Granbury, who forwarded it on to General Cleburne. Cleburne had received other such notes of captured Federals who had strayed into the camps of the regiments in his division, so he personally went to General Cheatham to propose he awaken his men and stand ready for quick action, either preemptive, or in rapid response to any Federal attack. Cheatham demurred, allowing that General Hood was well aware of the situation.

In fact, three times during the night General Hood was awakened. The first time was by General Stewart who commanded the corps that was coordinating with Cheatham near Spring Hill to complete the blocking of Schofield's force. He was confused over orders from Hood that required him to change his front significantly and went seeking confirmation of the orders. The second interruption to Hood's rest was by General Forest who sought permission to engage the Federals near Thompson's Station, further south. It wasn't until Hood's sleep was interrupted a third time that he heard about the sounds of Union troops on the Columbia Pike and that lost Union soldiers were being scooped up near the pike.

That intelligence did not reach Hood until he was awakened by a short, dark haired private, who on his own initiative had sought out the general.

Somehow the private talked his way past all the sentries, and walked into the bedroom of Absalom Smith's home where Hood and several staff officers were sleeping. The private shook the commanding general awake.

"General, I done come here to tell you that the Yanks are out there movin' on the pike. I seen 'em and we captured one of 'em. They are out there and they are in a confused state on the pike. Now is the time, General. Now is the time for us to get 'em. Don't wait 'til mornin'. By morning they'll be gone. It's gotta be now, General. Sir."

Hood had been in a deep exhausted sleep, but he sat up, rubbed his eyes, and grunted as he tried to focus on what the private was saying. He didn't question how the private came to be standing by his bed, and didn't question the man's story.

Hood did do three things: He thanked and dismissed the private without ever asking who he was or what regiment he was in; he awakened his chief of staff and directed him to write an order for an immediate night attack by Cheatham's corps. Lastly, Hood fell back to sleep as soon as he spoke to his chief of staff. That officer, exhausted and still more asleep than awake, scribbled the order, folded and sealed the paper, and stumbled back to his cot without remembering to summon a courier to deliver it.

No one else awakened the commanding general to tell him that 20,000 of General Schofield's men were marching through the night to the safety of the fortified town of Franklin, passing within two hundred yards of the sleeping brigades of Cleburne's and Brown's Divisions.

Come morning, if anyone doubted that the Federals had simply marched quietly past the Confederates' camps, all they had to do was look at the debris that littered the Columbia Pike. The dirt highway was strewn with parts from wagons and artillery limbers, the dropped gear of marching infantrymen, and even dead mules that had been cut out of their harnesses after they collapsed from fatigue. Schofield had cleanly sprung Hood's trap while the Confederates slept.

General Hood called for a gathering of his commanders the next morning and let his fury be seen and heard. He cast blame far and wide among the army's corps and division leaders, especially on Generals Cheatham, Brown, and Cleburne. To compound the dismay of these subordinate generals, Hood suggested that the men of the Army of Tennessee had grown soft and reluctant to attack, having grown dependent on the breastworks behind which they had fought time and again during the summer campaign under the command of General Joe Johnston, before Hood took command. To end the conference, Hood ordered his entire force to immediately pursue Schofield's men north towards Franklin.

Chapter 37

November 30, 1864, On the Southern Outskirts
of Franklin, Tennessee
11 Men Present for Duty

"Bain, I don't like this," Jesús softly said as he and Gill stood in the formation, staring down the long slope towards the town of Franklin. They were looking north and the ground dropped away towards the buildings over a mile in the distance. Two dark lines were visible between Jesús and Bain and the building roofs.

"Me neither, Jesse. I reckon those are the Yankee earthworks out there, the short one out front and the long one behind it."

"Looks to me like we're right in front of both of 'em," Jesús answered.

"Yea, our lucky day. We'll get to dig the bluebacks out of two holes, not just one. But be quiet now."

Jesús leaned forward and looked right and left down the long line of Confederate soldiers. The unbroken line stretched as far as he could see in both directions, and there were too many flags to count. It was clear that this was not a feint, not a diversion, not a flank attack. The men in the ranks knew that General Hood had ordered a hammer blow to the Union defenses on the southern edge of the town of Franklin. Jesús could easily see that

271

Granbury's Brigade and the rest of Cleburne's Division were in the center of the long battle line.

"Bain, I never seen so many of us all together. It's the whole army. It's everybody. We ain't never done nuthin' like this before," Jesús said.

Word was already going up and down the line that the two divisions General Hood believed were most guilty of letting the Union army slip by the night before were being offered a chance to redeem themselves in battle. Moreover, the rumor was that Hood had told his generals he was ordering the attack to rid the men of their reticence to attack enemy breastworks. Hood was convinced the army had lost its aggressive spirit during the Atlanta campaign. If the last battles around Atlanta two months earlier under General Hood hadn't persuaded the men they were now under the command of a fighting general, today would. Today, 20,000 Confederate infantrymen would roll over the Yankee breastworks in a straight-ahead massed assault.

Sergeant Degas stepped up to Gill's side and reminded him to keep alert and watch the guides. It would be a long advance and Degas wanted to be sure his men stayed elbow to elbow and that the line not break apart as they moved through the fields. The nine men from San Antonio stood together, some shifting from foot to foot. Corporal Gill was in his customary place at the end of the company. Private Hawkins was directly behind McDonald, and Anderson stood tall in the center of the company next to San Miguel. Private Braden was next to them. Lieutenant Navarro paced nervously behind the line, but stopped when he saw General Granbury riding to his left in front of the regiment. Granbury reined in his horse and stopped as General Govan approached him. They both dismounted and passed their reins to aides who remained mounted and led the horses behind the lines of troops.

The two brigadier generals shook hands and separated, walking in opposite directions. Granbury strode briskly to the center of his brigade's line and shouted so all could hear him.

"Men of Texas, you have fought many hard battles, but this will be the worst of all, the enemy being entrenched and in plain view. Now if I have a man not willing to go in this charge, let him step to the rear."

That was all. That was all that was needed for the 1,100 men standing before Granbury to let loose a chorus of shouts and take a step forward, assuring their commander that they would not waver. Granbury drew his sword, turned to face the town of Franklin and stood, waiting for the order to advance on the enemy behind their breastworks. Granbury's long unruly hair stuck out at odd angles under his kepi, and if his hands trembled as he gripped his sword, or if his bowels were queasy and rumbling, none of his men knew it. Nor would any of them have begrudged their gangly commander his personal struggle with any premonition of the hour ahead. Every man in the brigade was a combat veteran, yet, to a man, they were all wrestling with their private fears as they stood and waited.

Granbury had sent his old regiment, the Seventh Texas, forward as skirmishers. That line of dispersed riflemen was already working its way over the open fields, men pausing to kneel, fire, and reload before moving forward again.

A flag waved atop Winstead Hill near the Columbia Pike. Seeing the signal to begin, the major generals commanding the divisions, the brigadier generals and colonels commanding the brigades, and the colonels, majors, and captains commanding the regiments shouted commands that were heard and echoed up and down the two-mile long line of Confederate soldiers. Regimental drummers beat cadences, and brigade bands played behind the long battle lines. The lively sounds of Dixie and the Bonnie Blue Flag dueled for the ears of the troops in front of the bands. The color guards of nearly one hundred and fifty regiments in twenty-nine brigades stepped ten paces ahead of the ranks, and the red and blue battle flags of the Confederacy punctuated the formations. Colonels, majors, and captains took their places in front of their regiments and companies. Sergeants and lieutenants formed a loose cordon behind the ranks to keep scared men from lagging or running. At last, the long line of soldiers started moving forward.

The Federal cannonade began as soon as the Confederates cleared the first rail fence. Every regiment in the attack had been the target of artillery before, and every man had seen others torn apart by solid shot and exploding shells.

"Bain, I feel like ever' one of them cannon shells is comin' straight at my *cabeza.*"

As Bain began to tell Jesús to quit worrying about his head, an artillery shell exploded behind the company, just a few yards away. The fuse of the shrapnel shell had been cut slightly too long, so instead of exploding over the Confederates, it landed and exploded on impact with the earth, still sending iron shards flying outward. By random chance only Corporal Gill was hit. A piece of iron drilled through the back of his stolen Yankee knapsack, piercing his blanket, rubber blanket, and the seven letters from his mother that were stacked and tied together. The iron shard still had the force to tear through the other side of the knapsack, penetrate Gill's jacket and shirt and lodge in his back, halfway between his spine and his shoulder.

273

Gill dropped to the ground, knocked unconscious, his bleeding wound not immediately visible as his knapsack was still held in place by the two shoulder straps, even though there was a jagged hole in the back of it.

Private McDonald stumbled as Gill fell against his legs, and he started to tell Bain that the artillery shell behind them had been close. Then he realized his friend was down and men were stepping over him. Jesús immediately stopped and took a step back, bumping into Private Hawkins, but moving quickly to where Gill lay unmoving on the ground. Jesús knelt next to Bain and rolled him over. Then Jesús felt himself being pulled up and backwards.

"He's gone, Private, get back in line!"

McDonald swirled around, his left hand holding his musket, and his right hand moving to the hilt of his belt knife. Then he felt a tight grip on his right wrist and heard Sergeant Degas, "Your friend is dead. You must leave him. You must avenge him now. Let's go."

McDonald remained still, staring down at Gill, where blood from his wound was beginning to pool under him. The company was moving quickly away. Degas was about to jerk McDonald forward, when Lieutenant Navarro spoke, "Jesús, *mi amigo*, stay here while you say a prayer to our friend, for all of us, and then rejoin the company. Ambrose and Bernard need you, and Henry and I must go now."

Degas glared at Navarro, but said nothing. McDonald nodded, still looking down at Gill, and softly said, "Bain told me that I wouldn't run. He told me that I would keep going," Jesús looked up at Lieutenant Navarro and said, "I'll catch up."

The lieutenant nodded to the sergeant and the two men jogged forward to resume their positions behind the company, leaving Gill bleeding on the ground and McDonald standing over him. The sergeant and lieutenant rejoined the company as the battle line approached the first Union earthworks. They didn't see McDonald kneel and cradle Gill's head in his lap.

Jesús held onto Bain for a minute, arms wrapped around his friend, swaying slightly, not thinking of anything, not hearing the cannonade continue. He didn't even look up when the next line of soldiers stepped around him, as they advanced as the second wave of Hood's mass attack. Finally, McDonald started to ease Gill's still form to the ground. It was time to prove Bain's confidence in him was not ill-founded. It was time to keep his promise to the lieutenant.

At the movement, Gill's eyelids flickered and he groaned. Jesús jerked back startled, and Gill's head dropped the inch or two to the grass. Jesús pulled his canteen around to splash water on Bain's face and wet his lips.

Jesús patted Gill's cheek and begged, "Bain, Bain, look at me, *Amigo*."

Gill opened his eyes and with effort focused on Jesús. He asked, "Am I bleeding? What hit me? My back's on fire."

"*Sí*, Bain, you are bleeding, but you are alive, and I need to look at your back. A cannon shell exploded behind us and knocked you down."

"Who else got hit?"

"Nobody else, Bain. Just you. Now let me take your pack off so I can see your wound. Maybe pour water on it."

Jesús unhooked the knapsack straps and helped Bain sit up. The sound of the fighting behind them continued, the roar of the cannons now joined by the sounds of hundreds of muskets firing as the Confederates approached the first Union breastworks.

When Jesús started to pull Bain's jacket off his shoulders, Bain flinched and yelped. Jesús stopped, pulled his knife, put the point of the blade in the hole in the jacket, and sliced upward to the collar. He pulled back the flaps of the dirty material and saw the wound. The small jagged piece of shrapnel was partly visible with blood oozing around it.

"Bain, I can see it. I'm goin' to pour water on it now."

Gill nodded and gasped as he felt the water, sharp, then soothing, on his back.

"Bain, I'm goin' to pull it out."

Again Gill nodded, and clinched his teeth. McDonald first tried with his fingers, but couldn't get a grip on the hot iron shard. He pulled out his knife again, put the point against the visible piece of metal, and pushed slightly into the wound seeking the end of the shard and the leverage to ease it out. With one hand McDonald pressed with the knife and with the other he poured more water on the wound to wash away the blood so he could see. Gill tensed and groaned, but sat still.

"Got it. You want it? It's still hot," McDonald asked as he held up the jagged piece of iron.

"Damn, that hurt, but thanks, Jesse. Nah, I don't want it. Toss it."

Instead of tossing it aside, Jesús dropped the shard into his own haversack and poured more water on Gill's wound. While he waited for the bleeding to lessen, he pulled a greasy cloth bag from his haversack and tore a piece out of it. He put the cloth on top of the wound and wrapped his red scarf under Bain's armpit and around his neck. He thought the wound would need stitching, but he knew the surgeons would be busy with more

275

severely wounded men. He furrowed his brow in thought, and finally said, "Bain, you sit here. I gotta go. I gotta catch up. I promised the lieutenant I would. But I'll come back for you after we're done. I won't leave you long. You'll be safe enough if you just sit here."

"Nah, Jesse, I ain't sitting here. We're going up there together. Help me up."

Jesús sighed, but stood and pulled Bain to his feet. Bain swayed a few seconds, but didn't fall. Jesús collected both rifles and handed one to Bain.

"Can you walk?" Jesús put his arm around Bain's waist, and Bain, being taller, easily rested his arm across Jesús' shoulders. Arm in arm, they slowly walked after the company, towards the sounds of the battle.

As the pair went forward, they passed prostrate figures, men dead or dying on the ground. Some appeared asleep, others were grotesque forms, missing limbs or with gaping wounds in their torsos. Even after two years of seeing dead and wounded men, Gill and McDonald were both taken back by the amount of blood and the stench. One officer was headless, victim of a solid shot from the Union artillery. They passed other men who were hobbling towards the rear, some holding dirty bandages to bloody wounds. Others sat on the ground in a stupor.

Captain Albert Tilton was scared. He had recently inherited command of the Fifty-first Illinois Regiment, which today fielded about 300 riflemen. Tilton had been in other hot battles during the campaign to take Atlanta. But never had he ever imagined that so many Rebels might be charging straight at him. He couldn't imagine there were so many Secesh still alive after all the killing Sherman's army had done over the past fifteen months. Yet, he saw the endless line of enemy moving forward, all too quickly crossing the fields, closing up their lines as men fell from artillery explosions. He couldn't deny it was real, but he was still in awe there could be so many of them all together at this one place, this one afternoon, and a large number of them coming right at his regiment. He counted five blue Rebel flags directly to his front.

Tilton reflected that half his men were green replacement soldiers, having arrived only a couple of weeks before, and the other half were veterans who knew their three year enlistment period was up in three months. Tilton worried that his veterans spread among the new men would not be willing to hold these forward works when the safety of the second line of defense was so close behind them.

The captain stepped over to the color guard, and put his hand on the shoulder of the teenage sergeant who bore the national flag, rough cut pole

276

held upright in both hands. "Sergeant, are you firm in your resolve? Our colors must remain here. They must be visible to the men. Are you steadfast today, Sergeant?" asked the captain.

"Yes, sir. I'm a mite scared, but I'm steadfast. I'll stand here, sir, until you tell me otherwise," replied Sergeant Louis Genung.

"Good man. You watch me. I'll let you know when to retire," replied Captain Tilton.

Tilton turned to find another captain saluting him. It was Captain John Johnson from Company E.

"Sir, my men can't shoot because that knob out to our front is blocking our view. But when the Rebs get past it, we can fire obliquely and hit them hard. I'm asking your permission to let my men turn their muskets into shotguns."

Tilton was impatient and replied, "Do as you please, Captain, but fight them. Fight them!"

Johnson ran stooped over back to his company at the end of the regiment and ordered his men to double or even triple load extra lead bullets into their muskets. He reminded his sergeants not to let any man fire until he gave the order.

Captain Tilton paced back and forth behind the color company in the center of the regiment. He kept his eyes glued to the advancing line of Confederates. His hearing was already dulled by the cannons' ongoing firing. He knew that his brigade commander wanted the whole brigade to hold their fire until the Rebs were too close to miss. Tilton agreed with the principle, but feared his men would not wait that long. He knew that one nervous new recruit could fire early and set off the whole regiment. Tilton prayed the command to fire would come soon, come now.

The runner from Colonel Conrad was panting and tried to take a deep breath before he spoke, but Tilton asked him first, "Now?" The man nodded and Tilton immediately shouted, "Fire by Battalion! Ready, Aim, Fire!" The volley was ragged as company commanders heard and repeated the order. Nonetheless, within seconds nearly three hundred muskets belched smoke that covered the space in front of the Union troops of the Fifty-first Illinois Infantry.

A hundred yards away, over fifty Texans in Granbury's Brigade fell. The Rebel line staggered as the men closed ranks around their fallen comrades, and then the steady Reb advance turned into a running charge. The Texans knew they now had precious seconds to close the gap while the Yanks reloaded, so encouraged by shouting sergeants and officers, they leapt forward and dashed towards the low pile of freshly dug earth that hid their opponents.

"Reload! Independent Fire!" shouted Captain Tilton. But hardly any of the men in his command heard that order. Instinctively, whole companies of men rose and ran to the rear, towards the safety of the next line of earthworks. A few sergeants managed to keep some of their men in place. Some were killed by musket fire as excited Confederates fired for the first and only time during the charge. Seconds later, as the first Rebs cleared the piled dirt in front of the shallow trench, other Union defenders were knocked down by hard swung musket butts.

Captain Tilton turned to order his color guard to withdraw, only to see them twenty yards away running hard to the rear. Tilton needlessly shouted, "Withdraw!" as he too began to run to safety.

Sergeant Genung thought he was going to make it to the gap he could see in the earthworks. Then he saw a cluster of Confederates running at him from his left. He gripped the flag staff tighter, determined to protect the national banner that had been entrusted to him. He looked back to his front and pumped his legs even harder. Then he felt the pain as a bayonet entered his side and dug into his abdomen. As Genung fell, he felt the flag pole being pulled from him, and could hear a high pitched yell from the man standing over him.

Private Hawkins went over the low earthworks and into the shallow ditch, stepping on the back of a fallen Union soldier. He fell sideways, slipping off the man's torso, but Private Anderson grabbed his elbow and pulled him upright.

"Come on, Ambrose. You can't rest here," Anderson shouted as he pulled the slight teenager forward.

"Close 'em up, Sergeant, keep the men close together!" Lieutenant Navarro shouted as soon as he regained his position behind his platoon of Company A-K. The whole brigade was surging forward, now chasing the fleeing Yanks, making it difficult for the NCO's to keep the men in each company together.

Major Fisher paused on top of the piled dirt long enough to shout as loudly as he could, "Now, men, fire! Shoot the running bastards! Fire!" Most of the men around him did just that, halting just long enough to take quick aim and shoot towards the mass of fleeing Yankees in front of them. In a ripple effect, other men saw and did the same, until most of the riflemen in the 6th-15th Texas Consolidated Regiment had fired before charging onward with empty muskets.

Navarro could see that other men from Bexar County besides Gill and McDonald were now missing. He hadn't recognized any of them on the ground where the first Union volley had taken down so many, but he knew some of his troops must be casualties from that terrible initial strike by the Yankee infantry. The companies, and even regiments, were now intermingled, but Degas and Navarro kept some of the Bexar men together as they ran forward, most of the men yelling. Navarro could see the blue jackets of the men they chased climbing over the next line of earthworks, many of the fleeing men being roughly pulled up and over by the defenders. Navarro watched a running man in gray bayonet a Union standard bearer and hoist his flag up high, waving his trophy. It seemed to Navarro an unlikely vision: a gaunt Reb in rags waving the stars and stripes in the midst of a battle. Many Confederates were catching up to the Union soldiers and either swinging their muskets at them like clubs or thrusting bayonets into the back of any man they could catch. A few were yelling, trying to get Yanks to surrender. Nowhere were the Federals trying to fight, to make another stand this side of their main earthworks.

Navarro could not see the ends of the earthworks, for this second line of defense stretched from the north edge of Franklin on the Harpeth River in a long semicircle, going close to several buildings, including Mr. Carter's house and his cotton gin. The earthworks ended on the south edge of Franklin on the banks of the same river. It was a complete line of works with no exposed flank. Moreover, these works were not built in haste. The ditches were dug long before the battle, with thick logs and timbers added to the barricade. Artillery emplacements, both on the parapets of the earthworks and further behind the works on low rises, dotted the formidable defensive line.

McDonald and Gill angled towards the Columbia Pike, the road on which the Union army had escaped during the previous night. Once they reached the dirt road, they continued on it, Bain by now walking without leaning on Jesús, but the wound in his back making each step increasingly painful. They silently approached the forward Union earthworks, the battle sounds coming from further beyond the works, out of their sight. About one hundred yards out, the pair stopped at a line of fallen Confederates, victims of the first mass volley of the Federal soldiers in the defenses. They looked to the right and left and saw scores of men on the ground, some crumpled, some still writhing in pain, some calling for their mothers or sweethearts. Clinching their rifles tighter in both hands, Gill and McDonald kept going until they reached the Yankees' ditch. They did not pass very many more fallen Confederates, for all the Federals had fired at the same time and then had peeled back from their cover and run.

"Bain, look at that poor *hombre*," Jesús said as he looked at a figure who was kneeling on the ground in the middle of the Columbia Pike. The pair could only see the back of the kneeling body, but they could see that he wore an officer's uniform. The dead man was facing the direction of the attack, his head on his chest, frozen in death. The corpse was hatless and the long wavy hair on the back of its head was matted in blood and bits of bone and brain tissue. A wound the size of a silver dollar was visible in the midst of the gore.

"I see him, Jesse. Let's keep going," Gill replied as he tried to pull Jesús to the side to avoid the corpse in the road

"No, wait, Bain. Bain, that's the general. That's our general. That there's General Granbury," Jesús almost whispered to Bain. "He's been shot dead. Shot in *la cabeza.*"

Private McDonald pulled loose from his friend and took the few steps to General Granbury and knelt in front him. McDonald reached out to touch the general as he gaped at the kneeling corpse.

"We gotta keep going, Jesse. We gotta catch up. We can't stay here."

Jesús put his hand on Granbury's shoulder, then reached up to touch a long blood-clotted hank of Granbury's hair. "It looks like General Hood done punished this good man as much as a man can be punished."

"Yea, Jesse, him and a danged sight more. So let's go now and do our part. Come on, it's gonna be dark soon, and we got to find Lieutenant Navarro and the others. Like you promised you would."

Captain Tilton was breathing hard and dismayed that his regiment was scattered. Yes, many of them had reached the safety of the main earthworks near the cotton gin, but his troops were now scattered among the other regiments. In the confusion of the battle raging just yards to his front, Tilton couldn't even find his color guard to set them as a rallying point for the sergeants to gather the men together. But he did see his sergeant-major.

"Sergeant Major, where are the colors?" Tilton shouted in his ear.

"I saw Sergeant Genung get bayonetted on the other side of the wall. He's down. The national banner is lost. I don't know where Corporal Brady is with the regimental colors."

"All right. You start gathering the men here. Right here."

"Sir. I will, but it won't be easy to find many of them. And I don't even recognize the new men yet, and that's half of us."

280

"Just…" Tilton started but didn't finish. For now he saw a wave of Rebs coming over the breastworks not thirty yards away. The Union soldiers at the wall didn't break and run like his regiment had, but they were giving ground step-by-step as more and more Confederates crossed the earthworks. Most of the soldiers on both sides no longer had loaded muskets, so the fighting was brutal hand to hand. Knives, bayonets, musket butts, sticks, rocks, and bare knuckles were the weapons now. Men rolled on the ground and were stomped or stabbed. Men pounded each other with fists and rocks. Skulls were bashed in with gun butts and clubs. Men strangled and bit each other and gouged eyes.

Captain Tilton took in this scene, raised his sword, and loudly shouted, "Charge!" to anyone who could hear him in the maelstrom. A dozen men, including his sergeant-major, went forward with him.

Captain Johnson had somehow held together most of Company E, and he saw Captain Tilton running towards the melee. Johnson raised his own sword in his left hand and held his Remington pistol in his right. He too shouted, "Kill the damned Rebels! Charge!" He jumped forward, leading the twenty men around him into the fight at the cotton gin. Men in other regiments joined the sudden rush, until a cluster of over sixty Federal soldiers led by half a dozen earnest captains and lieutenants hit the melee like a moving wall.

Private San Miguel jumped down from the log wall and saw a Federal soldier just a few feet away raising his musket to aim at a man coming over the earthworks. With both hands, San Miguel threw his unloaded musket at the Yank, pulled his belt knife, and leapt forward. The musket hit the man in the side and knocked his aim off, and then San Miguel piled into him. San Miguel thrust his knife into the blue cloth of the man's coat and fell with him to the ground. The Texan then felt someone step on his leg, but he was never aware of the gun butt that crashed down on his head, caving in the side of his skull.

Lieutenant Navarro and Sergeant Degas went over the earthworks together. Navarro, looking ahead, saw a large group of Union soldiers running towards them, led by several young officers waving swords. The Union officers seemed to be screaming, but the din of the battle was such that to Navarro they seemed to be miming. Degas looked down to see Private San Miguel's furious last seconds, and he shot the man who killed San Miguel. He then leapt to the ground and looked for other Bexar men.

Navarro finished crossing the barricade and found himself in a group of Rebels who were moving forward to meet the new wave of Federals. Like the Union officers, Navarro shouted as loudly as he could, "Kill them! Charge!"

Like snarling yard dogs the men in blue and gray crashed together, stabbing, slashing, and clubbing. Some officers were shooting pistols at close range into the faces and torsos of the enemy. In the initial clash, no one asked for or offered surrender. If a man wore the wrong color, others tried to shoot or stab him. If he turned, he was shot or stabbed in his back. If he fell, he was stomped. If he pressed close, he was kneed in the groin, his eyes gouged, or his face bit. The first impact of the two groups hitting each other took many men to the ground, some desperately wrestling, some wounded and dazed.

Navarro stabbed a man and pulled back his sword, now bloody. He was packed into the mob too tightly to raise his arm to swing the sword down, so he moved it to a port-arms position across his chest. As he did so, a bayonet was thrust at him. Holding the hilt of his sword in his right hand and the blade in his left, Navarro frantically pushed the tip of the bayonet down and to the side, keeping the parry going to bash his right fist and sword hilt into the face of his attacker. The man pulled his head back in pain, so Navarro threw his shoulder into the man's chest, knocking him down. The Texan shoved his sword point into the fallen soldier and then stepped back to see that his comrades in gray were surging further forward trying to reach yet another line of earthworks. When Navarro felt someone bump into his back, he turned, raising his sword to slash at his attacker. Instead, he saw a familiar face, young Adam Braden, who still didn't know his wounded twin had been killed in a train wreck.

"Private Braden... Welcome!" Navarro panted.

Also short of breath, Braden replied, "Huh? Glory be, Lieutenant, I'm sticking by you, sir, if that's alright."

"Come on, then, that way," Navarro said pointing with his sword as he pulled Braden forward by his elbow, "We have another set of works to take."

Braden and Navarro continued forward, still packed closely in a group of Rebs who were piercing through the Union defenders near the cotton gin, their mass and inertia forcing the Federals to give way. In spite of their blood-won progress, these Confederates were met by far more Union soldiers who were surging forward in a counterattack. The Union soldiers soon flowed around both sides of the group of Rebels that included Navarro and Braden. The Union defenders were shredding the outside ranks of the attacking Rebs, shooting and bayoneting the attackers from three sides.

"Come on, Adam, we're almost..." Navarro didn't finish urging on Braden because he was clubbed to the ground. Navarro looked up to see a Union private standing over him and a Federal Captain pointing his pistol at his head. Navarro let go of his sword and sagged backwards, saying nothing.

"Just lie there, Reb, if you want to live. And keep your man there, still, too," Captain Johnson said.

Navarro glanced to his left and saw Braden standing next to him, his rifle on the ground, his face contorted in anger, and a bayonet held against his ribs.

Gill and McDonald walked on, leaving the road and veering to the right, where they thought their regiment had gone. The distance was not far at all, no more than a pleasant afternoon stroll across a farm pasture. But the horrifying landscape of the dead and wounded became ever more grisly as they approached the main Federal earthworks. Canister from the cannons behind the barricades had swept down clusters of Rebs, leaving rows and piles of mutilated bodies. There were still corpses of men wearing blue coats and trousers, but most were in gray and brown. Jesús was so jaded with the sight of dead men and gore, he thought nothing more could faze him. Then he saw one more dead man, one he recognized.

"Aw, Bain, no. Not him too. Not old Pat, too. No."

Major General Patrick Cleburne was lying on his back, his red silk sash around his waist. Still holding his embroidered kepi and his sword by his side, Cleburne was dead on the ground, a small bullet wound over his heart, eyes frozen wide open. Gill could not imagine how their division commander had come to die here and his body left alone while the battle continued not a hundred yards ahead, but there he was. Gill had nothing to say and pulled McDonald by the arm towards the fighting, away from the dead general.

Soon McDonald and Gill found themselves in the midst of General Lowrey's Brigade. They recognized the general urging his men onward, but were not close enough to tell him of seeing General Cleburne and General Granbury dead on the field behind them. Intent on finding and rejoining their company, the two men slowly worked their way to the front of the Mississippians. When they had passed through two companies of the Eighth Mississippi Regiment, the two Texans stopped and stared at the Union earthworks directly in front of them, imposing in their size. The ground before the barricade was covered with Confederate casualties. Even though it was nearly dusk, Gill could see three blue and white battle flags from

Cleburne's Division fluttering near the earthworks, but still on their side, the outside of the barricades.

Gill and McDonald rushed with the soldiers in Lowrey's Brigade and reached the ditch in front of the earthworks. Rifle fire was loud and close, and the continued roar of cannons shooting canister rounds into the Confederates could be heard to either side. Gill slid down into the deep ditch and crossed hurriedly, stepping on the backs of dead men until he fell against the far side of the ditch. He looked back to see McDonald more gingerly stepping over and around the corpses to cross the ditch.

Gill asked a sergeant kneeling near him where Granbury's Brigade was, and the man pointed left and said these were Govan's Arkansas regiments. Bain nodded and he and Jesús started crawling on hands and knees. Their progress was slow as several times they had to freeze or hug the ground when they saw enemy muskets come over the barricade above them. Federal soldiers would stand up on the parapet and shoot down into the mass of Rebels gathered in the ditch and on the sloping exterior wall of the earthworks. Some Rebs fired back and a few men even tried to grab the barrels of the Yankees' muskets when they suddenly appeared over their heads. Gill saw one Reb vainly trying to extend his bayonet all the way up to stab at a Yank, but he fell backwards, shot while he stretched up, his head exposed. Gill and McDonald had to crawl over corpses and men who were curled up, clutching at wounds. Jesús gave his canteen to a man who was begging for water.

As they worked their way along, crawling and hugging the outside slope of the parapet, they came to an opening in the earthworks where two artillery pieces had been firing double canister rounds at an enemy who were just a few yards away. Here, Gill and McDonald were stopped by a mound of bodies piled nearly waist high. Most of the corpses were eviscerated, missing limbs or heads, and the ground was slushy with blood and offal. McDonald and Gill waited huddled over, frozen in fear and horror, next to the dam of mutilated dead men, until a cannon fired. While it was being reloaded, they squirmed their way over the shattered corpses. The pair couldn't help but put their elbows, knees and hands into the warm bloody slop of human tissue and rags.

In this section of the defenses near Mr. Carter's gin, stored bales of cotton had been added to the barricade. Bits of cotton were being torn loose by the constant musket fire and cotton floated in the air, settling like snowflakes on the living and the piles of corpses.

Sergeant Degas had not followed the lieutenant when Navarro had pressed on beyond the main earthworks. As soon as he stepped off the parapet on the inside of the works, Degas saw Bernard Anderson's head above the mob to his left and tried to work his way to Anderson, while fighting for his life with every step. Degas was a veteran of gang fighting in New Orleans, where knives, pocket pistols, and spiked brass knuckles were lethal weapons when men crunched together in dark narrow alleys. Now Degas used his belt knife in his right hand and small revolver in his left, having dropped his empty musket on the parapet after avenging Private San Miguel. Degas didn't try to slash or swing his knife, but stabbed and twisted his blade into any blue coat, and fired his small pistol as he was pressed against other men.

He reached Anderson as the big Texan was lifting a Union soldier up as he would lift a sack of grain, to throw him into other Federals who were trying to thrust forward their bayonets. The thrown man wasn't impaled, but he did land across two muskets knocking them down and opening the way for Degas to lunge forward and shove his blade into one chest and fire his pistol into another. Anderson, hatless, eyes wild, his beard flecked with his own froth and bits of cotton, reached out with one huge hand and pulled a musket from the grasp of a Union soldier. With his other fist he smashed the man in the face, blood spurting forth from the man's ruined nose. He bayoneted another soldier and left the musket dangled from his victim's chest.

Anderson was beside a cannon whose crew had fled or already died. He stooped and retrieved the iron tipped swabbing staff from under a corpse. With his back to the wheel of the piece, Anderson spread his feet and gripping the five foot long staff in both hands, he swung at the head of Union officer. The iron tool shattered the man's skull, and without adjusting his grip, Anderson swung the staff backhanded and caught another man on the shoulder, breaking his collar bone and knocking him down.

Captain Tilton had led his charging men all the way to the main works and saw the huge Confederate next to the cannon, wielding the long staff. Tilton's revolver was empty, and he dared not close with the Reb to use his sword. As Tilton watched, the big man had no more enemies left standing near him, so he stepped away from the artillery piece toward the nearest group of Union soldiers. His long reach with the iron capped staff quickly cleared a semi-circle before him until he suddenly crumpled to the ground, shot three times in the chest.

Degas had moved a few steps away from Anderson as Bernard picked up the cannon implement. The little pistol was empty, so Degas pocketed it and pulled a musket from a corpse's grip, saw it was primed, and looked around. In the gloom of dusk, he saw Private Hawkins sitting, leaning back against

285

the earthworks, holding one hand around his other arm, blood seeping through his fingers. Degas had intended to cover Anderson's flank with the musket, but he saw the big man unmoving on the ground, blood soaking through his coat. Immediately dismissing Anderson as lost, Degas instead took the few steps needed to reach Hawkins. With his free hand Degas yanked the private hard to his feet. He kept a tight fist on Hawkins' coat and climbed up the parapet until he found a narrow gap in the logs on top. He dragged the little soldier with him, pushing aside branches, ignoring scratches to their faces. The pair reached the far side of the earthworks, and Degas shoved the young private onto his face against the dirt on the side of the embankment. Degas fell next to Hawkins and put his mouth next to his ear.

"Ambrose, we had to get back to this side of the wall. Too many Yankees on the other side. We must wait here until more of us can go over the wall."

Hawkins turned his head slightly and looked at Degas' face just an inch or two from his. "Sergeant, why are we alive? Why ain't we dead yet? I saw Bernard die. I saw Bain die, way back there. I seen Andrew die on the wall. Why ain't we shot?"

"Not our time yet, but now we must protect ourselves." Degas crawled over Hawkins, moving off looking for another discarded musket. It was nearly full dark now, making the sounds of the fighting more frightening and the cries of the wounded more pitiful

Gill was crawling, wanting to call out as he and McDonald traversed the forward slope of the earthworks, but he feared any sound would draw fire from above. Instead, he whispered "Sixth Texas?" as they crawled past other men who were huddled against the wall. After several efforts, a voice replied, "Yea, Company G. You?"

"Company K."

"Keep going."

"Yea."

Gill began to whisper, "Co K?" until he heard a familiar voice.

"K here," as an arm reached out. Gill took the extended hand and let himself be pulled further up and closer to the log barricade.

"Bain? Bain? Is it you, Bain? I saw you fall. I nearly tripped over your body. Tell me it's you, Bain," Hawkins said excitedly. Immediately, a rifle appeared over the top of the wall, pointed generally down toward the voice, and fired. The bullet went a few feet beyond the living men into the ditch where it hit a dead sergeant.

This time Hawkins whispered, "Bain, you hit? Bain, is that really you?"

"Nobody else, Ambrose. Nobody else," replied Gill in a hoarse whisper, "Unless you count Jesse. He's here, too."

From the dark, Jesús grunted as he slithered up to lie next to Hawkins.

"Who else is here, Ambrose?" Jesús whispered.

"Sergeant Degas dragged me back to this side of the wall. Bernard and Andrew are dead on the other side. That's all I seen."

"Quit talking," Degas whispered from beyond Hawkins, "Use your bayonet now. Next rifle comes over the wall, stab through the logs under the rifle." As Degas finished, another rifle came over the wall and fired blindly, but no one reached up to stab at it with a bayonet.

"They keep shooting down on us 'cause we're not firing back," Gill whispered, "Everybody be sure you have a loaded musket. I'm going to slide up and fire over into the Yanks. Then you pass your muskets up to me, one at a time." The others nodded, and Gill climbed up, until his head was just under the gap beneath the head log.

Gill quickly slid his musket through the gap and raised his head so he could see the interior of the log barricade. He saw a dozen Federal soldiers within a few yards, pointed the musket at the nearest man and pulled the trigger. He ducked down and exchanged muskets with Jesús. Without pausing except to step a foot to his left, Gill rose up, poked the musket through the gap and fired a second quick round where he had seen several Union soldiers. As he fired, a bullet thudded into the head log inches from him. Gill dropped down again, his back on fire from his wound which was bleeding again. Ignoring his pain, Gill took Hawkins' rifle and stepped back to his first spot, raising up to peer through the gap. He saw a face right in front of him on the other side of the wall. Gill pulled the trigger as he was still sliding the musket forward. The bullet whizzed by the man's skull, but the fiery muzzle blast caught him full in the face, throwing him backwards as he screamed. Gill dropped down beneath the gap, then slid down the wall into the ditch.

Seconds later, six Union soldiers, led by a lieutenant with a revolver, appeared above the head log, each man quickly firing into the area below them. Firing blindly in haste, the volley from the six muskets did not hit any of the four Texans. But the Federal lieutenant stayed in place, peering over the top of the barricade as the smoke from the muskets dissipated. He had re-cocked his Colt revolver and clearly saw the group of Rebs below him.

The lieutenant yelled at them to surrender. In reply, Degas snapped off a quick shot from the hip. Degas' un-aimed bullet went into the logs below the lieutenant, and the Union officer fired, hitting Gill in the neck as he looked up from the ditch. Without pause, the lieutenant cocked his pistol and fired yet another round that grazed McDonald's cheek before he dropped down to safety on the interior of the rampart.

McDonald slid down into the ditch, his cheek bleeding, but forgotten. He stopped next to his friend and leaned over him protectively as he got close enough in the dim light to see the wound in Bain's throat. As Jesús held Bain tightly, Bain looked up at Jesús. Their eyes locked before Bain's eyelids closed and his body went limp. Blood dripped from the wound on Jesús's cheek onto Bain's face

Degas and Hawkins slid into the ditch, and together they pried McDonald off Gill's body. Without trying to comfort him with words, the pair forcibly pulled Jesús away. Degas and Hawkins, dragging Jesús between them, crawled along the bottom of the ditch.

When they reached a spot several yards distant, they stopped. Hawkins kept his arm around McDonald as Jesús let out a primal howl, a guttural sound of loss, nakedness, and rage that frightened Ambrose as much as the horrific place in which they were trapped. Ambrose embraced Jesús tightly as his friend trembled, then violently shook, crying, gasping for air, unable to any longer restrain the enormous wave of pain built up over three years: three years of random disease, senseless hatred, dying without reason, and endless killing by men who were not murderers.

After a time, Jesús was silent and still, but Ambrose continued to hold him. Degas disappeared into the dusk and came back in a few minutes with a musket in each hand. The sounds of the fighting were lessening as dusk had turned to the full blackness of night. Still, men were shouting and the flashing of musket muzzle blasts all along the earthworks kept the battlefield in a flickering yellow light. Degas tugged at the other two men, forcing them to separate, and together they crawled further away from the shooting.

When they reached a slight dip in the ground, Degas set aside his musket and working prone, pulled a few corpses into a pile, building a protective wall from the ongoing Union musket fire. The three men from Bexar County then stayed still, listening to the wounded cry out for help. Even Degas made no effort to find other men from their company or return fire towards the barricade where the Yanks kept firing over the wall into the ditch. The night grew bitterly cold, and the trio shivered together in the blood soaked mud, hoping they would not be random victims of the blind firing from the earthworks.

At dawn Degas roused the other two out of their stupor. They looked around and saw a Confederate captain slowly making his way through the corpses. Degas stood. The officer saw him and said, "The Yanks are gone. They crossed the river in the night. Find your regiment."

Degas looked at the earthworks less than forty yards from them. The ground was littered with bodies, too many to count. Hawkins and McDonald joined Degas staring at the carnage all around them. After a moment, the three slowly made their way to the barricade.

They found Gill as they had left him. His skin was now pale bluish. Shreds of ice were on his closed eyelashes, the blood on his neck wound frozen into dark pink crystals. McDonald sat next to the corpse and put his hand on Gill's cheek, stroking it, saying softly, "Oh, Bain, it should have been me, not you. Not you. It should have been me." Hawkins patted Jesús on the back, then carefully pulled the red and brown scarf from around Gill's shoulder.

Degas and Hawkins left McDonald mourning over Gill's remains while they made their way up and over the barricade. The interior of the earthworks was even more strewn with dead men than the outside. Degas searched for the still forms of Andrew San Miguel and Bernard Anderson. Both were partly buried beneath the corpses of Union soldiers. They checked the pockets of the men's jackets for any letters, but found none. Then they walked further into the yard of the cotton gin and looked for other bodies they might recognize.

As the morning sun rose, scores of other Confederate soldiers, as well as teamsters, cooks, body servants, and civilians from Franklin, formed work parties to scrape out shallow ditches for mass graves. Degas, Hawkins, and McDonald, joined by Matt Quinn, put Gill's body on a rubber blanket and carried it through a gap in the barricade and laid him out in one of the burial trenches close to San Miguel and Anderson.

The tally of missing men from the Sixth Texas was long, and included Private Adam Braden and Lieutenant Eugene Navarro.

Chapter 38

It was almost dark when Private McDonald and Private Hawkins sat down by their campfire to fry a piece of pork. Hawkins' arm was bandaged, but McDonald's cheek wound was a dark strip of clotted blood. No one else was close by. Jesús had just begun giving one word answers to questions, after a week of being silent, sullen, and withdrawn. For days Jesús had trembled beyond the cold and rejected any effort by Ambrose to comfort him. Ambrose was not much better, but he displayed a resilience that belied his age and size.

Sergeant Degas appeared in the gloom and sat down across the fire from them. Without preamble, Degas said, "I'm leaving tonight. You boys want to come with me? I'm asking you two because you have been good soldiers and you're still alive. I figure it's time to stop dying for a dead cause."

Hawkins spoke, "Maybe. But I never thought you would skedaddle, Sergeant. You funnin' with us?"

Degas replied, "No, Ambrose, I am speaking the truth. I'm walking out tonight. I'm going back to New Orleans. We are beaten. General Hood has done his best to kill us all. I'm through."

"But, Sergeant, you done led us this far, why now?"

"If I thought the war might still be won, I would stay. But it's over, Ambrose. We are but a handful of men trying to hold back the tide. It may have been nothing but foolishness all along, but now, nothing can stop the blue wave. The Confederacy is lost, and we are lucky to be alive. I'm not going to give General Hood one more chance to kill me for nothing but his stubborn pride. I'm sick of the stubborn ways of men. The stubborn ways of men like me."

Hawkins replied, "Sergeant, that's more words than I heard you say in three years. We may be losin' the war, but there's still provosts and Yankees that may catch you, even if you make it to New Orleans."

Degas was silent for a moment, then said, "McDonald, do you remember the drawing of the bathing woman you saw the day we ate the tomato fruits last spring?"

Jesús looked up at Degas as if just seeing him, and nodded.

"That drawing came in a letter from my brother. He's made arrangements with a steamship company in New Orleans. He's paid for me to go home to France."

Hawkins interjected, "Sergeant, we thought your home was San Antone."

"My mother was a Creole, from New Orleans, and she married a Frenchman and went home with him. I'm a born Frenchman."

Most older men would have waited to see if another man would say more, but Hawkins asked, "How'd you get here then, from France, I mean?"

"My mother died in France when I was a boy. So I did what many boys do when they lose their mother. I turned bad, so bad that my father sent me off. Far off, across the ocean, back to my mother's people in New Orleans. My mother's brother took me in, but they were hard people. I gambled, and I drank and stole and fought, and one day I found it wise to seek yet another home, far off. San Antonio, where no one knew me."

Now that Degas had opened up, there was no holding Hawkins back, "Then, how'd that letter from your brother in France find you up in Tennessee?"

"A girl in New Orleans. A soiled dove, as some say. We shared a room. I promised I would send for her one day. I wrote her once after we got out of prison camp. And I have maintained correspondence with my brother, so she sent me his letter. It took many months and much good fortune for it to reach us in Tennessee. Edgar and I were close after our mother died. He said in his letters that he is now an artist, and his paintings are in great demand and sell for a crazy number of francs. The drawing you saw of the naked woman, it's a sketch for a painting. He sent it to me to show off to his big brother, perhaps. And maybe to entice me to come home. I agree with you, Jesús. It is a drawing of a truly beautiful woman. Perhaps she would like me."

"What about your girl in New Orleans?"

Degas shrugged, "I don't know. It's been a long time, so maybe she has found another man. She does not like being alone very much. And my brother did not arrange passage for her to sail to France."

After a silent moment Jesús spoke the first sentence he had said in a week, "Sergeant, I don't blame you for walkin' out of here tonight. You ain't alone in your thinkin' of how bad this war has got. I've lost...we've lost everyone but us three. Even the hairy pig...even Bain. They're gone. All gone. There ain't hardly nobody left. But I'm stayin'. Can't speak for Ambrose, and there ain't nobody else left that I care about. But I owe it to Bain, and the lieutenant, and Bernard, and Andrew, and some others, to stay and see it through."

Jesus paused a long time staring at the fire. Then looking up and trying to smile, he said, "Besides, I'm plannin' on sparkin' Bain's sister when I get home. How could I do that if I went back before it was over, after losing Bain? She'd spit in my eye. Nope, I'm staying."

Degas considered McDonald for a long moment, then asked, "Ambrose, you staying too?"

Without hesitation Hawkins answered, "Sergeant, Jesse, he's, he's my family. I ain't got nobody else. I'm sticking with him."

Degas had no reply, as if he had used up all the words he had in telling his story. He just nodded, stood and held out his hand to the two young men. Jesús thought Degas wanted to shake hands, but when he held his hand out, he saw Degas was holding a folded paper.

"It's the bathing lady. You take it. It will help keep you warm 'til spring. I plan on meeting her in person." Hawkins and McDonald could not see the rare smile on Degas' face.

"Ambrose, you take it. Susan would use a knife if she found such a drawing in my knapsack when I get home."

Private Hawkins, who had not seen the drawing of the bathing woman but had often thought about what bathing women might look like, eagerly reached out and pocketed the folded paper. When he looked up, Sergeant Degas had walked away in the darkness.

Chapter 39

December 13, 1864, South of Nashville, Tennessee
5 Men Present for Duty

"I sure could use a bath," Hawkins said to McDonald. The two men were side by side, both cold and wet from sleet, both still aching from their wounds, both hungry and exhausted, but neither had fallen out during the hard marching. McDonald was conspicuous in the red and brown scarf wrapped around his neck.

"Ambrose, you never had a winter bath in your whole life," Jesús said as he looked over, surprised to see the little teenager smiling as he marched.

"Yea, but before last week I never knew what a bathing woman looks like," Ambrose countered.

"Just because you're pining now for a bath, don't mean there's gonna be a nekkid bathin' woman right there in the room with you. Or in the creek with you, since you never bathed indoors in your life, neither."

"Aw, Jesse, can't a man dream of life after all this freezin' warrin' is done?"

"I suppose so, Ambrose. Just don't be dreamin' none about no girl named Susan."

"Jesse, I wouldn't dream of dreamin' such a dream. You know that."

The brigade column came to a stop as commanding Captain Broughton received his deployment orders. His men were to construct a lunette on top

293

of a wooded hill that overlooked a deep railroad cut through a ravine. The Texans would share the little fort with a battery of four artillery pieces. Together the infantry and cannons were the extreme right flank of the Confederate army. The Texans bivouacked on the hill and worked all the next day digging a long deep ditch and building wooden walls to protect the riflemen and artillery crews.

December 15, 1864

"I sure miss an unhurried breakfast," Hawkins said to McDonald as the two men stood on the firing step and gazed outward, their muskets resting in front of them under the head log.

"*Sí*, I can't remember the last time I ate *tortillas and frijoles* off a real table, sittin' on a real bench," McDonald replied.

"Jesse, you guess anybody else in this army has ever even seen a hot corn *tortilla*?

"Nah, nobody else, I reckon."

The cannons fired without warning and both young men instinctively ducked. They recovered their composure and peered through the gap to see lines of Union soldiers down the hill and on the far side of the railroad cut. It was a brigade of US Colored Troops, commanded by Colonel Thomas Morgan. The rising sun was reflecting off hundreds of bayonets as the early morning fog evaporated. While the fog had hidden the Union brigade from the Texans until they were close, the fog had also misled Colonel Morgan, whose scouting patrols had failed to recognize that the wooden palisade on the hilltop was a daunting obstacle blocking their advance.

The Texas riflemen began firing, adding to the casualties that were rapidly being inflicted by the Reb artillery. The troops in the forward regiment of the brigade were caught between the steep walls of the railroad cut when the cannon shells began exploding in their midst. Many of the Union soldiers were encountering an artillery barrage for the first time, and they began breaking away from their formation to seek a fast way out of the death trap. Within minutes, the regiment became a retreating mob.

Morgan ordered his other three regiments forward. These regiments cleared the railroad cut, but were soon stymied by the intense fire from the lunette up the steep slope from them. A firefight developed in which the Federals substantially outnumbered the Confederates on the hill, but the Texans were making full use of their protecting logs and they were veterans who could load and fire with deadly proficiency. Moreover, the men on the hill held vivid memories of their own merciless exposure to the enemy's musket fire at Franklin just two weeks before. They were ready to turn the table. By noon the attack had played out and the Federals withdrew beyond the range of the hilltop cannons.

By late afternoon, Cleburne's Division was called upon to reinforce the opposite end of the Confederate line. The Texas Brigade, now led by Captain Selkirk after Captain Broughton was wounded during the day's fighting, put on knapsacks and started marching. Finally, daylight gave way to dark, and General Hood was still unsure where he wanted Cleburne's Division, now commanded by General Smith. The army was retiring in a mix of order and confusion and, without firm instructions, General Smith allowed his exhausted men to fall by the roadside and rest in the dark while they could.

December 16, 1864

Their rest time had been short, only a few hours, and the cold made sleep a scarce luxury. The division was now the strength of a small brigade, each brigade still functioning as a small consolidated regiment. They started the day marching to the southeast. Finally, after marching and countermarching for half the day, the men in the brigade found themselves on the far right end of the Confederate army. Again, they were on a hilltop, this one large enough for a name: Overton Hill. This time the Texans arrived as the fighting began and joined a division of soldiers from Alabama defending well-constructed earthworks

The Confederates on Overton Hill were well placed behind logs and had two batteries of artillery pieces firing shrapnel and canister down the hill, in addition to enough infantry to man the fortifications with riflemen packed in elbow to elbow. They faced Union troops who had also fought the day before, including some of the same US Colored regiments who had confronted the Texans.

"Jesse, ain't them fellers down there darkies?"

"*Sí*, I believe they are, but that don't matter none a'tall, cause they're wearin' blue and carryin' rifles. That's all that matters," Jesús replied as he loaded his musket once again.

"If they're the same fellers that came at us yesterday, they're soldiers, that's for sure, 'cause we sure killed a lot of 'em yesterday," Ambrose said as he slid his musket over the top of the logs to fire again.

In his peripheral vision, Jesús saw Ambrose flinch and drop his gun outside the barricade. Then Ambrose sat down holding his left upper arm with blood flowing through his fingers.

Jesús slid down next to Ambrose, where he took off his knitted scarf and stuffed it under Ambrose's hand to wrap it around the ugly wound. As he did so, he saw white pieces of bone, broken and jagged, protruding from Ambrose's arm.

Jesús immediately recognized that Hawkins would lose his arm to a surgeon's saw, and maybe die. Ambrose saw it too, and sat back with his eyes closed, grimacing, but determined not to cry out. Jesús was exhausted, still emotionally numb, and shaken by Ambrose's wound. Not knowing what else to do, he leaned over and kissed his friend on the forehead. Then he took his musket, stood up, and resumed his methodical loading and firing at the attacking enemy, not aiming, barely looking over the logs as he pulled the trigger, before he began to load again.

A few minutes later Matt Quinn and another black man hurried forward and knelt by Private Hawkins. Quinn replaced Jesús's blood-soaked scarf with a bandage he wrapped around Ambrose's arm, better staunching the blood flow. After handing the scarf back to Jesús and affectionately squeezing his shoulder, Matt and his partner carried Ambrose away.

The casualties taken by the Federal regiments attacking Overton Hill were even greater than during the failed attempt at the railroad cut the previous day. The Union troops never were able to press their attack through the fallen trees and the sharpened stakes implanted on the slope of the hill. But the failed attack on Overton Hill was only a Federal diversion to pin down the Confederates on the right end of their defensive line. The main Union assault came further to the left where the Rebs' defenses were stretched too thin. There the Confederate soldiers gave way again, the line dissolving under the fierce assaults of the Union troops. The Army of Tennessee, now an empty broken shell, retreated. Hood's grand strategy to beat the Federal army piecemeal in Tennessee had failed. The only maneuver left for the remaining Confederates was to run.

Part 5

Chapter 40

Late December 1864, South Tennessee
3 Men Present for Duty

I t was snowing again. Those men who could, those who had few enough wounds or ailments to do manual labor, had spent the day cutting small tree trunks to finish their winter huts. The three men were silent and still, all three wrapped in ragged blankets, sitting around the dying embers of the campfire. One man wore homemade moccasins made of partly cured cowhide that had been wrapped and tied around the remnants of his old shoes. The cowhide had dried stiff and shrunk to a tight covering. The man hoped the moccasins would hold together for at least a week.

The three men didn't know each other well, having been in different regiments just a month before. This evening each was thinking about the past two months, the friends of three years now gone, the recent horrors that had scarred them all. None of the trio was feeling obliged to share his thoughts with the other two. One man picked up a stick and stirred the fire, tossing the small branch onto the coals. Flames quickly flared up, reflecting off the solemn faces of the trio. The oldest of the three softly started humming the tune to a favorite hymn, one which had given comfort to him over the years since he was a boy.

Another of the trio stayed in his reverie for another minute, listening to the man's low voice, before he joined in the second verse of the old song. The third man knew that in the past month he had already shed all the tears one man was allowed on this earth, so with dry eyes he joined in the last verse:

> "You must go----------------------and stand your trial,
> You have to stand ------------------it by yourself.
> Oh, nobody else-----------------can stand it for you;
> You have to stand------------------it by yourself."

Their low voices carried in the night air into the captain's tent, which was just a few feet away. He heard their singing and let his thoughts slip away from the throbbing wound in his shoulder. He fell asleep still listening, wondering what trial could have been worse than their trials in Tennessee.

February 1865, Camp Chase, Ohio

Lieutenant Navarro and Private Braden were POWs for the second time. They had been crowded into a cattle car and taken north once again. Navarro was soon separated from Braden and loaded onto a different train with the other captured officers, including Major Fisher. Their train was bound for Fort Delaware, far to the northeast. The destination for the enlisted men's train was Camp Chase, Ohio.

It was mid-winter and colder than either man could remember, even colder than the night in Tennessee when they had all been ordered to get up and stand around their campfires.

"Sun's coming up," Sam Baldwin said.

Braden was pressed against Baldwin's back, both on their right sides, hips and shoulders numb against the bunk's slat board bottom. Two other shivering men were lying in the same position behind Braden. The four men had been spooning for warmth all night, with one thin wool blanket under them and two blankets stretched over them.

"Don't matter. You know they won't bring the food ration 'til midmorning," Braden replied.

"Yes, but the line will start now," said Baldwin, still the corporal, prodding his men to not shirk their duty.

"And it's my turn. I know. I'm going, but I'm taking my blanket," said Braden. The daily distribution of raw fish and rice was the main activity of the day at Camp Chase. The amount of food per man had twice been halved over the past few months, and often the men at the end of the line went away empty handed.

"Maybe it will be thick beefsteaks this morning," said one of the other two men in the bunk.

"You hush up that talk, Frank. If I can't have nothin' but two bites of boiled fish, I sure don't want to be salivating over the thought of beefsteaks," came a voice in the bunk above them.

"I can't salivate. My spit's frozen to my teeth," said another voice.

The three tiers of bunks were occupied by a dozen men from Granbury's Brigade, all captured at the Battle of Franklin, two months before. The windows in the one story barracks had no glass or curtain, and there was no stove in the barracks for warmth or cooking. The camp quartermaster had deemed the provision of stoves as "too costly." Therefore, the men built small campfires each day to cook the daily ration, which was usually a small square of white fish to be boiled and a few pieces of hardtack per man. It was rumored among the prisoners that the reduced rations were in retaliation for the treatment of Union POWs in southern prison camps. Whether it was revenge or simple graft, the prisoners at Camp Chase were half starving in the early months of 1865. The camp cemetery expanded daily as the weak and sick succumbed.

Early April, 1865, Rural North Carolina

Private Ambrose Hawkins did not die when the surgeon sawed off his arm and cauterized the stump just below the shoulder. He awoke in great pain, but endured it. He was transported by one of the last Confederate ambulance wagons to leave central Tennessee. In Georgia, Hawkins was discharged from the army and was taken in by a Methodist preacher who had been a Confederate chaplain until he caught yellow fever and was sent home to recover. In gratitude, the pastor's wife turned their small house and barn into a safe haven for the recovery of men who had been maimed, but were not dying from infections. Ambrose stayed in their barn and helped as he could, learning every day how to work with just one arm.

In late March, he profusely thanked the couple and started walking to find the army that he had heard was now in North Carolina. Hawkins was determined to find Jesùs, so they could go back to Texas together. Near the end of April, Ambrose caught up with the army and began to doggedly visit every camp of soldiers until he found the few remaining Texans from Granbury's Brigade. Ambrose saw Jesùs squatting by himself next to a campfire where a small fry pan of yellow-gray mush was sitting lopsided on the hot coals and burning around the edges.

300

"Dammit, Jesse, didn't you ever watch your mama cook? That, that, whatever it is, is done," Ambrose said as walked up behind Jesús.

Jesús looked over his shoulder and a smile split his face in two. He leapt up and reached Ambrose in one bounding step, hugging the one-armed man and ignoring the pan of mush that burned black on the fire.

On April 26th, the war ended in North Carolina. The Confederates' weapons were stacked and a final roll call made. Private Jesús McDonald was one of two men from San Antonio to answer, "Present."

301

Epilogue

This night's meal was special since it was the sixteenth birthday of the couple's oldest child. The honoree was seated at the head of the table, in his father's normal chair and place. In the eyes of his family, as of that day the young man was no longer a boy. He was already taller than his father and his hair had a redder tint than did his father's, whose full head of hair was now going to gray. After the blessing was said in English and repeated in Spanish, the family passed the many dishes around the table and silence reigned for at least three or four bites. Then the mother, grandmothers, and sisters all began to chat among themselves, leaving the father and son on an island of silence, which was just fine with both of them.

Without comment the father reached down to the floor, picked up a small package wrapped in brown paper, and handed it to his son.

"Pop, what's this? You and Mother already gave me the saddle. That's enough."

"Open it, please."

The conversations around the table quickly faded as ladies and girls saw another gift was being presented. Everyone was looking at the father and son seated next to each other. Without further protest, Bain Gill McDonald slipped the string from around the package and unwrapped it. He dropped the paper and held up a red and brown knitted scarf.

Jesús' mother was the first to speak, "Jesús, why did you give Bain that old scarf. It's raggedy. I could have made him a new one for his birthday."

"*Si*, Mama, you could have done that, and I hope you will for his birthday next year. But today, on his sixteenth birthday, I want him to have this scarf."

"Why, Papa, why that scarf?" chirped Maria, the couple's oldest daughter.

While Jesús swallowed and tried to think of how to reply, his wife, Susan, answered gravely, "Because, Maria, your Grandmother McDonald knitted that scarf and gave it to your father when he joined the army and left for the war.

Then with a sparkle in her eyes and lilt in her voice, she added, "And he was wearing it the day he rode up the road to our house to ask Papa for my hand in marriage."

Jesús smiled at his wife, and again swallowed in preparation to speak. But this time Susan's mother spoke first,

"And he was wearing it the day after he got home from the war. The day he knocked on our door, standing there skinny as a rail. It was the only time I ever saw Jesús speechless. He was there to tell us about our son...to tell us about Bain, the soldier, and how he died."

"You mean Uncle Bain? The one you talk about?" asked a still younger McDonald boy named Ambrose.

Finally, Jesús spoke before anyone else could, "Yes, *muchacho*, that Uncle Bain. Before Bain was your uncle, he was...he was my corporal in the army. And he was *mi amigo*, my good friend. He took care of me when there was nobody else. He watched out for me. And he fussed at me like he was my big brother. Like this Bain does to you, little one."

By now, sixteen year old Bain had unrolled the scarf and had put it around his neck. In the light, several dark stains could be seen on both ends of the scarf.

Another daughter exclaimed, "Papa, it's dirty! You should have given it to me to wash."

"No, I think not, Consuela. I think this scarf will always be stained."

Young Bain now added, "It's not dirt on the scarf, Connie, it's stiff and ..."

"*Si*, Bain, it's blood. It's the blood of three men, one who was a very bad man, who once took the scarf from me because...because he could."

"Did you let him take it, Papa?"

"No, *Mijo*, I didn't let him take it." Jesús smiled awkwardly at the memory, "He didn't exactly ask my permission for it."

"How did you get it back, Papa? Did you kill the bad man for it?

303

"No, I didn't kill him. In fact, I think that bad *hombre* is probably still alive. Folks say snakes live a long time. But, he gave the scarf back to me later, after he had it for a while."

The younger children by now were losing interest in the new gift and were busy with their spoons. The three women at the table were each lost in their own thoughts, all three of them remembering back nearly twenty years ago, to the last time each of them had seen young Bain Gill. It had been the day he and Jesús had marched away in their new uniforms, brash and confident, expecting to be home in three months, not three years.

Jesús now sat surrounded by his beloved family, yet was never far from his memories of those times of "warrin' and loneliness" and his friend, Bain, whose remains lay in a mass grave in Tennessee, a grave unmarked and overgrown by weeds many years ago.

Jesús looked at the scarf his sixteen year old son now had draped around his neck. He could see the stains, but he couldn't tell which stains came from which man whose wounds had marked the scarf; they overlapped and were now just intermingled dark spots on the red and brown stripes of the tattered old scarf.

Afterward

The Alamo Rifles was a real company of Confederates recruited in Bexar County, Texas and the city of San Antonio. The story line of this novel closely follows the historical path of the actual Sixth Texas Infantry in the Confederate army. The novel is both "historical" and "fictional," allowing the main characters to be a mix of names drawn from the original company roster and fictitious men. The officers carry the names of the real men in those positions during the war, but Bain, Jesús, Bernard, and even Sergeant Degas are all fictional characters. Leon Fremon and Ambrose Hawkins were real teenage soldiers whose names I pulled from the original roster of the Alamo Rifles. In fact, Ambrose Hawkins is one of only two members of the historical Alamo Rifles who were present at the final surrender in 1865. I apologize to his descendants to having replaced him with Jesús. I also confess to creating a link between the fictitious Degas and the historical French artist of the same era, Edgar Degas, whose mother was an American Creole. Edgar is indeed still famous for his paintings of nude bathing women.

A few men make short appearances in the novel because they wrote memoirs or diaries chronicling personal experiences that screamed to be included. I couldn't steal the tales of feisty William Oliphant, who was another actual teenage Reb who wrote of his wartime adventures, including his time in the prison camp pox house as a nurse, and his failed escape attempt from a train and near execution after becoming a POW a second time. To bind together other favorite vignettes from memoirs and diaries, some action has been shifted to the Alamo Rifles from other regiments and companies. Though never named as characters, I feel especially indebted to the reflective Captain Samuel Foster and the adventurous Lieutenant R.M. Collins for their unabridged writings about Granbury's Brigade.

Finally, I want to thank whoever invented the internet. When searching for primary source information about Federal regiments that did fight, or might have fought, the Sixth Texas, it was amazingly easy to connect to regimental history websites that included officers' names and personal anecdotes. Not all of the Yankees named in the novel are based on real men, but several are.

While not a formal bibliography, I must acknowledge the many print resources I used to maintain a historically accurate context for my fictional story. Three of the memoirs and diaries are from soldiers in the Sixth Texas Infantry:

Only A Private, The Memoirs of William J. Oliphant, edited by James M. McCaffrey.

The Civil War Diary of Charles A. Leuschner, edited Charles D. Spurlin.

The Unpublished Memoirs of Sergeant Robert Chalk, Co. G of the Sixth Texas Infantry, provided by Dan Snell.

Four other memoirs and diaries came from soldiers in other regiments in Granbury's Brigade:

Chapters From the Unwritten History of the War Between the States; Or, the Incidents In the Life of a Confederate Soldier in Camp, R.M. Collins, Lieutenant, Fifteenth Texas Cavalry (Dismounted), unedited.

The Bugle Softly Blows, The CSA Diary of Benjamin M. Seaton, Tenth Texas Infantry, edited by Colonel Harold Simpson.

One of Cleburne's Command, the Civil War Reminiscences and Diary of Captain Samuel T. Foster, Granbury's Brigade, CSA, Twenty-fourth Texas Cavalry (Dismounted), edited by Norman D. Brown.

Cleburne And His Command, by Captain Irving A. Buck, CSA, Adjutant to General Patrick Cleburne, edited by Thomas Robson Hay.

Additionally, several history books about Granbury's Brigade, the Confederate Army of Tennessee, and specific battles and campaigns provided guidance to track the many engagements in which the Alamo Rifles fought:

This Band of Heroes, by James M. McCaffrey.

Granbury's Texas Brigade, Diehard Western Confederates, by John R. Lundberg.

Arkansas Post National Memorial The Arkansas Post Story, by Roger E. Coleman

Chickamauga and Chattanooga, The Battles That Doomed the Confederacy, by John Bowers.

Mountains Touched With Fire, Chattanooga Besieged, 1863, by Wiley Sword.

The Shipwreck of Their Hopes, the Battles for Chattanooga, by Peter Cozzens.

The Finishing Stroke: Texans In the 1864 Tennessee Campaign, by John R. Lundberg.

Shrouds of Glory, From Atlanta to Nashville, The Last Great Campaign of the Civil War, by Winston Groom.

The Confederacy's Last Hurrah, Spring Hill, Franklin, and Nashville, by Wiley Sword.

Soldiering in the Army of Tennessee, A Portrait of the Confederate Army, by Larry J. Daniel.

Author Philip McBride is extending his writing interests into historical fiction in this, his first novel, *Whittled Away*. For over a decade McBride has been a contributing writer to the *Camp Chase Gazette* magazine, writing dozens of articles about Civil War soldiers, and the hobby of Civil War reenacting.

McBride is a retired teacher and high school principal and is an avid consumer of military historical fiction. He lives with his wife Juanita and yellow dog Dixie in Lockhart, Texas, not so far from the Alamo.

The author welcomes comments or questions about *Whittled Away* and the Sixth Texas Infantry Regiment in the Civil War, and may be contacted at pmcbride@austin.rr.com.

Made in the USA
Charleston, SC
22 June 2013